The Chiawaukas

Prequel to the
Keepers of the Universe Trilogy

Alexandria Chiaro

Hardcover ISBN: 979-8-9873179-4-5
Paperback ISBN: 979-8-9873179-5-2
EBook ASIN: B0GDGC52QD

Cover Design and Illustrations by Gretchen Caughey

Dedication

Heidi Weiss
Whose smile lit up a room and her warmth
filled you with love.

Sam Maness
Who left laughter and smiles wherever he went.

Michael (Mick) Spence
A friend and brother to all...greeting others
with Christ's love and kindness.

I am thankful to have known each of you.

Each of you will be dearly missed.

Thank you to my family and friends who love
me...encourage me...inspire me...
God Bless You all in All You Do.

The Chiawaukas

Prequel to the
Keepers of the Universe Trilogy

Welcome to the prequel of Keepers of the Universe Trilogy
where it all begins....
I wrote this adventure to transport you out of our galaxy
and into your heart.

Chiawaukas

High Priest Alaric
High Priest Akshai (Ak-shy)
High Priestess Imara
High Priestess Ammerie (Am-meer-ee)
Victor Viana Zane Omar Ollie Zeek Roark Raya
Ryleigh Razel Piper Pixel Celestial Blazer Stellar Luna
Tayen Alo Mateo Paxton John
Weston Emerson Hunter Vincent Sean Earl Ava Zaria
Dezi Ivan Lydia Graham

Cryptolores

The Warlord Alchodor (Al-ko-door)
Scaleon (Scaa-lee-on)
Erometh (Air-row-meth)
Avaridia (Av-are-rid-ee-a)
Lusper (La-sper)
Degula (De-goo-la)
Iram (Ear-rum)
Suvidia (Sue-vid-dee-a)
Garule (Ga-rule)

Planets So far Discovered in the Estellas Galaxy

Chiaras (Key-r-us)
Soleil (So-lay-el)
VeNoma (Ve-No-ma)
Acheeas (Ah-shae-us)
Tertammi (Ter-tam-mi)
Kareenia (Ka-ree-knee-ah)

Constellations

Star Points
Julianne
(A stunning maiden with long flowing hair in a beautiful long gown)
Italias
(The Archer who loves Julianne)
Agreadon
(Half Man/ Half Dragon) (A-gree-a-don)
Mount Valoroso

Enjoy the Journey!

Sincerely,
Alexandria Chiaro

Chapter 1

CHIAWAUKA SISTERS

You can hear the feet of two beings hitting the dirt as they run along the tree-canopied trails.

"I'm going to catch you and pass you one of these days!" a young female voice shouts out.

When the two reach the clearing, the river spreads wide before them. They stand in awe at the incredible beauty of the mountains on Chiaras. They breathe in the mountain air and listen to the sounds from the crystal-clear mountain river rushing by.

"You know I am gonna beat you one of these days!" Ryleigh insists gazing up at her older sister, Razel.

A big smile decorates the face of the beautiful aqua-blue Chiawauka, Razel. She reaches around the shoulders of her younger sister, Ryleigh. "You just may!" Razel delivers with love and encouragement.

"So, can I ask you something?" Ryleigh questions her older sister.

"You bet, sweetie." Razel beams with love for her sister.

"So, when I get older, and leave for the academy, will you still be there? What do we do as Supreme Guardian Beings? Well...I know what we do...I look forward to serving together!" Ryleigh communicates.

"Aw, I may be on a mission by the time you are at the academy, but once you have completed the academy, maybe we will serve on missions together. That would be so fun!" Razel assures.

"That will be great! I will zap any adversary that jeopardizes our peace!" exclaims Ryleigh as she enacts her words.

Razel, getting a kick out of listening to her younger sister, reminds her, "Zapping others is at the bottom of our priorities. We Chiawaukas (key-a-wau-kas), were created to love and give to each other." Razel pauses and peers across the river contemplating what she will say next. "Ya know, life is such a beautiful gift. It is an honor to be created as Supreme Guardian Beings."

"I cannot wait to meet a human! I wonder if they hug like we do since they have two arms like we do," Ryleigh exclaims.

Razel cannot restrain her laughter.

"And...I don't think there are ANY bad guys, are there?" Ryleigh carries on.

"To answer your questions, yes, humans give hugs like we do. And no, so far, no bad guys. We are very fortunate to be blessed with a peaceful life on this majestic planet!" Razel contends.

"Wait! The Chiarians (Key-r-ee-ans) are humans, aren't they!" Ryleigh's eyes light up. She grins.

Smiling from ear to ear, Razel answers, "Yes, though taller than most humans."

"Yeah...they *DO* hug just like we do." Ryleigh nods and giggles, realizing she has been hugging the Chiarians her entire life.

The sisters return to their home.

"Did you girls have a good hike?" Raya asks her daughters.

2

"We did! I am going to serve on a mission someday with Razel! At least, I hope to!" Ryleigh exclaims.

Roark walks into the room behind his daughters and leans over to kiss Ryleigh. "I hear your sister Razel just received another honor from the academy." Roark smiles at Razel.

Razel exhibits a very large smile, feeling honored and humble.

"I think it is time we pray and give thanks we are created as supreme guardian beings of this incredible galaxy," Raya conveys.

Roark leads his family in prayer.

Chapter 2

ELSEWHERE ON CHIARAS

Two male Chiawaukas are entering the outskirts of town from their daily run.

"I do not see why we must do any form of exercise. We are supreme guardian beings with unlimited powers," Zane grumbles.

"It is not about that...it is about discipline," Victor claims.

"I see no point in it," Zane continues using arm gestures.

"That is unfortunate. Supernatural gifts without discipline can lead to chaos...self-gratification...and separation from the body," Victor maintains.

"Maybe I don't want to be a part of the Chiawaukas...." Zane makes an elaborate gesture, then adds, "I think chaos might be fun...and self-gratification...for sure...big brother. Who does not want to relish in what they want? All sounds like fun to me."

Victor cringes. He cannot believe his ears. "I do not see how it is possible you and I share the same bloodline. Being born a Chiawauka is one of the greatest gifts there is. To be born a supreme guardian being...to serve others and protect the humans...to live in peace...that is what we are created for. In addition, we are uniquely designed...we are all connected. Although, from the words you speak, I am questioning that I am connected to you at all."

"I am just telling ya how I think. I think I could be on my own just fine without the high priests...and without all this discipline you want to instill in me. I believe I can be a great leader," Zane expresses.

"Zane...not you, nor anyone can be a great leader until they master serving others...or until they can be a good team player. If you cannot be a good team player...you will never make a great leader," Victor asserts.

"Says you," Zane continues to challenge his older brother.

"A...no...says common sense. To be a great leader you must be a good team player and understand the fundamental aspects that goes into being a team. Without that...the only leading you will do will resemble more of a dictator or being a bully over others," Victor contends.

"That works. Bottom line is...I would be the leader." Zane laughs. "Lighten up Victor, I am messing with you. You are always so serious."

Victor inhales a deep breath and wonders how the blood of his parents could create such a challenging Chiawauka.

"Besides...one of these days I plan on joining myself to Razel...and we will lead together," Zane boasts.

"Interesting...have you asked Razel?" Victor queries.

"Not yet. But how can she resist being at my side...forging a forever bond with me?" Zane boasts while he smacks his chest with the palms of his hands.

Victor refrains from exhibiting facial expressions and from engaging in any further discussion.

Chapter 3

AFTER A CLASS AT THE ACADEMY

The Chiawaukas are dismissed for the day. Stellar, Luna, Razel, Celestial, Tayen and Viana join each other and walk to the beautiful park nearby. Victor, Piper, Blazer, Alo, and Zane follow behind at some distance.

"Hey, I am gonna catch up with Razel. I want to hang with her for a while," Zane communicates to his brother and friends.

Zane jogs ahead. "Hey…Razel…wait up."

The female Chiawaukas stop and giggle.

"I think someone likes you, Razel." Luna smiles.

"I know. We have grown close these years at the academy," Razel voices. "I will see you guys tomorrow." Razel steps away from her friends and waits for Zane.

"Hey, how are you?" Zane stops next to Razel. "Want to go for a walk?"

"Sure," Razel answers.

The two proceed on the cobblestone sidewalk under the canopy of the mature trees, over the hill and down to the lake.

"I didn't think you liked to walk," Razel playfully comments.

"I like to walk with *you*. I don't like all that excessive nonsense my brother deems necessary to be disciplined," Zane exaggerates using his fingers to make quotation marks when he speaks the word 'disciplined.'

"Ah, I see." Razel smiles at Zane.

Zane reaches for Razel's hand and gazes into her eyes. "I like YOU Razel. Our time at the academy is coming to an end. We will be given assignments. I am hoping...well...." Zane gets down on one knee. "Razel...I would like us to be a forever couple and have our own little ones...I love you, Raz."

Razel is astonished. She knows Zane and she are *extremely* close, perhaps she does not realize the depth of his feelings, or maybe she does and she just pushes them out of her head.

"Oh, Zane." Razel places her other hand on top of Zane's hand and kneels so they are peering into the eyes of each other. "I care about you SO much. I am incredibly honored you want to be forever joined with me and have a family with me."

"Oh boy." Zane's eagerness shifts to apprehension.

"Zane...we have grown very close during our years at the academy. I thought you knew I want to travel on missions and serve with our fellow Chiawaukas," Razel details.

"I thought we could do it as a family...like your family does," Zane explains.

Razel slightly tilts her head. "Aw...Zane...you are a beautiful soul and I love you. Can we just put this on hold for the time being?" Razel gently pulls Zane's head next to hers so their cheeks are touching. She turns in to kiss his cheek.

"No." Zane takes her hands in his and lowers them. "I don't want to wait, Razel! I want us to be a team and rule the galaxy and have little Razels and Zanes...with you!"

"You mean serve?" Razel raises an eyebrow.

"Yeah. Sure...yes. That's precisely what I mean." Zane bends his arms at his elbows and realizes he made a word slip.

Razel leans back on her calves, sighs, and lowers her head. She then raises her head to peer directly into Zane's eyes and

7

reaches to hold his hands. "Zane, I love you. I do. My focus for now is on our upcoming missions. Serving the Chiawaukas…serving the humans…and maybe even one day…being chosen to be the high priestess." Razel pauses. "But you know all this." Thoughts race through Razel's mind. "Are you trying to keep me from it?"

"No! I want to be there to share all of it with you!" Zane snaps, pulling his hands from hers.

"I am not going anywhere. We can become a forever couple anytime. Why must it be now?" Razel questions with gentleness in her voice.

"Never mind. I am not waiting." Zane stands. "Have a good life!" Zane grumbles.

Razel stands. "The way you are speaking to me is not of love."

"If you can't see my love for you, you're blind!" Zane barks.

"If you must rush me…I feel you have ulterior motives," Razel replies. "I do want to serve on missions with you. I am honored you want me as your life partner. I do not understand why we must join now."

"Save it. I'm done." Zane, with wounded feelings feeding anger, storms off.

Razel feels pain rushing through her heart and sadness in her spirit. She remains standing while she watches Zane briskly walk over the hill out of her sight.

······⚬⚭⚬······

Razel is in disbelief. She sees her friends on the other side of the crystal clear mountain lake. She walks along the sidewalk, but decides to just transport herself to them.

"Oh Razel! We saw Zane on one knee…." Luna comments.

"And then both of you…did he propose?" Tayen asks.

Razel sighs. Tears form in her eyes, one tear trickles down her cheek. All the Chiawauka females instantly place a hand on

Razel. They vividly see and hear the exchange between Razel and Zane.

"Oh, sweetie. I agree with you. He has ulterior motives. I always suspected he wants to control you. He strikes me as that type, though disguised very well," Celestial shares.

"I know you two have grown very close. I am sorry, Razel," Viana voices. Viana feels the weight of Razel's heart.

"You know, Razel, you did nothing wrong. If you continue to put our Creator first...all the right people will be at your side...forever," Stellar conveys from her infinite wisdom. "You believed Zane's heart is as pure and noble as your own."

Razel nods. She wipes her eyes and gazes into each of her Chiawauka sister's eyes. "You guys are the best! I really thought Zane was great, but I am beginning to see what you see. I could *sense* his intentions are not pure and honorable."

"Aw, honey," Luna expresses while she reaches to hug Razel.

"Thank you, guys. I have the best Chiawauka family ever!" Razel declares while she sniffles.

The female Chiawaukas exchange hugs, then head to their homes for the evening.

……⊙ℬ⌾……

Razel can see Ryleigh out front of their home as she draws near. Ryleigh presses her hands over her heart then extends her hands to Razel. Razel feels a jolt of energy, which causes her to briefly be off balance.

Ryleigh runs to Razel. "Are you alright?" Ryleigh embraces Razel with a powerful hug.

Razel leans her head onto the top of Ryleigh's head. "Yes, I am. What gives? What was that?"

Ryleigh steps back and gazes into her older sister's eyes. "I could *feel* your heart pain. I wanted to send you energy, so that is what I meant to do," Ryleigh explains.

"Well, thank you. It worked. How did you learn to be so powerful?" Razel grins at her younger sister.

"Great training from a superb teacher, I guess!" Ryleigh winks at Razel. "Oh, we have company inside for dinner."

Razel slightly sighs.

"It will be alright...it is Ollie and Omar," Ryleigh discloses.

Razel perks up. "I love them!"

"Yes! They are an outstanding Chiawauka team!" Ryleigh maintains. "And by the way...Zane did not have pure intentions deep down. I sense he is up to no good, and he was going to draw you into his web!"

Razel is awestruck at the wisdom of her younger sister. "You amaze me!" Razel expresses with a huge smile. Razel places her arm around Ryleigh, and the sisters walk up the steps and into their home, where they enjoy a delicious dinner with their parents and friends.

......⟋⟍......

After an incredible meal and rewarding conversation, Roark and Raya escort Omar and Ollie to the door. Razel and Ryleigh follow.

"Thank you for the lovely evening," Ollie expresses.

"It is always a joy to be in your company," Raya contends.

Omar and Roark shake hands.

Ollie reaches for Razel's hand and takes it into her hands. "And Razel...all will be well. Zane, though an extremely handsome Chiawauka, lacks integrity. His words are smooth...but they lack substance. Remember that," Ollie imparts.

Razel sweetly smiles. "Thank you for that."

Ollie exchanges a hug with Razel, Ryleigh, and then Raya. "We love you," Ollie voices while she and Omar descend the stairs.

Roark closes their front door. Raya and Roark place their arms around their daughters. They squeeze them tightly. The family basks in its powerful connection.

······◦჻ઠ······

Later that evening, Roark knocks at Razel's door. "May I come in?"

"Yes," Razel replies and sits up in her bed.

Roark sits beside his oldest daughter. "You know, honey…what is meant for you…well…nothing will be allowed to prevent it. I know you feel heartbroken right now…but that does not change the gifts and abilities you have. You will be aligned with something greater…something true and real."

Razel smiles at her dad, realizing he is trying to comfort her. "Thank you. Ya know…when the words came out of his mouth, 'I am done'…the initial sting and shock, it did overwhelm me. But honestly, deep in my soul…I know my purpose and direction. I will not waver." Razel sniffles. "Not even for one of the very most charming, handsome Chiawaukas in all the land…." Razel releases a nervous laugh and cries.

Roark and Razel exchange a smile while peering into each other's eyes.

"Thank you, Dad," Razel voices.

"Anytime. I am thankful you appear to be handling this well," Roark conveys.

"I am. Like I said…initially…the shock and sting…ugh…I wanted to cry. I am hurt that he apparently never listened to my aspirations, but after spending time with my Chiawauka friends…and dinner…oh, and Ryleigh…." Razel grins. "She sent energy from her heart to mine when I was almost home."

Roark grins. "Yep! She is feisty."

Razel giggles and wipes her eyes. "She is!"

Roark leans and kisses his daughter's forehead. "Sleep peacefully. You made the right decision."

Razel lies back and smiles. "I know. I feel at peace. Thank you."

Chapter 4

FACING THE NEW WEEK

Victor stops to speak with Viana after he finishes teaching one of the classes.

"I am concerned about my brother," Victor confides.

"I know he had a falling out with Razel," Viana softly voices.

Victor nods. "Yes...there is that. Moreover, I see a dark side developing in him. He says he is just messing with me...and believe me...he enjoys that, but I sense there is more."

Viana acknowledges, "He does like getting under your skin. He did mention to Razel he was hoping to rule the galaxy with her...."

Victor expresses astonishment. "How did Razel respond?"

"Razel simply questioned... 'you mean serve'?" Viana recounts.

Victor shakes his head.

"If it helps calm you, Zane did say, 'Yes...that is what I meant,'" Viana adds.

"No. I do not feel calm. He has so many unique gifts. I do not understand his attitude," Victor shares.

Viana places her hand on the forearm of Victor. "I will pray for him."

"Thank you," Victor acknowledges.

·······᧧ℓᦂ·······

Midweek, a group of many Chiawaukas gathers. Zane is standing among Sean, Earl, Ava, Zaria, Dezi, Ivan, Lydia, and Graham, speaking to them of their potential. "We can form our own group. Yes, there are the Verndari…and we were born Chiawaukas." Zane extends his arms outwards. "I believe there is infinite abilities that we all possess."

"We have unlimited capabilities now," Sean comments.

The others nod in agreement.

"We do, but we would not be under the rule of the High Priests!" Zane expounds.

Just then, Ava spots Razel across the way, walking with some other Chiawaukas. "Oh, she is such a beautiful Chiawauka! She is always so kind to me and everyone she encounters." Ava's eyes are fixed on Razel.

"She is so full of love for everyone," Zaria adds. "I always feel better after I hang out with her."

Zane clenches his fists at his sides. He lifts his head up into the air and contains his hurt, angry feelings. "Yes. She is a remarkable Chiawauka, but each of you are!" Zane extends his arms and peers into the eyes of each Chiawauka. "Someday, if we form our own group, we will not be in anyone's shadow!"

"We are not in anyone's shadow now," Sean explains. "To be clear, the only one of us that perhaps feels he is in someone's shadow is you, Zane. Your older brother, Victor, is revered. He has received the highest rankings for his achievements. Maybe *you* feel you are in *his* shadow."

Zane clenches his fists again and lets out a scream, "Aargh!" He then composes himself. "I see. I get it. You are correct. My older brother *does* overshadow my shine."

13

"Does he really though?" Lydia bravely speaks forth. "We are all called to shine, which means we are *not* in the shadow of anyone. We each bring unique gifts."

Zane shakes his head. "Well…clearly you all are happy being pawns of the high priests. One day, I plan to break away! It will honor me if each of you will join me." Zane extends his arms to include everyone listening.

"I do not feel or believe I am a pawn. I am thankful to be chosen and created as a Chiawauka," Zaria articulates with resolve.

Several Chiawaukas nod their heads in agreement.

"Maybe I selected incorrectly," Zane retorts.

"Do not use your manipulation tactics on us. You laid your case before us. It is not happening today. You have given us something to think about," Sean rationalizes.

"Yeah, I do not appreciate being manipulated. That is not our way," Graham concurs.

One by one, the Chiawaukas depart the gathering.

"Zane…you and I have been friends for a long time. I can see your vision, but as Chiawaukas, we were created to lead, serve, and protect. We are Supreme Guardian Beings," Sean reminds.

"And you are alright with that?" Zane questions.

"Well…yeah, we have unimaginable supernatural powers. We are guardians…." Sean details.

Zane slightly shakes his head. "I guess there is a part of me that wants to use the powers for myself."

"And *that,* is where the fall will be…." Sean asserts.

Chapter 5

SOME OF THE CHIAWAUKAS MEET UP

Later in the week, after an awards ceremony, Chiawaukas gather at the majestic Crystal Lake Park.

"I see you got another award." Zane smirks at Razel when he approaches Razel and her younger sister.

Victor and Viana are close behind.

"I guess I did." Razel smiles.

"Hand it over! I want to see it," Zane insists.

"Hey, I don't like your tone with my sister!" Ryleigh retorts as she steps in front of her sister.

"No one asked you, little girl." Zane leans over a bit and growls at Ryleigh.

Razel swiftly places her hands on Ryleigh's shoulders and quickly relocates Ryleigh behind her, separating Zane from her younger sister. "Here, you can see my award. Quit being a bully," Razel calmly states.

Zane grabs it from the hand of Razel and tosses it around.

"Zane, stop!" Victor demands.

"What are you gonna do about it?" Zane challenges.

"Man, you're a mess!" Ryleigh spouts off from behind her sister.

Razel quickly turns and looks at her sister. Razel calmly and quietly conveys, "Ryleigh...stop...let me handle this."

Ryleigh folds her arms while she glares at Zane.

"What **ARE YOU** going to do about it...RaaaaZel?" Zane antagonizes.

Razel shakes her head and rolls her eyes. "You are unbelievable. Keep the award if that makes you feel better. Everyone knows whose heart is where. Your actions are a tell...."

Razel reaches for one of her sister's hands to lead her away.

"I thought so...you can't handle any heat!" Zane dishes out.

Razel keeps walking with purpose with Ryleigh next to her.

Victor is fuming. He feels embarrassed because of his brother's behavior.

Viana remains quiet for now, though great concern floods her body.

"I don't even know why we have female Supreme Guardian Beings! You are NOT tough at all!" Zane continues to elevate his voice.

That did it. Razel chooses to no longer contain her outrage. She stops, turns, and extends her body to a height of eleven feet. She roars so ferociously that flames shoot out of her mouth, purposefully landing inches from Zane. At the same time, Ryleigh positions her arms like she is holding a bow. She then releases an invisible arrow. It sails, making a direct hit to the center of his Zane's palm.

"OW!!!" Zane drops the award from his hand. He shakes his hand in pain and grabs his sore hand with his other hand to rub it.

Viana reacts rapidly and catches the award.

Zane scans the area and sees nothing that would cause pain to his hand. He clenches his fists and continues to jeer at Razel. "You think you are tough? I am telling the high priests that you blew fire at me! You almost scorched me...are you nuts!"

Razel quickly composes herself and sternly states, "Zane, be my guest...shout to the entire galaxy what I did...the fruits of our spirits speak volumes." Razel then turns, takes Ryleigh's hand in hers, and walks away with confidence.

"You'll be seeing me! I am not done with you!" rages Zane.

Razel releases Ryleigh's hand, turns, continues to take steps backwards, raises both of her arms, and follows up with, "Bring it!" Razel then turns and resumes walking away with Ryleigh.

"I will! You can count on that!" Zane slightly jumps up onto his tiptoes and back down while he points his index finger at Razel and Ryleigh, though they do not see his gesture.

"You are truly an embarrassment to our family name and to our purpose," Victor voices.

Victor and Viana glance at each other, nod, and blink. They then vanish.

The many Chiawaukas that are present...disperse.

"Never turn your back on me!" Zane continues, though he has no audience.

Razel and Ryleigh approach their home. Razel is shaking from experiencing the intensity of the confrontation. She is not accustomed to such negative feelings. It goes against her grain to engage in discord.

------⁂------

"Wow! You are amazing!" Ryleigh exclaims.

"That is not a good way to be amazing. It is everything we are not supposed to do. I am still so furious that he even attempted to twist things and accuse me of scorching him and accuse ME of being nuts! UGH! The gall!" Razel inhales a deep breath. "And being a Chiawauka has *nothing* to do with being tough. We were created to love...serve...and protect."

"Are you alright?" Ryleigh places her hand on her sister's arm.

Razel peers into the eyes of Ryleigh. "I am. I feel terrible that I allowed you to see me lose my temper. I also feel terrible in my spirit, that I lost my temper." Razel folds her right hand together like a fist and places it over the left side of her chest.

"Don't be. I also observed how you contained your frustration...then...there came a point that you just couldn't, well you chose not to. I think you behaved honorably," Ryleigh claims.

Razel slightly shakes her head. "I did choose to respond. I should have continued to walk away...I wonder what our high priests will have to say."

"Razel...you are amazing. *THAT* is what they will say! Defender of what is right! And besides...like you said...the fruit of your spirit speak volumes. The high priests most likely witnessed what went down," Ryleigh conveys.

Razel grins and gazes at her sister. "In all likelihood, you are probably correct regarding they no doubt know what happened. I will still meet with our high priests about it."

Ryleigh and Razel reach their home. Ryleigh darts up the porch steps and into their home exclaiming, "You should have seen Razel! She is the best! She received another award!"

Razel slightly shakes her head before she enters their home. She does not want to disappoint her parents or the high priests for the altercation she encountered with Victor's brother, Zane. Thoughts of astonishment of how Zane and Victor can be brothers cross her mind.

Chapter 6

ASSIGNMENTS ARE DESIGNATED

Time passes. The high priests stand before the assembly of Chiawaukas.

"We are pleased to announce some new assignments," Alaric declares.

"We are thankful for each of you," Imara assures.

"Victor, Viana, Omar, and Ollie…you will be stationed on Kareenia," Alaric discloses.

"Roark and Raya, we will be sending you to Tertammi. Your daughter Ryleigh will accompany you. Razel, you will remain on Chiaras," Imara voices.

"Piper, Celestial, and Blazer, your assignment is on the planet Acheeas," Alaric reveals.

"Alo, Tayon, Stellar, and Luna, for now, you remain on Chiaras with assignments," Imara instructs.

"These assignments will begin after the inauguration of the new high priests and ordination of our newly elected bishop," High Priest Alaric informs.

"We thank each of you for your tremendous service to our galaxy," High Priestess Imara commends.

......ᏩᎧ......

"I can't believe I did not get selected to lead a team! I am going to speak to the High Priests." Zane confides to Sean.

"Do you think that wise?" Sean asks, as he raises an eyebrow.

"Perhaps they have not seen my abilities! There are so many of us...I do think it wise to bring it to their attention!" Zane asserts.

......ᏩᎧ......

Zane enters the embassy and proceeds directly to the stairs.

"Sir...Zane...." the receptionist stands and firmly communicates.

Zane reaches the steps. He glances over to the receptionist. "You can let them know I am on my way up."

The lips of the receptionist roll around. The Chiarian receptionist contacts the high priests that Zane is on his way up.

The high priests exchange a look.

"Do you wonder what he wants?" High Priestess Ammerie questions Akshai.

"No. I believe he is going to question our decision," Akshai contends.

Zane knocks once upon opening the door.

The high priests stand at the end of the conference table.

"How can we help you?" High Priest Akshai inquires.

Zane walks about halfway along the length of the conference table when he stops. He tosses an arm forward with his palm up. "I want to know **WHY** you did not assign me to a planet? I am ready! In fact, Razel and I would make an incredible team with our combined strengths and leadership abilities!"

"Yes." High Priest Akshai nods. "We are very aware of your gifts."

Zane jumps in. "See, so you *do* know we would be outstanding leading a team! What's the holdup?"

"Zane…." High Priestess Ammerie is interrupted by Zane.

"Save it. You will tell me you have your reasons. Well, I am here to inform you I am going to gather a team. We will form our own chapter of the Supreme Guardian Beings! You will see! I will be at the planetary leadership meetings!" Zane points at the high priests.

"It is not our way to rebel and separate. We were created to work together, Zane," High Priest Akshai reminds.

"Precisely! You will be working with me as leader of my Chiawaukas," Zane describes.

The high priests remain somber and stand tall.

"Rebels are not tolerated. It is not our way," Akshai maintains.

"You will see!" Zane slaps his palm on the conference table, turns, and storms to the double doors. He grabs the handles on each door and flings them open at the same time. Zane exits the room.

The high priests turn and stare into the eyes of each other.

"You know where this is leading…." Akshai quietly voices.

Ammerie nods. "I do."

Chapter 7

THE INAUGURATION AND THE ORDINATION

High Priestess Imara and High Priest Alaric stand before the assembly of Chiawaukas and Chiarians on the planet Chiaras. Leaders from other planets are also in attendance. They are preparing to ordain the Chiawauka, John Henry Lanzreth, as a bishop. The high priests will also inaugurate the Chiawaukas, Ammerie, as high priestess, and Akshai, as high priest, of the Estellas Galaxy.

"It is with great pleasure that we ordain John Henry Lanzreth as bishop. He will serve with Bishop Weston and Bishop Mateo. He will join them in presiding over our fellow brethren at the monastery on Mount Abdiel. He will also serve on the advisory committee of Details and Protocol for the Chiawaukas. John Henry, it is with great honor we ordain you as Bishop John Henry Lanzreth." Alaric, Imara, Mateo, along with Weston, extend their hands above the head of John Henry with their left palm up and their right palm over John's head. "May you serve with gladness. May you lead with reverence for life. May the blessings of our Holy Father, God, Creator of the Universe, be with you forever.

Amen...." High Priest Alaric slightly bows, making the holy sign, then places his palms together as in prayer.

Bishop Lanzreth also bows with hands gesturing prayer.

High Priestess Imara bows with palms pressed together, as do Bishops, Mateo, and Weston.

Bishop Lanzreth raises his hands to the assembly. "It is a tremendous honor to serve you."

Bishop Lanzreth steps next to the high priests.

"It has been a great honor to be your High Priest and serve you to the fullest of my ability," High Priest Alaric sincerely shares.

"Our time has come to step over and present to you our new high priests," Imara expresses. "Akshai will be our new High Priest."

Akshai steps in front of the bishop and high priests.

"And Ammerie...you will be commissioned as our new High Priestess, serving our galaxy, protecting all from harm, ensuring peace...do you accept this appointment of service?" Alaric asks.

Ammerie stands next to Akshai in front of the high priests and bishops. "I do," Ammerie assertively answers while she slightly bows her head with her hands placed together.

"And Akshai, serving our galaxy, protecting all from harm, ensuring peace...do you accept this appointment of service?" Alaric questions.

Akshai respectfully bows his head with hands pressed together and voices, "I do."

High Priest Alaric and High Priestess Imara raise their hands and place them above the heads of Akshai and Ammerie. "May God lead you both, now commissioned...to be our reigning high priest and high priestess." Alaric again makes the holy sign then places his hands in prayer.

The head vocalist leads the assembly in a powerful, reverent song, which immediately shifts into a glorious, holy chant.

Servers holding processional candlesticks lead down the aisle. High Priest Alaric and High Priestess Imara are directly behind them in the procession side by side. Bishop Mateo and Bishop Weston are side by side behind the high priests followed by newly ordained Bishop John Henry Lanzreth. Just appointed High Priest Akshai and High Priestess Ammerie, also side-by-side, are directly behind the bishop. The procession continues down the aisle and out the large double doors. They quickly make their way to the commons area for a celebration with food, fellowship, and conversations. The area rapidly fills with Chiawaukas, Chiarians, and visiting leaders from planets in the galaxy.

Chapter 8

PREPARING FOR GOODBYES

R oark and Raya finish packing.

"Ryleigh, honey…do you have everything you want to bring to Tertammi?" Raya asks.

"I do." Ryleigh frowns. "I don't want to leave Razel. Can't we bring her?"

Razel smiles and hugs her sister.

Roark steps next to his daughters. "For whatever reason, the high priests deem it wise for Razel to remain on Chiaras."

Ryleigh repeatedly shakes her head. "I don't like it. Can we all be assigned to the same mission?"

Raya places her hands around her daughter. "Ryleigh, all will be well. Razel has completed the academy with the highest accolades along with summa cum laude. I imagine she is on her way to achieving her goals…her dreams." Raya winks at Razel while she embraces Ryleigh.

Razel is glowing. She gazes into the eyes of her sister. "We can visit each other. Your mission on Tertammi, most likely will not be long. Some missions are only for short bouts…and we can face communicate," Razel reassures. "I will miss you so much! I will miss all of you!" Razel stretches her arms around her mother and sister.

Roark extends his arms to envelop his family. "May our Creator watch over us, guide us, keep us safe in His care. May we serve as we are called to do and reunite soon."

Ryleigh embraces Razel in a powerful exchange of love and energy. Tears swell in her eyes.

"You are the best sister ever! You have so many gifts Ryleigh. I will deeply miss you!" Razel whispers.

Ryleigh, still embracing Razel, conveys, "You are the best sister ever! You have taught me so much. I hope to shine with leadership qualities for the safety of others like you do!"

"You already do." Razel kisses Ryleigh on top of her forehead.

Razel hugs her parents. Razel then escorts them to the transport vessel.

······◦❧◦······

Zane rushes to catch up with his brother. "Victor, I really am happy for you. Maybe by my remaining on Chiaras with Razel, we will be able to repair and restore our relationship."

"Perhaps. Zane, you have so much to offer. I am proud of you and I love you, brother," Victor shares his heart.

"Ya know…I see why you are so serious. You are meticulous and want things done right. I appreciate you consistently trying to instill in me a moral compass and discipline. I know it will rub off on me. I guess I have felt in your shadow at times…the Great Victor…." Zane discloses. "Honestly, I just wanted to derail you…get under your skin…I am sorry for the grief I have given you. I hope you will forgive me."

Victor cannot believe his ears though he senses a true, genuine spirit in the words of Zane. Victor reaches to hug his brother and states, "Of course I forgive you. I hope you will forgive me for coming across perhaps staunch and possibly even pompous at times."

Zane grins. "Victor…you cannot help yourself. The thing I know about you is you hold sacred our purpose and mission in life…and you do not waver. Very commendable attributes. I was wrong to be so jealous of you. You are right…I do have my own skill set and gifts." Zane sincerely smiles at Victor.

Victor cracks a smile.

"There it is…that smile. I love you, brother. Be safe on your mission and I will see you…soon." Zane reaches to embrace Victor.

"This is what I have been yearning for…friendship and closeness with you," Victor confesses.

"You have always had it. To be fair, I was entirely a pill," Zanes chortles.

Victor mists up. He feels grief that so much of their time together, Zane was causing friction. Victor now feels sadness of missing out on many good times with his brother. "Well…I treasure moments like this. I believe in you, Zane. You are a gifted Chiawauka. I look forward to serving with you," Victor expresses.

"I look forward to serving with you," Zane admits.

The brothers exchange grins and meaningful eye contact. Victor departs and continues toward the launch pad.

······◦ℛ◦······

High Priestess Ammerie and High Priest Akshai stand at the base of the transport space ship to greet each team and bestow blessings over them.

Viana, Victor, Ollie, and Omar arrive at the transport vessel and are greeted and blessed by the high priests.

"We are in for another adventure, old friend." Omar pats Victor on the back.

Victor nods. "Yes. It is always good to travel to different planets and speak with their leaders to maintain a strong camaraderie."

The Chiawaukas nod in agreement. Ollie and Viana lock elbows and ascend the stairs together.

"The four of us…together again." Ollie glows.

"Yep." Viana smiles from ear to ear.

······ঔৡ৩······

Piper, Celestial, and Blazer arrive at the transport vessel. Ammerie and Akshai greet them and bestow a blessing on them.

"I am looking forward to our assignment," Celestial sweetly voices with her raspy voice.

"Yep, I am, too. I want to fish at their lakes," Blazer mentions.

"Now that's funny. You always have been an outdoorsman." Piper grins.

"It calms me," Blazer shares.

"You know me…I am always curious to how things work," Piper reminds.

Celestial and Blazer both nod.

"I am looking forward to working with Briele, Reigna of Acheeas," Celestial voices.

"Yes. She is a remarkable human and leader," Piper notes.

The three aboard the vessel.

······ঔৡ৩······

Roark, Raya, and their daughters arrive at the transport vessel. The high priests greet them.

Ryleigh slightly frowns at them. Roark gently places his hand upon Ryleigh's back.

"I am sorry for frowning at you," Ryleigh addresses the high priests.

"Oh, sweetheart. We understand. We want your sister to remain here so we can amplify her training plus have her teach some classes. I do hope you understand," Ammerie lovingly expresses.

"I am sure you can work out visual communication arrangements to see each other. Plus, on occasion take leave," Akshai communicates.

Ryleigh perks up and nods.

The high priests bestow a blessing over the family.

Razel and Raya exchange an endearing hug. "I am so proud of you, sweetheart. You are a magnificent force." Raya kisses Razel. "Be safe, daughter of mine."

"You be safe. I could not do life without you," Razel conveys.

Razel and Ryleigh peer into each other's eyes. They hug, exchanging powerful thoughts and sentiments through their thoughts.

"You're the best!" Razel smiles at Ryleigh.

"YOU'RE the best!" Ryleigh smiles right back.

The sisters giggle.

Roark steps up. He places one hand on each side of Razel's head. He leans in to kiss her forehead then gazes into her eyes. "I am so thankful. I have been truly blessed to love and protect your mother, you, and your sister. Life may not always be easy…but it is always worth your best effort. I love you, sweetie." Roark embraces his oldest daughter.

"I love you, Dad." Razel closes her eyes as she rests her head onto her dad's shoulder. Tears begin to fill her eyes. After a powerful hug exchange, they release their arms.

"We will be seeing you," Roark encourages.

"I look forward to it! I love you guys!" Razel discretely wipes her tears while she waves to her family as they climb the stairs into the space craft.

Chapter 9

LIFE ON CHIARAS

The initial sting of separation from her family wears off as time passes. Razel continues to miss them, but not with the intensity she initially experiences. Visual communication with them puts her mind at ease knowing they are safe and enjoy working with the leaders of Tertammi. Razel and Ryleigh often end up talking for an hour after Razel visits with their parents.

......⚬≈⚬......

It is not long before Zane resumes wooing Razel.

"Hey wait up," Zane hollers at Razel as they leave the academy.

Razel hears a familiar voice. She stops, turns, and waits for Zane.

"Hey…thank you for waiting. Were you teaching a class today?" Zane asks in an attempt for dialogue.

"I was." Razel nods and resumes walking to her family home.

"Cool. I am sure you shine at that," Zane contends.

"Thanks," Razel voices.

"Hey will you sit with me a minute?" Zane points to a bench.

"I guess." Razel sits beside Zane.

"Wow! I never thought you would give me the time of day, but thank you. I apologize for my behavior to you. I hope you will find it in your heart to forgive me," Zane pleads.

Razel does not display emotion. She replies to Zane, "I appreciate that. I forgave you long ago."

"Alright then. Well...thank you," Zane stammers while moving his arms. "Hey...I thought you would like to know...I made peace with my brother before he left on assignment."

"That's great, Zane. I am happy for you," Razel calculates her words to keep her guard up.

"Okay then. Hey...did you receive the flowers I sent?" Zane questions.

"I did. That was thoughtful," Razel expresses.

"Yeah...hey...can we maybe...well can we have lunch or dinner sometime...or go to the lake like we used to? I really miss our friendship and time together...." Zane bears his heart.

The lips of Razel slightly curl. Her forehead creases and her nose wrinkles.

"That is quite a variety of facial expressions...and does not appear good. I did not realize that by my sharing, that I want to hang out together, would have such an adverse effect on you," Zane sighs.

Razel remains silent for what feels like extended minutes.

After an uncomfortably, awkward, long silence, Razel communicates, "I appreciate your gestures...flowers...notes slid under my office door...and now this...."

"Oh, boy...." Zane slightly shakes and lowers his head.

"Zane...my aspirations are still the same. In fact, earlier today the high priests informed me they are sending me to Mount Abdiel to study from Bishop Lanzreth and the others." Razel reaches for Zane's hand. "So...although I do appreciate your effort in wooing me...my focus for now is to be the best

Chiawauka I can be, and embrace each assignment that I am sent on, as an adventure."

Zane pulls his hand from Razel's hand. "So, we are really over?"

Razel inhales a deep breath and exhales. "My position remains the same, Zane. For now, I am not ready…and you do not appear willing to wait. It has nothing to do with my love for you." Razel tenderly places her hand on Zane's arm.

Zane shakes his head. "I was a fool. I do not know what possessed me to act so self-centered to you…to my brother…to my family…I have nothing now."

"What are you talking about? Zane, you are an extremely gifted Chiawauka! Speak to the high priests, maybe they will have a direction for your path if you cannot discern it," Razel suggests.

Zane shakes his head again. "I don't know." Zane stands and offers his hand to Razel.

Razel takes his hand with a firm grip. She stands in front of him.

Zane gazes into her eyes. He quietly voices, "Seems like old times…being next to you."

Razel continues to peer in his eyes, almost feeling as if she is in a trance. His mesmerizing voice coupled with his handsome physique is a combination difficult to resist. Just then, she hears the voice of High Priestess Ammerie. Razel places her index and middle finger to her left temple. "Yes. I understand. I can do that. Thank you," Razel communicates.

"What is it?" Zane inquires.

Razel peers into the eyes of Zane. "I must go pack. The high priests changed my leave date. I am leaving tomorrow." Razel begins to walk away.

"Wait! So, is this it? Can I contact you?" Zane requests.

Razel stops and turns to look at Zane. "Zane…if you are not willing to wait… then what is the point?"

"But I love you, Raz," Zane confesses.

"I love you. It is not about love…it is about timing," Razel explains.

"I am trying to understand. Just…just be safe and take care of yourself," Zane conveys.

Razel takes a few steps back to Zane's side. She hugs him and kisses his cheek. "You take care as well." Razel releases her arms and hurries to her home.

Zane stands watching the love of his life dash away. Various emotions rush his brain.

Chapter 10

MOUNT ABDIEL

High Priestess Ammerie and High Priest Akshai travel with Razel to Mount Abdiel.

"Everywhere on Chiaras is so beautiful." Razel breathes deeply. She feels peace from the breathtaking scenery that surrounds her. "Did you aspire to be appointed high priests?"

"I did," High Priestess Ammerie answers, then giggles. "You remind me of me. I was very ambitious."

Razel grins.

High Priest Akshai smiles. "You were." He comments on Ammerie's statement. "If I remember correctly, there was a very outstanding suitor that wanted to be joined with you after graduation from the academy."

Razel's eyes widen.

High Priestess Ammerie slightly blushes, then in her fashionable, whimsical manner she declares, "Yes. He was a Chiawauka worthy of my love."

"Aww, what happened?" Razel eagerly questions.

"Ammerie did not believe it was the appropriate time to form a forever bond,"

High Priest Akshai recalls.

Razel relates.

"Life has turned out very well for us, though," Ammerie voices.

"It has indeed." Akshai nods.

Razel wonders, but does not question if *they* were the couple.

"So, do you have a special assignment for Zane? I know he would like to oversee something, or be involved somehow," Razel discloses.

"Zane has great potential. He will be given assignments to strengthen his gifts," Akshai reveals.

Razel nods. She peers over the edge of the mountain road they are traveling on up to the Monastery on Mount Abdiel.

......⚬꠷⚬......

"Welcome," Bishop John greets.

Weston and Mateo also greet Razel and the high priests.

"Hello." Ammerie nods.

"Good to see you." Akshai firmly shakes the hand of Father John, Weston, and Mateo.

"Welcome to our Monastery, Razel." Father John extends his hand to hers.

"I am so pleased to be here, Bishop," Razel expresses with exuberance.

"Please, call me Father, or Father John," Father requests.

"I will. Thank you!" Razel's smile decorates her face.

Father John leads the others and shows them around. He also introduces Razel to Chiawaukas she does not know. That evening, there is a quiet dinner, followed by conversation on the large balcony that overlooks the mountains and valley below. From their view, several lakes are visible. The sounds of the waterfalls can be heard in the distance, along with the roar of the winding Agape River.

"We will depart in the morning. This has been such a lovely evening," Ammerie comments.

"I am glad you are able to stay with us," Father John conveys.

"Yes." Akshai nods. "Thank you for allowing Razel to observe and study here."

"Oh, you are most certainly welcome. It is our pleasure," Father John graciously imparts.

"Yes...it will be like old times when we had the both of you here, not to mention, Alaric and Imara," Weston indicates.

They hear footsteps coming up cobblestone steps.

Every Chiawauka stands to welcome back Zeek.

"Welcome back, brother." Father John extends his hand to Zeek.

"It is good to be back." Zeek sets his pack on a nearby table.

The high priests and bishops along with Razel observe the interaction with curiosity.

Zeek greets the high priests and bishops and his eyes catch and lock onto the eyes of Razel. He steps toward her and extends his hand to shake hers. "Welcome, I am Zeek."

Razel is caught off guard by his tall, muscular stature, sporting a midnight blue color. She smiles and extends her hand to his. They firmly shake hands, exchanging an almost immediate profound energy connection.

"It is nice to meet you." Razel glows.

"The pleasure is mine." Zeek slightly bows his head.

"What did you bring?" Akshai questions.

"Oh, yes...." Zeek steps over to his pack and opens it. He pulls out beautiful rocks, artifacts, and gemstones that he was in search of on his quest. He also removes a book from his pack.

All Chiawaukas gathered have their eyes on the contents that Zeek removes from his pack and lays out to display on the table.

Ammerie smiles. "I see you continue to keep a journal."

"Always." Zeek smiles. "I find documenting information to be rewarding. I also keep a journal of the places I explore, humans, and Chiawaukas I encounter, not to mention, where I uncover artifacts."

Akshai pats Zeek on the back. "Well…if it was not for you, and the other Chiawaukas here, the Ancient Writings would not be in a book. We very much appreciate your gift of journaling!"

The others nod and various forms of affirmations are communicated.

"I am honored to serve," Zeek proclaims. He glances over with wonder to see if he has captured the attention of Razel.

Razel sweetly smiles at Zeek.

Zeek grins. He continues to describe each item from his pack.

Conversations continue for hours before they walk to their rooms to sleep.

In the morning, High Priest Akshai and High Priestess Ammerie say their goodbyes to Father John, Weston, Mateo, and the others. They hug Razel goodbye and return to the embassy.

Chapter 11

THE OTHER CHIAWAUKAS

High Priest Akshai and High Priestess Ammerie work closely while training Zane, Sean, Earl, Ava, Zaria, Dezi, Ivan, Lydia, and Graham, among other Chiawaukas. They give them assignments on planet Chiaras which include some of them as instructors at the academy. As months roll by, Zane becomes agitated that he has not yet been assigned off planet. In his frustration, he again campaigns to solicit a bond with certain Chiawaukas who he believes to be loyal followers, or does he mean friends? He meets with the high priests again.

Zane rushes the stairs of the embassy placing a foot on every other step as he ascends the stairway. He barges into the conference room.

The high priests stand.

"This is unacceptable behavior of a Chiawauka!" High Priestess Ammerie stands and voices with assertiveness.

"I have asked you to give me a leadership position with Razel. You have yet to deliver. I will be leading a team. We will be leaving Chiaras!" Zane informs.

"That is rebellion!" High Priest Akshai pauses. "Zane, you are too gifted to make such a decision. Please reconsider," High Priest Akshai pleads.

"I have. I reconsidered me NOT telling you! Consider this my notice!" Zane turns and briskly departs the conference room.

Akshai and Ammerie exchange eye contact and reveal their thoughts telepathically.

Chapter 12

RESTLESSNESS CREEPS IN

"Sean, I am sick of being stationed on Chiaras and all this extensive training without an end in sight. Does it not bother you that our high priests have overlooked us regarding assignments off planet?" Zane grumbles.

The two Chiawaukas continue their journey on the outskirts of town.

Sean slightly shakes his head with each step. "Zane...I am on assignment! Here on Chiaras. I am learning valuable information and have no doubt they are training me to be a great servant and leader."

"Ha!" Zane tries not to be so disrespectful, but he does not appear he can help it. "You? A leader? The only leading you will do is...."

Sean stops and interrupts Zane, "If you are going to insult me, who you call a friend, I have better things to do with my time."

"Look, all I am saying is...we can be our own high priests. I will be in command, and with me...you will be second in command. We can form our own Chiawauka guardianship and be stationed on other planets. We can appoint our own teams…decide our own missions….” Zane details.

“But who will we ultimately be serving?” Sean questions.

A look of puzzlement displays on Zane's face. “What? No one. We would be serving ourselves!”

A notable cringe overtakes Sean's face. “We were created to serve and protect.”

With confidence, Zane stands tall and expresses, “We will be! We will be serving and protecting ourselves and whatever planet we choose to rule.”

“You mean serve….” Sean corrects.

“Yep. That's what I said,” Zane asserts.

Sean rolls his eyes knowing Zane said what he meant.

“We could go to VeNoma,” Zane suggests.

“VeNoma?! That planet is still desolate from centuries ago,” Sean claims.

“If it is…we will just use our powers and bring it back to life!” Zane maintains. Zane gestures with his arms and hands. “It will be great! You will be second in command! We would still be best friends,” Zane pleads his case.

Sean shrugs. “I don't know…it does not feel right.”

“Come on…think how cool it will be! Best friends leading together…having a say in the hierarchy of things…and if you want to form groups of what you believe in…you can…but still, second in command to me,” Zane persuades.

The forehead of Sean creases. He sighs. “I will think about it.”

……⚬❦⚬……

Zane and Sean part ways for the day. Zane spies Zaria and approaches her. “How's it going?”

Zaria looks up from a book she is reading. “Good. How about yourself?”

“I am simply amazing,” Zane laughs.

"Well, alright then. No encouragement needed," Zaria notes.

Zane sits down beside Zaria and then he reaches with his hand to slightly move a piece of her hair to the side. "You know...I have always observed you. I find you to be very impressive."

"What do you want, Zane?" Zaria sees through his smooth demeanor.

"Aw, can't a guy just think you are great?" Zane questions, tilting his head slightly.

Zaria barely smiles. "I suppose."

"Zaria...I have been thinking...I would like to blo...." Zane catches himself and rephrases, "I mean, leave Chiaras and lead some of our people to be founders of restoring VeNoma to life. I have spoken to Sean and he is on board. *I* will be leader and Sean has agreed to be second in command. We will be like the high priests, and I would be honored to have you at my side."

"You want to break away from our high priests and form a new Chiawauka group?" Zaria quizzes with surprise.

"You know me so well. Yes...I thought to myself...how can my powers be of a greater use...and I thought of the planet VeNoma. It could sure use our tender, loving care, and then I thought to myself...I can lead a team...even hundreds. Our mission would be to restore VeNoma to life, so humans can once again thrive on that planet," Zane elaborates.

A curious expression paints Zaria's face.

"I can see you are thinking about it. I will discuss it in further detail later." Zane stands.

"Wait. What about Razel?" Zaria inquires.

"What about Razel?" Zane responds.

"Have you run this past her?" Zaria quizzes.

"Well, sure...we may have our relationship on hold for now...but I still tell her everything. She is on board," Zane fabricates.

"Wow! That is surprising. She has always struck me as the type that loves what she does," Zaria conveys.

"Well…I did not say she will be joining us…she has her own aspirations, but yeah…she totally supports my idea," Zane deceives.

Zaria nods. Her spirit softens. "Alright. I will consider it. Thank you for thinking of me."

"Oh…thank you!" Zane pats the arm of Zaria.

Zane continues throughout the day scouting and grooming unsuspecting Chiawaukas for his plan of rebellion.

Chapter 13

CHIAWAUKAS ARE SENT OUT OF THE GALAXY

"It is time we send a team on an exploration mission," High Priest Akshai communicates.

High Priestess Ammerie agrees. "Do you know who you have in mind?"

"I do," Akshai voices.

"I do as well," Ammerie adds. "I think the team should consist of Zeek and Emerson."

Akshai nods. "Agreed. I think we should include Hunter and Vincent as well."

"Splendid. That will bring four different skill sets to make a strong team. I will communicate to the monastery our selections. The teams can leave on the mission at once," Ammerie indicates.

......⚮......

Zeek strolls out to the gardens to speak to Razel. "Are you busy?"

Razel looks up and sees Zeek standing before her. Her eyes widen and she smiles. "I am not busy."

"What are you reading?" Zeek asks.

"Only the thickest, most informative book ever...." Razel replies.

"Ah...The Ancient Writings...tough read," Zeek remarks and slightly tilts his head. "Wanna take a walk with me?"

Razel gingerly sets the book beside her and stands. "Yes! I would enjoy that."

Zeek and Razel stroll through the grounds of the garden pathways that span across a multitude of acres.

"I want to be the first to tell you...I received an assignment today...." Zeek begins.

"That is great news!" Razel declares.

"It is...I am being sent on an exploration mission into the Novias Galaxy. Emerson, Vincent, and Hunter will be with me," Zeek details.

"Oh, Zeek! I am so happy for you. Wow! What an incredible assignment," Razel expresses.

"Thanks. It will be pretty cool. I want to tell you; I am very glad we met. I have enjoyed our time getting to know each other," Zeek conveys.

"Aww...me too, Zeek. Maybe when you return, we will serve on a mission together," Razel imparts. "At least...I hope so."

Zeek grins. "I'd like that."

The Chiawaukas continue to stroll through the pathways between the gardens and circle around, returning to where they began.

"I'll leave you to it." Zeek smiles at Razel and points to the book.

"Yeah...it is a good read. So much information," Razel notes.

Zeek and Razel stand before each other, both slightly feeling awkward. Then they both giggle.

"Well, it's...." They both speak the same words.

The two laugh and smile.

Zeek extends his hand to Razel.

Razel grins. "That feels awkward too."

"I know." Zeek feels flushed.

Razel blushes.

Then they reach out to give each other a hug, not too tight, not too distant.

Razel steps back. "I am glad to have met you. Be safe out there."

"I will. The honor to have met you, is mine. I will send communications when I can. See you in a hundred years or so...." Zeek laughs.

"I hope you will not be gone that long. Good thing we will still be in our thirties." Razel grins.

"Yep...forever and eternity...." Zeek states.

The two exchange a more comfortable embrace. Zeek walks away and prepares for boarding the exploration ship. Razel sits back down on the bench to pick up where she left off, but her thoughts are sidetracked, at least for a while.

Chapter 14

RAZEL RETURNS FROM THE MONASTERY

Razel's orders to return to the academy comes within days of the departure of the exploration team.

"Welcome back, Razel." High Priestess Ammerie greets with a kiss on Razel's cheek and places her hands on Razel's forearms.

"Thank you, and thank you for assigning me to the monastery. I have learned so much from the bishops and other Chiawaukas." Razel slightly bows.

"We believed you would greatly benefit from your time there," High Priest Akshai comments.

"I did. I am thankful you chose me," Razel addresses the high priests.

"We are assigning you to teach some classes. In addition, we want you to continue to inspire others, as you have done," Ammerie instructs.

"I will do my best," Razel assures.

"That is all we ask. We are also going to have you lead a team for reconnaissance training. There will be three teams. You will be in the wilderness and take turns tracking and scouting," Akshai presents.

Razel lights up. "I look forward to it!"

"Go home…take a few days off. We will see you back here in three days," Ammerie directs.

"Thank you, both of you, for believing in me." Razel slightly bows then turns to exit the conference room.

Chapter 15

REBELS FORM

"So...you're back." Zane closes the gap between Razel and himself.

"I am." Razel stops.

"What awards did you receive at the monastery?" Zane smirks.

Razel shakes her head with disbelief. "I keep believing in words you speak...but then you rattle something off that is not in alignment with your previous words."

"What? I was just asking if you won more awards. Is that a bad thing, to show interest in your achievements?" Zane articulates so convincingly.

Razel controls all the eye rolls she wants to exhibit. "I do not win awards. I earn them."

"I see. Did you *earn* any?" Zane presses.

"I was there to study," Razel communicates.

"Well...there must have been an award for each category...." Zane harasses.

"That's it! You nailed it, Zane." Razel tosses her arms in the air. "I WON an award for every category imaginable." Razel sighs with frustration. "What is it with you and awards? You profess you love me, yet you exhibit jealously."

"Maybe I do. You are off gallivanting around and I have been stuck here," Zane scoffs.

"Zane...that is an attitude problem. You are not STUCK here. You are chosen to be here," Razel explains.

"I think the word *stuck* is more appropriate, but that will not always be the case," Zane boasts.

"Well, very good. I am happy for you." Razel tries to remain civil.

"In fact, I will soon be leading a team." Zane swaggers in a circle around Razel.

"I am happy for you. All the best to you." Razel steps around Zane and continues toward her home.

"So that's it...you're walking away...again?" Zane drills.

"The Zane I knew...well...I am beginning to think the caring, kind Chiawauka you showed me was merely a ploy. I wish you all the best, Zane." Razel turns and walks away.

Zane elevates himself to his tiptoes and shouts, "Did you meet someone else? Is that it?" He points with his finger.

Razel does not see his gestures. She rolls her eyes, curls her lips, shakes her head, and thinks to herself a variety of words she will never speak aloud. She does not turn around this time and continues with a fast pace to her home.

······⁂······

Zane searches for every Chiawauka he has approached regarding his idea to form their own group. He deceives each one by saying that the others agree. His lies extend to the highest level. He insinuates the high priests ordered it. He solicits his scheme very successfully.

······⁂······

Razel returns to her family home. It is as though she never left. She misses her family and decides she will initiate a video call. She goes to the communication sphere and transmits.

"There's my daughter!" Raya smiles.

"Hey, Mom." Razel gazes upon the beauty of her mother. "I sure miss you."

"Oh, honey, we miss you," Raya lovingly voices.

"Hey, Razel!" Ryleigh exclaims, "I can't wait to see you!"

"Me too, kiddo! Look at you…man, you have grown into a lovely young teen!" Razel notices.

"Razel, how was your time at the monastery?" Roark inquires.

"Everything I ever imagined and more. I met some fabulous bishops and Chiawaukas…I am very fortunate to be given that opportunity," Razel shares.

"Very good," Roark responds, "I am hoping we will return home, at least on leave for a bit."

"That will be wonderful! I am about to head out for another mission in the wilderness," Razel informs.

"Oh, very good. Sounds like the reconnaissance training," Raya speculates.

"Yes. Scouting, tracking…wilderness. I am looking forward to it, but I do not want to miss your visit," Razel expresses.

"We will schedule a time when you are home," Roark assures.

"Or you come here!" Ryleigh chimes in.

Razel smiles. "I would like that! Either way…I will see you soon! I love you guys!"

"We love you, sweetie," Raya voices.

"I love you, Razel." Ryleigh smiles.

"I love you!" Razel smiles with an endearing love.

"You be safe out there. I am so proud of you. I love you." Roark begins to choke up.

"Thanks, Dad. I love you." Razel reaches to touch the sphere and end the transmission.

Razel sits back, then she decides to go to her room and sleep. She thinks to herself, *sleep is healing. Our spirit and our body heal during sleep.* She snuggles under her covers. She closes her eyes and smiles as she recalls memories when her family was together. She thinks about and prays for Chiawaukas and humans she knows, and drifts off to sleep.

Chapter 16

REBEL CHIAWAUKAS FLEE

After successfully coercing his Chiawauka comrades, they confiscate a space ship. Zane is masterful and resourceful. He possesses the ability to cleverly deceive. His charm is disarming.

The high priests are notified by ground control. They walk over to the window that spans the length of the conference room.

"Did you see this coming?" Ammerie questions Akshai.

"Not of this magnitude," Akshai voices. "However, I am not surprised."

······ ❦ ······

Santos makes communication with the rebel Chiawaukas. His face fills the entire screen. "I am Santos. Leader of the Verndari. Zane…we have been watching. Get out of the ship now. You have nowhere to go…no place to run. No purpose apart from the Chiawaukas…."

"We will remain Chiawaukas…under our own authority." Zane closes communications.

"I thought you said we were assigned to this mission," Sean states.

Without haste, Zane orders Graham, the navigational officer, "Set in a course for VeNoma."

The rebel Chiawaukas flee the planet Chiaras.

The Verndari pursue, launching periodic strikes to scare them, not harm them.

·····⚮·····

The high priests contact Roark and Raya through the communication sphere.

"Hello. How may we help?" Roark asks.

"We want to be the ones to tell you that a group of rebel Chiawaukas have left the planet. We are tracking them," Akshai details. "It appears they are heading to VeNoma."

"Oh my! Is Razel alright?" Raya asks.

"Yes. Razel excels in every area," Ammerie voices. "You raised her well, she is teachable. Akshai and I want to tell you the leader of the rebels is…well…it is Zane."

Roark and Raya are aghast.

"You need to have a contingency plan. No telling what direction this disaster will take. Whatever back-up plan you come up with…add it into the Ancient Writings," Roark suggests.

"Thank you, Roark. That is a wise recommendation," Akshai acknowledges.

"Give our daughter a hug for us," Raya requests.

Ammerie nods. "I will."

Chapter 17

SUMMON THE VERNDARI

"I am tracking the rebel Chiawaukas. How can I assist you?" Santos, the leader of the Verndari questions.

High Priest Akshai expresses slight surprise. "Alright...so you are aware of the rebels...."

"Yes. Nikolai, my first officer, has been observing what has been happening." Santos divulges.

Akshai nods. "Very good...then you are aware we attempted communication with them; however, they blocked our signal."

Santos nods. "Yes. I **did** communicate with them before they departed Chiaras. They refused to negotiate. We are in pursuit of them now. We will not tolerate such action among supreme guardian beings. We will offer to them a peaceful return, but if they refuse, we will remove the powers they possess as Chiawaukas. They will remain on the planet VeNoma forever.

High Priestess Ammerie displays concern.

High Priest Akshai nods. "We understand."

"I'm curious, if they not only refuse to return as peaceful supreme guardian beings, wonder if they choose to attack?" High Priestess Ammerie poses the question.

"They are renegades. If they launch an attack against us, we will deem it necessary to destroy them," Santos sternly outlines. "But...because they are supreme guardian beings...created to protect the humans of our galaxy and to serve, we will refrain from such a measure and only use it as a last resort." Santos pauses. He adds, "I think a contingency plan is called for. Nikolai and I will help formulate one."

Akshai and Ammerie both nod with reverence to Santos, leader of the Verndari.

Chapter 18

THE VERNDARI MAKE CONTACT

When the Verndari reach the atmosphere of VeNoma, Santos communicates, "Zane...and rebel Chiawaukas...I am Santos...leader of the Verndari. You have violated the vows of the Chiawaukas and are now in contempt. Surrender yourselves peacefully."

Sean, Zaria, Graham, and Ava, along with the other Chiawaukas, express panic and concern.

"Zane...you told us all was cool...that the high priests ordered this," Graham recounts as he turns his head to glance back at Zane, momentarily taking his eyes off of the helm.

"I do not want to lose my powers! My abilities to help and serve," Ava contends.

"We are not going to lose anything," Zane assures.

"Your time to choose is coming to an end. Your powers will be stripped from you!" The stern, penetrating voice of Santos resonates throughout the Chiawauka ship that sits on the surface of the planet VeNoma. "I urge you to reconsider your choices and return peacefully."

"Follow me!" Zane commands.

The Chiawaukas rush from the ship.

"We will hide in those caves." Zane points. "They surely cannot strip our powers hidden in these caves."

Sean frowns. "I don't know, Zane...the powers of the Verndari are mighty."

"Wait here," Zane commands. Zanes navigates his way safely back to the ship. He rushes to the control room and flips on switches, presses buttons, and aims a laser directly at the Verndari ship that hovers in the atmosphere. He then sets a timer and races to get out of the ship and return to the caves.

......⚭......

"I don't think I want to be here. I miss our friends. I miss the high priests," Zaria sighs.

Ava and Lydia express the same concerns.

"Look. We are here. Maybe we *can* restore VeNoma, so humans can thrive here once again...then we will have made a difference," Sean proposes.

"That sounds good in theory, but it does not change the fact that our so-called friend coerced us all," Graham reminds.

"That is true." Earl nods.

Zane enters the cave. "Brace yourselves."

"Oh, Zane...what have you done?" Ivan quizzes.

The Chiawaukas spread out in the dark cave. Scotopic vision is one of their abilities.

There is an explosion above them.

"What is happening?" Ivan questions.

Ava meditates, so she can determine the source of the explosion. She closes her eyes. She opens her hands and turns her palms up. Not much time passes before Ava raises her voice, "You shot at the Verndari with a laser!" Ava is livid.

"What! I was hoping for a peaceful resolution," Lydia voices.

"Look...we need to make the best of this situation," Dezi suggests.

"Our names are mud!" Zaria throws her arms about. "We will be written in the Ancient Writings as traitors…rebels! I am *NOT* okay with this!" Zaria professes.

Just then, they feel movement under their feet. They hear more explosions. Continuous…non-stop explosions…one after another…after another. Suddenly, the surface under their feet begins to shift. Some Chiawauka rebels try to position themselves between the stalagmites. They place their hands behind them on the cave walls and secure their footing. Others search to find shelter under a ledge. No place is safe. Stalactites break off and fall from the cave ceiling. The surface of the planet in the cave begins to break apart.

Another blast penetrates the cave! Debris from the explosions makes visibility impossible.

"What was that?" Earl shouts.

"What was what?" Sean questions.

"Something is crawling on me!" Graham yells.

Multiple stalactites and rock fragments plummet from the collapsing ceiling of the cave, striking the Chiawaukas. Each Chiawauka drops to the surface floor from the impact. There is a powerful, quick, bright flash from some form of energy. Experiencing agonizing pain, the Chiawaukas scream out! They hear sounds of rubble striking the surface, along with slithering and crunching surrounding them.

"Beam us out of here!" Lydia pleads.

Zane attempts to beam them out. He cannot.

All goes silent. The air is thick with dust and debris.

……⟨∾⟩……

Particles in the air settles and clears. Bodies arise. Zane and the others stare at each other. Fright and dismay consume them.

The handsome Chiawauka who is Zane, steps forward. The sound of his pleasing voice has changed. For the first time, Zane and the others hear Zane's eerie voice when he expounds, "I am the Warlord Alchodor. I am the leader of the Cryptolores." He raises one of his arms, notices, and examines his disproportionately long fingers.

The others follow his lead.

Ava takes a step. "I am Avaridia…at your service."

"My name is Scaleon," Sean asseverates. "I am second in command."

Earl addresses the group, "I am Erometh."

"I am Lusper," Zaria informs.

Dezi slightly bows. "I am Degula."

Ivan nods. "I am Iram."

Lydia voices, "My name is Suvidia."

"And, I am Garule," states Graham.

The Chiawaukas remain standing. They notice significant changes in their appearance and detect they possess unique, disturbing, supernatural abilities.

"We have much to do!" The Warlord Alchodor articulates.

Chapter 19

THE CRYPTOLORES ESCAPE VENOMA

The warlord plots their course to Tertammi. The Cryptolores flee VeNoma.

"Our first mission as Cryptolores will be taking care of some Chiawaukas!" The Warlord Alchodor bellows.

The Verndari shadow and launch assaults with their weapons.

The Cryptolores vanish. They manage to escape unscathed and swiftly navigate to the area where they believe the Chiawaukas reside on the planet Tertammi. Scaleon and Avaridia swoop down. They scout the premises to pinpoint the exact location. They discover that the Chiawaukas, along with the humans, are asleep. Scaleon reports their findings to the Warlord Alchodor. Alchodor orders Iram, Erometh, and Garule to enter the sleeping Chiawaukas through their mouths. This way, the Cryptolores can end the life of the Chiawauka family by suffocating them while they sleep, choking their airways from inside of their throats.

"We will hide on Acheeas until we attack Chiaras," The Cryptolore Warlord communicates his plans of assault. The hideous beings take flight to the planet Acheeas after their diabolical mission on Tertammi. The Verndari quickly pick up their trail and continue the chase, launching more assaults with their weapons.

Again, the Cryptolores vanish from their sight. The Cryptolores land on Acheeas. They make short work of robbing a few Chiawaukas of their life.

Chapter 20

RAZEL'S NIGHTMARE

Razel tosses. She turns and shifts her body. She moves about like she is in a struggle for her life. Abruptly, she wakes and sits up with her hands on her throat as if she is choking. She is breathing heavy and fast, in a panic, then she begins coughing. Sweat drips from her forehead. She taps her forehead to help herself focus. She scans her surroundings and realizes it must have been a nightmare. Her senses are on full alert, though she lays her head back down.

Chapter 21

DARKNESS STRIKES TERTAMMI

M alini, the first lady of Tertammi voices, "I am surprised Roark, Raya, and Ryleigh are not awake."

"That *is* unusual. I will go check on them." Teryk stands. He walks down the tile floor hallway to their quarters. Teryk knocks. He knocks a second time. "Roark? Raya?" Teryk wrinkles his forehead. *Curious,* he thinks to himself. Teryk rushes back to the kitchen to retrieve the key to the door.

"Are they alright?" Malini questions.

"I don't know. There is no answer," Teryk expresses panic.

Malini gets up and quickly follows him. Teryk places the key into the lock. He opens the door. Anxiety surges through his body when he enters the quarters. He and Malini swiftly sweep each room with their eyes while they rush to the hall of bedrooms. Malini opens the door of Ryleigh at the same time Teryk opens the door of Roark and Raya.

Malini catches sight of Ryleigh snuggled under the blankets on her bed. She darts to her side. Malini reaches to touch Ryleigh and realizes she is lifeless. "Noooo!" Malini screams out. She caresses her face. Malini laments. Malini kisses the forehead of Ryleigh, then runs to the bedroom of Roark and Raya.

The heart of Teryk breaks when he hears the scream of his wife. He too, finds Roark and Raya with no breath. He examines them to see if they are injured. He finds nothing.

Malini sprints to Teryk's side. She clasps her hands over her mouth then drops to her knees next to Teryk and weeps. "How can this be? They are Chiawaukas…immortal…supreme guardian beings…."

"I do not know." Teryk steps away from the bed, pats the shoulder of his wife, then dashes to examine Ryleigh.

Malini stands. She leans over her beloved Chiawauka friends. She caresses the forehead and face of Raya, then she kisses Raya's forehead. Malini then lays her hand on the forehead of Roark. Malini offers prayers for the Chiawaukas.

Great sorrow fills Teryk when his eyes cast upon the beautiful, young Chiawauka. Teryk inhales a deep breath to get a grip on his emotions.

Teryk leaves the room at the same time that Malini exits the other bedroom. They abruptly meet in the hall. They stop. They gaze into the eyes of each other. Tears continue to stream down the face of Malini. Teryk gently leads his wife into his arms.

Malini whispers, "You knew Raya was expecting a little boy. They were going to name him Ryker."

Teryk caresses the back of Malini's head with one hand while holding her firmly with his other. "I know."

Outrage burns through every inch of Teryk's human body. Witnessing the horrendous scene of their cherished friends is incomprehensible. He whispers, "I need to notify the council."

Malini nods. She steps aways from his comforting embrace. "Yes…go."

Teryk promptly walks to his desk where the communication sphere is located. He transmits to the high priests along with all the leaders of the Estellas Galaxy under the emergency guidelines. Once everyone has checked-in, he begins, "The lives of Roark, Raya, and Ryleigh have been robbed. I inspected their bodies for foul play and have found nothing, so far. Their appearance is of a grey hue. Their lips appear to have a black film on them. I recommend we meet immediately. Action must be taken!"

ALL the planetary leaders, including the high priests, express shock and disbelief.

"I am going to send Weston and John to you. I am also sending Paxton. He can examine them. After their investigation is done, send the Chiawauka family home. We will bury them on Chiaras," High Priest Akshai instructs, then adds, "Roark and Raya made a video for Razel in case something should happen to them. You will find it amongst their things," Akshai recalls.

"It is in a box on the hidden shelf in their closet," Ammerie discloses.

"You are to secure it in a safe, weather-proof container beside their memorial stone on Tertammi. They were clear about their instructions and that Razel is not to come to Tertammi until the Ancient Writings are fulfilled.

"I understand." Teryk nods and ends the transmission.

······⚮······

Ammerie and Akshai stare at each other.

"I have no words." Akshai lowers his head.

"Nor do I," Ammerie mutters.

Silence engulfs them. They walk over to the large window and view out.

"What is to come of our peaceful galaxy?" Ammerie ponders.

"This is devastating...but we will be victorious. Do not doubt that," Akshai consoles.

Ammerie turns her head. She peers at Akshai. "You know, they were expecting a little boy."

Akshai's lips press together. He then answers, "Yes. Ryker was to be his chosen name."

Ammerie and Akshai both return their gaze to view out the window.

"We cannot tell Razel," Ammerie voices.

"No. We cannot. Roark and Raya were very specific in their instructions," Akshai concurs.

"They were planning on telling her during their visit," Ammerie comments.

"Yes." Akshai's heart sinks. "We need to contact Ollie and Omar. They need to return...to be here when we break the news to Razel."

"Oh, I agree. They were best of friends with Roark and Raya...well...everyone was," Ammerie expresses.

"Briele may have already briefed Omar and Ollie along with Victor and Viana," Akshai suggests.

"Perhaps. We need to bring them home now before we notify Razel," Ammerie communicates.

The High Priests contact the leader of Acheeas using the communication sphere.

"I am here," Briele transmits.

"Very good. Have you informed the Chiawaukas stationed on your planet?" Akshai inquires.

"I did. I do not believe that was overstepping," Briele offers.

"Not at all. We are requesting Ollie and Omar return at once," Ammerie conveys.

"They have already left. Victor and Viana choose to remain until further instructions," Briele outlines.

"Very good. Our wise Chiawaukas...they know what to do," Ammerie indicates.

"Yes, for now, Victor and Viana stay with you, on Acheeas." Akshai states.

Briele nods.

Akshai ends the transmission. "Now, we wait."

"John, Paxton, and Weston should be on Tertammi by now," Ammerie speculates.

"Yes…their investigation, I am sure, is well underway," Akshai notes.

......⚬ℛ⚬......

Hours pass. The high priests are in prayer when they hear the planetary communication sphere chime.

"We are here," Akshai reaches to press the visual button and answers.

The screen displays John, Paxton, and Weston along with Teryk and Malini.

"Our investigation is complete. They were suffocated. Actually, choked to death from within. Residue of an unknown filmy black substance is evident in all their throats, as well as on their lips," Paxton reports.

"Is that all?" Akshai questions.

"No. Their lives were robbed while they slept. There was no way they could protect themselves," Paxton details.

"We believe these murders were perpetrated," Father John solemnly discloses.

"Very well. Please clean off the residue from them and return the Chiawauka family to Chiaras. Place them in the ice lockers. We will have a burial for them next week," High Priest Akshai requests.

The team nods.

"I also collected samples of the residue of the filmy substance so I can study it," Paxton communicates.

"Well done. Excellent idea." Akshai nods.

"There is something else," Father John relays.

"What is that?" Akshai asks.

"On the window, the words, 'We are the Cryptolores,' was written with a black filmy substance. The same substance we found on the lips and in the throats of the Chiawaukas," Father John details.

"Who are the Cryptolores?" Puzzlement casts across the face of Akshai.

Father John presses his hands together as if in prayer and begins, "If I may…." Father John slightly bows. "Akshai…when I placed my hand on the forehead of Roark…I could see the Chiawaukas that rebelled and broke away. They have somehow transitioned into a type of filmy cloud formation. It seems they possess the ability to shift to matter," Father John explains, using his hands, positioning his palms up. He slightly tilts his head, "The rebel Chiawaukas hid from the Verndari in a cave on VeNoma…and they emerged as…the Cryptolores. At this time, we can only speculate that an unexplainable phenomenon befell the rebels after the attack of the Verndari, transforming them into these black filmy cloud-like creatures.

Akshai remains silent. He lowers his eyes and inhales a deep breath. He then raises his eyes and peers into the eyes of Father John. "I see."

"It fills me with great sorrow to inform you the leader of the Cryptolores is Zane. He now refers to himself as the Cryptolore Warlord Alchodor. Sean is second in command. He goes by the name, Scaleon," Father John reveals.

"I am grateful for your abilities Father John," Akshai earnestly conveys. "Now we know *who* we are dealing with."

"Thank you. I am grateful to be of service." Father John slightly bows. "…and yes…now we know who we are dealing with."

……·ᘓᏝᏬ·……

Ammerie and Akshai exchange eye contact.

"My heart feels great pain from the loss of this beloved family…." Ammerie dabs tears away.

The double doors swoosh open and startle the high priests.

"Oh! I did not mean to startle you," Ollie voices.

Ammerie rushes to Ollie. They exchange a hug. Omar and Akshai exchange a firm handshake.

"We came as soon as we heard. Roark and Raya have told us their wishes from forever ago...that if they have children, and something should happen to them, we are to be their guardians," Omar accounts.

"Yes, they made known to us that information as well. Razel clearly does not need a guardian due to her age...but she will need emotional support," Ammerie conveys.

"Yes." Ollie nods. "I will hold her as my daughter."

"Have you told her yet?" Omar asks.

"No. We were waiting for your arrival," Akshai answers.

"I will call her in now. We think it best to deliver the news here instead of the peace of her home," Ammerie explains.

"I agree." Ollie nods.

······⟳······

Razel arrives at the academy. She is excited about her upcoming assignment. Her smile quickly dissolves when she hears Ammerie's voice. Razel stops and places her index and middle finger to her left temple. "Razel, please come on over to the embassy. We will be in the conference room."

Razel communicates through telepathy, "I will be right there." Razel senses something. She cannot put her finger on it, but anxiety begins to grip her. She exits the academy out the side doors and rushes across the sidewalk to the embassy. Razel enters the embassy. She swiftly ascends the stairs to the first floor and continues to the door of the conference room. She opens it and enters.

"Razel!" Ollie smiles and quickly steps over to hug Razel.

"Gosh! It is great to see you two!" Razel's smile is back.

High Priestess Ammerie, High Priest Akshai, and Omar move closer and stand next to Razel and Ollie. Razel notices their somber expressions.

"What's up?" Razel hesitantly questions.

"Razel...." Ammerie begins.

"Razel...your family won't be coming home," Akshai gently voices.

"What?" Razel begins to quiver and sniffle with an expression of bewilderment.

Ollie reaches for the hands of Razel. She lifts Razel's hands into her hands and holds them firmly. Ollie gazes directly into the eyes of Razel. "Honey, they have died."

"What!" Razel takes a few steps backwards and hits the conference table. "I just had a video call with them! We were discussing when we would see each other."

"I know. This is the worst news ever," Ammerie softly voices.

Razel's head lowers. Her mind overflows with emotions and questions, "Wait...we are immortal...how did they die?"

"Razel...they were murdered," Omar delivers.

"WHAAAAT!" Razel shakes and expresses disbelief. "How? By who?"

A crease forms across the forehead of High Priest Akshai. "Razel...they were suffocated...choked to death from inside their throats by the Cryptolores."

Razel partially collapses and leans against the table with her hands upon the edge of the table to support her. Trying to make sense of it, she remembers her nightmare. She grabs her throat. She sighs and murmurs, "I felt them."

"What, Razel?" Ollie asks.

"I FELT IT!" Razel extends her arms. "I had a nightmare last night! I felt I was being choked...suffocated! I woke up with sweats and holding my throat! I must have felt what my family was experiencing!" Tremendous anguish surges through Razel. "WHOOOO are the Cryptolores! I don't even know WHAT to say!" Stress lines form on the forehead of Razel. "Do you have pictures? I need to see pictures!" Razel demands.

"We do…but…." Ammerie begins.

"No buts!" Razel wipes her eyes. "Show them to me now! Please."

Ammerie, Akshai, Ollie, and Omar exchange quick glances. Akshai walks over to his desk, reaches for the envelope of photos, and returns to Razel. He extends his hand with an envelope for Razel to take.

Razel snatches the envelope from his hand. She holds the envelope in one hand while she pulls out the 8 x 10 pictures with her other hand. She sets the envelope down so she can grip the photos with both hands. She quietly examines each photo. Her demeanor is stoic while she studies the photos. Tears form in her eyes. Her vision impairs while she studies the photos of her family. Razel wipes the tears from her eyes to see clearly. She inspects the details of each picture, placing one picture behind the other. She gasps. The photo of the Cryptolores evokes fright. "Teryk was able to capture these on film?" Razel questions.

"Yes. He has security cameras all around the embassy and their home." Akshai nods.

"They are a hideous, terrifying sight!" Razel continues to flip through the remaining photos. "So…." Razel sniffles. "The filmy, black substance on the lips of my family, along with their grey coloring is a sign of the Cryptolores?"

"Yes." Akshai nods.

"Who did the investigation and autopsy?" Razel inquires.

"Paxton, Father John, and Father Weston," Ammerie informs.

"I see." Razel turns and faces the table. She meticulously lays the photos next to each other in two rows on the conference table with the utmost care. She gently touches each photo. She inhales while she casts her eyes upon each photo again. She tilts her head forward and places her forehead in the fingers and palms of her hands. A storm of anxiety rushes through her mind. She closes her eyes and massages her forehead with her fingers. While her eyes remain closed, she very concisely articulates, "And who *ARE* these Cryptolore beings?"

Ammerie and Ollie want to wrap their arms around her, but they know Razel appreciates a straight shooter.

"Razel, it is our belief the Cryptolores are the rebel Chiawaukas. We believe Zane to be their leader," Ammerie divulges.

Razel gasps as if she has been gut-punched. Her head lowers. "I see." Razel's emotions spin between disbelief, shock, heartbreak, and outrage. "And their service?"

"...will be next week. Their bodies will arrive shortly. A planetary meeting is about to begin...." Akshai informs.

"May I leave?" Razel politely asks.

"Of course, Razel," Ammerie softly voices.

Razel briskly leaves the room, sails down the stairs, and runs out the large double doors of the embassy.

"We'll follow her," Ollie imparts.

Ammerie nods.

Razel runs a few blocks over to Crystal Lake Park. She stops at the edge of the clear mountain lake. Razel screams. Her scream is that of a wail. She drops to her knees. She uncontrollably sobs and screams shifting from one to the other. Razel laments for quite some time.

Ollie and Omar beam themselves to a bench at the park. They want to be there for her, though they recognize she needs her space, for now. They sit, experiencing grief as well. They pray and watch Razel's excruciating pain spill out.

······⌘······

After further discussion, the high priests decide they need to bring Viana and Victor home.

Akshai and Ammerie step to the communication sphere to make a visual contact with Briele, Reigna of Acheeas.

"Hello. How may I help you?" Briele questions.

"We need Victor and Viana to return to Chiaras immediately. Have them report to us," Akshai requests.

"I will," Briele communicates.

"We will be assigning other Chiawaukas to you," Ammerie conveys.

"Thank you. I appreciate that," Briele communicates.

Chapter 22

A PRIVATE MEETING

The high priests summon Victor. He enters the large conference room. The high priests are at the end of the table.

"Join us, Victor." High Priest Akshai stands and welcomes Victor with a firm handshake.

Victor sits in the chair next to the end of the table.

"It is so good to see you, Victor," High Priestess Ammerie voices.

"Thank you. I appreciate all the assignments you have entrusted me with," Victor humbly submits.

"Victor, it is with great sadness that we bring this to you. Your brother Zane led some Chiawaukas to revolt. They confiscated a starship, fled to VeNoma, and launched an attack against the Verndari," Akshai chronicles.

Victor is aghast. "Is he alive?" Victor questions.

"It is our belief he is. He led the rebels to the planet of Tertammi. They killed Roark, Raya, and their daughter, Ryleigh," Akshai details.

"Are you saying he murdered them?" Victor expresses disbelief.

Ammerie and Akshai frown.

"Yes. He either led the attack or was one of the ones that...." Ammerie stops speaking.

"Have you captured him? Will he be stripped of his powers?" Victor quizzes.

"Victor...he is now a Cryptolore," Akshai informs.

"I have never heard of such a name," Victor admits.

"Nor have we. Our investigative team has concluded they can shape shift from a filmy cloud-like form to that of substance," Ammerie details.

Victor sets his elbows on the conference table and presses his fingers into his forehead and firmly rubs his forehead.

"Does he have a name? What is a Cryptolore?" Victor probes.

"Yes. We have been told he now refers to himself as the Warlord Alchodor of the Cryptolores," Ammerie divulges.

"We will soon meet with the high council," Akshai informs.

"Does everyone know about Zane?" Victor peers at the high priests.

"Not everyone. Not yet," Ammerie indicates.

Victor slightly nods while he tries to process all the data.

"We are sorry about your brother...." Akshai begins.

Victor slaps his hand on the table. "I have no brother." Victor stands. "If you do not mind, I need to go."

Akshai and Ammerie stand.

"Of course, we do not mind. Take whatever time you need. We would like you at one of the meetings with the leaders," Akshai imparts.

Victor nods. He quietly voices, "Thank you. I will be there." Victor turns and walks out of the conference room.

Chapter 23

THE ESTELLAS GALAXY HIGH COUNCIL MEET ON CHIARAS

"We must formulate a plan," Teryk of Tertammi states.

"I agree. The devastation that these creatures have caused...ugh." Briele sighs. "I tend to agree with the Verndari," Briele, Reigna of Acheeas sternly voices.

"It is not our way to eliminate life. It is our belief to give every opportunity for beings to return their lives to live in accordance to our Creator of the Universe," High Priest Akshai advocates.

"Yes...but we are dealing with murderers!" Kehlani (Ka-law-knee) of Kareenia stands. She slaps one hand on the conference table and asseverates, "And...they just murdered Chiawaukas on Tertammi!" Kehlani waves her arms about.

"Augustus, Caprina...what is your position?" Teryk asks.

Augustus of Chiaras frowns. Creases on his forehead appears. "It is alarming. The devastation that has occurred...lives lost...I believe the Cryptolores to be a threat to the lives in our galaxy and maybe one day reaching into the universe. I see them as an imminent danger." Augustus pauses. "With that being said, if the Chiawaukas have a contingency plan, I am willing to hear it and consider it."

"I believe the Cryptolores to be sinister and malevolent. No life is safe with them lurking about the galaxy, but if the Chiawaukas have a fail-safe plan, I am open to it," Caprina voices.

Santos, leader of the Vernadari, communicates, "I will adhere to the plan of the Chiawaukas…but if they escape…we will pursue them…and destroy them all."

"I agree to your terms, Santos," High Priestess Ammerie voices.

High Priest Akshai nods. "Thank you, Santos. If our plan should fail then it falls to you."

"I understand," Santos maintains. "But if we encounter the Cryptolores before you implement your plan…we will attack. Our last visual contact with them was when they departed Tertammi. It is our belief they were heading to Acheeas." Santos stands. His tall, large muscular stature is a sight to behold. "I want you all to remember…do NOT say our name aloud. We can hear it and will assume you need our immediate assistance in battle. Our name…the Verndari…is only to be spoken when you are in imminent danger. Is this understood?"

Everyone at the planetary meeting nod regarding the request of Santos, leader of the Verndari. Nikolai, his second in command, also stands. Nikolai, along with all the Verndari, sports a tall, large muscular stature.

Santos adds, "I will appoint members of my squad to assist in execution of your plan."

The high priests exchange a barely noticeable glance at each other.

High Priest Akshai slowly nods. "We welcome the Verndari to assist us."

Each member of the Estellas Galaxy High Council and Court stand and bow with respect to the revered leader of the Verndari. Santos and Nickolai leave.

Chapter 24

CAPTURING THE CRYPTOLORES

High Priest Akshai and High Priestess Ammerie consult the elders. They summon the former high priests, Alaric, and Imara, along with seasoned Chiawaukas, and the bishops. The human leaders of Chiaras, Augustus, and Caprina, also sit in on the assembly. The leaders of the Estellas Galaxy are in attendance as well.

"What do we know about these Cryptolores?" Alaric questions.

Akshai walks around the table and hands out pictures of the Cryptolores. "These are images taken of the Cryptolores. The rebel Chiawaukas fled to VeNoma. When they left VeNoma...not only was their bodily form changed...their names changed as well. They refer to themselves as the Cryptolores."

"We know they kill life," Kehlani sternly expresses and points with her index finger. "What they did is an atrocity!"

"Though it is believed the rebel Chiawaukas were stripped of their supernatural powers...after the attack from the Verndari, something mysterious seems to have transpired...not only restoring powers to them but transforming them into these Cryptolore beings," Mateo theorizes.

There is a knock at the double doors. A Chiawauka stands and opens the door. It is Paxton.

Paxton rushes through the doors. "Excuse me for interrupting. The lab tests I ran are complete and I have the results on the samples we removed from the Chiawaukas on Tertammi. We can now verify from this discovery, what we initially believed…that they can, indeed, shift from a filmy cloud-like form, to that of substance. It is our theory from the pathology results…that they must find a live host to sustain their life, whether it be human or animal."

"I recommend we capture them, use a forever anesthetizing gas and imprison them deep in a cavern on the planet Soleil," Akshai presents.

"How do you propose you will capture them?" questions Briele.

The leaders and seasoned Chiawaukas are perplexed.

Silence sweeps the room.

Some begin jotting down notes and theories. Some appear to be in deep thought. After many thought-provoking minutes, a Chiawauka speaks out.

"I've got it!" Weston stands. "I think I have the answer!" Weston raises one arm in the air while he walks over to the display board. He draws out a design. "I suggest gel. A gel net. It will act like adhesive to their molecular structure, then we will instantly create a stainless-steel barrier that will contain them," Weston suggests.

The others nod in agreement as they glance around the conference table at each other.

"Wait…the fact remains their form, at times, is that of a cloud. We cannot catch a cloud. I suggest we wait until they inhabit an animal or…." Alaric interrupts Mateo.

"We are not going to sacrifice animals or humans. I know where you are going with this Mateo, and in theory it makes sense…to wait until the Cryptolores have chosen a host." Others in the room nod, understanding what is being said. Alaric continues, "But the lives of the hosts would be sacrificed. They would have to be imprisoned as well," Alaric maintains.

"Who led the rebel Chiawaukas?" Imara inquires. "Are his powers strong?"

"Very. He was an extremely gifted Chiawauka. His name was Zane, the brother of Victor," Akshai answers. "He now identifies himself as the Cryptolore Warlord Alchodor."

"I have no brother!" Victor stands. "I request from this day forward…none of you speak his name to me."

Some in the room tighten their lips. Some deeply inhale. Some slightly nod. All understand and each acknowledge they will comply to Victor's request.

Victor sits back down.

"I believe we need to implement an alternative plan," Briele recommends.

"Yes, we have one in the…." Akshai is interrupted.

Abruptly, out of nowhere, they feel a rapid vibration due to seismic waves traveling through the planet. Concern casts across their faces while they keep their mouths closed to equalize pressure. Instantaneously, they hear an explosion on Chiaras following the jolt!

All those in attendance quickly rise from their seats and rush to the large window to view out. They witness Cryptolores flying about with the Verndari close behind launching their weapons.

The Vernadari ship zigs, then zags. They circle tightly in pursuit of the Cryptolores. The Verndari fire different weapons.

Trees break in half, some completely burst apart. Rocks slide down mountains. Grass and dirt particles are sucked into the air. Holes on the planet surface develop. The Verndari launch one of their most powerful weapons. Upon impact, a transient crater forms immediately.

Ammerie and Akshai exchange eye contact and nod. Simultaneously, Ammerie leads the others to enact their plan of capture while Akshai places his index and middle finger to his left temple. "Santos…stop the attack! We have formulated a plan to capture the Cryptolores and imprison them for eternity."

The other Chiawaukas vanish. They follow Ammerie to implement the proposed plan.

The team of Chiawaukas form into a circle and position themselves above the embassy. "Weston…we will try your plan. We are…after all…Chiawaukas. Improvise if you must, to make this mission a success!" High Priestess Ammerie commands.

The Chiawaukas nod.

The Vernadari flight crew that Santos assigns to the mission transports to the Chiawauka cargo ship.

"Akshai…we will withdraw," the words of Santos are heard by Akshai and Ammerie. "I DO NOT understand why they appear unharmed. I *KNOW* our weapons hit them." The brows of Santos furrow. "This makes no sense." Santos paces the bridge of his ship with his arms behind his back.

The Verndari ship tilts to the left, turns, and departs the atmosphere of Chiaras. Santos orders his navigational team to have his ship hover over the planet in case the Chiawauka plan fails.

The Chiawaukas transition themselves to be undetectable to the Cryptolores and strategically implement their objective. They soar high and spread out to encompass the Cryptolores with a massive invisible gel net. The Cryptolores fly in different directions as if in a frenzy, not knowing where to go. They swarm and veer off. The Chiawaukas maneuver to match the Cryptolore flight pattern. Again, the Cryptolores shift trajectory. The Chiawaukas mirror their movements. A mountain is in close range. Another idea comes to Mateo. He places his index and middle finger on his left temple to communicate to his comrades, "I have an idea. Trust me. Be ready to capture them."

"Are you sure?" Weston questions.

"Yes. I think this will work. I will see you again someday. It has been my honor to serve with you and all the Chiawaukas...." Mateo expresses.

"Wait...." Weston beseeches.

"We appreciate you, Mateo. Your service has always been honorable," High Priestess Ammerie transmits through telepathy.

"Let's hope my idea works," Mateo inhales and voices.

Mateo soars to a boulder high on the side of the mountain. He leans back, watching, waiting, for the Cryptolores. Chiawaukas remain invisible while they hover in position. They wait, and wait, patiently.

Mateo feels a thump in his body. He reacts quickly and places his index and middle finger to his left temple. He announces, "They are here! Be ready!" Then he feels another jolt, and another, one by one, by one by one. The Cryptolores enter his body through his eyes, his nose, his ears, and his mouth. Soon all the Cryptolores have invaded and now possess the brave, selfless Chiawauka.

Ammerie places her index and middle finger on her left temple to communicate. She whispers, "I do not recall there were so many rebel Chiawaukas that turned into the Cryptolores. The number of Cryptolores that entered Mateo's body is too numerous to count."

During Ammerie's communication, Mateo manages to stand. He leaps off the boulder, plummeting through the sky. The Chiawaukas swoop in with the invisible net. Swiftly they execute their plan to encapsulate the Cryptolores that inhabit Mateo and flood the chamber with an anesthetizing gas. The cylinder does not expand and encompass Mateo. It malfunctions. The Chiawaukas immediately beam Mateo with the Cryptolores and themselves to the cargo ship. The Verndari flight crew instantaneously depart the atmosphere and lock in coordinates for Soleil.

Ammerie returns to the embassy. Akshai and Ammerie scour the map of Soleil ensuring the geographical longitude and latitude of the cavern. They correspond the data to the team.

The Chiawauka cargo ship reaches the atmosphere of the planet Soleil. Chiawaukas touch their emblem on their uniform and beam with the anesthetized Cryptolores deep into the cavern beneath the planet surface of Soleil. The Chiawaukas meticulously survey the underground chamber to ensure there is no air that will compromise the anesthetizing gas. After a thorough inspection is complete, the Chiawaukas hold out their hands and a protective mask manifests in each of their hands. They place the mask over their faces and fill the chamber with an anesthetizing gas. The team departs with the belief the Cryptolores which inhabit their comrade, Mateo, will eternally remain imprisoned.

Chapter 25

INVESTIGATION

A team of Chiawaukas and Verndari do a ground sweep, investigating for any remnants of blood from the Cryptolores. Santos, Akshai, and Ammerie join the team and sift through the ground cover and debris from the recent attack launched on the Cryptolores.

"I know our ship's weapons hit them," Santos articulates.

"I have no doubt," Akshai acknowledges. "If there is blood here...it will be found." Akshai pats Santos on the back.

"Over here." Mason sees something suspicious.

Akshai, Santos, and Ammerie trek over to the area Mason is at.

"Look...there appears to be an olive-green color matter attached to some black filmy slime." Mason points to several places across the ground.

Nikolai brings a container in which to collect the samples. He unscrews the lid and stoops over to carefully pick up the filmy olive-green substance with a tool. Nikolai then scrapes it into the container.

They see the span is greater than they thought. Others join in collecting the olive-green matter splattered across the ground and rocks.

Nikolai stands. "They do bleed. We hit them."

Santos and the high priests exhale a sigh of relief.

Chapter 26

A DAY OF REMEMBRANCE

The Chiawaukas, humans of Chiaras, and planetary leaders gather to honor their beloved Mateo along with the highly regarded and cherished Chiawauka family: Roark, Raya, and Ryleigh.

Former High Priest Alaric addresses the assembly, "It is with great honor that I speak today for our beloved Chiawaukas. First...I served with Mateo for decades. If you were fortunate enough to know Mateo, you would know Mateo was a Chiawauka with ideas. Some of his ideas made us laugh...some were very innovative. A most recent idea he had...was his last. He improvised...thought outside of the realm...he sacrificed his life to save countless lives." Alaric raises his hands to the sky. "Mateo, you have always been an outstanding and beloved Chiawauka. May God...Creator of the Universe, grant you eternal peace and rest."

High Priest Akshai then addresses the assembly, "Our hearts are also heavy with the loss of our beloved Roark, Raya, and Ryleigh. Roark was one of the finest Chiawaukas I have had the pleasure of serving with. He and Raya were not only disciplined...they were able to be flexible. Their youngest daughter, Ryleigh, was a joy to be around and aspired to be like her parents and older sister, Razel. It is with great sorrow we bury our people today. May God, Creator of the Universe, grant them eternal peace and rest. May we be granted what we need to forge forward with the mission we were created for."

The service ends. The vocalists lead in beautiful chants.

The high priests follow the Chiawaukas who carry the tall processional candlesticks. Directly behind the high priests, are the Chiawauka pallbearers who follow the procession down the aisle, wheeling the cylinder-shaped caskets. The caskets for the Chiawaukas are flat on the bottom. Each end is about twenty-six inches in height, with a clear slight dome for the top, so you can view the body. Omar, Ollie, and Razel follow. The rest of the assembly fall in behind and head to the large double doors.

......⚬⧽⧼⚬......

They reach the Garden of Remembrance. Holes for the caskets have been prepared. The caskets of Roark, Raya, and their daughter Ryleigh, are laid beside each other. Each casket base is lowered into the prepared area so the clear dome top is merely inches above ground level. This makes viewing the departed Chiawaukas easy for those who visit the garden. Cobblestone pathways weave through the garden of beautiful flowers, shrubs, and trees. The garden also sports all types of foliage. The memorial stone engraved for Mateo is situated across from the Chiawauka family.

Chapter 27

VICTOR AND RAZEL INTERACT

After the burial, humans and Chiawaukas mingle. Victor sees Razel and approaches her.

"Hey," Victor voices.

Feeling tremendous heaviness, Razel rolls her lips. "Hey."

They exchange eye contact.

"Razel, I cannot even begin to convey the depth of condolences I want to express to you," Victor begins.

"Thank you. I feel the same for you. I can imagine what you must be going through, as well," Razel comforts.

Victor slightly nods his head.

The two stand in silence next to each other gazing across the magnificent terrain.

After quite some length of time, Victor voices, "I am sorry...."

Razel does not let Victor finish. "Victor, you have nothing to be sorry for. We both believed in him. You lost your brother; I lost my family."

"Please...." Victor wipes a tear from his cheek. "Please do not mention his name. It sickens me what he has done. I have no brother. He is dead to me."

Razel casts her eyes down and slightly nods. She places her hand on the forearm of Victor and turns her head to look at him. "I understand. Somehow, I wonder if this is my fault since I declined his proposal, and...."

"Razel, don't. You did NOT do this. You did nothing wrong. For whatever reason, Zane has bullying tendencies, insecurities, and problems with authority. He has for a very long time...long before you entered his life," Victor solemnly assures Razel.

Razel wipes tears from her eyes. "I don't even miss him, Victor," Razel avers.

"I understand," Victor expresses with compassion.

Razel breaks down. She begins sobbing uncontrollably and gasping for breath, crying out, "I miss my family SOOO much! How can I do life without them? This is my fault! I shouldn't have responded to him...saying, 'bring it'!"

Victor wraps his arm around her and leans his head into her head. Razel shifts her stance and weeps into the shoulder of Victor. The two grieving Chiawaukas exchange a healing energy transference through their hug.

······⚬⧓⚬······

Ollie and Omar observe the exchange between Victor and Razel. When they believe it is the appropriate time, they stroll over to the grieving Chiawaukas.

Razel lifts her head from Victor's shoulder. She gazes at Ollie and Omar and rushes into Ollie's arms. Ollie comforts Razel and gently caresses her long blonde hair with one hand while she holds her tightly with her other hand.

Ollie softly whispers, "Omar and I want to be your parents. I know you are too old to be taken care of, but we would still like to be considered your family. Your parents asked this, of us, long ago, if something should ever happen to them."

Razel nods while her head remains buried on the shoulder of Ollie. "Thank you. I would love for you and Omar to be my family."

Ollie tightens her embrace around Razel with an endearing hug. Omar places one of his hands on the back of Ollie and one on the back of Razel.

While Razel is in the arms of Ollie, she extends her hand to the hand of Victor. Victor exchanges eye contact with Razel and takes firmly ahold of her hand. They feel each other's piercing pain.

Omar reaches for Victor's arm and slightly pulls Victor in for a group hug. Viana walks up and joins with her friends. She positions herself beside Ollie and Razel. The energy exchange they create is so powerful that the Chiawaukas illuminate.

Chapter 28

THE HIGH COUNCIL MEETS TO DISCUSS A CONTINGENCY PLAN

The Chiawaukas on the planet Chiaras meet in the conference room at the embassy. They wait for the arrival of the planetary leaders and the Chiawaukas stationed on other planets.

"It is good to see each of you. Thank you for coming," High Priest Akshai addresses.

"Has everyone reviewed the back-up plan we previously sent you, that Roark and Raya suggested…along with Nikolai and Santos?" High Priestess Ammerie asks.

Everyone nods or verbalizes, "Yes."

"We will write our contingency plan into the Ancient Writings as Roark recommended," Akshai informs.

"I am wondering, why do we need a contingency plan?" Kahlani questions. "The Chiawaukas and Verndari established protocols to ensure the safety of our galaxy long ago."

"Good point, Kahlani. I believe a contingency plan is necessary to ensure the protection of the humans on the planet Soleil and throughout the galaxy. We have enjoyed a peaceful galaxy, but now, with the Cryptolores…I know, I personally feel at rest knowing we are going to have a contingency plan," Briele discloses.

Kahlani nods. "I understand your viewpoint. Thank you for sharing your perspective."

Briele smiles at Kahlani.

"I think this plan is well thought out," Imara voices. "Thank you, Santos, and Nikolai, for bringing this to us."

"When we mentioned we were going to come up with an idea, Akshai shared with us what Roark and Raya had been working on. Their exceptional insight assisted us in formulating this plan. I believe Briele and others also recommended we have a contingency plan." Santos glances around at the members of the council.

Alaric nods. "It is brilliant! Always good to ensure the security of our galaxy and universe."

The entire Estellas High Council approve.

"When we anoint Augustus and his wife Caprina, the powers of our DNA will extend to their children," High Priest Akshai details while peering into the eyes of each in attendance.

"Very good." High Priestess Ammerie nods with approval. "In addition…that is how it will be passed through the bloodlines of the humans on Soleil."

"Yes…oldest daughter of the family," Akshai specifies.

"And once the two families meet…well, at some point in their generations…there will be a marriage. That is when they will fully have their powers." Ammerie envisions.

"There will be an anointing by the Chiawaukas onto the families once they are joined," Briele outlines.

"The child of that couple will have the purest form of powers," Akshai indicates.

"Both families we anoint with our DNA will have supernatural abilities," Ammerie communicates.

"Yes, but the strength of their powers is determined by what degree, if any, that they are tapped into their supernatural abilities and senses," Akshai adds.

High Priestess Ammerie nods. "Very good. I think we have reviewed most of the details."

"Sounds like a solid plan. I like it!" Kahlani voices.

"I agree. I am pleased with this proposal," Teryk communicates.

"Indeed," Akshai agrees.

"I like this very much," Imara expresses.

"The strategy is well thought out. Now it is time to go forth and execute it," The former High Priest Alaric indicates.

"It still puzzles me, that we witnessed so many of those Cryptolore beings enter Mateo. I do not recall there were that many rebels," Ammerie reiterates.

"Perhaps VeNoma still had inhabitants, and they joined forces with the rebel Chiawaukas," Kahlani suggests.

"That does not explain their ability to fly, transform into a cloud, nor possess a life," Teryk contends.

Everyone around the conference table gestures in agreement.

"I would say we have before us an intriguing mystery." Imara stands.

"That it is," Teryk concurs. Visible crease lines form in the center of his forehead and between his eyebrows.

"I will not rest until I figure out a way to rescue Mateo," Paxton asseverates.

"We appreciate your dedication, Paxton. Keep us apprised," High Priest Akshai acknowledges.

"Though the circumstances are grave, it is so good to see all of you again," Alaric imparts. He stands. "Until we see you again, peace be to you all." Alaric nods and glances around the room at everyone.

Imara smiles and waves.

The others in the room respond with the same gestures and sentiments.

Alaric and Imara leave the conference room.

"Alright." Santos stands. "Nikolai and I will return to our ship. Remember, do not say our name aloud unless it is an emergency," Santos reminds.

Those gathered nod at his request.

······⸱⸱⸱⸱⸱⸱

Augustus, Carpina, Teryk, Malini, Kahlani, and Briele rise from their seats and walk to stand in front of the large window that spans the length of the conference room. They position themselves into a circle. High Priest Akshai and High Priestess Ammerie levitate themselves above the leaders. The high priests perform the ceremony to transfer their DNA to the human planetary leaders of the Estellas Galaxy. Akshai and Ammerie move their hands in a figure eight while softly chanting. Golden droplets release from their hands and drop onto the heads and bodies of each planetary leader. The golden droplets absorb into the skin of the human leaders. A blast of energy illuminates the room with gold, and golden droplets fill the room. The ceremony is complete.

······⸱⸱⸱⸱⸱⸱

After extensive reconnaissance on the planet Soleil, two human families of noble quality are chosen by the High Council. High Priest Akshai and High Priestess Ammerie prepare to embark on their journey to the planet Soleil. They will perform the ceremony to release the DNA of the Chiawaukas through the golden droplets on two human female girls.

Chapter 29

MEMORIAL ON TERTAMMI

Teryk and Malini return to their home, Tertammi.

"Do you want to place their memorial stone under the two trees that canopy on the east end of Lake Kasmira?" Malini asks.

"Yes. I believe that is an appropriate place. We sure enjoyed a lot of picnics with them at that lake," Teryk reflects. "We can place the video Roark and Raya made for Razel in a box that is weather resistant, then we can build a square brick pillar that encompasses a stainless-steel compartment with a door, and place the container with the video inside."

Malini ponders. "When it is the right time, Razel will be led to find it."

"I agree." Teryk nods.

Teryk and Malini notify the best mason to construct the brick pillar, along with engraving the memorial stone to honor the Chiawauka family. Malini and Teryk place the video into the weatherproof container, then they open the door to the stainless-steel cylinder, and set the container inside. They close it up and step back casting their eyes onto the memorial stone. Malini rests her head onto Teryk's shoulder. Teryk wraps his arm around his wife.

Chapter 30

THE HIGH PRIESTS VISIT SOLEIL

On the planet Soleil, human, Genie Arabella arrives at the home of Anna. After Anna opens the door, you hear a voice, "My mother says I can stay over tonight!" Genie Arabella exclaims.

"That is great!" Anna Grace expresses with enthusiasm. "Mom, Dad…we are gonna play outside awhile before we come in for the night," Anna voices to her parents in the kitchen. Anna steps out on the porch and takes Genie Arabella's bag. "Here, I will set it inside until we return," Anna informs.

"Sounds good," Genie Arabella replies.

The two best friends set off running on the trails alongside of the crop fields.

"This summer has gone by fast!" Anna Grace comments.

"It has," Genie Arabella remarks.

"After this…let's go back to my house. It will be time for the sun to set. We can watch the stars come out," Anna suggests.

"Sounds like fun!" Genie Arabella voices.

The girls hold hands while they skip and sing back to Anna's house.

"You two must be beat," Anna's mother mentions. "I have some cobbler and milk if you would like a bedtime snack."

"Oh, yes please." Genie Arabella smiles and sits down at the table.

The girls enjoy the cobbler and milk then retreat to the bedroom.

"Your mom is such a good cook!" Genie Arabella acknowledges.

"Thanks." Anna smiles.

The girls take turns in the bathroom. They change into their night clothes then leap into their beds. Anna's room has twin beds positioned so they can look out the large window and observe the night sky. Anna's parents step in and say goodnight. After that, the girls tell stories and giggle while they observe the stars appearing. After a while of star gazing, Genie Arabella glances over to Anna and notices she has fallen asleep. Genie Arabella positions herself on her stomach with her head resting in her hands at the foot of the bed and sets her sights on the night sky. She is not tired yet. She meditates with wonder how their lives will turn out, who will they marry, where will they live, when she notices a snow globe-like object descending from the starry sky. She thinks to herself, *what is that? I have not ever seen anything like that...oh wait! It looks like it is getting...oh my goodness!* Genie Arabella quietly and quickly slides off the bed and swiftly crawls under the bed to hide. *I need to wake Anna*, Genie Arabella thinks, but fears the object is about to break the window. It does not. Instead, the snow globe object comes through the window and hovers in mid-air. Genie Arabella is gripped with fear and awe at the same time as she peers out from under the bed. Two tall figures emerge from the sphere. They walk over to Anna Grace. One is a male and one is a female. Genie Arabella notices they are adorned in beautiful priestly garments. The female has a tiara on her head. Genie thinks to herself, *they are tall like humans, but they appear to be shades of blue. It is hard to tell since it is dark with only the light from the moon.* Genie

Arabella lies very still under the bed observing the two beings that appeared from the night sky. She witnesses them placing their hands above Anna Grace and moving their hands in a figure eight over her body. Genie Arabella hears them begin to chant. She notices they have pleasant voices. She knows they are chanting something, but she cannot make out the words. Just then, Genie Arabella witnesses golden droplets release from their hands and fall onto Anna Grace. Genie's eyes widen as she quietly observes. She witnesses the golden droplets absorb right into her best friend. The two tall beings turn and walk to their sphere. The entire room lights up with colors of gold and golden droplets. Genie Arabella, unhesitatingly, extends both of her arms as far out from under the bed as she can. She hopes she will not be detected. Golden droplets descend upon her arms and absorb into her skin as well. Genie Arabella does not feel sick, or weird, or any discomfort. She is curious and has no idea what she just encountered, but a strong sense of peace flows through her body and calms her. She watches as the snow globe shaped object sails right through the window without breaking it and ascends quickly into the sky, then it vanishes. She quietly scoots out from under the bed and climbs onto the bed. She covers up with the blankets and lies on her side. She stares at Anna Grace and wonders what has just happened. *Do I wake you now to tell you? Do I ever tell you?* Thoughts race through Genie Arabella's mind. Not knowing what to do, she closes her eyes and finally falls asleep.

Chapter 31

GENERATIONS PASS

Years pass. On several occasions, the human, Genie Arabella, considers telling Anna Grace what happened, but never does.

Anna, Aurora, and Arabella are best of friends. They grow up and they marry.

One year, while out in the field working, a storm develops with forceful winds. Genie Arabella's husband, Gabe, is caught out in the field with William and Dimitri. An airborne limb strikes Gabe, ending his life.

William, Dimitri, Anna, Aurora, and Genie Arabella build a home for Genie Arabella high up on Mancini Mountain. They build the home arranging the Aspen trees vertically to ensure the home blends in with the surrounding environment.

They live out their lives. One by one by one, they pass away, except Genie Arabella.

Chapter 32

PAXTON STUDIES INTENSIFY

Paxton diligently continues to work in his lab, studying the results of his findings from the residue left behind by the Cryptolores. He hopes to soon solve the riddle of how to rescue Mateo.

Chapter 33

DEATH OF A LOVED ONE

The news of the passing of Sophia Montanelli's grandmother, Anna Grace Casella, spreads quickly.

Queen Marcella, along with Sarita Mancini, arrive at the same time to visit Sophia.

"Oh, sweetie...I am so sorry. We all loved Anna Grace. She was a true gem," Marcella conveys after she embraces Sophia.

"Yes, I think it was just last week that I saw her at church. She was just doting on Antonio," Sarita quietly voices.

The words Sophia hears soothes her grieving heart. She smiles and glances over to her three-month-old baby, Francesca Gianetta. "I am so thankful my grandmother was able to meet my Francie. Francie will not experience first-hand the wisdom of her great-grandmother, but I will teach her through stories."

"That sounds lovely, honey," Sarita comments.

"Where is Antonio and Theodore?" Sophia asks.

"I left that little prince of mine at home so I could focus on you," Marcella confides.

"I left Antonio with Don. They will be alright for a short time. Antonio is a year-and-a-half now, I am sure Don will keep his attention," Sarita informs. "I too, just wanted to see you, Sophia."

"Thank you both. We spoke with our priest, the funeral will be in three days," Sophia shares.

"Very good. Is there anything we can do for you?" Sarita asks.

"No. Just the fact you both took time out of your day to come and visit me speaks volumes. I am blessed with your friendship," Sophia assures.

"I take it, Leonardo is at the store?" Marcella questions.

Sophia nods. "Yes. That is how he sorts through everything...work."

"That's understandable." Sarita nods. "Aw, look at your precious daughter. My goodness, she has thick brunette, hair." Sarita pauses, placing her hand gently on the sleeping baby. "Maybe my son, Antonio, and your daughter, Francie...will marry someday."

The ladies giggle.

"If it were that easy!" Sophia smiles.

"I know...we always want the best for our children," Marcella adds.

"You never know." Sarita smiles.

The ladies enjoy a pleasant, heartfelt visit.

......⚭......

Leonardo finishes tying his tie. Sophia brings Francie out from the bedroom with an adorable dress sporting the colors of autumn.

"Your grandmother outlived your parents," Leonardo states in hopes to comfort Sophia.

"She did. I am thankful we have a large enough home to have her live with us," Sophia remarks.

"Sophia, I would not have it any other way," Leonardo assures.

"Thank you." Sophia carries Francie through the door. Leonardo holds his daughter while Sophia gets into the wagon then hands Sophia their daughter. He then climbs up and leads the team to the church. After the service, all those gathered go to the Garden of Remembrance where they bury their dead.

Sophia sways while holding Francie during the words of the priest. Afterwards, people pay their respects.

One lady with very long, wavy light brunette hair approaches Sophia and places her hand on Sophia's arm. "Hello, Sophia. I was best friends with your grandmother, Anna Grace, ever since we were little ones."

"Hello. Wow! You do not look a day over thirty-seven. What is your name?" Sophia inquires.

"Well, thank you. I have met you before. My name is Genie Arabella. May I hold your daughter?" questions the petite woman while she reaches for Francie.

Sophia allows the woman to hold her baby.

Francie snuggles right into the shoulder of Genie Arabella.

Somewhat surprised, Sophia comments, "Wow, she sure has taken to you."

Genie Arabella smiles a beautiful smile while she nestles her head next to Francie. She whispers, "You will have great powers, Francesca Gianetta Montanelli. Life may not always be easy, but your inner gift of great strength and charisms will always keep you grounded while you search the stars."

Sophia tries to hear what the lady is whispering to her daughter. Sophia quickly relaxes when she reminds herself the woman is just paying respects to one of her best friend's family.

Genie Arabella returns Francie back into the arms of Sophia. "You have a beautiful baby girl, Sophia. Peace be with you."

"Thank you for that. Will you come to visit? I would love to hear stories," Sophia invites.

"I am sure your grandmother has told you many stories, maybe someday. Take care, Sophia." Genie Arabella places her hand on the arm of Sophia, and slides it down to her hand, then walks away.

Sophia sways her baby in her arms while she stands next to the graves of her parents and her grandparents. Thoughts of wonder continue to ripple through her mind of the mysterious lady, as does curiosity, with regard to her youthful appearance.

Chapter 34

THE NEXT FEW YEARS

Over the course of the next few years, Queen Marcella, King Franklin, their son, Theodore, along with Don and Sarita Mancini, their son Antonio, Sophia and Leonardo Montanelli, with their daughter, Francie, do many things together as families. They enjoy game nights, dinners, outings, sleigh rides, among a variety of things. Theodore is older by a few years of Antonio. Antonio is a year and three months older than Francie.

By the time Francie turns four, she no longer sees Antonio. He is homeschooled by his mother and when he is not in school, he is at his pop's side watching and learning about horses, their cattle ranch, including their Krystyleen mine. Antonio does see Prince Theodore, because the king and queen bring Theodore out to the ranch to ride horses. Sullivan Carlisle is also a young boy close to the age of Theodore. Sullivan, Antonio, and Theodore grow to become very close friends. Don along with the king, and Sullivan's father teach their sons how to ride horses including all the skills that will be useful when they become adults.

Francie is five when she begins school. She meets a girl named Katherine and a girl named Eloise. Both girls are older, but they all mesh. Francie meets many children her age. Two boys in the same grade, Steve and David, become her very best friends. Their personalities complement each other and bring different elements to their friendship.

Families celebrate together plus share in each other's losses. They work together as a community to build strong families. They believe they have a huge purpose being born as humans by the Creator of the Universe, and they strive to raise their children with a sense of purpose, well-being, respect for others, and an appreciation for all.

Families enjoy activities together, including the quarterly get-togethers that Chamberlain Kingdom hosts. People from all around plus neighboring realms attend.

Francie, Steve, and David enjoy being the best of friends as they grow.

Chapter 35

PRINCE THEODORE HAS A SISTER

K ing Franklin smiles at his wife while gazing into her eyes. Their bundle of joy is wrapped in a blanket resting in the arms of Marcella.

"She is so beautiful…as you are." Franklin kisses the forehead of his wife.

Marcella is beaming.

Doctor Gerard steps out of the room to get their son, Prince Theodore.

Theodore enters the room and quickly walks to stand next to his father's side by the bed. He gazes upon his sister with love. "What did you name her?"

Franklin places his arm around Theodore. "We like the name Tabitha."

Theodore nods. "Yes. I like it too. How about Marie for her middle name?"

"Tabitha Marie," Marcella repeats. "That has a beautiful ring to it. What do you think Franklin?"

"I think Princess Tabitha Marie Chamberlain is perfect." The king stands proud. He then embraces his son and places his hand on his wife's shoulder.

"I love our family," Marcella sweetly voices.

Franklin leans in to kiss her.

Chapter 36

THE EXPLORATION TEAM RETURNS

T he exploration team assigned to explore the Novias Galaxy return safely home. Zeek, Emerson, Hunter, and Vincent report to the high priests, Akshai and Ammerie. After a lengthy debriefing, the team returns to Mount Abdiel.

······◦◊◦······

"Hey Paxton, do you ever sleep?" Emerson jests.

Paxton turns around. "Well, welcome back!" Paxton and Emerson exchange a hug with pats on the back.

"What are you doing here?" Vincent questions while he walks around the laboratory scanning the data written on the display boards and occasionally stops to glance at notes.

"Well, I think I have figured out something. I need to run it by the high priests before I disclose the details," Paxton explains.

Vincent and Emerson both nod.

"We will leave you to it," Emerson states.

······◦◊◦······

"Paxton, it is good to see you again," High Priest Akshai welcomes.

"Please, sit. Enlighten us on your discovery," High Priestess Ammerie voices.

"Alright. Thank you." Paxton walks energetically to the chair next to the high priests. He places his hands on the conference table. "I have been working on this for some time. I believe if the Cryptolore's host is dead, they will flee," Paxton communicates with enthusiasm.

"Am I to understand you want us to kill Mateo?" Akshai questions.

"No...well...yes, but technically...no. We will immediately beam him out and flood the chamber with the anesthetizing gas. It has been effective for all these years. We will flood the cavern with a fresh batch!" Paxton outlines with eagerness. "As soon as we beam Mateo out, we will administer life revitalization to restore his life."

"I do not want to endanger any more lives," Ammerie advocates.

"Well, that is the beauty of this plan. I hypothesize we use a laser, cut a direct hole into the chamber...then we will use our powers, while on board one of our ships that is hovering in the atmosphere, and strangle him or suffocate him. We will use the arc, which will enable us to have a complete visual. As soon as Mateo is lifeless, the Cryptolores will flee. We then, will instantly beam Mateo out while we seal up the hole formed by the laser AND fill the cavern with the anesthetizing gas!" Paxton takes a breath. "This will require a couple of teams. Each team will work simultaneously with a different mission! I propose we assign Stellar, Luna, Alo, and Tayen."

"I see. What is your theory behind using a laser instead of beaming in?" Akshai questions.

"To ensure no lives are jeopardized," Paxton asserts.

Akshai and Ammerie peer at each other.

"I have to say, Paxton, this is a well-formed plan. My first thought was to beam someone in…however…a laser, paired with the use of the arc, will be equally effective," Akshai commends. "There will be no time lost by having two teams."

"Just brilliant. Thank you, Paxton." Ammerie reaches out and pats Paxton on his hands.

"We will assign Alo and Tayen to use the laser. Stellar and Luna will utilize the arc to implement measures so the Cryptolores believe that Mateo has passed. The Cryptolores will flee his body. At that very instance, Alo and Tayen will flood the chamber with the anesthetizing gas and seal the hole while Stellar and Luna beam Mateo to the safety of our ship. We will appoint Celestial and Blazer to restore life into Mateo. We will then transport him to the monastery where Celestial and Blazer will remain with him until he fully recovers," Akshai outlines.

·······⊙ℓ⊙·······

Within a short time, the rescue mission for Mateo unfolds. The execution of the strategy goes precisely as Paxton described to the high priests.

Mateo is safe at the monastery on Mount Abdiel under the care of Celestial and Blazer. For now, the rescue mission is only known by the ones involved.

Chapter 37

ETCHING WORDS ON A CAVE WALL

One day, when Francie, Steve, and David are eleven, on their way home from school, the kids stop by David's home, and then by Steve's home. From there, they head to the mercantile. Francie and her friends go inside.

"Hi, Mom! We want to go for a hike. Do you mind?" Francie asks permission.

"I'll give you until dark to be home." Sophia smiles at her daughter. "You kids be safe."

"Oh, we will, Mrs. Montanelli," Steve assures.

David, Steve, and Francie run from the store to the outskirts of town.

"What do you guys wanna do?" Francie asks.

"I want to go explore up there." David points.

"I have heard there is a cave. My uncle Ron has told me stories when I was younger," Steve recalls.

"For entertainment purposes?" David asks.

"I don't know…maybe…let's go." Steve motions.

The three friends trek up the trail that hosts a rather steep incline at times. They soon reach another trail not visible from the base. It is protected from sight by a canopy of trees. The kids branch out, scout the area, and notice all the cool scenery.

"Hey guys…this looks like a cave entrance." David spies.

Francie and Steve quickly come to his side. The three stand with marvel in front of a cave opening they see beyond some bushes.

"Did anyone bring their lights?' David questions.

"Yep," Steve answers.

"Yes." Francie removes her back pack, kneels, and reaches in her pack to grab her Krystyleen torch. She stands. "My parents told me to keep it with me always."

"Very good." Steve nods.

"Wait…what about a wild animal?" David cautions.

"I think we will be fine," Steve maintains.

The three eleven-year-olds enter the cave with reservations, yet anticipation.

A surge of curiosity mixed with apprehension rushes through their minds.

They inch their way into the cave while each one holds their Krystyleen torch before them. They move the lights in all directions to clearly navigate the cave.

"Wow! This is so cool!" Francie relaxes.

"Man! This is great, but I do not need to explore those other tunnels," David expresses.

"Yeah, I'm with ya," Steve concurs.

The three friends stand in a large room of the cave in awe of the size.

"Aww, fireflies." Francie holds one hand out.

Steve and David stand by observing the fireflies.

"They must like your hand. I have never seen so many fireflies," Steve comments.

"You must be magical. I have never known fireflies to be so bright." David witnesses.

"Wow, Francie! That is incredible!" Steve exclaims.

Francie stands mesmerized. "This *is* incredible."

"Ha, I always thought you had magical powers." David laughs.

Francie blushes. "I don't know...this is just cool."

The friends watch the fireflies continue to land on Francie's hand. The light from the fireflies enhances and radiates at least three times their normal little light.

"This is just amazing," Steve asserts.

"Hey. Let's write on a wall what we learned at school today," David suggests.

"I like that idea." Steve nods.

"Wait...we have to make it sound cool," Francie voices.

"Okay, how about, Steve, Francie, and David, forever friends are we...." David begins.

"Yes...I like that," Francie agrees.

"From sun to sun...." Steve suggests.

"Oh yes! Followed by moon to moon...." Francie adds.

"Okay...I got it!" David begins to carve words on the wall. Francie and Steve go behind him to perfect it.

The kids successfully carve into the cave wall,

'Steve, Francie, and David,

forever friends are we-

from sun to sun and moon to moon-

we are one...fidus Achates.' (A faithful friend or devoted follower.)

They step back to admire their work. The three smile.

"Best day ever!" Francie smiles.

"You seem to always say that when we are together," David comments.

"Well...yeah...I guess I do." Francie pauses to think.

Steve grins. "Another great adventure!"

"Yep." David nods.

"I love us!" Francie exclaims.

"Did you and your friends have fun on your hike today?" Leonardo asks while Sophia passes him the pitcher of tea.

"We did. We love exploring! I am so thankful we live in such a cool kingdom! Thank you!" Francie is grateful.

"You are welcome, sweetie. Ya know, your mother and I believe it is time you have your own horse. What about inviting David and Steve with us to pick out one next month?" Leonardo outlines while he smiles at his daughter.

"Oh gosh! Thank you! I love that idea!" Francie exuberates.

Chapter 38

THE WIND SWIRLS

Some of the Chiawaukas that reside on Mount Abdiel, have been working intently putting together more documents into the Ancient Writings. After the documents have been thoroughly investigated and discerned, some will be added into the book, some will not. They have documents neatly spread out over a couple of large, handcrafted, wooden tables when they hear winds begin to roar.

Mountains tend to have their own weather pattern. Gusts reach extreme speeds. Some debris breaks one of the beautiful full-length windows. Glass shatters across the room. Documents fly from the wind that barrels in. Wind is blowing so hard, the rain is coming down sideways, and blankets the room. The Chiawaukas instantly place a protective covering over the wet scattered papers. They use their powers to seal up the gap the broken window left.

After the storm, they form into teams. One team sprints down the stairs to the basement to gather materials that they keep on hand. They move with purpose and quickly build a new window.

One team volunteers to clean up the debris and rainwater, while another team collects the documents that have been dispersed by the strong winds. They carefully dry each paper and lay them across the table. They immediately work on restoring the book of The Ancient Writings.

"When you complete this, I will deliver it to the high priests," Father John informs.

......⚬🙖⚬......

"It is so good to see you both." Father John bows before the high priests.

"It is good to see you, as well," High Priest Akshai addresses.

"Always a pleasure to be in your company." High Priestess Ammerie smiles.

Father John extends his arms with the book of The Ancient Writings in his hands. "It has been restored. We experienced a hiccup during the process one day. A storm came up, broke a window...pages flew about the room...what a mess. However, our faithful Chiawaukas immediately took action. After they completed restoring it, Weston and I went through page by page again, making sure all the discerned documents were there."

"Well done, brother." Akshai nods.

"What an extraordinary, beautiful leather cover for the words that breathe life," Ammerie expresses.

Father John bows to the high priests. "I am pleased to be a part of The Ancient Writings."

Chapter 39

PICKING OUT A HORSE

Francie, Steve, and David load into the Montanelli wagon and head towards the Chamberlain Stables to select a horse for Francie. A herd of majestic Wintuckets just arrived from the Martinelli Kingdom.

Leonardo brings the wagon to a halt. Everyone dismounts and walks over to the stables. Charles, the man in charge of the castle stables, approaches.

"Welcome! This herd just arrived," Charles mentions while he points over at the paddock.

Don Mancini is standing beside the fence watching the horses when he glances over and sees his friends. Don tips his hat, "Sophia, Francie...good to see you both." Don and Leonardo exchange a handshake. "I think you're gonna find just what you're looking for."

"I'm sure we will." Leonardo nods.

"Where is your son, Antonio?" Sophia inquires.

"He stayed at the ranch with some horses we are keeping," Don informs.

"Are these the rejects?" Leonardo questions.

"Not at all. In fact, there are a couple here I want for myself, but thought your daughter may want one of these," Don reveals.

Leonardo laughs under his breath. "So...you are sacrificing."

Don grins, "I guess I am. Anything for you."

Francie is already admiring the horses and reaches her hand out to see which one comes over to her.

Steve and David are at her side.

"Ah, hi girl." Francie reaches her hand to gently stroke the nose of a beautiful grey Wintucket mare.

Steve reaches his hand toward the mare as well. "She sure seems to like you."

"Yeah." Francie smiles. "I think this one is it."

Sophia and Leonardo exchange a smile.

"You made a great choice, Francie. She is one that I wanted to keep for myself," Don shares.

"I am glad you brought her here," Francie conveys.

Don steps into the paddock to bridle the horse Francie chose. He leads the mare out of the paddock and over to another paddock. "Francie, come with me. I will let you lead her around. Do you have a name picked out?"

"No. Not yet," Francie discloses.

Francie leads the mare around in the paddock. She feels very comfortable with her.

"Where will we keep her? Where can I train her?" Francie queries.

"You can keep her here at the castle stables and train her here," Charles informs.

Leonardo nods. "Thank you for that."

"It's no trouble at all," Charles replies. "I will teach Francie. Be here tomorrow at seven in the morning."

Francie nods. "I will."

"I'll be getting back to the herd." Charles tips his hat. "Nice to see you all." He walks away.

"Well, Don, we were hoping you and Antonio would teach Francie," Sophia voices.

120

"I would sure like to. Our free time is burning at both ends right now, with the cattle, the mine, the horses, not to mention, the fields," Don details.

"Oh, Don. I am so sorry to hear that," Sophia compassionately responds.

"It's just part of life," Don states. "Francie, you are in good hands. Charles is a superb horseman."

Francie nods.

......⟡......

In the morning, David and Steve decide they want to watch Francie at her first lesson.

"What are you going to name her? David asks.

"I don't know. It'll come to me," Francie remarks.

"I imagine like a bolt of lightning," Steve supposes.

"You may be right! In fact, that is it! Her name is Aspen!" Francie exclaims.

David and Steve glance at each other. Steve raises an eyebrow.

"Okay, how did you come up with Aspen from Steve saying a 'bolt of lightning'?" David asks.

"Easy! When he said it'll come to me like a bolt of lightning...I immediately thought of trees...and how sometimes they split when hit...then I thought of an Aspen tree...and how magnificent they appear in the fall...with colors of yellows...golds, reds, and oranges...so Aspen it is!" Francie beams.

"Glad I could be of service!" Steve grins.

David nods. "Yep...that makes sense to me." David slightly shakes his head and grins.

"I cannot wait to tell my parents what I named her!" Francie expresses.

Over the course of the next few years, Francie becomes an experienced rider. She even trains with Aspen for jumps and some other tricks. On occasion, she performs for the kingdom at annual events. David and Steve always attend and cheer on their comrade. The three grow into their teenage years.

Chapter 40

SUMMER AT UNCLE RON'S RANCH

"Come on, I think we should ask her to go to your uncle's ranch with us," David pleads with Steve. "You know it will be a blast!"

"I agree. Sounds like fun being together one last summer before we leave for the guard." Steve nods while he carries gear from his house to his Uncle Ron's wagon. "Let me run it by my uncle."

"There ya go." grins David.

Steve and David approach Steve's Uncle Ron.

"How I can I help you?" Ron inquires.

"Can Francie come with us?" Steve just blurts it out.

Ron stands tall with his shoulders squared. He searches the eyes of each teenager. "This would please the two of you?"

"Very much," David, without any hesitation, answers.

"It would. Next year we leave for the guard, it just wouldn't be right not hanging with her this summer," explains Steve.

"I see. Well, I am sure your Aunt Cheri will be alright with the idea. How about we go over and speak to Francie and her parents? She may not want to hang with you guys for the summer," jests Ron.

"I doubt that," David quietly puts forth.

The three approach the mercantile and then enter on arrival.

"Ah, good to see you, Ronnie!" Sophia briskly moves from behind the counter and greets Ron with a hug. "What brings you in?"

"Well, Cheri and I came into town to get my nephew here, and his sidekick. And these two, have the notion that they want Francie to also join us at our ranch for the summer. So, here we are, asking if that will be alright with you," outlines Ron.

"Oh, she will be thrilled! I do not mind. I know you will put her to work. Let me go get her and Leo." Sophia quickly walks to the back of the store. "Leo, Francie, we have customers."

Francie dashes to the front to wait on the customers. Sophia gently places her hand on Leonardo's forearm.

"What is it?" Leo asks Sophia.

"Ron and Cheri are in town getting supplies, they are also picking up Steve and David for the summer," Sophia informs.

"Yeah, well…that's nice." Leo shrugs.

"There is more…." Sophia quietly conveys. "They would like Francie to join them."

"What? With two teenage boys? Absolutely not!" Leo snaps.

"Leonardo! These teenage boys happen to be our daughter's very best friends! Next summer they leave for the guard. Let's give her this. I trust them all. Those boys have always shown Francie honor. At least think about it." Sophia gazes up into Leo's eyes.

"How long do I have?" Leo questions.

"The length to reach the front of the store," Sophia replies, glancing at Leo.

Leonardo shakes his head and continues to walk to the front of the store.

"Well, there he is! How are you, Leo?" Ron extends his hand.

Leonardo reaches out and shakes the hand of Ron. "Long time. I am doing well, thank you. I hear you guys have a cockamamie...I mean to say...I hear you guys have an idea."

"We do. I am bringing my nephew, Steve, and his sidekick out to my ranch for the summer, and we would love it, if Francie would be allowed to join us as well. Of course, I will pay her for any work she does," Ron outlines.

Leonardo studies the faces of the two teenage boys and glances at the overwhelming excitement in the blue eyes of his daughter. Lastly, Leo glances over to his wife. "I think that will give our daughter an excellent opportunity to be on a ranch for the summer. Thank you, Ron, for including her." Leo extends his hand to shake Ron's hand once more.

"Oh, Daddy! Thank you!" Francie leaps into Leo's arms to hug him.

David is beaming from ear to ear and a grin plasters across Steve's face.

"How soon can you be packed?" Ron asks Francie.

"Oh, it won't take me long! Are we bringing our horses? Can I bring Aspen?" Francie rattles off questions.

"Yes. Steve and David will get Aspen. You collect your gear and we will pick you up in fifteen minutes," Ron instructs. "Sophia, also good to see you. I will take good care of your daughter." Ron and Sophia exchange a hug.

"I am going to go with Francie." Sophia pats Leo in the middle of his chest.

······ঔৡঙ······

"Be sure to pack one dress. You never know when you will need it. Maybe on Sundeis," Sophia suggests.

"Yes. I have it. I am also taking my journal. Everything I need." Francie double checks her bag.

"Wow! This is a pretty big deal for you. My fourteen-year-old daughter will be fifteen when you return," Sophia comments.

Francie stops what she is doing and looks at her mother. "I am sorry I will not be here to celebrate with you, but thank you for having me! Thank you for letting me go!"

Sophia smiles and hugs her daughter, "It is quite all right. This will be a wonderful experience for you and a lovely way to bring in your fifteenth birthday!"

"Thank you, again, for letting me go! It will be a great way to spend one last summer with my guys," Francie comments as she stuffs one last shirt into her pack.

"What makes you think it will be your last summer together?" Sophia tenderly pries.

"Well, you know...next summer they leave for the guard, then who knows when they will be back. And...life changes. We will all grow up. They may even meet girls when they are away," Francie speculates.

"Are you going to be alright with that?" Sophia inquires.

Francie pauses and gazes into her mother's eyes. "I guess I will have to be. Yes! Of course! There is no way I could ever commit to just one of them. I would never choose one over the other. It is truth that I know in my fiber...though I don't know why I sense that. I feel at peace...but it is weird that I just know...I mean maybe someday...it just depends on timing."

Sophia nods. "Trust your internal voice, sweetie. God gave it to us for a reason."

"Well...they are both the best guys a girl could have as her best friends! If there was only one of them, then I would be the first in line...." Francie laughs at her own words, "but they are both my best friends."

"You have a marvelous time this summer, honey!" Sophia sweetly smiles and runs her hand down the arm of Francie.

The two leave Francie's bedroom that has adorable sweet pink wallpaper with stripes, white polka dots, and flowers which assist in creating a very cheerful environment. They walk to the front door. Leonardo is waiting in the front yard to hug his daughter goodbye.

"You be safe, honey. Enjoy your summer," Leonardo whispers in the ear of his daughter.

"I will, Daddy! Thank you!" Francie releases their embrace and smiles at her dad. She steps to her mother to give her another big hug. "I love you both!"

Sophia and Leonardo stand smiling at the crew as they climb onto the wagon.

"We will take good care of these three." Cheri smiles and waves.

Ron tips his hat. David, Steve, and Francie wave as they ride away with their horses in tow.

⁓⁓⁓ ❦ ⁓⁓⁓

They have been traveling for hours it seems.

"I don't remember it being so far away," Francie mentions.

"Yeah, they own property in three kingdoms: Chamberlain, Alpine, and the corner of Martinelli," reminds Steve.

Francie nods. "That's right! I remember."

"We will be home soon." Cheri turns to the kids. "Are you all hungry?"

David, Steve, and Francie nod.

"There it is," Ron informs the group.

"Wow! It looks like you have changed your approach, Uncle Ron." Steve notices.

"We *have* changed the approach. We have also built a huge shop that you cannot see from here. We also added on a couple of bedrooms," Ron discloses.

"This is a great spread, Sir," comments David.

"Thank you," acknowledges Ron as he leads the team down the long drive and pulls up close to the house. "Let's unload, get your horses settled in, unhook this team, then I will show you around."

"Would you like me to help you with dinner?" Francie asks Cheri.

127

"No, honey. You go out with the guys. Ron has something to show the three of you," Cheri informs.

"Alright. Well, I will help you clean-up," Francie insists.

Cheri smiles.

Francie glances over to the door and sees the guys waiting.

"Come on." Steve motions.

Francie joins her friends. They walk outside. Ron is waiting at the base of the deck.

"After we take care of these horses, I have a surprise for you. It is in my shop. Come on." Ron signals with his hand.

The three friends swiftly go down the deck stairs. They help Ron with the horses, then they walk alongside him.

"I think you're gonna like this surprise," Ron mentions.

"Uncle Ron, I like everything you have done," Steve remarks.

After leaving the stables, they walk quite some distance across the immaculate landscape that surrounds their ranch home to the shop. Their home and shop are secluded in a sanctuary of trees.

Ron unlocks the door of the large shop, flips on a light, and the kids follow him inside.

"Wow! This is incredible, Uncle Ron!" Steve compliments.

"I thought you would like it. Follow me," Ron states.

The three teens follow Ron to the middle of the shop. He reaches down to a corner to lift the cover and carefully begins to pull it off. David and Steve also take a corner to help remove the large cover.

Francie, David, and Steve stand in awe.

"Pretty sweet, don't you think?" Ron beams.

"A…yeah…what is it going to be?" asks Steve.

"This is going to be an all-terrain vehicle. Also known as an ATV. All you must do is put it together." Ron grins as he places his hands on his hips.

"You want *us* to put it together?" David quizzes with a little laugh cracking in his voice.

"Well, I know you two enjoy hands-on projects. I thought before you go into the guard, this would be a great project and fun for us all," Ron replies.

David and Steve glance at each other with curiosity.

"How long do you think it will take to construct it?" Steve asks.

"Well, nephew. That depends on you and your crew. I can tell you…the quicker you get it completed, the longer you'll have to learn how to drive it," chuckles Ron.

"Alright. I think I can do this. Thank you for believing in me," expresses Steve.

"Well, I could have put it together, but your Aunt Cheri and I thought it would be a good learning experience for you and your friends," admits Ron.

"Yeah! This is great, Uncle Ron!" exclaims Steve as he walks around examining the pieces laying across the floor of the shop. "There *are* instructions…right?"

Ron nods while walking to some built-in storage against the south wall. He pulls out a manual from a drawer and hands it to Steve. "I will assist you with anything you need. When you have a question or need physical help, let me know, but I trust you can do this. I have taught you through these years how to use all my tools, so I am confident in your knowledge."

"Yes, Sir! You can count on me! Thank you, Uncle Ron!" Steve communicates.

Ron smiles and pats his nephew on the back. "You're most welcome. I think your crew here will be quite an asset," Ron asserts while he winks at Francie and David. "Your aunt probably has dinner ready. You guys can begin this project in the morning. Let's go up to the house."

The three teens nod, smile, and walk out of the shop. Ron turns off the lights and locks the place up. They traverse back up to the house.

Chapter 41

ON A MISSION

Steve and David are busy screwing bolts and nuts in place. Francie has spent the week handing them what they need and reading the directions aloud.

Ron walks into the shop after his morning chores. He is astonished when he sees the project nearly completed. "Boy! You three are quite a team. I figured it might take you two weeks to knock this out, but it looks like it is almost done!"

"Yeah...and I don't think we will have many pieces leftover," laughs David.

Ron chuckles and pats David on the back. "That is always good to hear."

Steve comes up from working on the engine. "Man! This was kind of a nightmare at times. Sometimes we would have to study the directions when it didn't make sense to any of us, but honestly, you were right, Uncle Ron, this has been fun and the three of us make a great team!"

Ron grins. "Well, I am really glad you figured it out. Do you mind if I inspect it before we take a drive?"

"No! By all means…please!" Steve outstretches his arm with his palm open toward the ATV.

"Yes, inspect it before we drive it!" David concurs.

The three teens stand next to each other anxiously awaiting Ron's approval. After thoroughly inspecting the construction from top to bottom and back to front, Ron eventually completes his inspection and turns to face the kids. "I knew you could do it! This is safe and perfect. I realize I had to come out and oversee at times, and help with a few heavy things, but you three should be very proud of yourselves. How about we go out and I teach each of you to drive?"

With anticipation, the three teens glance at each other and all exclaim, "Yes!"

Ron walks over to the double-doors of the shop, pushes a button, and the door rolls up. He returns to the ATV. Ron and the three teens load up in the newly constructed ATV with a piece of Krystyleen as its power source. Ron places the key in the ignition. The vehicle starts right up, quickly settling into a low rumble. Everyone smiles with excitement, just the sound of the rumble is invigorating!

Ron puts the ATV in gear and slowly pulls out of the shop. Steve hops out and closes the door. Then the four put their safety harnesses on and Ron slowly leaves the drive. He heads for some trails that are wide enough for an ATV.

"Oh, my! This is so fun!" Francie exclaims. "I love Aspen, but this is thrilling!"

The guys laugh.

"God and our angels, keep us safe," David quietly voices.

Steve is visiting with his Uncle Ron.

"Now look. I want you all to pay attention. You are each going to get a turn at driving this today," Ron communicates.

The three teens nod.

Ron lets his nephew drive first. David and Francie remain in the back while Ron and Steve trade places.

Steve places his foot on the accelerator. He then glances over at his uncle.

"Nope! You keep your eyes on the road! You have lives in here!" scolds Ron.

Steve expresses a slight cringe and immediately keeps his eyes on the trail road.

"Look, I want you all to know…this is for our enjoyment, and the first priority is to be safe, so we can play another day. When you are the driver, you keep your eyes on the road. You do not need to make eye contact while you are behind the wheel. You have the lives of others along with your life in your hands. Safety and fun makes for a great team…alright?" Ron instructs.

Francie and David are both nodding their heads.

"Yes. Absolutely," David replies.

Steve nods without making eye contact as they were all taught, and keeps his sights on the road.

After they drive around awhile with Steve at the wheel, Steve comes to a stop to let one of his friends take over.

"Francie, you're up," Ron insists. The kids change spots in the ATV. Ron instructs Francie on where the brake and accelerator are located. Francie has listened to all his instructions and proceeds after Steve is securely strapped in the back with David. A large smile casts across the face of Francie once her foot hits the accelerator. Not only, is Francie glowing, a streak of playfulness shoots through her. "Hold on!" Francie laughs.

David and Steve glance at each other. Ron is smiling with pride knowing he is teaching the kids how to build things and how to drive. Francie increases pressure on the accelerator and cannot believe how free she feels. She sees the road is straight and revs up the speed until she spies a hill. Francie slows WAY down.

"Hey, what gives?" Steve asks.

"I don't want to go airborne!" Francie is gripping the steering wheel.

David and Steve grin at each other and laugh.

David expresses, "That's our girl."

Steve nods.

They go down the hill and it gives them a jump in their stomach.

Francie drives for a bit more around some curves then comes to a perfect stop. As she unbuckles, she turns her head to look at David and Steve. "Okay...that hill scared me! I did NOT want to go airborne!" She laughs a little, then glances over to Ron, "That was incredible! Thank you so much!"

"You're quite welcome, Francie. You seem like a real natural," Ron commends.

"That was just sooo fun!" Francie states while she climbs out and trades places with David.

"Oh man! Hold on for dear life," teases Steve as he reaches up for a safety handle and pats David's arm.

"Yeah, yeah...make fun of me...." David grins.

Steve and Francie exchange a big smile.

"Alright, my guess is you were paying attention to my instructions to the others," comments Ron.

David nods. "Yes, I think I have it."

David takes off and enjoys driving the four of them on the trails through the trees, then back into the fields. With the breeze hitting their faces, Ron decides he needs to install a windshield onto the ATV.

"Man, this is great, Ron," David chimes.

"You're doing a great job. How about you driving us back to the shop now," instructs Ron.

"Yes, Sir." David nods. He stops when they reach the shop, so Ron can open the door.

"Do you feel comfortable driving it in?" Ron asks.

"I do, but I'm gonna let my buddy have the honors," replies David. He puts it in park, unbuckles, and steps out of the vehicle. Steve gets out of the backseat and returns to the driver seat.

With such a serious expression, Steve proceeds to drive the ATV into the shop and parks in the location where his uncle directs him. Steve turns off the vehicle. Francie and Steve exit the ATV. As they exchange smiles, great delight fills their souls.

"Let's go get some dinner," recommends Ron.

Steve, Francie, and David, walk with Ron out of the shop. Everyone is discussing what an excellent time they experienced.

Chapter 42

FRANCIE'S BIRTHDAY

"**I** hope she will love this!" Cheri comments to Ron.

"I am sure she will." Ron pats Cheri while he peers over her shoulder at the beautiful white on white cake that is decorated with trees, a river, mountains, and a horse. "You are an artist," Ron compliments and kisses Cheri's cheek.

"Alright, I am going to hide this in the refrigerator," Cheri voices while she rearranges food to make space for the birthday cake.

"And you made breakfast...yum...." Ron never tires of being impressed by his wife.

"No, Steve and David made breakfast to surprise Francie when she wakes up," Cheri informs.

"Where is he?" Ron asks.

"I think he went to get David to make sure they are in the kitchen when she walks in," Cheri details.

Ron nods. "I see."

⸱⸱⸱⸱⸱⸱◦ℛ◦⸱⸱⸱⸱⸱⸱

You can hear Francie's sock-covered feet running down from the upstairs while she glides her hand on the banister. She turns when she reaches the bottom step and slides into the kitchen.

"Good morning, birthday girl!" Cheri walks up and greets Francie with a hug.

"Thank you!" Francie joyfully expresses. She then glances past Cheri to see Steve and David standing in front of the stove.

Ron also gives Francie a birthday hug. "I know you're not with your parents this year, but we wanted to make sure to celebrate you properly so you know how much we all love you," Ron speaks like a father.

"Aw...that is so thoughtful of you! I am so fortunate to be here. Thank you," Francie communicates.

"It is our pleasure," Ron assures.

"Yes. I love you being here! It is like having a daughter." Cheri smiles.

Cheri and Ron step back so Francie can clearly see Steve and David.

Steve sports a big grin on his face and David has a smile.

Steve opens his arms wide for Francie to enter. She steps into his open arms. He gives her a big birthday hug. "Happy birthday! I made you scrambled eggs along with bacon and sausage."

"Oh my...thank you! Yum! It smells SOOO good." Francie beams.

"I made you waffles," David boasts. "I think you're gonna like 'em."

Francie's eyes light up and she places her hand on the arm of David, then peers into the eyes of her best friends. "You two are just the best!"

David extends his arms around Francie to give her a birthday hug. He quietly voices, "Happy fifteenth birthday!"

"Thank you!" Francie closes her eyes and replies while she is in the embrace of his hug.

"Well, let's eat," Ron directs.

Francie grabs a plate off the stack because they are serving cafeteria style.

"Nope." David reaches and takes her plate. "Steve and I will serve you. Go sit down."

"Gosh, I feel like a princess." Francie smiles from ear to ear.

Steve sets before Francie a plate full of food he and David made.

Everyone in the kitchen sits down around the table. Ron leads them in prayer.

"So, birthday girl…an ATV ride, or a trail ride?" Ron asks.

Francie is lit up from the tender love she is being shown. "Whatever you all want to do."

"No…this day, we are celebrating you," Steve candidly voices.

David and Cheri both nod.

"Well…let's go on a trail ride. I want to share my day with Aspen. I love her so much. Let's ride to the river…or the lake," Francie suggests.

Ron nods. "We can do that."

Cheri is also beaming. "I love that idea."

"And tonight…David and I are going to grill. Uncle Ron has taught us so much about mixing seasonings…we have a surprise for you this evening as well," Steve communicates.

"Gosh…I feel so loved and honored. Thank you. All of you…if I die…please know how much I love all of you! You guys are the best friends a girl could have!" Francie heartfully shares.

"Oh, honey, you are too young to think of such things," Cheri responds.

"Maybe, I just get filled with so much thankfulness…well…I am very grateful and want you each to know how much this all means to me…how much each of you means to me," Francie bears her soul, then she bites into the scrambled eggs, followed by a bite of waffle. Her eyes speak for her. "This…." Francie uses

137

both hands to point at her food, "...is the best breakfast I have ever had! You two are great cooks! Yum!"

Steve grins with joy that he put a smile on her face and made her stomach happy. David smiles with accomplishment that his waffles are delicious and she loves them.

······· co⟩o·······

There is nothing like the sound of many hooves clip-clopping on the trail, and hearing the songs of the birds while the summer sun warms them. They reach a bend in the river where it widens. There is easy access to walk across the rock bank to the river's edge. All of them remove their boots and socks, then roll up their jeans. David, Steve, and Francie have a wonderful time playing in the water. They look for beautiful rocks and even some gold nuggets. Cheri and Ron laugh as they splash each other and feel like kids themselves.

"Should we do a birthday dunk?" Steve puts forth.

"No! Never dunk me!" Francie's laughter instantly shifts. She becomes serious just as she stumbles on a rock and begins to fall. Steve and David both grab one of her arms to keep her from going in. Ironically, the three find themselves in knee-high water. From the force of each of the boys grabbing an arm of Francie, they lose their footing and they all fall into waist-deep water, then begin laughing.

"Francie...." Steve voices.

"Yeah?" Francie looks at Steve.

"I was just kidding around. I want you to know, I would never dunk you...only David." Steve laughs at his words.

"Thanks for that, buddy." David grins.

Francie and her best friends navigate their footing on the rocks in the waist-deep water.

The three friends continue to laugh until their stomachs hurt. They are soaked with the cool mountain river water.

Francie raises her arms into the air. "Best birthday ever!"

"Good thing I packed towels," Cheri quietly speaks to Ron. Ron grins. He enjoys watching the kids. "Yes, good thing."

······⌒⧸⧹⌒······

"I must say, you boys sure paid attention. These steaks are incredible," Ron compliments.

"Thanks, Uncle Ron. We appreciate everything you have taught us," Steve communicates.

"Indeed, we have," David reiterates.

Cheri steps onto the back deck with the cake in her hands. She leads them in singing happy birthday to Francie.

"Oh my! I do not know what to say! You guys have shown me so much love!" Francie gasps. "Look at the beautiful artwork on this cake! I don't even want to cut it!" Francie declares.

"I am glad you like it, sweetie. I remembered you love a delicious white-on-white cake, so that is what I made you, decorated with some of your favorite things," Cheri imparts.

After Cheri sets the cake on the table, Francie reaches to hug Cheri. They exchange a powerful embrace.

"Thank you all, for being a part of my life," Francie speaks from her heart.

Everyone raises a piece of cake on their fork and Ron makes a toast, "To family and forever friends."

In unison, with their forks raised, they exclaim, "To family and forever friends!" Each one places the first bite of cake into their mouths. Their facial expressions describe it all. "MM…delicious!"

Chapter 43

THE REST OF THE SUMMER

Over the course of the summer, the three friends help Ron and Cheri around their ranch. They ride horses. They continue to grill and experiment with flavors as Ron taught them and, of course, they make time for using the ATV to explore the vast property that Ron and Cheri own.

"Since we will be returning you to your homes tomorrow, how about you take the ATV out for one last spin?" Ron suggests.

Steve, David, and Francie light up.

"Yes, Sir. Thank you, Uncle Ron," Steve conveys his gratitude.

"Do you not need us for anything else at the house today?" Francie asks.

"No, you kids go enjoy yourselves. Be back by ten," Cheri instructs.

"It'll be dark then," David comments.

Ron grins, "Yes, don't worry, the ATV has headlights and it is about time you three learn to drive in the dark. Watch for wildlife."

"You will be able to see all the constellations, so enjoy yourselves," Cheri adds.

An expression of concern casts across the faces of the teens, but they eagerly accept. Hugs are exchanged. Steve, Francie, and David head over to get the ATV.

"I don't know that I like this idea," David remarks. "We are not even supposed to be driving...anything but horses, let alone in the dark."

"Stop worrying. It will be alright. It has headlights," Steve assures.

"That's just great...then we will be spotted and your aunt and uncle will get in trouble," David continues.

"Dave, buddy...no one is out here. They live in the wilderness. Relax, man," Steve attempts to reassure his best friend.

The kids grab some water and snacks from inside the shop and some blankets. After loading them up, David opens the shop door. Steve drives out the ATV, David closes the door, then Francie and David climb into the ATV for their last adventure of the season.

"Well, I am glad that your uncle installed racks for rifles," David notes.

Steve grins. "Yep, I am glad he taught us very well, years ago, how to use them."

David and Francie both nod. They hit the trails and take turns driving all over the family property, going up and down and around, navigating the mountainous terrain.

"Well, hmm...." Steve brings the ATV to a stop at a fork in the road. "Which way to go...." Steve thinks aloud. "Let's take the trail to the right."

Francie curls her lips and squinches her face up.

"Do you not like that idea?" Steve glances over to her.

"I do...it will be a beautiful drive with canopies of trees that drape over the trails...but we will have to turn around and eventually take the left fork," Francie details.

Steve's eyebrow raises. "How do you know that? I don't think we have been here before."

"I do not know how I know it…but there is a large tree down on this trail blocking the passage," Francie insists.

Steve's set of very white teeth show during his big grin. "Alright…now I AM curious and have to go this way."

David whispers to himself, "I bet there is a tree down."

"What's that, buddy?" Steve quickly glances back at David as he takes his foot off the brake.

"Nothing, I am game. Let's take this trail," David agrees.

Francie glances over at Steve with a smile. She notices he has so much confidence in his driving abilities.

"Wow! This trail is beautiful with canopies of trees, as you described," Steve mentions.

"Yeah. This is pretty great!" David comments from the back seat.

"I LOVE this! It is so peaceful to be out here with you two! I can just be me." Francie extends her arms upwards and inhales. She loves the scent of the pine trees that surround them.

"Well…who else would you be?" David playfully questions.

Francie laughs. "You know…I mean I do not have to explain myself to you guys. You just get me. I feel so at peace here."

David and Steve both smile as an inner peace swells inside them.

They enjoy the breathtaking scenery of the somewhat challenging trail when around the next switchback, there it is, a large Aspen tree is down, prohibiting further travel.

"Well, I'll be…." Steve cannot believe his eyes. He places his foot on the brake and comes to a slow and easy stop. Steve turns his head with kind of a tilt and peers into the eyes of Francie. "How did you know?"

Francie slightly shakes her head back and forth. "I do not know. I saw it…I don't know…I sensed it. I can't believe it myself. Here it is. Exactly how I saw it."

David leans up from the back seat positioning himself between his friends with his hands on the back of each seat. "Unbelievable, I think you must have a gift...some sort of charism that some people are born with."

"What?" Steve quizzes. He opens the door and gets out to walk around a bit.

David and Francie also get unbuckled and get out of the ATV.

"Yeah, you know we have heard it in Sundei teachings...gifts that we were given and born with," David explains with one palm up.

"Yeah, yeah. I just never gave it much thought." Steve glances at each of his friends while he walks around inspecting the size of the Aspen tree. "You know...maybe he is right and you *do* have some sort of special sense. I honestly thought you were pulling my leg," Steve comments peering over at Francie.

"I don't know, guys." Francie shrugs her shoulders. "I just know that sometimes I sense stuff...or I can see it," Francie reveals.

"So...you know how everything is going to turn out?" Steve questions.

"No. Not at all. It is only sometimes that I have a strong sense of something or see a scene I have never encountered...and then poof...a day...a week...I am there. Not always...just sometimes. I cannot even predict when it is going to happen...and honestly, I never thought it was a big deal," Francie admits.

"I'd say it is a pretty big deal," David concludes while he, too, walks around the area.

"I don't know...maybe...it just seems normal for me and I figure everyone has it," Francie theorizes.

"We all have special gifts, *that*, I believe," David adds.

"Well, let's load up and turn around," Steve suggests.

"OR...we could move this tree and journey on up," Francie submits an alternative idea.

Steve nods. "We could, but let's do that another time. And by the way...I agree...we all have special gifts."

David and Francie both nod in agreement and get back into the ATV.

"Okay, how about we head to the lake?" Steve proposes.

"I like that idea! We can eat there and lay out the blankets and look at the stars when night casts across the sky," Francie agrees.

"I like that idea, too." David smiles. "And see...another gift...you have a way with creating a scene with your words." David pats Francie on her shoulder.

"Affirmative!" Steve nods.

Steve maneuvers the ATV with skill and gets them turned around. Their destination is the lake. Steve drives with precision down and around the switchbacks until they reach the fork. This time, they take the left fork which leads them to a trail that winds to the lake.

"Oh, wow!" Francie exclaims when they peak a small incline on the trail and the lake spreads out before them. "Absolutely breathtaking!"

After they park, they gather the blankets from the back and spread one out and toss the others down on a sandy shore between rocks. They also pull out the food storage and carry it over, along with containers of water. They set the supplies near the blanket. Francie reaches in the storage cooler and passes out food.

"Thank you." Steve nods.

"Thank you, Francie." David also nods.

"Nothing better than this summer. We built an ATV. We have learned to drive. We have gone on a lot of horseback rides. We have learned how to up our game at grilling food...." Steve inhales while he stretches his arms into the sky then places his hands behind his head as he leans himself back against a large rock.

"That about sums it up. Here is to the best summer ever...well, so far...." David grins while he raises his container of water.

Steve and Francie also raise their containers of water. The three friends clink their containers of water together while they smile at each other. They then scan the beauty of the landscape.

"Hey, I will be right back. I am going to run over to those pines. I have to use the restroom," Francie comments.

"I will go with you," David states.

"I do not need help, David." Francie laughs.

"No, of course not, but I will feel better if I am on guard," David asserts.

Francie smiles. "Yes, you are a guard and protector by nature."

The two trek some distance to the pines where Francie finds a private spot. David stands by. The moon now shines brightly and lights their return to camp.

Steve takes a couple of blankets and rolls them for a cushion for their heads. One blanket he throws across the top of the base blanket in case they get cold, to cover up with. The three teens lay down looking up at the stars as the night sky unfolds before them.

"I think this has got to be one of the best summers I have ever had," Francie remarks.

"I agree." Steve inhales a deep breath of the mountain air.

David reaches his arm to the sky and begins to point. "Every galaxy has legends of the stars that decorate the night sky. One legend of the constellations in the Estellas Galaxy is the Archer. Look over there, it is Italias. He is protecting his love, the beautiful maiden, Julianne, from Agreadon. If you look right there, you can see Agreadon...and there is Julianne," David continues describe details and point to the constellations. "Agreadon is half man, half dragon. Agreadon, wanting company, kidnaps the lovely Julianne. Italias seeks for direction in his prayers. He follows Star Points which you can see is becoming visible over there. Star Points leads Italias to Mount Valoroso."

"Oh! I see Mount Valoroso!" exclaims Steve.

David continues, "There, on Mount Valoroso, Italias finds Agreadon and Julianne. Italias shoots Agreadon with his arrows."

"What happens?" Steve asks.

"Oh, I know!" chimes Francie. "According to legend, Julianne feels compassion for Argreadon. She removes the arrows and nurses Agreadon to health. Agreadon releases Julianne into the love of Italias. Italias thanks him. Julianne and Italias ask Agreadon if he will join them. Argreadon is touched and deeply moved. Agreadon becomes their protector, and they all live together, forging a forever bond of friendship."

David and Francie turn their heads to glance at each other. Their eyes exchange an unspoken, unexplainable deep connection. They smile and begin giggling.

"That is quite a story," Steve reflects.

"I like to think we are three, forged in forever friendship." Francie lifts her arms to the sky.

"We are," David states.

"We are, indeed," Steve reiterates.

The three friends experience a great peacefulness that sweeps through their developing bodies and minds. Their senses are filled, hearing the distinct sounds of the gentle splashes of the water hitting the rocks. The scent of the pine trees and the beautiful night sky whisp them into reflection on life.

In the distance they hear the hoot of an owl.

After quite a while of enjoying the quiet and sounds of nature, Steve breaks the silence. "We should probably head back."

They all abruptly sit up when they hear the howls of wolves.

"Yep, that's our cue!" David hops up and reaches for the hand of Francie at the same time Steve does. They both grab a hand and help her up.

"You guys, I don't need help up." Francie laughs.

"We know," Steve submits.

"That's just what we do," David reminds.

"I am the luckiest girl to have you two!" beams Francie.

The three friends grab the blankets and put them in Francie's arms. David and Steve pick up the water containers, toss them on top of the food cooler, and each of them grab a handle. The three teens run to the ATV feeling a bit of panic racing through their bodies from hearing the howls of wolves.

Steve declares, "I'm driving!"

David and Steve hoist the cooler and containers into the back, then David reaches to Francie, and helps her toss aboard the blankets. They quickly leap in and buckle up. Steve starts the ATV, flips on the switch to the lights, and away they go! Steve proficiently navigates the mountain terrain. His skills in precision are tested and achieved as he swiftly drives his friends to safety.

When they reach the ranch, after parking the ATV, and locking up the shop, they stroll arm in arm.

"Best summer ever! Plus, we all have become pretty good chefs! I am so glad your aunt and uncle taught us so much about cooking and grilling!" exclaims Francie. "That is a rare asset to have!"

"Yep, my aunt and uncle have taught all of us a lot." smiles Steve.

David leans his head into Francie's head, who is in the middle. "Best summer ever!"

Chapter 44

PLANNING A WEDDING IN THE KINGDOM

Long before the Annual Fall Around, over the course of several months, families have been planning for a winter wedding of Sullivan Carlisle and Katherine Anne Achee.

"Oh, Francie! I cannot believe you have not met Antonio Mancini!" Katherine exclaims. He is going to be Sullivan's best man. You will meet him at our wedding!"

"Yeah. David, Steve, nor I have met him…well, my mother tells me when we were toddlers we met," Francie maintains.

Katherine turns to Francie and takes her hands, "You will be my maid of honor, won't you?"

"Oh, Katherine! What an honor! Yes!" Francie hugs Katherine.

Katherine giggles. "I couldn't think of any other friend I would rather have."

"The honor is mine. Thank you." Francie is very moved and humbled.

"Well, over the summer while you were off with Steve's aunt and uncle, I got my dress, and yours. I hope you do not mind the color. Since everything is already decorated with the winter flowers of red, I wanted you to have a red dress standing next to me, in my white dress," Katherine details as she walks to her closet and pulls out a beautiful full length lace gown over satin. She turns with the dress in front of her to show Francie. "I hope you love it! Your mother and I believe this shade of winter red will go beautifully with your skin and blue eyes. Plus, my dress." giggles Katherine.

Francie lights up and lifts the bottom of the gown while Katherine is holding the top of the gown. "It is just gorgeous! I love it!"

"I was hoping you would." Katherine smiles.

"So does this mean that Antonio, the best man of Sully's will be in red as well?" asks Francie.

"No. Sully wanted a deep, midnight blue tux for Antonio. I think it will look sharp and reflect the colors of winter. White like the snow...red like the winter flowers...deep blue...like the winter, night sky...." Katherine inhales, and as she exhales, she smiles as she imagines how glorious her wedding will be.

"You have impeccable taste, Katherine," Francie assures.

The two girls giggle.

"Well, one thing is for sure...you and David and Steve will finally meet Antonio. I am frankly surprised you have not yet met him. He is homeschooled and goes on purchasing trips with his dad and come to think of it...I have never seen him in town." Katherine giggles. It dawns on her and becomes apparent as to why their paths have not crossed.

"That's alright, one of these days," Francie speculates. "And...like I said...I guess we met when we were toddlers because my mom and Sarita Mancini are close friends.

"So, tell me all about your summer getaway...." Katherine sits on her bed. She then pats the bed which invites Francie to sit beside her.

Francie plops on the bed next to Katherine and shares with her the fun they had, that is, everything except the ATV. The three friends made a pact to never mention it to anyone other than the people present.

Chapter 45

THE WEDDING OF SULLIVAN & KATHERINE

Francie wakes up and walks out to the kitchen.

Sophia glances over to her daughter, "Good morning sunshine." Sophia notices Francie looks like she is not feeling well at all and rushes to check her for a fever. "Oh, my, you are burning up," Sophia's sweet voice comforts Francie.

"How can this happen? I am rarely sick! And now...to be sick on the wedding day of Katherine and Sully! Of all the days to be sick!" Francie puts her head into Sophia's shoulder.

"I am so sorry, sweetie. You go back to bed. I need to get your dress over to Katherine," Sophia contends.

Francie walks to her room with her mother. Francie lays back down while Sophia gets the dress out of the closet.

"I guess she will have Eloise move up to maid of honor," Sophia supposes.

"Yes, and other than the dress being too long for Eloise, it should fit her nicely. Please tell Katherine I am so sorry." Francie feels too sick to even cry about it.

"I know how important this is to you to be in the wedding of your close friend." Sophia pats Francie on the leg then gently sweeps some curls of her hair off her face.

"Well, that really does not fix missing being the maid of honor in Katherine's wedding." Francie sniffles, coughs, and rolls over to her back, looking up at her mother.

"I know. I feel for you and I also feel I must get this dress to Katherine and let her know as soon as possible!" Sophia states.

Francie smiles at her mom. "Yes! Go! You are the best mom a girl can have!"

"Aw, thank you, sweetie." Sophia leans over Francie and kisses her forehead. "Okay, I will be back!" Sophia turns and dashes out of the room with the winter red dress draped over her arm. She rushes to get it over to Katherine.

······⊙⧜☉······

Katherine is peering in the full-length mirror of the bridal room at the church. While she gazes upon her dress in the mirror, she can see Sophia standing at the door with a dress draped over her arms. Katherine turns. "Oh, no!"

Sophia walks into the room. "Yes...I am so sorry. Francie is just sick about being ill. She has a fever and chest congestion."

Katherine lifts the dress from the arms of Sophia, then sadness sweeps across her face. Katherine slightly shakes her head. "Well, Eloise will be here soon. The dress is too long for her, but should fit elsewhere."

"That is exactly what Francie said. You know...I can run it to the sewing machine and stitch it up quick. I think three inches will work."

"Yes, thank you so much...." Katherine hands the dress back to Sophia.

Sophia skedaddles out the church and over to her shop where she keeps a sewing machine. She quickly matches the color of thread, weaves it into the machine, and hems up three inches of the beautiful dress. Sophia then rushes back to the church to find Eloise and Katherine waiting for her.

"This should fit you now, Eloise," Sophia states with confidence.

"Oh, thank you...I am so sorry Francie cannot be here with us!" Eloise conveys.

"Thank you. She is sick about it herself. We all are," Sophia caringly replies. "Are you going to have someone step into the spot of bridesmaid?"

"Yes, Caroline is on her way," Katherine answers. "She will fit nicely into the dress Eloise was to wear."

"Alright. It sounds like all is under control." Sophia walks over to Katherine and places her hands on the arms of Katherine. "You are a beautiful bride! God bless you and Sully with a fulfilling life."

"Thank you, Sophia. We think you are the best!" Katherine hugs Sophia.

Sophia smiles. "Alright, girls...enjoy this beautiful day together."

Both girls smile at Sophia.

"Give Francie our best. Tell her we miss her so much," Katherine instructs.

"I will," Sophia assures as she walks out of the room.

······⚬⧓⚬······

The wedding is flawless outside of not having Francie. Eloise is the lovely maid of honor. Katherine and Sully make a handsome couple and the colors they selected are very classy. David and Steve meet Antonio Mancini. The wedding and reception go smoothly with the guests enjoying themselves and congratulating the newlyweds. All is well in the Kingdom of Chamberlain. Winter turns to spring which turns to summer.

Chapter 46

THE FAREWELL

The day of departure for Steve and David arrive. Francie meets the two of them on the street before they head out on their horses with other young men.

David and Steve both exchange eye contact and a heartfelt smile with Francie as she approaches them.

"What did you bring us?" David asks while he grins.

"I brought your favorite cookies. I baked them last night," Francie informs.

"Well, we appreciate you spoiling us," Steve adds with a wink.

"I am sure gonna miss you guys!" Francie exclaims.

David and Steve both get quiet.

"Ah, don't quiet up on me!" Francie smiles at her friends.

"You're gonna be just fine without us," Steve maintains.

"Don't be so sure...." Francie winks.

Steve and Francie exchange a forever friend hug. Francie kisses Steve on the cheek. "Have I told you lately you're the best?"

Steve in turn kisses Francie on her cheek. "You are pretty great yourself. Take care of yourself."

"I will. You take care of you...and that one." Francie tilts her head in the direction of David.

"I will," Steve indicates. He then releases Francie from his arms and steps back.

David steps toward Francie and reaches for her. He gently draws her into his arms and gives her a big hug, with his head resting next to her head. "You know we love you, Francie."

Francie begins to mist up, smiles, nods, and whispers, "I know. I love you guys, too."

Francie requests while they are in a hug, "You two be safe."

David then pulls his head back from the side of Francie's head so he can look into her beautiful blue eyes. He repositions his hands and places one gently on the back of her head and one assertively around her waist. He then slightly tilts his head and leans in to kiss her.

David's kiss catches Francie off guard. She at first squirms, then feels a warmth of love and passion she has not yet encountered. She quickly relaxes and feels safe. She embraces David while she feels magically swept away.

David slightly pulls his face away to again gaze into her eyes. "We will forever be friends." He then rests his forehead onto her forehead and they experience almost a magical, unexplainable deep connection, like an energy transference.

Francie steps back and radiates with love for them both.

David smiles and gives Francie another embracing hug and whispers in her ear, "You know...I love you."

Francie whispers into his ear, "Me too, you."

They drop arms and step back.

Steve smiles at Francie. "You take care!" Steve mounts his horse.

Francie anxiously nods.

"Thanks for the cookies!" Steve conveys with appreciativeness.

"You guys are welcome! Write when you can!" Francie stands on her tiptoes and slightly elevates her voice over the noise. "I love you both! Be safe!"

The friends wave.

Steve winks at Francie one last time before riding off. "*You* be safe!"

Francie shoots a huge smile at Steve.

David exchanges eye contact with Francie. He reaches to hold one of her hands and grips it tightly. After what seems like communicating through their eyes, he releases her hand and nods his head. "I'll be seeing you...." He then turns, gets on his horse, and rides off with Steve, and the other young men that enlisted for the Guard of the Kingdoms.

Francie sighs and quietly voices, "Only in your dreams...you're leaving...." Thoughts of that kiss skip through her mind. She feels excitement and sorrow at the same time. She senses and thinks to herself, *this first perfect kiss...may be our last kiss...just due to timing.*

The parents wave and hold each other as their sons ride away. Sophia steps beside Francie and side hugs her.

Francie smiles at her mother. "Thank you." Francie leans her head into Sophia and holds her mother's hand.

Sophia keeps one arm wrapped around her daughter knowing this is just the beginning of heartaches and departures in her young life.

······◦&◦······

"What was that all about?" Steve quizzes as they ride side by side in the accompaniment of other young men to the academy of the Guards of the Kingdoms.

"What was all what about?" David replies clueless.

"You know what. Why did you kiss Francie?" Steve presses.

"Oh…that…I don't know. It just felt like the thing to do," David responds and then adds, "It was so powerful. I was not expecting that at all."

"I think that is messed up. You are leaving. We both are leaving. That is why I did not kiss her goodbye on the lips." Steve flings his arm toward David. "We may not ever come back. We may meet other women. I think you were being selfish," Steve matter-of-factly states.

"Maybe you are jealous I got the first kiss," David jests.

"Who are you? No. I made the decision not to complicate things. Francie knows this about me," Steve unwavering makes his case. Steve thinks to himself…*She is not a prize…I think you were led by…well, I don't know…selfishness!*

David contemplates. After some silence, he admits, "Noted. I see your point. Yeah, you are probably right…I should not have kissed her…plus, I may have lied to her by saying, 'I'll be seeing you'." David sighs. "It is highly likely we will meet other girls, and possibly not ever come back."

Steve and David both slightly shake their heads, for different reasons. They then reminisce on their lives and envision their future.

Chapter 47

LONGING FOR HER FRIENDS

It has been a little over a year since Francie's forever friends left for the guard, and it has been several months since Francie has received word from her childhood friends, David and Steve. She hopes they are well and happy.

⋯⋯⟋⟍⟍⋯⋯

"Have you written Francie yet?" Steve questions.

"No," David mumbles.

"Don't you think you should?" Steve questions.

"No." David shakes his head. "I can't. I wouldn't feel right about it."

"Unbelievable," Steve remarks.

"I have an idea…why don't you write? You are the one that is good with delivering messages.…" David counters.

Steve expresses disbelief. "So, you do not have enough regard for your friendship to write her yourself?"

"It's not about that. Not at all. I just cannot bring myself to tell her. Honestly…it kind of makes me sad," David explains.

"I thought you are happy with your decision," Steve responds.

"I am." David pauses, then sighs. "But writing to Francie and telling her...well...that makes me sad even thinking about it."

"So...you are telling me your sadness is greater than your news?" Steve tries to make sense of it.

David places his forearms on the railing of the balcony and leans over. "I guess it is. I can't tell her. In fact...thinking of telling her makes me feel like I am betraying my heart and words."

"To who?" Steve quizzes.

David slightly shakes his head. "To Francie...I don't know. I feel I have let her down...and even my own heart...but we *have* been away a year. Things change...if I write her, I will feel I am letting everyone down because writing it out makes it all real."

"Well...it is real. I will do it, but search your memories...Francie will be happy for us. She is a solid friend...always wanting the best for us," Steve reminds.

"She is. She will want the best for us," David agrees, pauses, then sighs. "I just don't want her to think she isn't the best."

"She won't. Don't worry," Steve assures.

······⌘······

Francie strokes the beautiful face of her horse, Aspen. She rests her head into Aspen and softly speaks as if Aspen can understand every word, "I sure miss those boys. Well...I suppose they are young men now. I wonder what all they are learning." Francie giggles, then endearingly smiles and moves from showing Aspen affection to brushing her coat with love in every brush stroke. Francie slightly sighs. "Wanna go for a ride, girl?"

Francie saddles Aspen then leads her out of the stables and climbs onto the saddle. "Let's go, girl." Aspen begins a walk, until Francie signals Aspen to gallop. Francie heads to the mountains on horse trails she has taken many times to enjoy the scenery and regroup her young soul. Nature always seems to energize Francie.

......⚬ℓ⚬......

"Where is Francie? I could use her help," Leonardo asks Sophia.

"It is such a beautiful day out, I told her to go enjoy herself," Sophia answers.

Leonardo nods. "Yes, I suppose that is a good idea. She has seemed kind of mopey for the most part over this past year."

"Yes, at times. She just misses David and Steve," Sophia discerns.

"I know, I know. There will be other boys. She is a beautiful young lady," Leonardo declares.

"Well, I do not believe she will consider that, at least not now," Sophia replies.

"I know. I do not see how she could choose one of those boys over the other. I believe she would have them both if she could." Leonardo quietly laughs to himself while thinking of his daughter. "You know, they might make the choice for her." Leonardo glances over the boxes of merchandise he is stocking on the shelves.

"You may be right." Sophia wrinkles her lips. "They are young men. If they do not know when they are going to be back, you are correct…they could very well meet girls that they may marry."

Their conversation is interrupted by Aaron Anderson, the delivery man in the mountain region.

"Good morning, folks!" Aaron greets as he enters their store with a satchel of mail, newspapers, and advertisements as to what is going on elsewhere.

Sophia walks over to the counter. "Just set everything right here. Thank you so much, Aaron."

"My pleasure, I certainly enjoy what I do…traveling from town to town throughout all the mountain regions. I always enjoy when I meet up with carriers from the coastal regions, it is just cool." Aaron grins with pride in his career choice.

"Well, we all appreciate your dedication and the great job you do," Sophia praises.

Aaron attempts to purchase a few items before he heads out, however, Leonardo and Sophia will not hear of it. They generously gift him what he needs.

"I really appreciate that!" Aaron expresses.

"We will not hear of taking your money. We appreciate your service," Leonardo assures.

"Thank you." Aaron tips his hat to Leonardo and Sophia. "I'll be on my way."

"Be safe, Aaron." Sophia smiles.

"See you next time." Leonardo nods.

"I think I will leave this for Francie to sort. She enjoys sorting and making sure it all gets to its local destinations." Sophia decides.

Leonardo nods. "Yes." He returns to stocking the shelves with merchandise.

······ᦆᦔᦆ······

Francie reaches the river and dismounts Aspen. "I just love this place. It is so beautiful. I can see the colorful rocks in the river. The scent of the pines surrounds me." Francie lifts her arms to the sky and exclaims, "I love life, Aspen! Thank you, Father God, for all you give us!" Francie takes her boots and socks off and rolls up her jeans as far as she can to get her feet wet in the water. "I pray you are well David and Steve! I love you guys!" Francie speaks aloud while she frolics in the river. She loves hearing the splashes and feeling the cold mountain river water on her calves. She bends down to pick up rocks and admires the beauty of some more than others. Memories of their summer at Steve's uncle's ranch dance in her mind and she smiles.

Francie walks home from the stables where she boards Aspen. "Hello, I am home." Francie steps into her home. Sophia and Leonardo are in the kitchen.

"Perfect timing, honey." Leonardo greets his daughter with a hug.

Sophia winks. "Hi Francie, I hope you had a wonderful day."

"I did!" exclaims Francie as she washes her hands then helps set drink glasses on the table.

"How was your day?" Francie inquires.

"Well, I stocked merchandise," Leo informs.

"Oh, Aaron Anderson came in today with a satchel full of stuff. I left it for you to sort through," Sophia communicates.

Francie lights up. "I will! Thank you for saving it for me! Do you mind if I sort what he brought, after dinner, instead of waiting until tomorrow?"

Leonardo shakes his head back and forth. "No, we do not mind at all."

"Great!" Francie beams.

Sophia sweetly smiles knowing her daughter is hoping there is a letter for her.

After Francie helps clean up, she dashes to their store to sort through all the items Aaron Anderson left. She hopes to find a letter from her forever friends. She quickly sorts through each piece and begins to feel disappointment, again, but then she spies her name, 'Francie Montanelli.' She beams with joy and eagerly opens the envelope. Her smile from ear-to-ear quickly subsides as she reads the words written:

"Dear Francie,

We hope this letter finds you well! David and I also hope this letter arrives before your birthday! We want to wish you a Happy 17th birthday! We are sorry we are not there to celebrate with you!

As you know, we do not know when we will be assigned to Chamberlain Kingdom. We want to let you know, well…here it is…Francie…David is getting married to a girl he met. Her name is Leah. I know you two will hit it off. I am not getting married, but I am dating a girl I met. Her name is Veronica. You will like her as well! It has nothing to do with how we feel about you, Francie. David could not even bring himself to let you know, but I felt you needed to know. I hope you will find it in your beautiful heart to accept this. You are a remarkable friend...please know that! Remember, nothing can replace any of our great memories, or our feelings for you! Take Care of Yourself!!

Forever,

Steve

Francie's heart instantly sinks. She literally feels sick to her stomach. She stares at the stack of stuff Aaron left and presses herself to sort all the mail, newspapers, and ads as she promised her parents. She wipes the mist swelling up in her eyes, refusing to let one drop trickle down her face. She holds in every tear of heartbreak racing through her. Her head is filling with great anxiety, she feels like she can vomit, she feels heartbroken. When she completes her task, she takes the letter and goes home. She quietly and directly walks to her room. Her parents are already in bed.

After Francie changes into her pajamas, she crawls into her bed and snuggles under her blankets wanting to cry, but will not allow herself to do so. Instead, she just feels a deep wound sweeping through her soul. Shortly, as she lays quiet in the dark room gazing out the window at the stars, a few tears form in her eyes and roll down her cheeks. She does not reach to wipe them.

Chapter 48

GROWING PAINS

Sophia and Leonardo are about to leave for the day. Usually, their daughter is up by now. "I am going to go check on Francie. I will be right back," Sophia lets Leonardo know.

Leonardo gets his things and proceeds to the front door.

Sophia quietly knocks on her daughter's door, and then lets herself in. "Francie, are you alright?"

Francie remains almost motionless and replies, "No, I am not feeling very well. I am going to stay in bed today."

"Well, can I get you anything? Is your throat sore? Where do you feel bad? Let me check your temperature," Sophia insists.

"No, I do not have a temperature. I just need sleep," Francie is adamant in her answer.

"Well...alright. Let me know if I can bring you...." Sophia is interrupted by Francie.

"No. I need nothing. Have a good day. Tell Daddy have a good day as well." Francie covers her head signaling to leave her alone.

Sophia steps back and retreats from her daughter's room. Her motherly instinct tells her something is up. She then reaches the door and conveys to Leo, "Let's go."

"Is Francie not coming?" Leonardo questions.

"No, she says she is not feeling well," Sophia answers.

The two leave the house.

"Well, do I need to check on her?" Leo quizzes.

"No, I literally just checked on her." Sophia expresses frustration.

"Alright, maybe it's a girl thing," Leonardo comments.

Under her breath, barely audible, already feeling frustrated she doesn't know what ails her daughter, Sophia sighs, "Ugh."

The Montanellis enter their shop.

"Well, she never fails us," Leo comments as he notices how everything Aaron dropped off is neatly sorted.

Sophia smiles. "Yes, we have a very sweet daughter."

Leonardo goes to the back and Sophia sets her bag behind the counter and proceeds to open the store. While returning to the counter she notices something on the floor. It is an envelope that has been ripped open. Sophia picks it up and turns it over and sees it is addressed to Francie from Steve. Sophia places the envelope next to her chest and whispers aloud, "So this is what ails you, my dear."

Leonardo comes out of the back ready to greet his customers. "What do you have there?"

"I think the answer to what ails our daughter," Sophia relays.

"What is it?" Leo inquires.

"A letter from the boys," Sophia states.

"Oh, it is probably just saying they won't be home for her birthday or anytime soon," Leonardo supposes.

"I hope you're right," Sophia remarks while her lips curl as she feels concern.

......⚬℘⚬......

The day presses on. Customers come in and out all day, then later, David's mother, Cecilia, walks into the store with a list.

"Good afternoon, Cecilia!" Sophia exclaims with a smile as she greets David's mother. "What can I help you with?"

"As you know, David is getting married, and I need the most beautiful gown for the occasion! It will be held in Zaltana where the bride is from." Cecilia bursts with joy. "You know, I always thought my David would marry your Francie, but I guess things didn't work out. I am sorry for that. We love Francie. And I guess Steve also has a girlfriend he met in Zaltana," Cecila chatters. "Life, ya never know. Anyway, it sounds like Steve and David will be away for some time. I know they were hoping to return to this kingdom, however, their orders keep them away."

"Yes, of course," Sophia calmly replies, expressing no signs of not knowing any of this information though thoughts race through her mind making sense of why her daughter was so distant this morning. "Let's look at this catalog for dresses and colors...we will get you fixed up."

Cecilia smiles. "I knew I could count on you to help me! Thank you."

"Well, it is not every day your only son gets married. I am happy to help," Sophia assures.

The ladies study the dress styles and colors. Cecilia makes her selection. "Very good. I am I glad I came to you, Sophia, you, and Leo never let us down," Cecilia compliments.

Sophia humbly smiles, "Well, we appreciate your business."

"By the way, tell Francie happy birthday for me. David mentioned in his letter she will be seventeen on Friday. He and Steve are truly sick they missed her sixteenth and now her seventeenth birthday," Cecilia communicates.

"I will be sure and tell her. Thank you, again." Sophia's sweet way about her stands out while she escorts Cecilia to the door.

After Cecilia leaves, Leonardo comes in from helping another customer carry supplies out.

"We have had a good day. What did Cecilia order?" Leonardo asks.

"Well...I think I found out why our daughter is sick in bed." Sophia stares into the eyes of her husband.

"What's that?" Leonardo inquires.

"Cecilia just informed me David is getting married to a girl from Zaltana and Steve is dating a girl from there. In addition, they will not be back to Chamberlain Kingdom anytime soon," Sophia details.

Leo nods, "Ah...I see, our Francie is heartbroken. She is resilient. She will be fine." Leo shrugs his shoulders.

Sophia explains, "Leo...Francie, David, and Steve have been BEST of friends since they were five years old. I imagine this is crushing her."

Leonardo digests what is wife is explaining. "She may hurt now, but I am sure she is sad for her loss and happy for them. Our daughter is a warrior and she will be alright." He places his hand on Sophia's right arm. "I understand her life is not going to be as she had, maybe, hoped...I still say she will be alright. She just needs time. Plus, we both knew she would not end up with either of them. They are childhood friends...she could never choose between them...at least not now, at this age." Leo raises his shoulders and his arms are bent at the elbows with his hands out, palms up. "I think her heart stings because the reality of them being away has sunk in...her life and their life is shifting into the next phase without daily access to each other. She is experiencing the pains of growing."

Sophia expresses a look of frustration and outlines, "I know time will heal. Sounds like you do understand the gravity of what she is going through. Ever since they departed to enter the guard, she has periodically mourned their absence. Now, she is grieving her loss."

Chapter 49

THE REST OF THE SUMMER

"Thank you so much for putting this shower together for our baby." Katherine hugs both Elosie and Francie. "You two are the best friends I could have. And Sophia...thank you for all your work, as well, and the exquisite cake."

Sophia sweetly smiles. "It is my pleasure." Sophia then excuses herself to the restroom.

"Quick...Francie...I heard about David getting married...this month! Are you alright?" Katherine quietly questions.

Eloise and Katherine feel so much empathy for their friend.

"I am...I knew it would happen. Well...I guess part of me was hoping it wouldn't...but I could never choose between them...I love them both as my forever friends." Francie slightly frowns.

"Any time you need to vent...I am here," Katherine insists. "Just so you know...you are the best, too!"

"I am here for you as well, Francie," Eloise conveys.

"I appreciate that. Thank you both. I want the very best for them. Now let's talk about you...Katherine. You look like you can pop any minute!" Francie smiles.

Eloise and Katherine giggle.

"I feel like I waddle everywhere. Quack, quack." Katherine giggles, then she snorts. "Now I need to go to the restroom," she states as she holds her stomach.

Sophia and Katherine exchange places in the bathroom.

Chapter 50

A BABY IS BORN

Katherine cries as she pushes one last time. The young doctor, George Gerard, catches the baby. "Oh, Katherine! It's a boy!" exclaims the doctor.

"Is he healthy?" Sully quizzes as he peers over the doctor to peek at his son.

"Yes. Yes. He appears to be healthy. Sully, why don't you leave the room while we finish things up here. The nurse will come and get you in a few minutes," Doctor Gerard suggests.

Sully kisses Katherine on her forehead, "I'll see you in a few minutes."

Katherine squeezes his hand and nods.

The nurse takes the baby and cleans him up while the doctor finishes with Katherine. The nurse places the bundle of joy into Katherine's arms. "Meet your son." The nurse smiles, then proceeds out the door to get Sully.

Sully quickly steps into the room and over to his wife and son, beaming with joy.

"Have you a name for him?" Doctor Gerard inquires.

Sully and Katherine gaze into each other's eyes and smile, then look upon their son.

Sullivan proudly announces, "His name is Benjamin William Carlisle."

"That is a very strong name. Congratulations!" the doctor expresses joy to his patient and friends.

Francie and Eloise show up.

"Oh, my! What a little doll!" exclaims Francie. She then smiles at Katherine. "I will babysit anytime you want."

"We appreciate that." Sully nods and pats Francie on the back.

"He is just precious." Eloise beams with delight and wraps her arm around Sully as they stand side by side.

Katherine introduces, "Meet our son, Benjamin William Carlisle."

Francie and Eloise both stand by Katherine's side experiencing the joy of new life.

Chapter 51

"I'm going to ride Aspen on my favorite trails today," Francie informs her parents. "That is, if you don't need me for anything."

"No, sweetie. It is another beautiful day. Go have fun." Sophia lovingly smiles at her daughter.

"I think you have done an amazing job with Aspen. You have accomplished teaching her how to jump, not to mention how to lie down. You two make quite a duo. Are you going to perform at The Annual Fall Around this year?" Leonardo inquires.

"I don't know, Daddy, maybe." Francie smiles then finishes her glass of milk. She stands and kisses each of her parents on their cheek. "Okay! I'll be back later!" Francie chimes as she rushes out the door, grabbing her backpack from the chair as she passes it.

Francie walks to the stables to get Aspen. She saddles her up. Aspen is always happy to see Francie. The two depart and quickly make their way to Francie's favorite trails. "I love you so much, Aspen. I am so fortunate to have you as my horse!" Francie takes in the wonders of autumn. Leaves that remain on the branches of the

Aspen trees decorate the landscape with yellows, golds, oranges, and reds. The scent of the pine trees is a fragrance that fills the air. The sounds of nature, paired with the river water moving over the rocks, sings. She also hears the waterfalls in the distance and the sound of Aspen's hooves with each step on the dirt trail. "Autumn is romance and energy," Francie states aloud while she feels her spirit recharging with each breath of the crisp mountain air. She recollects a few summers ago at Steve's aunt and uncle's ranch, *the trails are wide enough for an ATV...just like these trails.* Francie smiles while reminiscing about that fun summer as she dismounts Aspen. They both walk to the water's edge. Nearby is an old, rickety picnic table, yet strong enough to sit on. Francie gets her backpack and opens it. She feels inspiration to write. She pulls out a pencil and paper, but she sets the pencil and paper back down because first things first, she removes her boots and socks, rolls up her jeans, and steps into the river. She reaches over to Aspen and expresses aloud, "I love you so much, girl! And David and Steve...I love you guys, too!! I will forever! My daddy is probably correct...I could never choose between the two of you, but you will forever be my siblings in spirit! I pray God will bless you and keep you, and maybe one day we will reconnect and I will embrace your partners as my own." Francie smiles. She has made internal peace with her forever friends. She then tells Aspen, "I should write them! That is what I will do!" Francie steps out of the water and decides to sit on a boulder. She picks up her pencil and paper and begins to compose a letter to her two dear friends. As she writes, she takes moments to bask in her surroundings and the fall colors that encompass her. She smiles.

> *Dear David and Steve,*
>
> *I received your letter before my birthday. I apologize for the delayed response. Thank you for the birthday wish! Wow! What news! Congratulations to you both! You are both the BEST!! I will forever love you as my brothers and I look forward to meeting the partners you have chosen!! God Bless you both in all you do!*

Forever-My love & friendship-
Francie xoxo

Just as Francie is re-reading her letter, feeling at peace, she hears male voices and horses approaching. She quickly stuffs the letter and pencil into her backpack, stands up, and turns toward the intruders. Aspen begins to whinny.

Three of the four male riders get off their horses and approach Francie.

An eerie feeling swirls through Francie.

"My name is Devlin." He steps closer to Francie while another rider circles to the other side of Francie.

Francie gives a dirty look to the intruders and demands, "Stay back! There is nothing here for you!"

"There is water for our horses," one rider states.

"Not to mention your beauty is quite spellbinding." Devlin notices as he takes another step closer to Francie. "Are you from around here?"

"It is none of your business where I am from!" Francie asserts.

"I see your boots and socks are off. The river water is always nice to step in," Devlin attempts to make small talk.

The man in his early twenties who is circling behind, grabs the arms of Francie at the same time Devlin and one of the other riders charges her and grabs her legs. They lift her slender, tall teenage frame into the air and slam her onto the picnic table. They begin to move their hands all over her body. Francie puts up her most physical battle she has ever encountered! When one rider tries to kiss her, she spits. Francie screams, kicks, and punches with every ounce of strength she has in her. The three intruders continue to man-handle her while she screams, "Stop!" Francie becomes short of breath from a stress-induced asthma attack.

The rider who remains on his horse, hollers, "Hey, come on…that's enough! Let her go!"

Devlin crosses him and shouts, "No way!"

The rider dismounts his horse and grabs ahold of Devlin's shoulder and pulls him off. "I said, enough. We are not monsters. This girl does not deserve this."

Francie continues to scream and fight with all her might while the men continue their attack.

Aspen rears up and comes down on one of the men. Aspen stomps him to death. Another rider takes his hands from Francie, turns, pulls out his gun, and shoots Aspen.

Francie screams out in sheer agony, "NOOOOOOO!" She begins hysterically sobbing.

The rider that had pulled Devlin back and ordered to call off the attack, fast draws his gun and shoots Devlin along with the rider who shot Aspen. Blood splatters onto Francie. The men collapse. Francie rolls herself off the side of the picnic table and rushes to her horse. She drops to her knees and leans over Aspen, "Please, please…do not die on me! I love you! Please don't die." Francie uncontrollably sobs while she holds and kisses Aspen. Her cute white shirt is ripped. She has some bruises, along with residue of blood from the villains that were shot. They appear dead. Her physical integrity remains intact. Francie is still gasping for air.

The rider remains standing with his gun lowered by his side while he gazes down at Francie. "Miss, you need to calm down so you can breathe easily. I am sorry for these men. Including the harm they did to you and your horse."

"Pray for your soul! My horse will live!" Francie weeps.

"Well…Missy…your horse needs to be put out of her misery." The rider raises his gun. Francie turns and lunges toward him. She grabs both of his legs which results in him falling backwards. She snatches the gun. "Do you have a knife? Tell me now!" she screams while tears are streaming down her cheeks. She remains short of breath while she has the gun pointed at the cowboy.

"I do, it's in my pack," he calmly informs.

Francie backs up, keeping the gun pointed at the stranger. She removes one hand from the gun to wipe her eyes so she can clearly scan her surroundings. While keeping the gun pointed on the only rider alive, she reaches in his pack with her other hand and carefully feels around for the knife. She finds it and pulls it out.

"You…get up and leave this place and never return to our kingdom!" Francie demands.

He stands, brushes himself off, and begins to gather the reins of the riders' horses.

"No. Leave them. Take only your horse," Francie orders.

"You are pretty demanding for such a young one," the rider comments.

"Do not underestimate my youth," Francie sternly speaks.

"No, I suppose not. Again, I am sorry for these cowboys and I apologize for not stepping in sooner. We have been on the road a long time and they were swept away with your beauty," claims the intruder.

"No excuse for wicked behavior!" Francie stands tall with her shoulders back and the loaded gun steady in her hand, pointing at the surviving rider.

"Good luck with your horse, Miss. For what it is worth, I am sorry," The rider conveys while he stoops down to pick up his hat and brushes it off. He then gets on his horse and rides away. When he is out of sight, Francie rushes to her backpack and pulls out her first aid kit. "If I can stitch a dress, I can stitch you, Aspen! Hang on girl!"

Francie shifts from feeling the intense anxiety of the assault to taking care of business and attempting to save her beloved horse. She takes the knife and the first aid kit to remove the bullet and stitch Aspen up. Sobbing, Francie pleads, "Please don't die on me. Please don't die on me!" She knows it is too late. She lays her body onto Aspen's body, holding and caressing Aspen while tears stream down her cheeks. "I love you, Aspen girl. You're my baby." Francie laments as Aspen breathes her last breath.

The rider decides to canter into Chamberlain and look for the sheriff's office. He sits tall on his majestic Wintucket horse as they walk on the town streets until he spies the office of the sheriff. You can hear the hooves against the cobblestone until he reaches the office. He remains on his horse, in hopes the sheriff will notice him.

Sheriff Wesley Winslow does notice the rider and gets up from his desk and walks outside. "Welcome to Chamberlain. Can I help you?"

"No, but you can help a young lady that I suspect is from your kingdom. She is up past the C-Fork, on the Chianne River. Her horse…I speculate is dead. From the brief encounter I had with her, my guess is she will most likely not leave her horse's side to come home. I wanted to let someone know, so she is not alone overnight out there," the rider details.

"Can you give me a description?" Sheriff Winslow questions.

"Yes. My guess is she is five-feet-nine-inches tall, with long, brunette curls," the rider describes.

"Alright, I will gather some help and we will search for her. Thank you. Do you have a name?" inquires the sheriff.

"I do. Let's just say I am making right a wrong…at least attempting to." The rider tips his hat with gratitude. "Thank you for looking after her."

Sheriff Winslow nods.

The rider begins to walk away then pulls back on the reins. He stops and turns his body back toward the sheriff. "By the way, take shovels. She is not going to let anyone take her horse. She will want it buried right where it died."

"I understand. Much obliged." Sheriff Winslow tips his hat.

The rider leads his horse away.

Sheriff Winslow is quick to act. He rides to the castle grounds to enlist a few of the guards, in addition, he swings by the Veterinarian's office to bring the local vet as well.

Wesley Winslow's stomach feels sick inside. He is nearly certain it is Francie Montanelli. "Guys, hold up." He signals the other men. "I am going over to alert the Montanellis. Go on, we will catch up," directs the sheriff.

The guards and vet head out, while Wesley back-tracks to the store of the Montanellis.

Wesley dismounts his horse and bolts into the store.

Sophia senses trouble, stops what she is doing, hollers for Leonardo while shortening the distance between the sheriff standing at the door and herself.

Leo comes out from the back, "What is it?" He sees the sheriff and steps up his pace. "How can we help you?"

"Look, I am not certain, but I was notified there is a young lady at the Chianne River, and her horse is dead. From the description…well…I suspect it is Francie," details the sheriff.

Sophia gasps and places her hand on the arm of Leonardo. Leo exchanges eye contact with his wife. "We will both go with you," asserts Leonardo, making direct eye contact with the sheriff.

Wesley nods. "Alright, I thought you would. The vet and guards are on their way. I told them we will catch up."

"You got that right!" Leo exclaims as he walks Sophia out the door with his hand on her back, then turns to lock up. "Let's go!"

Sophia and Leo step up into their wagon and follow the sheriff, without wasting any time.

······⊙⅋⊙······

The Montanellis and the sheriff catch up with the others. Perhaps, the others were going at a slower pace which enables the other team to quickly join them.

Sheriff Winslow rides to the front and takes over the lead. He motions directions with his arm.

Francie is oblivious to the approaching distinct sound of the many hooves of the horses slamming against the dirt trail. Still lying over Aspen and holding her, Francie has fallen into a quiet rest after wailing for Aspen's life that was robbed from her. Also, her difficulty breathing has miraculously subsided.

Sheriff Winslow quickly dismounts his horse and rushes to Francie's side. He notices her torn top, bruises, and dried blood sprayed across part of her body. He silently kneels and places himself beside Aspen and Francie. "Are you injured?" the sheriff quietly questions.

Francie shakes her head, wipes her nose, and her eyes, and responds, "No."

The Montanellis arrive. Both Sophia and Leonardo expeditiously step down from their wagon and rush toward their daughter. They come to an abrupt halt as they scan the surroundings and recognize that something horrific occurred.

Sophia leans her head into Leo's shoulder. Leo places his arm around Sophia. They stand in silence, wanting to say something, but no words can convey their sentiments.

Francie soon raises her head from Aspen, and stands up. She turns and sees her parents. She begins crying all over and darts to her mother.

"Oh, my gosh! Are you hurt?" Sophia is aghast when she sees her daughter's blouse ripped and splatters of blood across Francie. Sophia places her hands on Francie's cheeks. "Are you hurt?"

"This is not my blood." Francie trembles, while she replies.

Sophia pulls her daughter close to her and holds her ever-so-tightly, yet remains quiet, while she embraces Francie.

Sheriff Winslow brings a blanket from his pack and wraps it around the back of Francie.

Francie sheds tears into her mother's shoulder, but tries to be quiet about it.

Leo envelops them both. He lays his head onto his daughter's head. After a few moments, he kisses the back of his daughter's head. He then steps toward Sheriff Winslow. The two men exchange eye contact and walk out of ear shot from the ladies.

They quietly exchange words while the vet examines Aspen.

"Have you seen any of these men before?" the sheriff asks.

"Not a one," answers Leo.

One of the guards who is bent down over one of the bodies comments, "I cannot be sure, but I think I saw this man when I was a guard in the kingdom of Estevan. He was a pretty good ranch hand if memory serves me well. I do not recall his name though."

"How long ago was that?" Wesley asks.

"I'd say about two years ago, then I was transferred to Chamberlain Kingdom," the guard replies.

Sheriff Winslow nods.

"I want to know what these men did to my daughter!" Leo demands.

Both the sheriff and Leo glance over to Sophia and Francie.

Wesley places his hand on the shoulder of Leo. "You may not get any answers right away, Leo."

"Yeah, you may be right. In fact, I may never know." Leo kicks some gravel while his eyes are fixed on his wife and daughter.

······◦❧◦······

Doctor Brett, the vet, stands and turns to Francie. "You know there is nothing you could have done. I see by the knife and your first aid kit…my guess is, you were going to remove the bullet."

Francie peers into the eyes of Doctor Brett, but remains side by side with her mother. Francie wipes her nose with her arm and nods. "Yes." Francie sniffles and wipes her nose again. "But it was too late."

Doctor Brett nods. "Yes, I can see Aspen was shot at very close range. There is nothing you could have done, sweetie."

After the sheriff inspects the other bodies lying nearby, he and Leo return to the proximity of Doctor Brett and the women.

"Sheriff...Leo," Doctor Brett addresses, "Aspen was shot at close range."

"I see. Thank you, Doctor," Sheriff Winslow conveys. "I appreciate the information. Had I known this was a crime scene, I would have brought our medical doctor as well."

"Well, I am able to examine them and determine a time of death," Doctor Brett informs.

"Boy, that would sure help me out," the sheriff responds.

"I can tell you their time of death...." Francie points to the intruder that was stomped. "That one died when they attacked me. Aspen stomped him to death! The other two men were shot by a fourth man...who was a very fast draw."

"How did you know she was out here?" Sophia quizzes.

"A rider came through town," Sheriff Winslow begins.

Francie becomes very focused on the sheriff's words.

"He just remained on his horse in front of my office. I went out and asked him if I could help him. He said, 'No,' but that I could help a young lady because he believes her horse is dead," outlines the sheriff.

Francie's lips moue.

"Did he give his name?" Leo questions.

"No. When I asked him his name, he said, 'Let's just say, I am making right a wrong...at least attempting to,' and that is all he said. Well, as he rode off, he did stop and turn to tell me to be sure to bring shovels because the brief encounter he experienced with her, he believed she would want to bury her horse right where it died," recounts the sheriff.

Sophia squeezes her daughter with a half hug.

Leo shakes his head with anger. He then walks over to Francie and places a hand on each of her upper arms and looks her directly in her eyes. "Are you physically hurt?"

Francie shakes her head several times. "No." She wipes her nose and eyes again.

Sophia is about to speak up and articulate that Francie is indeed hurt, emotionally, but she tightens her lips and refrains, for the sake of her husband and her daughter.

"Francie, you tell me, where do you want Aspen buried?" the sheriff asks.

Francie points. "Right over there."

"Alright then, and Leo, since your wagon is here, can we haul these men back to town in the bed?" Sheriff Winslow inquires.

"Be my guest." Leo throws up his arms. "I'd rather just leave them here for the animals to eat, but that wouldn't be the right thing to do now, would it." Leo shakes his head. He feels exasperation, while he takes a few steps around, going nowhere.

Sophia feels immense empathy for her husband and daughter.

The men load the bodies into the bed of the wagon. You can hear the wood as each body is placed onto the wagon bed. They grab their shovels and begin to dig a grave for Aspen in the designated location Francie chose. The two women sit on the ground. Francie lies across the lap of her mother. After some time passes, Francie stands and states, "I am going to help dig."

"Oh, honey, are you up for that?" Sophia asks.

"Yes!" asserts Francie. Francie runs over and grabs her socks and boots and quickly puts them on.

Francie moves with purpose, grabs a shovel, and begins to assist the men that are digging the grave for Aspen.

Leo walks over to his wife. "You know she is like this. She is not going to sit by while others work for her."

"I know. I just thought she could sit this one out." Sophia sighs.

"I know," Leo gently assures.

"Maybe, helping will be healing...perhaps, help with closure," Sophia suggests as she takes in a deep breath.

Chapter 52

THE FALL AROUND

A few weeks pass since the incident with Aspen. Sophia is filling boxes of merchandise they will sell at the Annual Fall Around. Francie walks into the store to help her mother. Sophia desperately wants to visit with her daughter about what happened, but still cannot bring herself to inquire. She does her best to not ask. She allows Francie to lead the way as to when she wants to talk about what went down. Leonardo, also, does not mention a word of it. Instead, he and Wesley visit about the incident and the mysterious fast-draw that appears to have protected Francie, though his efforts were untimely.

Sophia's sweet voice breaks silence, "Honey, have you considered writing a letter to David and Steve to let them know about Aspen? I mean, after all, they were with you when you picked Aspen out...and I think you were with them when you came up with the name for her...."

There is a long silence while Francie continues to help place merchandise in boxes to haul to the Annual Fall Around. Francie shrugs and replies, "I don't know. Mom...David is getting married...in fact, probably already married to a girl from

Zaltana, and Steve is dating a girl from there. So, I do not really want to bother them with any of it." Francie shrugs and slightly frowns while she ties a ribbon around some baked goods.

Sophia works alongside of Francie and formulates what next to say.

"I am so sorry, Francie, that your friends have met girls and are moving on. Is that what ailed you a couple of months ago?"

Francie sighs while she works. "It is." She ties off another bow and glances over to her mother. "I know you knew. I saw the dress receipt for David's mother, and I was certain she mentioned it to you."

Sophia nods. "She did...but I have been waiting for you to tell me."

Francie also nods and confides, "I wrote David and Steve a letter while I was at the river with Aspen. It is still in my backpack."

"Aww...are you going to mail it?" Sophia caringly asks.

Francie rolls her lips around, "Yeah. Might as well. It would be rude not to respond to the letter Steve wrote, though waiting for over two months to reply is out of character as well. Yeah, I will mail it out when Aaron Anderson returns." Francie nods. She feels at peace with the decision she made.

"Are you sure you do not want to mention what happened to Aspen?" Sophia gently pries.

"No. I am not sure. But as I said...they have their new lives and partners...they do not need to worry about me." Francie remains steadfast.

"Oh, honey, I think you will always be a part of them, and they will always be concerned with your well-being," Sophia tenderly assures.

Francie shrugs again and sighs. "I don't know...they have been gone for over fifteen months...it just seems like a lifetime."

"I know...but they will forever be in your heart, as you are in theirs. That is what makes forever friends. An unbreakable connection, my dear," Sophia shares in her ever-so-sweet comforting voice.

"I guess. I don't know." Francie finishes packing up another box of

merchandise.

Sophia sweetly smiles and contends, "Oh, I think you do know. Whether you are willing to allow yourself to feel, does not mean, it doesn't exist." Sophia pauses, "And…I am here for you, honey, whenever you want to talk about what happened at the river."

"No. I will deal with it myself," Francie answers.

"You do know, God did not create us to do things alone," Sophia maintains.

"I don't know. I believe you, but maybe all this stuff I have gone through is teaching me how to be alone…how to deal with everything on my own," Francie suggests.

"Oh, daughter of mine…so many people love you. You do not have to go through anything alone. Talking it out is beneficial and healing to your spirit," Sophia reasons.

"No. Other people have their own stuff they are going through. I will figure things out on my own," Francie remains adamant.

"So, if someone you know or even someone you do not know, has something hurtful happen to them, and they want to talk about it, are you saying you would not listen to help their healing?" questions Sophia.

"No! Of course not! I would gladly be there for anyone! I would *WANT* them to share with me, so I can maybe help them, and pray for them, and pray with them," Francie asserts.

"That is how people feel, also, for you. They want you to share…so maybe they can help you, or just be a listening ear…or pray for you. Look, I know your best friends left to better their lives with a great career, and…in doing so, you were left behind. That does not mean you are unlovable, Francie. All of you were just kids. People want the very best for you and want to help you if they can. I am pretty sure those young men do too, even if they are building their lives elsewhere," Sophia attests.

Francie begins to smile. "I hear you."

"I am glad." Sophia lovingly smiles at her daughter. "Well, we made short work of that! Everything is ready to transport to the castle grounds."

Francie smiles again at her mother. Sophia returns a heartfelt smile to her daughter.

.......ᘓᑈᓂ.......

The royals are getting ready for the Annual Fall Around. Marcella and Franklin are enjoying breakfast with their children.

"It's pretty cool the Fall Around is by your birthday!" exclaims Tabitha Marie.

Theo smiles and grins at his younger sister. "I guess it is."

"Eloise will be attending, won't she?" Marcella questions her son.

Theodore again grins. "Yes, Mother. She would not miss having an opportunity to enjoy time with us."

"We like her," King Franklin comments.

"I am glad. I plan to ask her to marry me," Theodore informs.

"Oh!" Marcella places her hands over her heart. "I love that!"

"Are you going to ask her at the Annual Fall Around?" Tabitha quizzes.

"That is what I am planning," Theo confirms.

"I trust you have asked her parents' permission," Franklin asserts.

Theo grins. "I have. They gave me their blessing."

"...and you have ours." Franklin smiles at his son, full of pride.

"I cannot think of a better young lady to be your wife and take our place someday," Marcella lovingly conveys.

"Can I be in your wedding?" Tabitha grins from ear to ear.

"Of course. What every prince wants is his little sister in his wedding." Theodore laughs. "Yes, Princess Tabitha, Eloise and I would not have it any other way."

Tabitha glows with love for her older brother.

Chapter 53

SEE ME IN YOUR DREAMS

A few months have passed since the incident that robbed Aspen of her life, and Francie has been trying to process everything that happened that day.

Francie awakens with a smile on her face and feels a peacefulness she has never encountered before. She lies quietly in her bed. She smiles and enjoys the calm and tremendous peace she is experiencing. She rolls over to her nightstand and quickly grabs her journal and a pen.

I will write a song. That's it! Francie sits up in bed, still smiling, with an overwhelming, peaceful energy that consumes her. She scribbles down what she dreamed...

> *I woke up feeling peaceful-from a dream I had of you-*
> *Holding me in your arms-in the yard lit by the moon-*
> *Our heads resting together-our cheeks touching-sends me chills-*
> *While we slow dance by the firepit-as the wind is standing still...*
> *I open my eyes and it's over-it was only in my dream-*

Our lives took different avenues-long before adult life
came to be-
You are the one my yes is for-I would dance with you
through life-
Resting in your arms-working by your side-
Holding me in your arms-in the yard lit by the moon-
While we slow dance by the firepit-I get tingles next to
you-
I open my eyes and it's over-It was only in my dream-
Which gave such a peaceful feeling-
Maybe you'll see me in your dreams...
Holding me in your arms-in the yard lit by the moon-
Slow dancing by the firepit-as the wind is standing
still...
Maybe...one day...our dreams will be real...

      By Francie Montanelli

Francie rereads her lyrics a few times and she thinks, *maybe, I will add more to the ending at some point.* She begins singing it. She hops out of bed, grabs her journal, and runs to the kitchen. She sees her mother making waffles. "I dreamed it! I feel all better!" Francie exclaims.

A baffled expression casts across the face of Sophia. "Well, that sounds very nice...what are you talking about?"

"Oh!" giggles Francie. "I had the most incredible dream!" Francie exclaims as she twirls on the floor in her socks and pajamas. "It was so ***real,*** I could ***feel*** it! I could ***see*** it!" Then Francie holds the journal in front of her with both hands, "Do you want to hear it?"

Before Sophia can get a word out, Francie adds, "Oh, please! It is just beautiful!"

Sophia smiles and turns off the heat. "Can I sit down?"

"Yes! Yes! But I will stand!" Francie's excitement fills the room.

"Alright then." Sophia pulls out a chair to sit down. She eagerly listens to her daughter read what she has written, but to her complete surprise, Francie begins singing her heartfelt words,

> I woke up feeling peaceful-from a dream I had of you-
> Holding me in your arms-in the yard lit by the moon-
> Our heads resting together-our cheeks touching sends me chills-
> While we slow dance by the firepit-as the wind is standing still...
> I open my eyes and it's over-it was only in my dream-
> Our lives took different avenues-long before adult life came to be-
> You are the one my yes is for-I would dance with you through life-
> Resting in your arms-working by your side-
> Holding me in your arms-in the yard lit by the moon-
> While we slow dance by the firepit-I get tingles next to you-
> I open my eyes and it's over-It was only in my dream-
> Which gave such a peaceful feeling-
> Maybe...you will see me in your dreams...
> Holding me in your arms-in the yard lit by the moon-
> Slow dancing by the firepit-as the wind is standing still...
> Maybe...one day...our dreams will be real....

Francie is so excited that she does not even notice her mother's expression.

"What do you think? Don't you love it! I love it! It is SOOOO Beautiful! And mom! I woke up feeling so much peace! I **AM** going to write Steve and David and let them know about Aspen! I know they have probably received my first letter of response to them meeting girls and getting married...but yeah...I am truly at peace now! You are right, Mother! We will be connected for life!" Francie expresses with such spirited energy and passion. "I think the root is I just miss having them around...then our lives took different directions. I will always love them and want the best for them!"

Sophia, deeply moved by, not only, the lyrics, but her daughter's energy, finally gets a word in. "Francie...." Sophia stands and places her hands on her daughter's arms. "That is the most incredibly powerful, not to mention...beautiful song I have ever heard. I am not just saying that because you are my daughter. I mean it. You have a real gift."

Sophia and Francie exchange a bonding hug.

"I am very glad you received a dream that brought you peace," Sophia conveys.

"I did! I just can't believe it! Out of nowhere, I had an incredible dream and I wrote it into a song!" Francie exclaims while she spins in a circle. Francie feels very thankful and amazed she finally feels at peace.

"Well...whoever the leading man is in your dreams...he is one lucky man." Sophia smiles as she finishes up breakfast.

Francie holds her journal close to her heart. She returns it to her room before eating breakfast. Francie smiles and thinks to herself...*he will never know....*

Chapter 54

AT THE MANCINI'S

A few months pass. Sarita and Don are finishing up breakfast. Then they get ready to meet the king and queen and their youngest, Tabitha, for a sleigh ride through the Chamberlain Mountain range. They will begin on Sunrise Peak.

"Antonio, I know you will hold the ranch down while we are gone. I just want to let you know how proud I am of you," Don conveys to his only son.

"Thanks, Pop. You and mom taught me everything." Antonio grins.

"Well, I...Sarita Mancini, do solemnly attest that we do have the greatest son! Oh, honey, I cannot wait until you meet your wife and make me a grandmother! I will teach your children the ways in which we taught you," Sarita exclaims. Sarita appears to always be full of loving joy.

Don grins at his wife and winks at Antonio. "Son...I hope you meet a woman as tender as your mother...and as fierce. I hope you meet a warrior and not a whiner. Someone who is full of zest...like your mother."

Antonio shakes his head feeling slightly embarrassed. "Guys, I haven't met anyone. Maybe someday. It is the furthest thing from my mind. Right now, I love purchasing horses, training them…looking after the cattle, not to mention, working at the mine. What more could I possibly want?"

Sarita smiles at her son. "One of these days you will meet someone to build a life with. Oh! I just get so thrilled thinking about it! You will bring me a daughter I can love as my own…and children…OOO! I cannot wait!" Sarita carries plates to the kitchen.

Antonio and Don exchange a grin.

Sarita's joy is infectious.

Don stands. "Well, it's time we get going."

Don and Sarita bundle up with their winter gear.

Sarita holds her arms open and reaches toward her son. Antonio steps into her arms and gives her a big hug.

"You guys be safe," Antonio conveys.

"We will! We have been doing this sleigh ride every year now, since Tabitha was two," Don comments.

"I remember when Antonio and Theo used to go when they were young," Sarita reminisces.

Don smiles. "Yes, they both wanted to lead the team…every year."

Laughter and good memories surround them.

Everyone steps outside. Don and Sarita descend the steps and head over to the sleigh.

"You guys be safe! I love you both!" Antonio calls out.

"Oh, we love you too, honey!" Sarita turns around and waves to her son.

Don turns back and waves, in a salute manner, at Antonio. "You take care! See you in a while!"

"I'll surprise you with dinner!" Antonio states.

"That'll be great!" Don responds.

Sarita leans her head into Don just before they reach the sleigh and quietly voices, "We have been so blessed with the best son ever!"

"We have." Don agrees. He assists his beautiful Sarita onto the sleigh.

"I do hope someday he will meet Francie Montanelli. Her parents are just lovely, and she is such a doll...so polite and helpful," Sarita continues.

Don nods. "She is. It is surprising they have never connected since they have gotten older. I agree with you. I think she would make Antonio a lovely wife."

Sarita giggles. "Francie Mancini. I like the sound of that. I think we should arrange them to meet...maybe send Antonio into town, to their store."

Don grins. "Not a bad idea."

"I will talk to Sophia tomorrow and make the arrangements. You know... Francie and Antonio did play together when they were babies and toddlers. I think Antonio was about five years old when he did not want to go with me anymore into town, he just wanted to stay by your side with the dogs and horses," Sarita reminisces. "I definitely thought he would meet Francie at the wedding of Ben and Laurie, but she came down sick."

"Yeah...and from kindergarten on, she was thick with Steve and David," Don comments.

"Yes...they were best of friends, but you know, life changes. I will meet with Sophia and we will plan our children to meet again," Sarita asserts with a smile on her face.

Don and Sarita enjoy the morning ride to the castle to pick up the king and queen and their daughter.

Chapter 55

AT THE CASTLE

Franklin, Marcella, and Tabitha descend the steps of the castle. The Mancinis are waiting in their sleigh.

"Well, hello honey." Sarita smiles to greet Tabitha.

"Hi, Mrs. Mancini," Tabitha addresses.

Franklin helps his daughter into the sleigh. He then assists Marcella into the sleigh.

"You know what? Franklin, trade me places. You sit up here with Don and I will sit with Marcella and Tabitha." Sarita turns and winks at Tabitha and Marcella.

Sarita gives Don a quick kiss on his cheek, then exchanges places with Franklin.

"Everyone ready?" Don asks.

"We are!" exclaims Tabitha.

The two families head off toward the Chamberlain Mountain Range to go on their annual sleigh ride on Sunrise Peak.

······ঔঙ······

"What do you think about a Septembria wedding?" Theodore asks Eloise while they stroll around the castle grounds in their coats and snow boots.

"I like that idea. How about the fifteenth of Septembria?" suggests Eloise.

"I like that idea." Theo smiles at Eloise. "I was thinking I am going to have Antonio as my best man, unless you want me to have Sully."

"Well, I could have Francie as my maid of honor…or Katherine…." Eloise expresses her thoughts.

"We will figure it out." Theo smiles. He wraps his arm around his fiancé.

"This is such a beautiful winter day. Next year, let's go on the sleigh ride with your parents and the Mancinis," Eloise hints.

"You would like that?" Theo questions.

"I think it would be fitting…and romantic." Eloise glances up into Theodore's eyes.

Theo kisses the top of her head. "Next year, we will go."

Eloise smiles and snuggles into Theodore. They continue to walk across the snow that blankets the castle grounds.

……⌾⧜⌾……

Tabitha is very happy to be sitting between her mother and Sarita. "I love this!" exclaims Tabitha.

Both women look at Tabitha. Marcella takes Tabitha's hand in her hand and tenderly smiles at her daughter.

Sarita wraps her arm around Tabitha and kisses her head. "I am glad you do, honey."

"Hey! Why are we not going up that trail today?" Tabitha points and quizzes.

"Look at the tree line up there. A lot of wind appears to be stirring about. Sometimes, it seems that mountains have a climate of their own. I prefer we steer clear of it and stay down here today," Don responds.

"I was concerned we would not be able to go, since it recently snowed, but this is an outstanding day," notes Marcella.

"Yes, Don and I had our concerns as well, but all seems to be well," Sarita comments. "Oh, and congratulations on your son and Eloise getting married! How exciting!" adds Sarita.

"I get to be in their wedding!" Tabitha exclaims.

"How special is that!" Sarita smiles.

"We love Eloise. She will be a very, well-rounded queen someday," Marcella states with confidence.

"And I will be Aunt Tabitha!" Tabitha chimes in.

"You certainly will, honey." Sarita expresses joy.

The families enjoy the scenery of the landscape when the horses come to an abrupt stop. The horses begin to stomp and attempt to rear. The team appears to be anxious.

"Whoa...there. It is alright," Don calmly voices, to assure the team, though fear begins to creep into his body, while he scans their surroundings.

"Did you hear that?" Franklin searches up to the high peaks.

Don, still trying to calm the horses, replies, "Yes. I must get us out of here now!"

"What is it?" Sarita leans toward the front.

Don glances back at his wife with a look of fear that she has never seen before. "It's an avalanche!"

Sarita takes her eyes from Don and casts them up the mountain. She sees a slab of snow rushing toward them. Sarita pats Don. "I love you. Do what you must to save us." Sarita turns and sets her eyes on Marcella and Tabitha.

Franklin gazes upon his wife and daughter. "I love you both so much!"

The women wrap arms around each other and Tabitha. Tabitha cries.

"Let us pray," Sarita insists. Tabitha tries to calm herself while she rests in the arms of her mother and Sarita. The women begin to unceasingly pray.

Don and Franklin exchange eye contact. Don once again tries to get the horses to go. This time they run. "That's it! Get us out of here!" Don exclaims.

Everyone braces themselves while the team attempts to outrun the slab of snow that is barreling with velocity, increasing in size, as it sails down the mountainside.

......⁕......

"Look!" exclaims Eloise, "An avalanche!" Eloise points toward Sunrise Peak.

Theodore takes his arm from around Eloise and runs a few steps. "NOOOO! It can't be!"

Theodore exclaims, "Come on!" He runs to the stables.

Eloise follows closely behind.

"Will you please ride into town and get the sheriff? Also, have someone ride out to get Antonio. I will gather the guards. We need all available hands to help," Theodore directs.

"Yes. I will do that!" Eloise voices.

Theodore saddles up horses with the assistance of their stable hand, Charles.

"After we are done here, Charles, help me gather all the guards," Theodore requests.

"I will," Charles replies.

Eloise takes off to get Sheriff Winslow. Theodore and Charles move swiftly to gather all the guards on duty.

Sheriff Winslow sends his deputy out to get Antonio Mancini.

The sheriff and Eloise arrive back at the castle and see the assembly of men Theodore and Charles have been able to gather.

"We have supplies and are ready to go," Theo states.

Sheriff Winslow nods.

"Eloise, please hang back and wait for Antonio to arrive. Tell him of the avalanche and tell him we are heading up on the Sunrise Peak Trail," Theodore requests.

Eloise nods. "Yes. I will do that."

Theodore and the sheriff exchange eye contact and lead the rescue mission.

Sheriff Wesley Winslow quietly discusses the matter with Theodore while they trek through the snow-covered trails. "You know, we may reach a point where we must go on foot. And you know, Theodore...I do not even...."

"You don't have to say it, Wes. I know very well we may not be able to rescue them." Theo shakes his head. He is driven with fear and anxiety. The thoughts of losing his family and his best friend's parents are more than he can bear.

"I'm sorry. I am just trying to prepare you...." Wesley submits and pats the back of Theodore.

"I know," Theo acknowledges. "Thank you."

They reach a point where there is a wall of snow against some boulders and trees.

"Well, I guess this is where we go on foot." Theo shrugs.

The sheriff signals for the rescue team to come to a stop. The men dismount their horses. Theodore and Wesley take a few steps. They navigate up the wall of snow to scan the terrain for any signs of the sleigh, the team of horses, and Theo's family along with the Mancinis. They also listen for any signs of life.

Eloise sees riders coming up the road to the stables. She rides to meet them. It is Antonio and the deputy. "They told me to tell you to go to Sunrise Peak Trail."

"Thank you, Eloise." Antonio tips his head and continues to ride with purpose.

The deputy also nods to Eloise and rides on.

Eloise wants to join the rescue party, but knows she can better serve at the castle. She heads up to the castle and enters. She alerts the staff as to what is happening. "There has been an avalanche. Please make food and gather blankets for the crew when they return. Please keep in your prayers our beloved king and queen and their daughter...and the Mancinis." The staff all nod and immediately get busy with preparations for the rescue team and any survivors.

Antonio and the deputy reach where the horses are tied up. They grab their shovels and trek up the wall of snow. They spy the men spread out, digging across the landscape. It appears though, for all the shoveling, no headway is being accomplished. Just piles and piles and piles and piles of snow.

Antonio scans the area and spots Theodore. He treks through the snow to his location. Theo raises his head from shoveling when he senses the presence of someone beside him. Theo and Antonio exchange eye contact. Theodore slams his shovel into the snow, so it remains standing, and reaches out to embrace Antonio. With tears in his eyes, he backs up a step and peers into the eyes of his best friend. "I think we have lost them. Our entire family, Tony." Theodore pauses, "I think I'm gonna be sick." Theodore takes a few steps away and vomits.

Antonio is in shock. He again, scans the snow-covered landscape. He observes all the men who are diligently shoveling. He witnesses his friend bent over, feeling overwhelmed with hopelessness. Antonio whispers under his breath, "How could you let this happen…God!" Antonio kneels beside Theodore and wraps one arm over his back. "Tell me what you want. I will lead the men to continue to shovel if you want."

Theo nods. "Yes. I will help you."

Antonio stands and reaches his hand to assist Theodore to his feet. The two tall young men look all around. Antonio formulates a plan. "You know, I was going to walk as far as I can, and search for their tracks…but the snow has erased all evidence. I like your idea…that you have men spread out shoveling. It covers more territory."

"Yeah, but as you can see…it doesn't even look like we are making a dent." Theo states.

"I know. There is so much snow." Antonio shakes his head. "Come on, let's find them!" Determined, Antonio takes his shovel to an area he thinks he may find them. He begins shoveling with a steady, fast-paced movement.

Theodore also resumes shoveling.

Hours turn into more hours. Darkness of the night casts across the kingdom. Men pull out their Krystyleen to light the work area. Not one person is complaining of being hungry, tired, or cold. They are all determined to find their beloved people.

The morning sun appears over the top of Sunrise Peak. Beams of light fan out over the peaks onto the landscape where the men have been shoveling all night.

Antonio, Theodore, and Wesley Winslow survey every inch of, what seems like, vast trenches shoveled out. They meet back after thoroughly inspecting all the areas for even a glimpse of something from their people, or the horses, or the sleigh. They find nothing.

While the three men discuss options, the other men stand by and observe their expressions.

"What do you two want to do?" Sheriff Winslow asks.

Theo and Tony stand staring at each other, both slightly shaking their heads.

"I have no words." Theodore gazes at Wesley and Antonio. "Is this it? Are we just supposed to give up searching for them with no glimmer of hope they are still alive!"

Antonio shakes his head the entire time that Theodore is speaking. "I don't know. I agree...are we just supposed to give up? Accepting their deaths? Leaving them out here without the proper burial?"

Wesley speaks with compassion, "If you want, we can begin shoveling again tomorrow, or, we can wait for the snow to melt to find their remains."

"Ugh, I hadn't even thought of that!" Theodore blurts. "It will be at least six weeks before we experience a significant melt."

"The longer we wait, the less likely we will find them alive," Antonio asserts.

Theodore and Wesley both nod.

"Well, as I said, we can pick up tomorrow…maybe give the men a day of rest." Wesley suggests.

"Yes, do that. I will continue to shovel, though," Antonio declares.

"I will as well," Theodore concurs. "Give the men a break to get rested and the two of us will continue to search for our families," Theodore communicates.

Wesley turns to the rescue team. "Thank you, each of you, for helping us. Go home. Get a day of rest and join us again tomorrow."

The men nod their heads, yet, do not leave. The group remains assembled with shovels in their hands. One of the men steps forward, "These are our people, too. Don nor Franklin, would never, ever, leave us if we needed them, neither would Sarita or Marcella. We are all in."

The men take their shovels and spread out again, shoveling, and searching.

······⌒⧓⌒······

Eloise awakens in a chair when the sun beams through the window of the castle. The staff are busy preparing for the day. She rushes to the kitchen. "No word?" She addresses the head chef.

Chef shakes his head, displaying a somber expression. "No."

"Alright. Please prepare food to go. We will take food to the rescue team. Maybe grab some change of clothes and dry socks," Eloise outlines, although she is aware that the people in their kingdom have boots that protect their feet completely from wetness and cold.

Eloise, Charles, some of the kitchen staff, and a few guards that remained at the castle, set out with food for the men.

They arrive at the wall of snow and dismount. Eloise looks up and sees it is a steep grade. Nevertheless, she slings a bag over her shoulder and climbs, using every muscle of her young, petite body to get up the bank. The others follow her.

They view as far as their eyes can see. They are astonished with what appears like an unending maze, shoveled in all directions. Eloise spies Theodore. Then she glances at the ones who accompany her. "Split up. Go and pass out food and water." Everyone nods and spreads out, giving food and water to the rescue team.

Eloise and the others patiently wait and watch.

Dusk sets in.

Theodore walks over to meet with Antonio. Sheriff Winslow sees the two young men and steps to visit with them. Theodore and Antonio speak no words. Trickles of sweat runs down their foreheads. They peer into the eyes of each other. Sheriff Winslow remains silent. After what seems like long minutes, Theodore and Antonio exchange a handshake and wrap their free arm around the other. Then, initiate a comforting pat on the back of the other. The two nod at each other.

"Sheriff, let the men know they can go. Antonio and I will decide tomorrow what steps to take moving forward," Theodore discloses.

The sheriff nods. He walks around announcing to the rescue team they may go home.

Eloise steps next to her fiancé and remains by his side. As the men descend the wall of snow, Theodore, and Antonio gesture and shake the hands of every person who helped. They thank each one by name.

Chapter 56

DECISIONS

"What's up, Celestial? Ever since you returned from your getaway, you have seemed preoccupied," Blazer notices.

Celestial and Blazer continue to stroll along the countryside of Chiaras before they gather for their assembly. Celestial shifts her stroll into a walk with purpose, yet her shoulders are rounded forward, her lips are tight, and her attention is elsewhere.

"I am a good listener. Did you at least have a good time away?" Blazer questions. "I know you needed it. The time we spent with Mateo at the monastery...well...I am certainly thankful he recovered."

"Yes! And yes, I did have an enjoyable getaway," Celestial answers with her soft, raspy voice.

The two continue to proceed toward the embassy.

"I just do not understand your silence. You are usually so chipper and share with me," Blazer continues.

Celestial remains silent until they reach their destination. She then turns and stares into the eyes of Blazer. "I am processing something. I am also discerning if I even should tell you."

"You can tell me anything, Celest. We are a team, you should know I keep confidences," Blazer assures.

"Oh, it's not that. This is on a much larger magnitude, Blazer," Celestial reveals. "Let me process it. I know you have always kept what we share between us...but as I said...this is...well...I do not even know what to define it under."

Blazer nods and opens the door for Celestial.

⁓⁂⁓

Theodore walks through the castle. He glances into the office. He can visualize his father taking care of paperwork. Theodore then walks over and peers out a window and envisions his mother playing with his younger sister, yet they are not there, only visions in his head of various family memories.

"Sir, can I bring you something?" the chef asks.

"No. Thank you," replies Theodore.

"Very well." The chef bows and returns to the kitchen.

Theodore decides to ride out to see Antonio.

⁓⁂⁓

Antonio opens the refrigerator and sees the food he quickly set in there when the deputy arrived at his door. Now, he does not even want to eat. Antonio reaches for the milk container and begins to take a swig, but then pauses. He can hear his mother telling him, "Don't you do it, honey. It's not a community mouthpiece on the milk jug." Antonio grins reminiscing. He sets the milk on the counter while he reaches for a glass. He pours himself half of a glass. He places the milk back on the shelf in the refrigerator, then decides to go out to the stables, to make sure all the animals have food and water.

While Antonio is tending to daily chores, he hears the hooves of a rider coming up the drive. Antonio stops what he is doing and walks out from between the stable and the barn.

Theodore dismounts his horse. He leads Champion over and ties him off in reach of the water.

The two best friends stand staring at each other. After what feels like some minutes pass, they both step toward the other and embrace, with intermittent pats on their backs. The young men step away from each other, both wipe their eyes.

"I can say I am honestly at a loss. I always knew one day I would be king, but I never imagined it would be like this. I have studied my parents well, and I know they believe in my ability...I...I just never imagined it would be now...before I am even married. I always pictured Eloise and I living on our own for a while, then moving into the castle...enjoying the lives of my parents and sister." Theodore chuckles a little. "Watching Tabitha grow into a beautiful woman...meeting someone...becoming Uncle Theodore." Theo smiles as he envisions how he thought his life would unfold. "I just can't believe they are gone."

"I feel ya. I have no doubt I can manage this spread and make my parents so proud. I just never thought I would be doing it without them here with me," Antonio discloses. "Oh!" Antonio raises his shoulders slightly with his elbows bent and palms up. "And there is the Krystyleen Mine to manage. Good grief. I almost forgot about that. Yeah...and that too...I will run."

"One thing is for sure, our plates are more than full," Theo acknowledges.

"Yeah, like the size of a banquet...a feast we both knew we would receive...but not at this price...not now," Antonio imparts. "I would rather have my parents than all of what I have!"

"I know. Me too. We were raised knowing what we will inherit, even taught how to manage, and take care of what our families leave to us...." Theodore pauses and surveys the spectacular Mancini Ranch. "Tony, by our hard work we will make it even greater to honor them. What they taught to us...*that* is how we will forever preserve their legacy they have raised us for," Theodore resounds with a renewed energy.

Antonio nods. "I agree. I will be the very best at what my mother and pop taught me. That is how I will honor them!"

"Me too! I will run our kingdom and build on the foundation I inherited from my parents. Eloise and I will make it even better…if that is possible," Theodore communicates.

"Alright. We have a plan." Antonio grins.

Theo smiles, then his lips become straight. "How about we ride out to the site and scan over the area again. We are going to need some closure before moving forward with our plans."

"I agree. We must find them and give them a proper burial," Antonio submits.

"Yes." Theodore agrees, but then he pauses, "Wonder if we do not find their bodies?"

"Well…we will just have to make peace with that…and have a memorial ceremony. We need to speak with the town priest," Antonio weighs in.

Theodore nods his head.

Antonio saddles up his horse and rides off with Theodore.

······◦૪◦······

Antonio and Theodore arrive at the snow wall. They dismount and tie off their horses. Grabbing their shovels, they climb up the bank. To their surprise, they see numerous men from town shoveling. They look around.

Antonio lightly taps the chest of Theodore with the back of his hand, "Come on. There's the sheriff."

Antonio and Theodore tread quite some distance over to where Sheriff Winslow is bent over investigating something. They reach him and stand next to him in amazement.

"Is that a crevasse?" Antonio questions.

Sheriff Welsey stands straight up. "I believe it is. Of course, we just uncovered this little segment. My deputy almost fell in, but this would explain why we have not been able to find evidence of the sleigh or your families."

"I did not even know we had a crevasse here," Theodore admits.

"My theory is, Don was driving the team to escape the avalanche, which explains why they are so far away from the normal trail. Out this far…well, most people do not travel to, so this crevasse could have been here a very long time. Anyway…my thought is, he was doing his best to protect everyone when the force of the avalanche caught up with them and swept them over and down. As the snow melts, we will be able to determine more. I'm sorry. It does not look like we will be able to retrieve their bodies," Wesley outlines. "Would you like me to join you to meet with Father?"

Theodore and Antonio again stare at each other, then solemnly shake their heads.

"No, you have done enough. Thank you so much," Theodore acknowledges.

"Yes. Thank you, Sheriff. We are astounded at the turn out again today for the help with searching," Antonio adds.

"You are both welcome. What you see before you, is a kingdom of people that love your families," Wesley affirms.

Theodore and Antonio both nod.

"Our kingdom will need you to take over as king as soon as you can," Wesley confides. "I will assist you, as I did your parents, in every way that I possibly can."

"I appreciate that," Theo expresses. "My wedding is not until Septembria. We will have no queen until then."

"Understandable. I will perform the coronation ceremony with Father next week if that is alright with you," outlines the sheriff.

Theodore nods. "Yes. Whatever we need to do to keep our kingdom safe and running smoothly."

"I assume you will take over your family ranch and mine?" Wesley addresses Antonio.

Antonio humbly nods. "Yes, Sir. I will do everything in my power to keep it as my parents, and grandparents, and great-grandparents would want me to."

"Very good. You both are exceptional young men, who, I have no doubt, will grow into great leaders. I want you to know…I recognize that, even though you are both experiencing great internal pain," Wesley commends.

Both young men nod and appreciate his encouraging words.

Chapter 57

WHERE ARE WE?

Sarita opens her eyes and notices Tabitha and Marcella next to her curled up, sleeping. Sarita sits up. She surveys her surroundings and spots Don and Franklin lying on the ground. She sees their team of horses, but no sleigh. She studies the mountains, but realizes these peaks are not *their* mountains. *Where are we?* She wonders. She positions herself onto her hands and knees. She quietly inches herself away from Marcella and Tabitha to stand. Sarita quietly tiptoes over to Don and kneels to gently wake him.

Don opens his eyes.

"Shhh." Sarita places her finger over her mouth, then stands and reaches for his hand. He too, stands.

They distance themselves from the others.

"What do you remember?" Sarita asks her husband.

"Going over the edge of the crevasse...I do not recall anything after that," Don recounts.

"Nor do I. Look around. I first thought, we survived the fall...and maybe, we are deep in our planet...but that just does not make sense. The sun is shining. Look around us. Mountains, valleys…fields….” Sarita attempts to grasp their situation. “There is our team of horses.” Sarita points.

Don also surveys the landscape and tries to remember. He walks in different directions. “I remember I was leading the team…trying to outrun the avalanche…get us to safety. Then I remember the blast of snow propelling us over the edge.”

“Yes! That is what I remember as well,” Sarita concurs.

“Where are we?” Don wonders.

“I do not know.” Sarita conveys puzzlement.

Just then, they hear Tabitha screaming, which wakes up Franklin and Marcella. They grab ahold of their daughter. “You are alright, sweetie,” Marcella assures. She then glances inquisitively at Sarita, Don, and Franklin.

“I do not recognize this scenery,” Franklin admits.

“Nor do we,” Don adds.

Marcella rubs her hands over the back and arms of Tabitha to comfort her daughter.

“So, we are not dead?” Tabitha questions.

“No, honey. We are all here,” Marcella comforts.

Tabitha scans the unfamiliar surroundings as well. “But where is here?”

The adults exchange eye contact with one another while questions whirl through their thoughts.

Chapter 58

LETTERS FROM HOME

S teve picks up mail from the store for him and David. He glances through and sees a letter from David's mother. Steve grins and nods. Steve arrives back at their house. "Hey buddy, you got a letter from your mom."

David stands up and walks over to Steve. Steve hands him the letter. David returns to a chair to sit and read it. "Hey, do you want me to read it aloud?"

"Well sure. I always like to hear what's going on back home." Steve grins.

David opens the letter from his mother and reads,

> *Dear David and Steve, I hope this letter finds you both well…and David, my darling, I hope you are enjoying married life to sweet Leah. Please let me know about Steve and Veronica…if, and when, they plan to marry.*

Steve smiles and nods. "Sounds just like her."
David agrees, "Yeah." Then he picks up where he left off,

> *Theodore proposed to Eloise. They will be married next Septembria. Tragedy struck our kingdom, King*

Franklin, Queen Marcella, Princess Tabitha, along with Don and Sarita Mancini met their fates in a deep crevasse while on their annual sleigh ride. There was an avalanche. Their bodies have not been recovered.

David and Steve exchange an expression of shock.

"That's terrible!" David exclaims.

"It is! Theodore and Antonio must be in shock and feeling devastated." Steve concurs.

"Wow. Well, there is more," David communicates.

"Yes, please, keep reading." Steve motions with his hand.

Oh, and I am sure Francie Montanelli has written and told you about Aspen...

Steve's posture changes as does David's. David abruptly stands and paces. He now clutches the letter with both hands, while he continues to read aloud,

But if she has not, here goes...Mid Septembria, Francie was out on a ride to one of her favorite places up past the C-Fork along the Chianne River. Apparently, some men...four to be exact, came upon her and Aspen. Aspen was shot. Poor Francie...well...the family kept it hush hush, but we saw the sheriff leading a posse. They returned with three dead bodies. Francie had blood splatters on her and bruises over her face and body. Word has it that the fourth man shot the other men, who were assaulting Francie, but no one knows for sure. Francie will not speak of it to anyone, and she is, of course, deeply distraught, over the death of Aspen. I knew you two would want to know. I imagine Francie has already written you and told you everything though. Alright, I will close for now. God be with you. With much love, your mother.

A surge of shock rushes through Steve and David. They stare at each other.

David continues to pace around the room. "Man, I hope she will recover quickly. I wish we would have been there to prevent it. I can't believe she hasn't written us and told us."

"Well, it did take her awhile to respond to the letter I wrote her wishing her a happy birthday and that you were getting married," Steve reminds.

"Isn't that just great." David flings his arms in the air then back down. "We abandoned her. No more celebrating her life or our lives together, then I get married." David pauses and stops. His thoughts run deep. "If I know Francie, she wrote us the letter that day when she went to the river…and just did not send it right away."

"I agree with that. She probably has been busy," Steve voices. "She knows we did not abandon her. She knows we wanted to be in the Guard of the Kingdoms."

"I know. I know. I should have stayed and married her. You know I wanted to…." David expresses.

"And all three of us knew the chances were high neither of us would marry her," Steve expresses. "We are all friends. Plus, we were kids."

David tips his head slightly to the left. "Well, I am pretty sure if there was only one of us…she would have. I should have stayed and asked her to marry me."

"None of that matters. What matters is, we all knew our lives would change, and we all know we carry each other in our memories and hearts, if you will," Steve assures. "And look…she was only fifteen, well, almost sixteen when we left home. Our first year in the guard prohibits us being married or even dating."

"Yeah, yeah. Maybe so…but doesn't it piss you off that someone did this?" David contends.

"Well yes! It makes me mad as hell! But there is nothing we could do. She knows this. I know Francie, and there is no way she blames us for anything…for not being there…for us moving on...you getting married or me having a girlfriend. She is not one to be mad or angry or hold grudges," Steve articulates. "She is very happy for us. Trust me."

David grins. "Yeah...that is one of many reasons why I think she is just the best."

"She is...but we have our own women now who are pretty great as well! And you are head over heels for Leah," Steve reminds.

"I am...but I have like a deep...like a spiritual connection...with Francie...it's unexplainable...so, I won't even bother," David asseverates.

Steve nods. "I hear ya."

"This is just crap!" David shakes his head.

"It is. Sounds like justice was done though," Steve consoles.

"Justice was done where?" Leah chimes in while glancing through the rest of the mail that is on the counter.

Both David and Steve are caught off guard, not realizing she arrived home.

"A friend's horse was shot back home...and we think justice was done," Steve answers.

Leah nods. "I see." She glances through the ads. "That's odd."

"What?" David asks.

"Oh, there is a letter that seems like it got glued to the ad. Let me peel it off." Leah gingerly pries the letter from the ad. "Oh, here Steve. It is addressed to Steve and David."

Steve takes the letter and glances at David.

"Well, open it. Let's hear it," David presses.

"Alright," Steve complies.

Steve opens the envelope and unfolds the letter. "Oh, it's from Francie."

"Imagine that," Leah smirks.

David's facial expression becomes cross.

Steve reads the letter aloud,

Dear Steve and David,

I have been putting off telling you some heartbreaking news. Aspen died. I had her buried where she died...by the Chianne River past the C-Fork. Well, she was shot by a bad man. It was an unfortunate event. I was there enjoying the morning and writing you the last letter I mailed congratulating you both. I hope you all are having a wonderful winter. God Bless You all, in all you do.

Forever friends~ Francie

PS- I look forward to meeting Leah and Veronica!

Steve folds the letter and places it back in the envelope.

David nor Steve utters a word.

"Who is Aspen?" Leah asks.

David kind of rolls his lips in a frown. "She was a beautiful horse."

"We were with her family when Francie picked her out. Francie named her Aspen," Steve details.

"Why does she still write you guys?" Leah quizzes.

Steve bows out. "Hey, I'll see you tomorrow." He exits through the door to his half of their house.

David walks outside onto their balcony deck.

Leah follows. "I just don't understand why she still writes you, knowing you're married."

"What!" David cannot believe what he is hearing. "She is a forever friend of ours. We will always be friends and keep in touch. Plus, she wrote us to tell us of her horse. As Steve mentioned, we were all together when she picked it out and named her."

"Does she have a boyfriend or a husband?" Leah presses.

"I have no idea. We aren't there. Look...we haven't seen her since we left for the guard which will be two years in like four months. She is like family. Please, there is no reason to ever be jealous of her. I made a vow to God when I married you. I will honor my vow because of who I am. So please, don't be all jealous on me.

Francie also honors her vows, and her friend's vows. Please don't be this way. If we get transferred back to Chamberlain, I want us all to be able to hang out together and enjoy life together," David passionately expresses.

"Wonder if she wants you?" Leah questions.

"What! Francie has never implied that! Look...I met you. I love you. I married you. I am keeping my vows to you, to God...because of who I am, and I highly doubt, knowing who you are, that you will ever leave me...because...well...I just do not see you ever leaving. As for Francie...our friendship goes back to when we were five. We will always have a friendship bond. I do not want to alienate her. I hope Steve and I like her husband, whenever she does marry. I know Francie will like you and Veronica," David carefully accounts. "And I am sure you girls will like Francie. If we ever do get stationed back home, I would want to have her and her family in our lives. Life is too short not to enjoy the people God gave us." David takes a breath. "Did you think that she wrote anything inappropriate?"

Leah frowns. "No, I heard nothing inappropriate."

"If you want me to forsake her...I will, though you have never met her," David offers. "If we get stationed back home, I will just give her the cold shoulder and be distant and not invite her to anything."

"Okay. That would make me feel better." Leah turns and goes back inside.

David places his forearms on the balcony and leans over. His heart is heavy. He does not want to alienate Francie from his life, in case they do live in the same kingdom again, plus, he enjoys exchanging occasional letters to catch up, but he also wants to honor his wife.

Leah steps back onto the deck behind David. "I suppose...I see your point. I would not like to be cut off from my grade school friends either. I apologize for getting so upset and being so jealous."

215

"Come mere." David holds open his arms and looks into the sky while holding his wife next to him. "Ya know, forever is a long time, especially considering we are eighteen. I am a man of my word. I promised Francie we would be friends forever, and I made a vow before God giving my life to you. In my world, there is room for both. I believe we are all connected. I hope you will be at peace with that."

Leah nods, peering up into the eyes of David. "I am. She is fortunate to have you as a friend, but I guess...*I AM MORE* fortunate to have you as my husband. I look forward to meeting her someday."

David sets his eyes back on the stars while he continues to hold Leah next to him. He hopes his words and actions will put Leah's insecure heart at rest. He also feels the sting of regret regarding his first female best friend.

Chapter 59

THE TRAVELERS

The five humans continue to stand. They spread out a little in each direction and scan their surroundings in the beautiful, yet unfamiliar place.

"Look! Over there! There is a cabin." Tabitha spies with her keen, youthful eyesight and points.

Don, Franklin, Marcella, and Sarita all look in the direction Tabitha is pointing and views what appears to be, a ranch.

"I say we go," Franklin states.

"I agree," Don concurs.

The men pick up the reins of the horses. They lead their families in a hike over to the ranch.

"Hello," Don calls out. He does not want to startle the owner.

"Wonder if they aren't human," Tabitha hesitantly quizzes.

Marcella wraps her arm around her daughter. "You have quite an imagination."

You can hear the soles of their boots as they step up onto the wooden deck and knock. There is no answer.

They survey their surroundings and see cattle grazing. They see some stables. Don knocks again, then he reaches for the door handle and turns it. He pushes the door open.

"Are you sure you should do this?" Sarita whispers.

"Hello...." Don enters the large cabin.

The others follow and scope out the place.

"Oh, look! There is a note on the table." Sarita notices while she walks around. She reaches for the note on the table, picks it up, and reads the note aloud,

> *"Dear Travelers, Welcome to the Northern Ranch. There are clothes for you, along with bedding. There are cattle you can eat, along with a well-stocked pantry. There should be everything you need to enjoy your stay here. There is a small town about four miles to the south. Make yourselves at home."*

Don steps over to his wife and takes the note into his hands and studies it himself. "Whoever wrote this did not sign their name. I guess...maybe... *we* are the travelers," He concludes as he makes eye contact with his wife and friends.

Marcella places her hands on the top of Tabitha's shoulders while standing behind her.

Tabitha begins to cry. "Are we dead?"

Marcella hugs her daughter. "No, honey."

"But how do you know?" Tabitha sobs.

Sarita takes Tabitha's hand in hers. "Do you feel my hand?" Tabitha nods.

"Well, honey...I do not believe any of us are dead. I cannot tell you where we are. Can you think of it as a mystery? I know you like reading about mysteries," Sarita softly voices.

Tabitha wipes her eyes and catches her breath. "Yeah. Maybe we can search for clues to solve the mystery."

"I like that idea." Sarita lovingly smiles while she pats and releases Tabitha's hand.

"I think you are right...*WE*...*are* the Travelers," Tabitha agrees as she peers at Don.

The adults exchange eye contact again.

"I think we are," Sarita caringly expresses. "The Travelers...I like that."

Chapter 60

ANOTHER GETAWAY

"Celestial, wait up. Where are you going?" Blazer questions.

Celestial finally stops and turns to look at her assigned partner. "Look, I cannot involve you."

"Well, I am already involved because I am part of your team...and maybe you could benefit from another point of view," Blazer maintains.

Celestial shakes her head repeatedly. "Oh, Blazer. I don't know what I was thinking...well...I do know...but this is huge. Okay...you can come with me...."

Blazer nods.

The two of them touch their emblem. A sphere encloses around them, which carries them off the planet of Chiaras.

Chapter 61

THE MEMORIAL SERVICE

Theodore and Antonio sit beside each other in the front row of the church. People from all over the kingdom arrive, plus some people from neighboring territories. The pews quickly fill up. The lead singer gestures for all to stand to sing the opening song. Father walks down the aisle. An eloquent, inspiring homily is given by Father Romano.

After the last song is sung, Theodore and Antonio follow Father Romano down the aisle, then the rest of the congregation file out.

Francie has tears in her eyes. Her heart is heavy as she thinks of Aspen and grieves what she has lost. She now feels empathy for Theodore and Antonio, though she has yet to meet Antonio. She whispers to her mother, "I have to leave."

"Alright, sweetie." Sophia understands the service has ripped the band-aid off her daughter's grieving heart.

Everyone relocates over at the commons area to gather and eat the food people bring in. Theodore and Antonio begin to feel overwhelmed. Members of the community, kingdom, and neighboring realms express their love for their families. Theo and

Antonio are immersed with a strong sense of love from those rendering homage. Though they feel overwhelmed, they have a deep sense of gratitude. The young men are at peace with their decision, to be the best they can be, to honor their families.

Chapter 62

CURIOSITY

"You have my full attention. Why did we come to this planet to watch a funeral service?" Blazer quizzes.

Celestial shakes her head and touches her emblem. A sphere encompasses them and they leave the planet to return home.

"Still no words? No explanation?" Blazer asks.

"I have no words." Celestial sighs with heaviness on her heart.

Chapter 63

ANTONIO MAKES A TRIP INTO TOWN

Antonio looks in his refrigerator and freezer, not to mention, supplies he has taken inventory on. He jots down a decent-sized list. He deems it necessary to go into town to the Montanelli Mercantile.

He grabs his saddle, but then realizes, and says aloud, "I can't ride my horse. I must team up the wagon. UGH." He gets the team ready and heads out for town.

He pulls up in front of the mercantile, climbs down, ties off his horses, and steps inside with his list in hand.

Sophia lights up. "Oh, Antonio!" She walks from around the counter and greets him with a hug. "My condolences. The funeral service was just lovely. Sarita was one of my best friends, as your dad was also. We just never saw much of Don or you, but loved it when we did see your parents! Are you holding up alright? If you need anything…please…please come to us. Your mother and pop would want that."

Antonio nods. "Thank you. I do have quite a list."

"Well, let me see it please," Sophia directs.

Antonio gladly gives her the list.

Sophia begins to go over it with him.

Antonio can hear her words, but he is mesmerized by the beautiful young lady walking from the storeroom in his direction. Sophia notices her words are not being heard and glances up at Antonio and tracks where his eyes are focused. She sees her daughter walking down the aisle carrying some merchandise to stock on the shelves. She smiles and quietly stands with the list in her hand watching a developing connection between Francie and Antonio. Leonardo steps out from the back and begins to walk to the front, when he too spies what is happening and abruptly stops.

Francie reaches Antonio and Sophia.

"Are these supplies for me?" Antonio does not even know what Francie is carrying. He is swept away with his connection to her eyes and her natural beauty. The way she carries herself, so tall and confident, casts him into a daze.

"No silly, these are for the store. Hi! My name is Francie Mancini." Francie giggles and is blushing while she reaches her hand to shake his.

"What? You have the same last name as me? I am Antonio Mancini," Antonio's expression is that of a pleasant surprise.

"What? Oh, my! I meant to say...I am Francie Montanelli." Francie is so embarrassed, red decorates her face. Hearing his deep voice seems to also affect her. "I must have been thinking that...you are you...I mean...that you are...a Mancini, and I just slipped...oh, my...."

"You're fine. It's alright. Kind of has a nice ring to it." Antonio grins and laughs. "I...uh...oh...this must be your mother. I gave her my list." Antonio shakes his head, smiles at Sophia and points with one hand to Sophia. Kind of in a smooth move, with one arm bent in the same direction that his other hand is pointing.

Sophia tries to contain a huge smile that is forming from within her dancing heart, while watching the two interact. Sophia sweetly conveys, "It is quite alright, Antonio. You have a lot on your mind."

Antonio nods and swallows. "I do. Do you want to help me get the items?" he stares at Francie.

Francie giggles. "Sure." Not taking her eyes from the eyes of Antonio, she outstretches her hand to her mother's hand. Sophia hands her the list.

Francie and Antonio stroll the aisles with a cart. They set items from the list in the basket.

"You know, we played together when we were toddlers…at least, that is what I have been told." Francie smiles and behaves kind of silly.

"Yeah, my mother has told me that before." Antonio grins, then runs his hand through his thick head of brunette hair. "I don't think I have ever seen anyone with long curls like yours." Now, Antonio is behaving giddy.

The two continue to walk the aisles and fill the cart that Antonio is pushing around.

"I'm gonna be nineteen next month," Antonio reveals.

"Cool. I will be eighteen in Juliah," Francie shares.

They reach their way back to the counter to check out.

"I will help you load all this," Francie states.

"No, I cannot allow that," Antonio expresses.

"I have arms. I help our other customers," Francie maintains.

"Well, if you want, but I don't like the idea," Antonio remains adamant.

Francie and Antonio exit the store when he glances back, "Thank you!" He hollers to Sophia and Leonardo, "I appreciate it!"

Leonardo and Sophia stand side by side with their arms around each other. They enjoy watching their daughter interact with Antonio.

"You know, I like that young man," Leonardo admits.

"Whoa, did I just hear you correctly?" Sophia laughs a bit and questions with her lovely soft voice.

"You heard me correctly. I like him. I have always heard good things about him, and being in his presence just leaves me with good vibes," Leonardo simply states.

Sophia laughs. "My husband is going off vibes now? I never thought I would hear you use *that* word!" Sophia is grinning from ear to ear.

"Well, yes. I like him. Plus, the son of our friends, Don and Sarita, has got to be top notch. I hope our daughter likes him," Leo shares.

Sophia casts her eyes back to Francie and Antonio and observes them load his wagon. "Oh, I am pretty sure our daughter likes him as he likes her."

"You have a vibe, don't you?" Leo laughs.

Sophia laughs again, "What is with the vibe? That is just funny coming from you." Sophia pauses. "Yes…they have good energy between them."

"See…I told you she would get over Steve and David," Leo boasts.

Sophia does a head roll. "They will forever be her friends."

"Yes, but this young man may be her forever…." Leo contends.

Sophia warmly smiles at her husband, then they return to witnessing the connection between Francie and Antonio.

"So, you wanna hang out sometime?" Antonio asks.

"Sure. What do you have in mind?" Francie asks.

"How about fly fishing? We can invite Sully and Katherine, and Theodore and Eloise, if that is alright with you," Antonio suggests.

"Wow! I love that idea!" Francie's eyes sparkle and her smile shines.

"Alright. I will get ahold of everyone. Let's plan on the second Saturday of next month," Antonio leads.

"I like that idea! Pick me up at six in the morning?" Francie asks.

"Yes!" Antonio smiles. He tips his hat. "It is sure nice to meet you."

"Likewise." Francie smiles so big, it seems all her teeth are showing.

Antonio climbs onto the wagon and smiles. "I'll be seeing you."

Francie is swaying back and forth. "Yes, you will."

Antonio rides away with a noticeable grin. He thinks to himself, *I like that girl!*

Francie watches him lead his wagon team away and then, out of the blue, the memory of when Steve and David left for the guard, dawns on her. David said those same words to her years earlier. Her reply to him was *only in your dreams, you're leaving.* She pushes the memory out of her mind and refocuses on that handsome, kind Mancini cowboy.

Chapter 64

THE CORONATION

People from the kingdom gather on the castle grounds to witness Prince Theodore being crowned their king.

Eloise stands quietly with the castle staff and relatives. Their best friends and families sit in the front rows. Royals from neighboring kingdoms are also in attendance.

Sheriff Wesley Winslow and Father Romano officiate the coronation. Father Romano leads all those gathered in prayer, followed by the Sheriff officiating the ceremony. Prince Theodore declares his vows as he transitions from Prince to King. Sheriff Winslow takes the crown of Chamberlain Kingdom and places it on the head of Theodore. "Theodore Franklin Chamberlain, you are now the king of this great kingdom. We trust you will continue to lead with the same vision as your father led."

"I will. In fact, to honor my parents, I plan to build on what they have done, to even new heights of prosperity, and to ensure a peaceful kingdom. I thank you all for being here. In Septembria, you will have your queen. Eloise and I will be married Septembria fifteenth. The entire kingdom is invited along with our friends from neighboring kingdoms."

The crowd cheers. King Theodore is led off the stage by Father Romano and Sheriff Winslow, followed by the royal guards.

Chapter 65

SATURDAY ROLLS AROUND

During the next three weeks, Antonio makes several appearances at the Montanelli Mercantile. He enjoys his visits with Francie and offers to help Sophia and Leonardo, if they need anything.

Saturday finally arrives. Antonio is outside of the Montanelli home at 5:50 in the morning.

Leonardo glances out. "Francie, your fishing date is here."

Francie spits out the toothpaste from her mouth and wipes her face. She runs out to the living room, just as Antonio knocks at their door.

Leonardo opens the door. "Hello, Antonio."

Antonio nods. "Hello, Sir."

Francie grabs some muffins from the kitchen her mother baked. "Bye Mom! Bye Dad!" Francie states.

"Is this your gear?" Antonio asks.

"Yes." Francie smiles.

Antonio reaches to pick up her gear, then opens the door for Francie. "Goodbye, Mr. and Mrs. Montanelli." Antonio nods.

"Oh, please…call us by our first names," Leonardo insists.

Antonio again nods, then gently releases the door. Francie and Antonio stroll side by side out to the wagon.

"I didn't know if you knew how to ride a horse, so I just brought the wagon," Antonio mentions, while he sets her pack in the wagon bed alongside his poles.

Francie graciously smiles, not revealing she knows how to ride.

He then assists her onto the wagon.

"You know, I am able to climb up the wagon by myself," Francie voices.

"I have no doubt, but any self-respecting gentleman will always assist a lady," Antonio declares, while he smiles at Francie.

The two leave the area and meet up with Theodore and Eloise. Next, they meet up with Katherine and Sully Carlisle.

"Alright, let's go." Antonio leads.

"Where are we going?" Francie asks.

"Mancini Lake," Antonio answers.

"Oh…I like that idea!" Francie smiles. She is full of energy.

After traveling up the scenic mountain trail, the view of the lake appears before them. Sun glistens across the mountain lake. Snow still decorates the tops of the surrounding peaks. The rich color of the pine trees paints the landscape, which sport game trails, and hike trails, that stagger throughout the terrain. The crisp air, paired with the scent of the trees, and mountain lake water, engages all their senses, as the spectacular scene spreads before them.

"Oh, Antonio! It is breathtaking!" exclaims Francie.

Antonio smiles and dismounts the wagon. He then reaches for Francie. "Come on. Let me lift you down."

Francie scoots over to the edge and turns herself as though she is climbing out, but allows Antonio to put his hands on her waist and help her down. They stand there just gazing into the eyes of each other. They both smile.

"Well, Cowboy…I like this idea of yours! Fishing out here with our friends," Francie comments.

"I am glad." Antonio confidently grabs her pack, his pack, his poles, and basket. He walks tall as the two stroll to the edge of the lake. Katherine, Sully, Eloise, and Theodore all carry their stuff down. There is a picnic table Antonio's father built. They set their gear on top.

"This is a great idea!" Sully breathes in the mountain air.

"I LOVE the fact you two finally have met!" giggles Katherine.

"Oh! I know!" exclaims Eloise.

Francie turns all kinds of red with a huge smile lighting up her face.

Antonio directs. "Alright…let's spread out. You girls can fish if you want or sit anywhere to watch. Whatever you ladies would like to do."

"Well, I just want to watch for now," Eloise remarks.

"Yeah…that sounds fabulous." Katherine giggles.

Francie smiles and winks at Antonio. "Go get 'em."

Antonio smiles with self-assurance. He and his best friends wade into the lake. Out of the blue, he hears the words of his pop enter his thoughts saying, *I hope you meet a woman as tender as your mother…and as fierce.* Antonio grins from the memory, then casts his line.

Francie brings a large blanket. She lays it out for the three of them to sit on.

"I love this! Finally…girl time…with our guys!" Eloise shares.

"I know. Me too!" Katherine agrees. "My parents are watching Ben for us today. It is so nice to have a date together."

"Is Antonio your guy?" questions Eloise.

Katherine and Eloise can't help themselves. They eagerly await a response from Francie.

Francie grins with a smile she cannot wipe off her face. "I like the fact Antonio is so confident. He is a gentleman…and most of all, I do not have to explain myself to him...which reminds me of David and Steve. They understood me. I never had to explain myself. I think that is what is so striking about Antonio...he seems to get me. Which is key...so I do not have to spend my lifetime explaining myself to him."

"Are you thinking...lifetime?" Eloise delights.

Katherine claps.

"I don't know, guys, this is our first official date." Francie giggles. "He has been coming to the store a lot to see me, and it creates an environment for my parents to get to know him as well. He tells me family is very important to him."

"Well, I can tell you...Antonio is a gem," Eloise adamantly states.

"He is. I agree. He and Sully are thick. I have gotten to know him very well. I like him, Francie," Katherine confirms.

Francie smiles again as the three girls sit and watch the guys cast their lines.

"You know...fly fishing...it looks like art," Francie comments.

Katherine giggles. "It does."

Francie begins thinking aloud and sings,

> *"Fly fishin'...it's what I want to do. Fly fishin'...I think it'd be my groove...casting my line out...in the mountain river...beneath the big blue sky...under the morning sun...."*

"Oh, my gosh! That is great!" Eloise expresses.

"Did you just make that up?" Katherine asks.

"Yep...it just came to me...." Francie continues,

> *"Taking my picnic blanket to the slab by the river... my friends and I sit quietly as they wade out and cast their lines...*
> *they are...fly fishin'...that's what I wanna do... fly fishin'...I think it'd be my groove...*

casting my line out…in the mountain river…beneath
the big blue sky
…under the morning sun.
Each one casts their line out-it sure looks like art-
we raise our drinks-exchange a clink-with a toast to
another catch.
Let's go fly fishin'…it's what I wanna do…
fly fishin'…I think it'd be my groove…
casting my line out…in the mountain river…beneath
the big blue sky…
under the morning sun…."

Francie finishes singing.

"That is fabulous!" Katherine asserts. "I LOVE THAT!!" Katherine claps.

"Oh, my! I love it, too! The guys will love it! I had no idea you were so talented, sweetie," Eloise discloses. "I mean…I know you are creative…I had NO idea of this gift! Bravo!"

"Thank you. Yeah…I will get an idea…and then…bam…a song will just come to me," Francie shares.

"Have you written others?" Katherine asks.

"I have. One about a dream I had." Francie reminisces. "My mother loved it."

"Oh, sing it for us," Eloise pleads.

Francie smiles. "Not that one…not today…."

"Alright, honey. But just wow! You have a gift!" Eloise expresses.

"You do!" Katherine concurs.

Francie shrugs her shoulders and expresses humbleness, "I guess…."

"Own it. God gave us all gifts. Clearly that is one of yours," Eloise asserts.

Francie smiles. "Okay. Thank you."

"Thank you for sharing!" Eloise and Katherine say the same words at the same time.

The three young ladies giggle while they watch the guys fish.

After a while, the three young men return to camp with their catch in their baskets. They clean the fish. The girls start the fire and get out a cast iron skillet.

Antonio winks at Francie while she works with Elosie and Katherine. Francie's smile is pasted on her face.

Sully and Katherine exchange eye contact and then glance at Antonio and Francie. Theo and Eloise also catch a glimpse of the couple. The friends not only witness, but feel the energy between Antonio and Francie. They are loving it.

After they eat, everyone takes part in clean-up and packing up.

"Man, always a great time coming here!" Sully pats Antonio on his back.

"Yep. Best time always." Theodore smiles.

The girls stand arm in arm.

"If we had music, we could dance," Theodore mentions.

"Oh! We do have music! Francie...sing it for them...please!" begs Eloise.

"What?" Antonio grins.

"Oh, yes, dear Francie...sing it for everyone. We will join in. I remember the words," Katherine persuades.

"Please, Francie. It sounds like quite a song," King Theodore encourages.

Francie takes in a big breath to calm her jitters. Then she giggles. "Alright...here it goes...wait! Just so you know...I do not have the best singing voice. Okay, here goes,

> *Taking my picnic blanket to the slab by the river...*
> *my friends and I sit quietly as they wade out and cast*
> *their lines...*
> *they are...fly fishin'...that's what I wanna do...*
> *fly fishin'...I think it'd be my groove...*
> *casting my line out...in the mountain river...beneath*
> *the big blue sky...*

under the morning sun.
Each one casts their line out-it sure looks like art-
we raise our drinks-exchange a clink-with a toast to
another catch...
Let's go fly fishin'...
it's what I wanna do...
fly fishin'...I think it'd be my groove...
casting my line out...in the mountain river...beneath
the big blue sky...
under the morning sun...."

Eloise and Katherine both sing some harmony. Francie is about to finish when the others continue to sing,

"Let's go fly fishin'...it's what I wanna do...fly fishin'...I think it'd be my groove...casting my line out...in the mountain river...beneath the big blue sky...under the morning sun...."

The friends laugh and clap.

"That is great!" Sully exclaims. "Did you just make that up?"

Francie nods. "I did."

"It's just wonderful!" Katherine claps again.

"Wow...if Eloise and I ever need a song written, we will be coming to you!" Theodore proclaims.

Francie, again, feels humble. A huge smile decorates her face.

Antonio steps close to Francie and gazes into her eyes. "You amaze me."

Antonio pauses and looks at each of his friends standing in a circle. "I want you all to know...I hope to make Francie...Francesca...my wife someday."

Katherine claps, and declares, "I'm loving it!"

Francie's eyes widen. She almost cannot swallow. "Is this...is this a public proposal?"

236

Antonio takes her petite hand in his, "No. This is a public announcement in front of our friends of my intentions. I, of course, will ask your father and mother for your hand in marriage…and then, I will come before you." Antonio lifts the hand of Francie that he has been holding, to his lips, and kisses the top of her hand. He then weaves his fingers between her fingers and lowers their hands.

Theodore and Eloise stand side by side, with arms around each other. Sully and Katherine also stand next to each other, arm in arm. The friends are all beaming. They can feel a kindred energy between Antonio and Francie.

After everyone packs up, the friends exchange hugs goodbye.

"I love you, Francie!" Eloise whispers. "I love you, Katherine."

"I love you both so much!" Katherine squeezes her best friends.

"I love you guys so much. My sisters and best friends!" Francie expresses.

Sully, Theo, and Antonio, all pat each other.

"This was a great day!" Sully attests.

"It was indeed!" Theodore agrees.

"I have the best friends anyone could have," Antonio confides.

Sully helps Katherine into their wagon. Theodore lifts Eloise into their wagon. Antonio asks Francie, "May I help you into the wagon?"

"Now you're asking?" Francie grins.

"I am," Antonio responds.

"You may," Francie answers.

Antonio hesitantly and gently reaches to place his hands on her waist, but then his confidence takes over and he lifts her up a bit off the ground to help her into the wagon. "You're right. With your long legs, you don't need my help, but I will always give it."

"I like that," Francie comments.

The ride back to town is in silence, but not an awkward silence. They reach Francie's house. Both remain in the wagon. Antonio and Francie have their eyes locked on each other.

"It's a good thing we have the same friends," Antonio breaks the silence.

"It is," Francie agrees and giggles.

"I sure liked your song. That was very cool," Antonio comments.

"I'm glad you enjoyed it," replies Francie.

After more silence, Francie makes a move, to leave.

"I better go," Francie decides.

"Alright." Antonio pauses. "Francie?"

"Yes?" Francie stays in her spot on the wagon.

"Look, when I first saw you in the store, I was captivated. I felt like God had gifted me. I felt your energy...I sensed you were like me. I can be around you and I don't have to talk non-stop or explain myself...and this may be our first official date...but I have been coming to see you almost daily to get to know you and your parents. For me...since I met you...I don't want to wait for my life to get started with you. I hope that when I do ask you to marry me...that is, if your parents bless me with their permission...well...life is short...and I do not want to short ourselves any of the days we have left," Antonio heartfully discloses his feelings.

"I like the fact I do not have to explain myself to you either. I like the respect you show me. I like that our paths finally came together," Francie exchanges.

Antonio climbs out of the wagon. He reaches up to help Francie out. She grabs ahold of his shoulders and he gently lowers her to the ground. The two just gaze into the eyes of each other. Antonio reaches one arm slightly to the side of her and into the bed of the wagon and grabs her backpack, then he offers her his other arm with his elbow bent. She takes it and they stroll up to the front porch.

He sets her backpack on the porch. "Well, goodnight...Francesca."

"My name is Francie," Francie states.

"I know. Do you mind if I call you Francesca?" Antonio asks.

"No...but why?" Francie questions.

"Because to me, you are a beautiful young woman. Everyone should recognize that and call you Francesca. My guess is you have earned that name. Plus, it is your legal name. To me...you are Francesca...and I hope everyone in town, including your parents will call you that."

"What do you mean I have earned that name?" Francie wonders.

"I mean, I can feel your energy. I can't explain it. I do not know how you grew up or your life events that formed you...but I sense that you are a very deep person. I admire that. I connect with that. That is what I mean by...you earned it. Maybe that was not the right way to describe what I meant...." Antonio gets quiet.

Francesca evaluates his words. "I hear you. I understand. Francesca, it is."

Antonio nods. "Well, alright then."

"Alright." Francesca nods and picks up her backpack.

"I'll see you another day," Antonio states.

"You will. Be safe on your way home," Francesca voices.

Antonio nods. "Thank you for the great day. It just seemed so...."

"So...natural?" Francesca finishes his sentence.

"Yes. I sure do like you," Antonio admits.

"I like you too, Cowboy," Francesca expresses a different kind of smile. She turns and walks in her house.

Chapter 66

TRAVELING IN THE GALAXY

"Where are we going now? This looks like we are heading to the planet Acheeas," Blazer communicates.

"We are." Celestial frowns. "You want to know what is going on. I am going to show you. I just can't talk about it."

They reach the planet Acheeas and Celestial navigates them to a beautiful mountainous valley region, similar to that on Soleil.

"We are not going to stop since we have to get back to Chiaras...." informs Celestial. "I just want to show you."

"Show me what?" Blazer presses.

"You'll see. Keep your eyes on the look-out," Celestial advices.

Celestial spies what she wants Blazer to see. She then turns, navigates toward the planet Chiaras, and leaves the atmosphere.

"Hey, wait. Is that it?" Blazer questions.

"Yep. Now we need to get back," Celestial maintains.

Blazer shakes his head.

They return to Chiaras in silence. Blazer expresses a look of puzzlement toward Celestial. They go about their duties and meetings with the other Chiawaukas.

Chapter 67

MOVING FORWARD

A few weeks pass since their fishing expedition. Francesca keeps wondering if Antonio has spoken to her parents. He still frequently comes to the store.

"Hello Sophia and Leonardo! Do you mind if I take Francesca out to my property for a while?" Antonio asks upon stepping into the store on one of his visits.

"That is quite alright, if Francie…I mean Francesca, wants to go." Leo smiles.

"I like what you said to her about her name. She explained it to us and we totally agree," Sophia voices.

Antonio grins. "Well…your daughter is a very special lady. In fact, if you give me your blessing…I will ask her to be my wife."

Sophia drops what she is doing and rushes over to hug Antonio.

Leonardo also steps close to Antonio and reaches to shake his hand. "Boy, I always knew I liked you. You have my blessing." Leo's lips form the biggest smile.

Sophia squeezes Antonio with a hug. "You have my blessing as well."

"You know…she can be quite spirited…and when she gets an idea…she may not even tell you…she may just do it," Leonardo informs.

"I kind of get that impression," Antonio releases a nervous laugh. "My Pop told me he hopes I meet someone as tender as my mother, and as fierce," Antonio recalls.

"Oh, yes…Sarita. We loved her and your pop so much! Yes…you are getting the same if our daughter says yes," Sophia contends.

"I'd say." Leonardo winks and then pats Antonio's arm.

Just then Francesca walks into the store.

"Hey there…I just got here. I was wondering if you would want to come out to the property today? Your parents said they do not mind," Antonio outlines.

Francesca lights up. "Sure. Sounds fun."

"You two have fun. Be safe." Sophia waves.

"See you back here…later." Leonardo also waves.

Antonio reaches to take Francesca's backpack from her and carry it himself.

Antonio helps Francesca into the wagon and they leave for his ranch.

"So, are you going to be in their wedding?" Francesca asks.

"Theodore and Eloise? Yes. Me and Sully," Antonio answers.

"Me too…with Katherine," Francesca comments.

They arrive at the Mancini Ranch. Most of the ride was in silence.

"Sorry, I don't talk much sometimes," Francesca reveals.

"Oh, I don't mind. I don't either. I figure your head is in thought somewhere," Antonio supposes while he steps off the wagon. He turns to lift Francesca down.

"Yes. That's it," Francesca concurs as she places her hands on his shoulders while he puts his hands on her waist and gently assists her.

242

"Me too. Sometimes I am just quiet, thinking of things," Antonio shares.

"Your parents...?" Francesca asks.

"Yep. I think of them often. They would simply love you. It saddens me they are not here to meet you. I mean...they know you...it's just...they didn't get to enjoy you and I visiting with them...out here...having game night or going on a trail ride," Antonio details.

"Game night?" Francesca lights up.

"Yep. That's what we do out here." Antonio smiles. "Come on. I want to show you the place. I guess...it is my place now...."

Francesca walks next to Antonio. They are greeted by fur babies. Francesca bends down and caresses each dog.

"Oh, they are sure loving on you." Antonio grins.

"They are very beautiful herding dogs," Francesca compliments.

"Let's go in. Antonio takes her in the side door. They step into the entry area. There is a washroom and pantry off to the left side. The kitchen spreads before them.

"Wow...this is great!" Francie comments.

"I'll give you a tour. Here is the dining room, on the other side at the front of the house is the formal living room. Over here is the family room," Antonio details the guided tour.

"Oh! Look at the magnificent stone fireplace! It should go all the way up," Francie suggests.

"Yeah, Mother always wanted to add an upstairs...but we didn't, yet."

Francesca lights up. "Well...I agree! I would add the upstairs to almost duplicate the main level.

"Funny, Mother said the exact same thing." Antonio nods while he leads her from the large family room to the hall, that sports three bedrooms, and two baths; one main bath and one master bath.

"Antonio...this is absolutely fabulous!" exclaims Francesca.

"Yeah. Like I said, Mother wanted an upstairs, so we could have many guests...or family...." Antonio shares.

"I can see her vision. I agree." Francie feels at home.

Antonio smiles.

"I would put a double glass door on the wall of the master bedroom that opens to the deck...and if you build an upstairs, I would have a wood railing...you know...a banister...so the top floor can see over onto the main level...and set the fireplace stone on up to second floor ceiling, out the roof," Francesca describes.

Antonio grins.

Francesca notices. "Did you not want me to speak my ideas?"

"No. That is you being you. You certainly do remind me of my mother," Antonio admits.

"I am honored to remind you of your mother! Wait...is that a bad thing or a good thing?" Francesca wonders.

"Oh...I think this is providential. I mean...finally meeting you." Antonio gazes into the beautiful blue eyes of Francesca. "You like to hike...right?"

"I do!" exclaims Francesca.

"Let's go. I am going to take you to a beautiful place. You strike me as a nature girl, even though, I originally thought you were a city girl," Antonio jests.

"I am an outdoor girl. I prefer a mountain river and trails any day to sidewalks and cobblestone," Francesca states.

Antonio takes Francesca by the hand and leads her out of the family room onto the back deck and down the wooden stairs. You can hear the sound the boots make on contact with each step to a trail that leads to the Chianne River. Antonio stops. "Can you hear it?"

Francesca listens, then gazes up into Antonio's eyes. "I can. It's the river!"

Antonio is around six-foot-one inch to six-foot-two inches tall. Francesca is five-foot-nine inches tall.

Antonio smiles. "Yep."

The two continue navigating the trail, hearing the rocks and dirt underfoot. They also hear the frogs singing their summer song as they trek along the trail, until the clearing opens before them.

Francesca runs to the water's edge. "I love this, Tony!"

Antonio smiles. "I knew you would." He walks to stand next to her.

Francesca leans into him.... "Thank you. I love this place!"

"You are quite welcome." Antonio confidently stands next to whom he deems as the most beautiful young lady he has ever seen.

Francesca sits on the rocks and takes her boots and socks off. She rolls up her jeans." I have to get in! This shallow pool right here next to the shore is so inviting...and these rocks are calling me!"

"I didn't bring a towel," Antonio mentions.

Francesca giggles. "I did...I try to always carry one! Ya never know when I will be at the water!"

Antonio grins.

After some time, they head back up to the house. Antonio pulls out some food and makes sandwiches for the two of them.

After they eat, Antonio escorts Francesca to the stables and barn as well.

"You have quite a beautiful place here," Francesca kindly comments.

"It's getting late. I better take you home." Antonio notices.

Francesca replies, "Yeah." Thinking to herself, *she is home*. Then a grin appears on Francesca's face.

"I like seeing you smile," Antonio remarks.

"Thanks." Francesca behaves giddy.

"Oh, shoot! I forgot something by the river! Do you mind if we go back before I take you home?" Antonio behaves innocently.

"Sure...it will be cool since the full moon is upon us," Francesca voices with

exuberance.

Antonio has Krystyleen in case they need it, but the full moon, indeed, lights their way.

Francesca notices some lights as they get closer. She whispers, "Antonio, is someone on your property?" Francesca begins to feel sick inside. Memories of the intruders back in Septembria begin to haunt her. She grabs ahold of his arm.

"It is all right, Francesca. I will keep you safe," Antonio comforts and places his hand atop of her arm that is holding his arm.

The fears Francesca is experiencing diminishes when they reach the campsite and she sees Krystyleen lights spell out 'Say Yes.' She turns to face Antonio when she realizes he is kneeling before her with a ring in his hand.

"Will you marry me...so we can spend our lifetime dating...getting to know each other...grow up together?" Antonio's deep voice is like music in sync with the sounds of the night.

Francesca has never been so touched by the gesture of someone. Well, David and Steve, not to mention all the other people, but this is on a new scale, an adult level. Francesca feels so honored and safe. She gently touches the side of Antonio's face with the palm of her hand. "Yes, Antonio Mancini...I say yes!"

Katherine, Eloise, Theodore, and Sully come out from the trees shouting, "Congratulations!"

Francesca takes a few steps to the side. Antonio stands and quickly places the ring back into his pocket.

"Oh, my! YOU guys lit the Krystyleen!" Francesca solves the mystery.

Sully is chipper and relays, "We did. Antonio had this day planned and we wanted to be a part of it...so we told him we would help."

"Well, what a surprise! I was kind of scared," Francesca discloses.

Katherine takes Francesca into her arms. "I am so sorry, honey," Katherine whispers, "I don't think Antonio knows what happened."

Francesca nods into Katherine's shoulder and whispers back, "It is alright. He is very forthright about protecting me."

"Well…yes, honey. He will protect you and love you…forever." Katherine places her forehead on the forehead of Francesca.

Eloise then hugs Francesca.

"Do you have an idea when you would like to get married?" Theodore asks.

Antonio and Francesca in unison answer, "Octobria."

Both feel surprised when they hear the other blurt out the same month, though they have never even discussed it. Their eyes dance as they study each other in astonishment.

Everyone begins to laugh.

"For real? You want us married in Octobria?" Francesca questions Antonio.

"Absolutely. I love autumn!" Antonio reveals.

"It's full of romance!" again, both Francesca and Antonio declare that statement in unison.

They smile at each other and giggle. Their friends circle around them. Francesca feels a deep peace she has not experienced since the dream she had months ago of her forever friend.

She feels her spirit open. She smiles and gazes up into Antonio's soft eyes.

He opens his arms and she walks into his embrace. "Oh." Antonio reaches into his pocket and pulls out the engagement ring. "May I?"

Francesca peers into his eyes and nods.

He places the ring on her finger, then tenderly kisses her forehead while giving her a loving embrace.

Chapter 68

ANOTHER CHIAWAUKAS MEETING

Chiawaukas gather in the conference room of the embassy. All stand when High Priest Akshai and High Priestess Ammerie enter the room. The high priests proceed to the head of the table where two chairs are positioned for them.

"Everyone, please sit. Thank you for attending." High Priest Akshai begins. "Today we will have another discussion on protocol, out in the field, in regards to humans."

"We want you all to remember, always…always…protect in a manner that appears natural, so they will remain unsuspecting," High Priestess Ammerie reminds.

"We are continuing to monitor the planet Soleil where the Cryptolores have been in captivity for many, many moons. There will be a day in the future when we will send a team to locate the two families who possess the Chords of Chiawaukas. While the team is there…we will also have them locate the coordinates where the Cryptolores are imprisoned," High Priest Akshai outlines.

"We will evaluate our plan of action depending on our findings," High Priestess Ammerie notes.

"What about human life?" questions Piper.

Celestial is beginning to feel like she is being targeted, although she is confident that no other Chiawaukas know what she has done.

"In what sense do you mean, Piper?" High Priest Akshai asks.

"I mean...if a human dies in our presence...do we save them? Do we intervene and prevent their death? Do we gift them with golden droplets and breathe life back into them?" Piper lists various questions. "I am just wondering."

Celestial is on the edge of her seat clasping the chair edge with her hands, trying to remain chill.

Blazer notices his teammate's anxious behavior.

"It has been our position to never interfere. Now...can there be exceptions? Perhaps. We will determine that at the time of a human death," High Priestess Ammerie explains.

"Wonder if we are best friends with the human...but not with another human...do we choose one over the other if they both were to die?" A younger Chiawauka in the assembly voices.

"I do not believe I know you. What is your name?" High Priest Akshai quizzes.

The Chiawauka stands and declares while turning many colors, "My name is Pixel. This is the first assembly I have been to."

"Pixel, while it is nice to meet you, you entered the wrong conference room in the wrong building. This briefing is for seasoned Chiawaukas in the embassy. I believe you are to attend the assembly for instructions at the academy...since you are entering the academy. They will also teach you how to control your changing of colors...to be less conspicuous," High Priestess Ammerie addresses.

"Well, gosh. I am sorry." Pixel grabs her notebook and then accidently scoots her chair too hard and it slides into Victor, who is a very seasoned, no-nonsense Chiawauka. "Oh, gosh, buddy. I am so sorry." Pixel stares at Victor and begins to wipe his knees, like that will help. "Assembly...embassy...Assembly at the academy...briefing at the embassy...boy did I hear wrong!" Pixel chatters aloud.

The Chiawaukas are finding this interaction very amusing though they refrain from expressions of such.

"Would you please stop. Enough already," Victor states.

Pixel tightens her lips and her eyes widen like she knows she has done it now. She begins bowing, repeatedly bowing, while she walks backwards to the door. "I apologize. I will get to where I am supposed to be. I am so sorry." She continues to step backwards until she smacks into the wall. She then turns her head and sees she missed the door. "Oops, my bad." She then makes a rectangle expression with her teeth showing, then she high tails it out the room.

Victor shakes his head and murmurs, "Unbelievable."

Viana, who is sitting next to Victor has her mouth tightened as well, and blinks her eyes.

"Pixel asked a good question. Do we save one life over another in case one happens to be close to us. The fact is...both humans are someone's best friend somewhere. All lives matter. All lives are worthy. Our policy is to not interfere with the death of humans...but I am sure there will be instances that may have questionable surroundings for us to evaluate," High Priest Akshai adheres.

When Celestial hears the words the high priest speaks, Celestial begins to relax, thinking to herself, *I think what I did was worthy...it would be under the umbrella of merit. I could not just let them die! Not after hearing the little one's scream...and their prayers for their families....*

Chapter 69

GOING INTO SUMMER

"**I** think I am going to gift Francesca a horse for her eighteenth birthday." Antonio considers while he and Sully are working on repairs to Sully and Katherine's barn.

"You know…it is about time she learns to ride a horse," Antonio assumes.

Katherine walks into the barn carrying Ben. "Wow! You two have made a lot of progress!"

Sully winks at his wife and son.

"Katherine, perfect timing. I was just telling Sully I think I am going to give Francesca a horse for her birthday. She will soon be living on the ranch and I figure she needs to know how to ride," Antonio discloses.

Sully glances at Katherine.

"Do you not think that is a good idea?" Antonio notices the apprehension in their expressions.

"We think she will love whatever you want to gift her," Sully expresses.

"Okay…you had me worried for a minute," Antonio responds.

"Oh, Antonio...Francesca will love whatever you gift her." Katherine smiles. "Oh, and she loves to dance."

Antonio smiles. "Good to know. Thanks for the tip."

Katherine sweetly smiles while she kisses Ben on his cheek. "Alright, I'm gonna take this little guy back inside and lay him down for a nap."

Sully nods and smiles at Katherine. "We should be done here soon."

"Nice to see you and your little one," Antonio comments.

"Yes. Nice to see you as well." Katherine nods and walks out the barn.

......⚬❦⚬......

"Alright...so you want your matron of honor in a deep purple?" Sophia asks her daughter.

"Yes, and I want my bridesmaid in a beautiful orange that will complement the purple...celebrating colors of autumn," Francesca details.

Sophia smiles. "Do you want the guys in brown? That is a fall color."

"Mother! Gross! That is my LEAST favorite color!" Francesca laughs. She knows full well her mother is playing around.

Sophia smiles and conveys, "Well, alright. I was just making sure." Sophia giggles.

"No brown. Never." Francesca laughs at the suggestion of her mother.

"So, what are you thinking for the guys?" Sophia questions.

"I don't know...maybe a beautiful blue suit...like the night sky...with maybe purple gingham shirts...I don't know...we will just have to look through fabric and catalogs to see...." Francesca decides.

"That is a good idea." Sophia nods and smiles. "Have you written to David and Steve to let them know?"

"Oh...no...I hadn't given it much thought." Francesca begins thinking.

Sophia raises an eyebrow. "Really?"

"Well sure. I have been busy with you and planning our wedding. I guess I can write Steve and let them know," Francesca supposes.

"You don't have to invite them," Sophia mentions.

"I know. I doubt they could come anyway, with their schedule," Francesca replies. "Life goes on. The loss I felt last year...well...I guess like anything...it diminishes."

Sophia slightly nods.

"Are you going to tell Antonio what happened to you and Aspen?" Sophia asks.

"Hadn't planned on it. It happened before we met," Francesca rationalizes.

"Yes, but sweetie...everything in our lives...the good and the bad...form us into who we are each day. Don't you think Antoino would want to know? He seems like a very passionate, loyal, devoted man...not to mention, head over heels for you," Sophia earnestly makes her case.

Francesca frowns. "I don't know."

"Well, I think when the time is right, you two should share memories about your lives...not to mention, your dreams," Sophia wisely encourages. "I'm sure you want to know things about him...."

"I do! Everything! What makes him...him." Francesca grins thinking of Antonio.

"I am sure he feels that much enthusiasm wanting to hear about your life," Sophia hints.

Francesca nods and takes to heart the wise words her mother speaks.

Chapter 70

BIRTHDAY SUPRISES IN JULIAH

Antonio has been working on the upstairs addition to the ranch home. Sully helps when he can.

"Looks like we are going to be done before the end of the month." Sully steps back, admiring their work.

"Yep. I want to surprise Francesca with the progress we have made," Antonio comments.

"Oh, she is going to love it," Sully confirms.

"I figure if we finish up here by the end of the month, we can go over to your place and make the additions Katherine wants." Antonio glances over at Sully.

"Yep. She will like that," Sully contends, still admiring their work.

⸻⸻

Leonardo and Sophia greet their daughter when she enters the kitchen. "Happy birthday, sweetheart." Leonardo hugs his daughter.

"I made waffles for you." Sophia sweetly smiles at her daughter.

Francesca hugs Sophia. "Aw, thank you, Mama."

"Now, tonight, we have all the preparations for a big dinner for you and your friends," Sophia indicates.

"We know you guys will probably leave and go somewhere, but we want to begin by having your birthday dinner here," Leonardo conveys.

"I think that is perfect! I have the best parents ever!" Francesca smiles as she pulls out a chair to sit and eat breakfast.

······· co ·······

Theodore leans back and stretches like he is at home. "This is one of the best meals I have had! Thank you, Sophia...and Leonardo. In fact, if we ever need a chef at the castle, I am going to call upon you." Theodore winks at Sophia while the others exchange smiles.

"Oh, yes!" Katherine giggles.

"Let me bring in the cake." Sophia scoots her chair back to stand when Leonardo pats her shoulder and interrupts her movement.

"I'll get it." Leonardo lights the candles, picks up the cake, and carries the cake to the table.

Everyone joins in to sing, "Happy Birthday to you, Happy Birthday to you, Happy Birthday, Dear Francesca...Happy Birthday to You!"

Francesca blushes and smiles from ear to ear. "God has truly blessed me with a magnificent family and wonderful friends who love me." She takes a deep breath and blows out her candles.

"Well done." Leonardo smiles and winks at his daughter.

After they enjoy the delicious cake and ice cream, they all pitch in to clear the table. Every person then finds a place to sit in the living room.

Francesca opens a gift from Katherine and Sully. She tries not to rip the paper and preserve the entire wrap.

"Francesca, just rip it." Sully laughs while he directs.

Francesca smiles and with that, rips the very well taped package open. She finds a decorative pink box with a mountain scene on it. She opens the box and there is an exquisite bracelet with a cross, a heart, and mountains on it. Francesca pulls it to her chest. "Wow! This is so beautiful. Thank you!" Francesca slides the bracelet onto her wrist. "It is perfect. I LOVE it! Thank you so much!"

Then Francesca opens a perfect shade of purple sack from Eloise and Theodore. She gasps. "Oh, my! How beautiful and thoughtful!" She runs her hands over the cover of a very soft purple leather journal. It has an engraving of a moon, stars, mountains, and a river with a few pine trees, including her name, Francesca, inscribed on the leather cover just below the river. "Wow! Two perfect gifts! Thank you!"

"Well, we know you are creative and figured you would use it to jot down your inspirations," Eloise sweetly communicates.

"You all are such blessings to me!" Francesca exclaims. "Thank you...each of you!"

"I have a gift for you, but it is out at the ranch...our ranch. I will show you this evening or tomorrow." Antonio smiles.

Francesca lovingly smiles at Antonio. "You...are my gift."

Antonio blushes a bit and proudly smiles.

Leonardo sets his hand on top of Sophia's hand, then she places her other hand on top of Leonardo's hand.

"Well, we better go." Sully stands. "We need to put Ben to bed. Thank you for an incredible evening!"

Katherine stands and picks up Ben out of a highchair. "Yes, thank you. Just another wonderful family dinner!" Katherine and Sully make the rounds of hugging everyone. Then Katherine kisses the forehead of Francesca. "I love you, sweetie."

"I love you, too," Francesca expresses.

Sully gives Francesca a hug, as well, then opens the door for his wife and son.

Theodore addresses Leonardo and Eloise, "If you two do not mind, we would like to stay a bit and visit with you about our wedding in Septembria."

"That is completely alright." Sophia smiles.

"Do you guys mind if we leave to go out to the ranch?" Francesca asks.

"Of course not." Eloise smiles and hugs Francesca. "Go and see what your man is giving you." Eloise smiles.

Francesca radiates, then gives her parents and Theo a hug goodbye. "Thank you, again, for the beautiful journal. So thoughtful!"

Theo and Eloise both nod.

"It is our pleasure." Eloise winks.

Antonio shakes the hands of Theodore and Leonardo. He hugs Sophia and Eloise. "Well, alright...I guess it is my turn to show this one what my gift is to her." Antonio winks and places his hand on the lower back of Francesca. He then reaches for the door with his other hand and opens it.

"See you guys later! Love you all!" Francesca enthusiastically broadcasts.

"You two be safe and have fun!" Leonardo articulates.

"Love you both!" Sophia voices.

Antonio assists Francesca onto the wagon. Francesca sits close to him for the duration to the ranch.

......⚬⚭⚬......

"How do you think Francesca will handle being given a horse?" Sully asks his wife.

"Hard to say. It is a subject she does not even want to discuss with Eloise nor I. She did not even want to tell David and Steve what happened...and she *loves* them as her forever best friends. So, I don't know. She really seems attracted to Antonio in every way," Katherine outlines. "So, maybe it will go well, and actually force her to communicate the heartbreak she experienced."

Sully nods. "Yeah…sometimes communicating is healing."

"I'd say most of the time." Katherine sweetly smiles and gazes upon her husband with love.

······◦∫◦······

Antonio lifts Francesca down from the wagon. "Well, I have two surprises for you. One inside and one out here. Your choice…which one first?"

"Let's go inside first. I need to use the restroom," Francesca voices.

Antonio takes her hand and they walk up to the ranch home. Francesca pets the fur babies that follow them. Antonio opens the door and motions for her to enter.

Francesca steps in, then begins to walk to the main bathroom when she sees the magnificent remodel. "Oh, my! This is breathtaking! Everything just as I have envisioned for our home!" She looks up and sees the high ceilings, now sporting a second floor with a balcony that overlooks the family room on the main level. She dashes to the stairs and is captivated by the stunning, handcrafted wooden stairs that have unique patterns on each step, and is finished with a beautiful stain. She sprints up the stairs and scans each room. She is in awe, as she admires the architectural details. It is, indeed, an exact floorplan of the main level bedrooms and baths.

She turns around and gazes over the railing while she stands beside the stone fireplace that goes through the ceiling of the second floor. "Wow! Your craftsmanship is remarkable! I would have helped you!"

Antonio looks up, "I know. You will be able to decorate and choose if you want carpet. There will be a lifetime of projects for you to work at my side. I wanted to do this to surprise you. Sully helped me when he could."

Francesca runs down the stairs and leaps into the arms of Antonio. She kisses his cheek. "This is everything I imagined and more!" Francesca hugs Antonio tightly.

He wraps his strong arms and large hands around her and they just hold each other.

"Mm." Antonio breathes. "I look forward to having you here with me every day."

They both melt into the arms of the other and their guards begin to lower.

"Wow! Best hug ever! THAT could heal a broken heart," Francesca whispers and lowers herself from her tiptoes.

"I have something else…outside. I would like to show you before it becomes dark," Antonio conveys peering into her blue eyes.

Francesca warmly smiles. "Yes…I am going to use the restroom really quick." Francesca comes out from the bathroom. "Alright, Cowboy…." and takes his hand.

Antonio leads her out to the stables. "If you will wait here, I will be right out."

Francesca nods. "Yes…I will wait."

Antonio enters the stables. He walks over to a filly and bridles her. He leads the filly out.

"Francesca…." Antonio gently voices.

Francesca turns from admiring the breathtaking scenery of the ranch and casts her eyes on a most impressive Wintucket filly. Francesca steps closer and caresses the filly's head. "Antonio…what is this?"

"Well…I figured since you are soon going to be Mrs. Antonio Mancini…that you need a horse of your own to love and learn how to ride. Now, I have not named her, but I have been working with her for months. You will grow with her. She should not be ridden for another year, but this way…you two can get to know each other…and by a year from now, she will be old enough to ride," Antonio details.

Francesca's eyes light up. She is in love with the beautiful Wintucket filly. "What shall I name you? Moondance? How about Autumn? Like when we will be married...."

Antonio's heart is full of joy as he observes Francesca bond so quickly with the filly.

"Well...maybe I will name her Moondance, and save the name Autumn for when we have a little girl." Francesca thinks aloud.

"Wonder if we never have a daughter?" Antonio questions.

"Yeah, you may be right. Who knows...I can't choose," Francesca voices her thoughts. "Yes...I think you are Autumn, aren't you sweetie?" Francesca strokes the head and nose of Autumn. "Autumn...a name fitting for your beautiful auburn, chestnut coat."

"Wait right here," Antonio requests. He returns into the stable. He bridles another horse and leads the mare out.

"Francesca...." Antonio quietly speaks.

Francesca is stroking the nose of Autumn, when she hears Antonio's voice. She moves her head next to Autumn and peers down the side of the horse and sees Antonio bringing another horse.

"Now, this mare is ready to ride. I have broken her, and she will be an excellent horse for you, now," Antonio explains as he leads the mare to Francesca.

Francesca can barely speak, "You are gifting me two horses?"

"Well...yes. One you can ride now and one you can bond with until she is old enough to safely ride," Antonio informs.

"So, hello, Moondance." Francesca shifts her focus from Autumn over to the Wintucket mare.

"How about I saddle her up and give you a lesson?" Antonio suggests.

Francesca grins. "You are such a generous, loving man...I am so thankful for you and for you loving me. Thank you...SO much for these wonderful gifts! These horses…our home…truly…it is *you*, that is my gift."

Antonio places his hands on the waist of his fiancé. Then he tilts his head and gently kisses her lips for the first time. "The pleasure is mine. I am pretty sure I am the one who is blessed and gifted to have you." he smiles.

Antonio leads both horses back into the stables. He returns Autumn to her stall and saddles Moondance. Then he saddles his horse, Shadow, and leads them out.

"I'd like you to meet Shadow. I named him that because when he was a colt…." Antonio laughs a little. "He would follow me everywhere. So, I said, 'boy, you are my shadow'…and that is how his name came to be."

"Ah…that is so sweet." Francesca caresses Shadow. "Nice to meet you, sweetie."

"I know how you came up with Autumn…but how did you come up with Moondance?" Antonio questions.

"Well…I love when the moon brightly shines…and I love to dance…." Francesca discloses. "Plus, her coloring…."

"Very good. I do have one more thing for you," Antonio mentions.

"What's that?" Francesca asks.

Antonio drops the reins of the horses and holds out his arms to Francesca. He wraps her with one arm around her waist. He places one hand in the middle of her back while he takes her other hand in his hand. He peers into her blue eyes as she looks up into his. "I want to dance with you." Antonio leads Francesca in a slow dance to the rhythm of the sounds of the summer evening on the ranch. The two begin to laugh. The connection between them deepens as they slow dance with a couple of twirls Antonio adds. Antonio then pulls Francesca in for another hug. "I hope you have enjoyed a very…happy…birthday."

Francesca gazes up into his eyes. "I have." Her heart melts.

He kisses her again with a little more passion than before and holds her firmly in his arms while he rubs her back.

When their kiss breaks, neither of them can speak. They only gaze into the eyes of each other.

"How about I help you up on Moondance and we go for a little ride?" Antonio asks.

Francesca smiles and turns. She places one foot in the stirrup. Antonio slightly lifts her while she raises herself up and places a leg over the stunning white mare with a few grey speckles.

Antonio then mounts Shadow. "Are you ready for a ride?"

A playful grin casts across the face of Francesca. "I am, Cowboy."

The two guide their horses from the stables and out into the field. "You are quite good at this. You must be a natural," Antonio compliments.

Francesca grins again, then she leans forward and whispers to Moondance, "Let's show him what we've got." Moondance takes off in a gallop.

Antonio is amazed and a little concerned. He wonders if Moondance is misbehaving, or does his fiancé know how to ride? He errors on the side of caution and catches up to them. "Are you alright?" Antonio reaches over to Moondance. Francesca slightly pulls back the reins to slow Moondance down.

"I am." Francesca smiles.

"You had me worried. One more thing that squashes my initial belief that you are a city girl...and look at you...riding with skills like that," Antonio expresses with a grin which brightens his face.

Francesca smiles and is turning a little red. "Yeah...I can ride...and...I may live in town...but I am a country girl at heart."

"I see that. I remember that from fishing." Antonio smiles. "One of these days I will give you a guided tour of our property."

"Your property?" Francesca asks.

"Our property," Antonio clearly states. "You will soon be Mrs. Mancini of the property. Should something happen to me...it will be your property and if we have children...then their

262

property," Antonio details. "You are to feel and believe this with all of your might. Promise me that."

"Okay. I promise," Francesca agrees.

They exchange eye contact and heartfelt smiles.

"Wanna head back and sit on the back deck for a while before you go home?" Antonio suggests.

"I'd like that," Francesca communicates.

The two return to the ranch. They enjoy the mountain scenery that backdrops the ranch. They take care of the horses and put them in their stalls for the night. Then hold hands as they trek to the house.

Francesca leans against the deck rail while Antonio gets them a couple of glasses of water.

When he steps onto the deck from the family room door, he is mesmerized by her beauty.

Francesca turns and reaches for a glass of water. "Thank you."

"I remain at your service. It was nice to see you ride. Maybe one day you can tell me all about where you learned to ride." Antonio wraps a blanket around Francesca.

Surprised at his genuine consistency, her heart remains open, and she softly replies, "Yeah…maybe one of these days. We have our entire life to learn what formed us into who we are today."

"I look forward to it." Antonio places his arm around her.

They enjoy the summer evening and the colors of the sky as the sun begins to set. They relish in the peaceful silence and the sounds of nature. After some time passes, Antonio faces Francesca. "I better take you home. It is getting late. I look forward to the day when this will be your home." He then wraps both his arms around her.

Francesca whispers, "Me too, Cowboy." They sway in the embrace of their arms.

"I love you, Francesca," Antonio professes.

"I love you, too." Francesca admits while her head rests on his chest.

Chapter 71

OFF PLANET

"Celestial. Slow down. Where are you going?" Blazer follows his comrade.

Celestial stops and turns. "Look...I cannot tell you. I can't even speak it."

"Right. I remember you telling me that before. Oh...wait a minute...it just occurred to me...you took me to Soleil to witness a funeral...then flew me to Acheeas to show me humans...Celest...are those...did you...?" Blazer deeply sighs. "I cannot speak it either. I am going with you. Regardless, if I know what happened, I am your assigned partner, and whether I know or do not know...I am bound to the outcome from your choice," Blazer explains.

Celestial and Blazer move with purpose out of sight from town. The two Chiawaukas exchange eye contact. "I never meant for you to be involved." Celestial sighs.

"I know, but as your assigned partner...I am," Blazer maintains.

Celestial touches her emblem and a sphere envelops them. They leave the planet Chiaras and set course to the planet Acheeas.

"How long do you think we have been here?" Don asks Franklin.

"I don't know, but we should be keeping track. Let's see if we can find a pen and paper somewhere in the cabin," Franklin suggests.

Don nods. "The food supply is great. Plus, feed for our horses and a great pasture. It is just incredible."

"I know," Franklin agrees. "Where do you think we are? I mean really...."

Don stops chopping wood and looks at his friend. "I don't know. I wonder at times if we did die...and we are at some transitional place, or maybe we died and this is our heaven...I don't know. I feel like I am alive. It is honestly the most perplexing situation I have ever encountered," Don admits.

"I agree...I replay that day...feeling confident we were going to outrun the avalanche...then the crevasse appeared...and over the edge we went...now here we are," Franklin details. "It baffles my mind beyond my comprehension at times. I mean, did we time warp somewhere after we went over the edge? I do not know." Franklin gestures with his hands. "When do you want to travel into town? Honestly, I think we will get our answers as to what kingdom we are in."

"You think we are in a different kingdom?" Don questions.

"That is the only plausible explanation I can grasp," Franklin confides.

Don nods.

Franklin walks up to the house while Sarita walks out to see Don. The two exchange a nod in passing.

"I can help you carry the wood," Sarita voices.

"Where do you think we are?" Don asks.

"Well...." Sarita scans their surroundings. "I think we are on a mountain-valley ranch...similar to ours...but different...why do you ask?"

"Franklin seems to think we are in a different kingdom," Don discloses.

Sarita and Don stare at each other.

"Well...I know my thoughts...and honestly...my gut tells me we are not on Soleil," Sarita calmly, but firmly voices.

"That is exactly what my instincts are telling me as well," Don conveys. He takes a few steps. "But *where* are we? And HOW could we be off planet?" Don curls his lips as he contemplates endless possibilities.

"I do not know. I am concerned about Antonio and Theodore. They must think we are dead. I just feel so badly for them," Sarita conveys.

"I agree. I have been sick about that as well. I wonder how they are coping...and what they are thinking...." Don shares.

Sarita steps next to Don and wraps her arms around him. She lays her head into his shoulder. Don wraps his arms around Sarita. The two embrace, exchanging energy and comfort as they search for rational answers.

......⚬⚭⚬......

Celestial and Blazer arrive on the planet Acheeas. They get out of the sphere and step onto the planet surface.

"I left them a note on the dining room table in that cabin over there." Celestial points.

"A note? What did you say?" inquires Blazer.

Celestial thinks of her response before she says a word. "I let them know that they have plenty of food and clothes and a town is about four miles south." She sighs. "I mean what else was I gonna say? Hey...I heard your screams and prayers. I didn't want you to die, so I put you to sleep, and safely relocated you on another planet to live out your life? Is that what I should have said?"

Blazer slightly shakes his head. "There is no good way to handle this situation."

"I know…right? Should we go meet them and explain?" Celestial questions.

"My first thought is to wait and let's think about it, but if they go to the town and speak to people in town…they will soon discover they are on another planet. I would hate for them to find out that way," Blazer expresses. "Plus, no doubt, someone will contact Briele, Reigna of Acheeas…then she will contact our high priests, who most certainly, already know."

Celestial frowns. "Oh, my! I didn't think of all of that. I know I may have saved them from death…but their families and friends think they are dead, and they probably wish they are, since they are no longer with them." Celestial kicks some dirt. "I think my good intentions may have some hefty repercussions."

Blazer frowns. "You may be right. But then again…we will work with the situation. Let's go introduce ourselves before they travel to the town."

"Sure…we will just stroll up there.…" Celestial remarks.

"Would you rather us pop in? Just manifest before their eyes?" Blazer submits.

"No." Celestial shakes her head. "That does not sound good either. We will walk." They begin to head toward the cabin when Celestial panics. "Wait. What height should we be?"

"I don't know." Blazer shrugs. "How about five-foot-six inches? I think that is a non-threatening height," Blazer suggests.

"Alright. I agree. Yeah…we will just waltz right up there…I am turquoise blue…and you…well…you look like you are sky blue." Celestial frets.

"Yeah…so? I like the colors we were created. Celest, it will be alright. Do you know what you're gonna say?" Blazer asks.

"NO! I am freaking out. I don't want them mad…not a good way to introduce supreme guardian beings…." Celestial carries on.

Blazer grins. "Well…it doesn't sound like you really have thought any of this out. I do understand why you stepped in. I think I probably would have as well."

"Really?" Celestial questions with her raspy voice.

"Yeah. Really. If I was on a planet vacationing and heard the scream of a little one and prayers for their families…yeah…I would have intervened as well. Don't worry. All will be well. Remember…if you had not intervened…they **would** be dead…from the life they knew," Blazer contends.

"Well…they **are** gone from the life they knew." Celestial drops her head and shakes it.

"All will be well," Blazer assures.

...... ✁ ......

"Wait." Celestial stops. "I do not want to alarm them. How can this be a good idea?"

"Look…they need to know what has happened and where they are," Blazer maintains.

Celestial curls her lips. "I know. I just do not think we should knock on the door. When they answer and see us…well…they might faint!"

Blazer chuckles a bit. "I think we look great!"

"We do…but…we're blue!" Celestial reiterates.

"Alright. We will hide and summon them out. I will lead," Blazer asserts. "We could make ourselves ten feet tall," Blazer jests.

"Okay…how about no on that height…and…thank you, Blazer. I can't believe I am so scared," Celestial discloses.

"It is alright. It is kind of unnerving. This is new territory for us," Blazer comments.

Celestial nods. They both hide and whisper their course of action.

......⌘......

Blazer casts an illuminating light, like a sunbeam, onto the front porch; then, with a volume that penetrates the walls yet pleasant on the ears, he voices, "Hello, travelers. Please come outside."

"Did you hear that?" Marcella inquisitively glances at the others eating their lunch.

"Hello Travelers. Please come outside," Blazer again throws his voice with an inviting tone.

Franklin and Don immediately stand. Sarita and Marcella also stand.

"No. You girls wait here," Franklin insists.

"I am coming with you," Sarita clearly asserts.

"Let us walk out first. If all is well, we will call for you. Otherwise, you three need to protect each other," explains Don.

"Alright. I see your point." Sarita nods.

Don and Franklin step onto the front deck into a bright illuminating light. They place their hands like a visor above their eyes.

"The light will not harm your eyes," Celestial, still invisible, assures.

Don and Franklin step off the deck and take a few steps into the front yard away from the cabin.

"We would like to introduce ourselves...to all of you. Our appearance may alarm you though," Celestial initiates.

"Who are you?" Don questions while scanning the property, yet sees no one.

"We are Supreme Guardian Beings of the Estellas Galaxy," Blazer states.

Sarita, Marcella, and Tabitha inch their way out of the front door with Tabitha behind her mother and Sarita.

"I am King Franklin Chamberlain of Chamberlain Kingdom on the planet Soleil," Franklin introduces himself.

"Yes. We know who each of you are. May we make ourselves visible to you?" Blazer asks.

Don and Franklin glance at each other and then at their wives who are behind them.

"Yes, please," Franklin requests.

Celestial and Blazer glance at each other.

Celestial whispers to Blazer, "Here we go...."

Blazer and Celestial materialize some distance from the humans.

Tabitha steps out from behind her mother and Sarita. "They're different shades of blue!" Tabitha points as she gleefully exclaims.

The adults stand in awe.

"We can be any form we choose. We have found this form is not so intimidating," Blazer voices. He steps forward and extends his hand to shake the hand of Franklin and Don.

Don and Franklin both step forward to accept the exchange of a firm handshake.

Celestial also takes a few steps forward. "Hello. My name is Celestial. This is my assigned teammate, Blazer. It is very nice to meet all of you."

The females step off the deck and walk to greet Celestial and Blazer.

"Was it you that left us a note?" Sarita questions.

Celestial smiles and nods. "It was. Honestly...well...I am having difficulty even explaining what happened."

"Why don't we sit down in those chairs," Don suggests as he points at some outdoor chairs.

Blazer and Celestial nod. The humans and the Chiawaukas saunter to the outdoor furniture. After they position the chairs in a circle, they sit down.

There is silence. Blazer and Celestial are formulating the words to describe the situation while the humans wait with anticipation.

"Alright. Here it is...." Sarita blurts out. "Are we dead? Is this our heaven?"

Celestial and Blazer both grin hearing Sarita's get-down-to-business attitude.

Celestial turns red.

"Look! She can change colors!" Tabitha eagerly points.

Blazer and Celestial take another moment. Celestial returns to her normal shade of turquoise blue.

Celestial inhales a deep breath. As she exhales, she begins to explain, "We are Chiawaukas, Supreme Guardian Beings of the Estellas Galaxy. I had a few days of leave and decided to spend it on the beautiful planet of Soleil.

The human families are intently listening.

"Anyway...on one of those days...you all were on your annual sleigh ride when I heard the screams of Tabitha and your prayers," Celestial pauses. "Well, I instinctively intervened when I saw the crevasse was about to swallow you and your horses up."

Sarita leans back in her chair and takes ahold of Don's hand. Marcella covers her mouth with one hand in disbelief and places her arm around Tabitha. Franklin sets his hand on top of his wife's thigh, just above her knee.

"I spread a substance over you that appears as a dark-blue confetti which placed you all into a deep sleep. I transported you to this planet...to this ranch," Celestial details.

"So...we are *NOT* dead?" Franklin inquires.

"No," Blazer assures.

"But we would have died if we would have fallen into the crevasse?" Marcella quizzes.

Celestial displays an expression of compassion and nods. "Yes."

"Surely our families and the kingdom believe we are dead...." Don speculates.

Blazer nods. "They do, and you would be, if Celestial had not instinctively stepped in to save you."

"But save us from what? Our death...where we transition from our human bodies into our life everlasting?" Sarita voices. "Our son believes we are dead. Our friends...our families...our people...."

"That is all true, Sarita. I am sorry for the grief this is causing you all. I just could not allow you to plummet to your deaths. Yes...it is true, your people believe you are dead from their world, and...they miss you terribly. I can assure you though...your sons made a pact with each other that they will live their lives in a manner that will honor each of you," Celestial accounts.

A gentle, loving smile decorates the face of Sarita as the grip of Don's hand around hers tightens. Sarita leans her head onto the shoulder of her husband.

"Exactly what planet *ARE* we on?" Franklin inquires.

"You are on the planet, Acheeas," Blazer enlightens.

"I see. Well...why did you not just rescue us and allow us to live on our own planet? Uninjured...setting us somewhere nearby...out of harm's way?" Franklin interrogates. "I just do not understand. Now we must live out our days here? My son thinks we are dead. The people of my kingdom...." Franklin sighs.

Celestial tenderly divulges, "In the split second I heard the cries of Tabitha and the prayers from each of you...you were already plunging over the edge of the crevasse by the force of the avalanche. Had I not intervened...we would not be having this conversation."

The humans absorb the information in silence with occasional glances at one another. Celestial and Blazer are mindful and remain quiet. Some time passes.

"Well...if I may...I am to understand that if you had not been visiting our planet for your few days off...you would not have heard us...and we would have died to the life we know as humans on Soleil and transitioned to our life everlasting. Instead...we are still alive...but dead to the life we knew...but alive still...on this planet to live out our days. Is that a fairly accurate account of what you explained?" Don inquires.

Blazer and Celestial both nod.

"I guess we should all be grateful that we have lives to live...because...regardless...our sons...and our people believe we plummeted to our death into the crevasse," Don rationalizes.

Blazer and Celestial nod again with empathy.

"Exactly what does that mean? How will our lives look? I mean...it is like a death to us as well. We lost everything...everyone we love...except each other. Maybe it would have just been easier to allow us the fate instead of relocate us," Sarita hypothesizes.

"Perhaps," Celestial's raspy voice chimes out. Her elbows are bent and arms out with her palms up. "I know I reacted quickly without thinking of the ramifications. I behaved instinctively and with love. I apologize if it causes you pain. My saving intuition kicked into high gear...and here we are."

"Here we are." The tight lips of Marcella soften.

"This planet will be your home. Tabitha will grow to adulthood. She will have friends...even marry one day," Blazer explains.

"Can we ever return to Soleil?" Franklin questions.

Blazer and Celestial glance at each other.

"It is unsure right now. Maybe...in an unforeseeable distant future we can figure out a plausible explanation of your return," Blazer speculates.

"Are there humans in the nearby town?" Marcella asks.

"Yes." Celestial nods.

"Can you tell us how our sons are doing?" Sarita pleads in her loving voice.

Blazer and Celest both nod.

"I can tell you Theodore and Antonio and the people of your kingdom dug for days searching for all of you. Theodore was crowned King. The wedding for Eloise and Theodore is set for Septembria fifteenth. Antonio met Francesca Montanelli and asked her to marry him. They will be married in Octobria. And, by the way...they fell together like they are one. The light in their eyes when they met...was bright enough to be a star in the sky," Celestial details.

Sarita places her hands on her chest, covering her heart, then hugs Don. "They met. They finally met. I will have the daughter I always wanted." Sarita experiences a peace hearing of their son and upcoming wedding to Francesca. "This brings my heart joy for them...but sadness for us...that we will not be there to watch them grow together and see our grandchildren." Sarita sighs and is torn from feeling joy to experiencing great sorrow.

"So...to be clear...." Franklin summarizes, "We would have fallen to our death resulting in transitioning to our eternal life everlasting...but instead...you swooped us up...." Franklin demonstrates a motion with his arms. "...and relocated us here to live out our days...in which we will then go to our eternal life everlasting. Is that correct?"

Celestial has her lips tightened and nods.

"Yes. That is correct," Blazer confirms.

"Sometimes, I think it would have been less painful if you had let us perish," Franklin asseverates.

Marcella places her hand on the arm of her husband.

"You wanted us to die, Dad?" Tabitha questions with confusion.

"Oh, sweetie." Franklin wraps his arms around his daughter. "Of course not. I am very thankful we are alive! And it appears a new journey awaits us. Are you up for it?"

Tabitha nods. "Yes. Let's make Theodore proud."

A humble smile breaks across the face of Franklin and he again hugs Tabitha. "I was merely addressing that it would have been less painful."

"For who? Because Theodore and Antonio are grieving just as we are. If we died from this life...you are right...it would be less painful...for us. Theo and Antonio would still be grieving...this way we can share with them in their grief and pray for them," Tabitha wisely articulates.

Franklin lovingly gazes upon his daughter, takes her hands in his hands, and looks directly into her eyes. "That is a very astute analogy, Tabitha. You are precisely correct. Your brother and Antonio *are* grieving our loss. We should be praying for them instead of mourning our loss as well."

"Well...we can be sad...but don't forget...they are sad too," Tabitha concludes.

"Yes, honey. You are correct. Thank you." Franklin places one arm around Tabitha and gives her a little squeeze.

Marcella and Sarita both have their hands folded as if in prayer.

"In your note, you mentioned there is a town to the south. Are the people...humans there...like us...that were meant to die, but you intervened and placed them here?" Don questions.

"No. This is the first time we have encountered this situation. The humans you will meet are from the planet Acheeas," Celestial answers.

"So, you are telling us, this is the first time *ever* you have rescued humans from inevitable death?" Don presses.

"It is. We are Supreme Guardian Beings and our mission is not to interfere," Celestial clarifies.

"But you did...this time," Marcella voices.

"I did. I apologize for the pain you are all experiencing. I instinctively protected you. And for now...maybe forever...I cannot return you to Soleil," Celestial admits.

"Thank you for being forthright," Marcella commends.

"Yes. Of course." Celestial nods.

"Thank you both for explaining everything. Can we call on you if we need something?" Franklin asks.

"You may," Blazer replies. "But know…we are stationed on the planet Chiaras…and we may not be able to arrive in a timely manner."

"But you can speak aloud to us. We will hear you," Celestial adds.

"It is a delight to meet you both. Thank you for telling us about our sons. I am so happy our son is going to marry Francesca. I, myself…and I am sure all of us, will deal with the pain we are experiencing which involves missing out on their lives…not hugging them…no more game nights and conversations…the list goes on…." Sarita sighs. "You will keep us updated though, correct?"

"Absolutely." Celestial nods with assurance.

Blazer extends his hand to shake the hands of Franklin and Don. "It is a pleasure to meet all of you, even though not under the most fortunate of circumstances."

"We are fortunate. You saved us!" Tabitha blurts out and reaches to hug Blazer and Celestial.

Celestial and Blazer both smile. "Peace be with you," Celestial and Blazer voice in unison. The Chiawaukas step back and vanish into their sphere. They transport from Acheeas, and return to Chiaras.

"And peace be to you…." Sarita quietly voices though the Chiawaukas have left.

Don wraps his arm around Sarita. They return to the cabin. Tabitha positions herself between her parents and takes ahold of a hand of each parent. The three stroll to the cabin.

Chapter 72

CONFESSING

"Celest?" Blazer questions.

"Yes?" Celestial responds.

"When are you going to tell our high priests?" Blazer wonders.

"Do I have to?" Celestial slightly jests.

"You know, very good and well, they most likely already know. If we know the names of the humans without meeting them...our high priests certainly know everything that goes on....it is just one of our gifts...to know things." Blazer reminds.

Celestial exhales out a little laugh. "I guess there is nothing to tell...they already know...problem solved."

Blazer slightly shakes his head. "You know that approach is not going to fly. They are most likely waiting for you to tell them."

"But see...if they KNOW I was going to do this...and I did...then why do I have to also communicate it to them? Don't you think that would be letting them know too often? Reminding them of something they already know I did?" Celestial attempts to bargain and rationalize.

Blazer again slightly shakes his head. "I know you already know the answer to your theory."

Celestial sighs. "I do. It just seems like an unnecessary step...'cause they know and I know...then I would be speaking about a matter we *all* know."

"There is nothing to fear. They are probably patiently waiting for you to be brave and tell them you stepped in to save some humans. There is nothing to fear of ever going to them and letting them know...even if they already know. It keeps the communication open between us and them. And remember...they never shut us off. It is us that want to keep our little actions private," Blazer surmises.

Celestial lets out a heavy sigh. "You are right. I will tell them." Celestial pauses.

"Boy, I hope Briele will forgive me...placing families on her planet without consulting her." Celestial shakes her head. "And the humans are consumed with the fallout of the 'dying' event...I have my own choices to worry about...."

"Celestial...you have nothing to worry about. You did what you believed necessary...just let our high priests know...align your mind with higher thoughts and fear will flee," Blazer assures.

Celestial nods. "You are right. Thank you."

Blazer feels an inner confidence believing he has helped his teammate.

Chapter 73

ANOTHER LETTER SENT

"That was extremely kind of Antonio to gift you two horses. We like him, honey," Sophia voices to her daughter while they shop for wedding supplies.

"Thanks. I like him too." Francesca slightly laughs. "You know, he reminds me a little of Steve and David. A perfect combination...really...of my forever friends." Francesca grins.

"You know...your dad has expressed the same thought to me as well," Sophia shares.

A large smile decorates the face of Francesca. "I did write Steve and David...to bring them up to date."

"Aw, I am glad you did. I am sure they will appreciate that," Sophia comments. "Did you ever tell them about what happened with you and Aspen?"

Francesca just stares at her mother with a vivid memory lurking through her brain. "No. I only told them Aspen was shot. They don't need to know anything else. They have their own partners to worry about."

Sophia nods. Empathy for her daughter is heightened. "Don't ever think they abandoned you or did not feel you were not worthy of them…the three of you were very close…close friends. You will always be connected."

Francesca nods while she picks up some more items for the wedding. "I know." Francesca displays a burst of energy. "In fact, it was like I had an epiphany! My love for Antonio, well, has not changed how I feel for my forever friends at all! It's kind of like having Katherine and Eloise, I love them both…they are all my forever friends."

Sophia sweetly smiles. "Aw, I am glad. It seems you have processed through all your feelings.

"I did. I guess you and Dad were correct. When they initially left for the Guard, I was missing their absence which shifted into grieving my loss…and I really didn't lose anything! We just transitioned into a different phase of our lives."

"I don't recall sharing that with you, but I am glad you clearly have navigated through your growing pains." Sophia looks with love at her daughter.

"I think these colors will be beautiful!" Sophia affirms while picking up some items.

"Yes! I LOVE these colors together!" Francie exuberantly expresses. "I am sooo thankful I finally met Antonio," Francesca confides. "We just mesh…like I did with my friends."

Sophia smiles and squeezes her daughter with a half hug. "Yes."

······⚬〰⚬······

Steve walks out of the mail store. He notices a letter addressed to him and David. He grins recognizing the handwriting. He places the letter inside a pocket and then meets up with David at their work.

"Hey. I got a letter from Francie today," Steve informs David.

"What did she have to say?" David inquires.

"I don't know. I haven't opened it yet. I was waiting for our lunch break or after work," Steve remarks.

David nods. "Alright. I wonder what she will tell us...probably that she is done being friends."

"What?" Steve can't believe his ears. "Enough. Our lives took the course that it did. That does not mean the three of us cannot remain friends." Steve shakes his head feeling a slight bit of impatience. "We have known her since we were like five...not once has she demonstrated petty behavior."

"Yeah. I know." David's lips curl.

........⚬୨୧⚬........

"So...Dad really thinks Antonio is a good combination of Steve and David?" Francesca asks with eagerness for confirmation.

Sophia sweetly smiles. "Yes, dear. He and I see them both in the character of Antonio. Of course...Antonio is his own person...but he does remind us of both of your friends...and why not? As humans, we gravitate toward people we mesh with."

"Yeah...me too, I agree." Francesca nods. "Oh, look! That is the perfect shade of purple!" Francesca picks up the lace tablecloth and unfolds it a little. "This is perfect to set our wedding cake on! I LOVE this plum color!"

Sophia recognizes her daughter is transitioning from being confident in her choices and at the same time wanting affirmation from her parents. "Oh, honey...that *is* a perfect shade of a rich, autumn purple."

Francesca sets the beautiful lace tablecloth in their cart. "This should be about all. I am so thankful, Mother, that we came on this shopping trip! It is nice to get away," Francesca voices.

"Yes." Sophia nods and smiles.

........⚬୨୧⚬........

"Let's hear it," David directs, as the two walk toward the river that runs through the middle of the town that they are currently stationed in. There is a sidewalk that leads down to the river and some benches placed along the river.

David and Steve sit on a bench.

Steve pulls out the envelope, unfolds it, and opens it. "Do you want to read it aloud…or do you want me to?"

"You go ahead," David answers as he leans forward and places his forearms on his thighs.

Steve smiles. "You know…I like her handwriting."

"Yeah, she has nice penmanship," David acknowledges.

Steve begins to read.

> *"Dear David and Steve,*
> *I hope life is treating you both well…and you are loving your life with your women! Theodore was crowned king several months ago…I can't remember if I wrote you that…he and Eloise will be married in Septembria…And I will be married in Octobria!"*

David sits straight up and glances at Steve.

Steve gives him a look and states, "I told you all would be well…." Steve continues to read the letter,

> *You are never going to guess…Antonio Mancini came into my parents' store…we finally met…and… we just meshed. The funny thing is…he sure seems like a combination of the two of you…which is super cool! Haha. You know I love autumn…well…so does Antonio…that is why we chose Octobria. You two, along with Veronica and Leah are, of course, invited…however…I understand if you cannot attend, due to your positions in the Guards of the Kingdoms. Thank you for your friendship and all the memories you gave me! Thank you for loving me and being my friend! Antonio and I both hope to hang out with you all if you are ever assigned to our kingdom! All the best to you both always- Forever Friends- Love Francesca.*

"Ah, she drew a smiley face on it," Steve adds.

David does not voice any words.

Steve raises an eyebrow. "Are you alright, buddy?"

"I am. Lucky guy." David pauses. "Yeah…I can see me in Antonio." David nods as he gazes across the river.

Steve laughs. "No, I think he is more like me."

"Are you for real or just trying to get under my skin?" David reacts.

Steve laughs. "Hey…we both liked Antonio when we met him and even mentioned he seems to be like us. So…let's be glad for Francie. I told you all would be alright."

"I *am* alright…and, it sounds like Francie is alright…and…you were right, alright?" David laughs a little at his choice of words. He casts his eyes across the river. He swallows. He ponders on his deep, unexplainable connection he feels in the depth of his soul, at times, regarding Francie, and files it under forever friends.

Chapter 74

THE WEDDING OF THEODORE AND ELOISE

Chamberlain Kingdom is busy with guests from neighboring kingdoms along with the people of Chamberlain Kingdom. The last time this many gathered was to mourn the loss of the royal family they loved. Today they gather to celebrate the wedding of the newly crowned King Theodore and his fiancé, Eloise.

The day happens to be a calm day, full of sunshine. Theodore is with Antonio and Sullivan.

"Are you ready?" Sully pats Theodore on his back.

Theodore nods. "I am."

They walk out of the castle down the steps and to the chairs that are set up for the wedding. Theodore stands in front of Father Romano while Antonio and Sullivan go to the other end to escort the matron of honor and bridesmaid.

Sully escorts his wife, Katherine. Antonio escorts Francesca. The music begins. All stand, turn, and their eyes behold the beauty of Eloise as she glides down the aisle in her beautiful white lace dress, sporting a long train.

Father Romano leads the service, then announces, "I present to you, King Theodore and Queen Elosie, Mr. and Mrs. Chamberlain."

Theodore takes the arm of Eloise and folds it into his arm. The two walk down the aisle.

The reception is a royal event, indeed. The food is a variety of cuisines, the music is lively and upbeat, inviting all to dance. Joyful conversations are heard throughout the grounds.

Chapter 75

OCTOBRIA

Sophia gazes upon her beautiful daughter. "That dress is just stunning on you, sweetheart."

Francesca smiles. "It is. I am so glad we found it! I love the fitted bodice and the way the rest just flows and has a little bit of a train, but not too much."

Sophia nods. "Yes. It is feminine, sporty...just simply elegant. The sweetheart neckline with short sleeves...Sweetie...you are truly gorgeous."

Francesca smiles and gives her mother a hug and kiss. "I can't believe I finally met Antonio...and we just meshed...I feel like a princess!"

Sophia lovingly smiles. "Your father and I feel very blessed to have Antonio be our son."

They hear a knock at the door. Sophia opens it. "Oh, my! You girls look stunning!"

Katherine and Eloise enter the dressing room of the church in their lace gowns.

Katherine giggles and smiles. "That dress shows off your figure, Francesca! You look like a princess!"

Francesca smiles and blushes. "Thank you. I was just telling Mother that is how I feel."

Eloise steps to hug Francesca. "It's time." Eloise kisses Francesca on the cheek. "You look sensational, honey."

Katherine and Eloise join Theodore and Sullivan. Father Romano and Antonio are at the front of the church. Once the wedding party proceed down the aisle and take their places, the music begins. People stand and watch as Leonardo escorts his daughter, Francesca, down the aisle. Leo whispers in Francesca's ear, "You are breathtaking, Sweetie."

Francesca glances at her dad and whispers, "Thank you."

When the ceremony is over, Father Romano announces, "I would like to introduce to you, Mr. and Mrs. Antonio Mancini."

All those gathered stand and observe the couple as they walk down the aisle and exit the church while the music is playing.

·······ᦔᢀᦞ·······

"May I have this dance, Mrs. Mancini?" Antonio slightly bows and extends his hand toward Francesca.

Francesca beams. "You may, Mr. Mancini."

The newlyweds step onto the dance floor to celebrate. They sweep across the floor in their first dance at the reception.

Antonio whispers into Francescas's ear with his deep voice, "You are radiant. Mm...you smell so good...I am looking forward to waking up to you every day for the rest of our lives."

Francesca lowers her head slightly and blushes. She whispers as she looks up and gazes into the eyes of Antonio. "I am looking forward to going to sleep in your arms, Cowboy...and all our adventures."

Antonio pulls Francesca close to his body. The couple enjoy the rest of their slow dance.

Francesca then dances with her dad. Antonio dances with Sophia.

The guests enjoy dancing, eating, and mingling.

David's mother and Steve's Uncle Ron and Aunt Cheri are also attending the reception.

Cecilia waits for an opportune time to approach Francesca. "Francie...Francesca...." Cecilia takes Francesca's hands in hers. "Honey...you are a light beaming brightly! I am sorry you are not my daughter-in-law, but I will always love you as my own." Cecilia kisses Francesca on the cheek.

Francesca sweetly smiles and embraces Cecilia. "Thank you for that. I will always consider you family."

"You better." Cecilia laughs. The ladies break their hug. "I can assure you they would be here if they could."

"I know. It is alright," Francesca assures.

The two smile at each other. Ron and Cheri step into the mix.

"Take care, honey. Please stay in contact with me," Cecilia insists as she bows out of the conversation.

"I will...and...thank you," Francesca warmly replies.

"Look at you...all grown up," Cheri comments.

"Francesca, we want you to know how happy we are you were able to grow up with Steve...spend time with us...and one year, the entire summer. We wish you and that young man of yours the very best...although we wish you were in our family." Ron grins and winks.

The three exchange smiles and laughter.

"We won't keep you...we just want to extend our best wishes and love to you...and please...keep in contact with us...you are family," Cheri voices.

Ron reaches out with his hand and places it on the arm of Francesca. "Absolutely. Bring Antonio out to visit sometime. You are always welcome at our home."

Francesca beams with a glow from her heart. "Thank you for that. I appreciate you both and love you so much! I also want to thank you again for the best summer ever!" Francesca exchanges a hug with Cheri and then with Ron.

"Oh, it was our pleasure! You be safe and take care of yourself." Ron nods. He and Cheri dismiss themselves.

"I will! Thank you for attending!" Francesca lovingly expresses.

"We wouldn't miss it!" Ron and Cheri express in unison.

All is as it should be in the Kingdom of Chamberlain.

Chapter 76

I LOVE YOU, MY SON

S arita wipes her eyes. She is misting tears of joy. "Thank you...so much...for allowing us to see our son be married. When you appeared and allowed us all to watch Theodore and Eloise get married, I was hoping you would do the same for us. I cannot convey how much this means to me. I love him so much," Sarita expresses while squeezing the hand of her husband.

"Ah, honey. I am glad we have the powers to show you. If I can do little things to help you...I will." Celestial places her hand on the hand of Sarita and assures with her raspy voice.

Sarita leans her head into the shoulder of Don. She then speaks toward the sky, "I love you, my son."

Don places his arm around his wife and caresses her. Sarita wipes tears from her eyes and drops from her runny nose. Don continues to gently caress his wife.

Marcella feels empathy for her best friend.

Franklin glances at Marcella and then winks at their daughter.

Tabitha steps closer to Sarita and places her hand on the back of Sarita. Sarita sweetly smiles and wraps one of her arms around Tabitha.

"Ah…and Francesca! My beautiful daughter-in-law!" Sarita places her right hand over her heart. "Again…thank you, Chiawaukas."

"Well…again…I am sorry for the grief my interference is causing you…but I could not let you all die when I heard Tabitha scream…and the prayers of your hearts…." Celestial maintains.

"I am speaking for all of us when I say we are grateful we are still alive. No…perhaps not as we had planned…but we are all healthy…and alive…we will build our lives here…and hold onto hope," Franklin assures.

The humans and the Chiawaukas nod and exchange eye contact with each other.

Chapter 77

THE NEXT DAY

"I knew going to sleep in your arms would be as peaceful as I imagined." Francesca smiles.

"And I knew waking up to you would be a sweet gift," Antonio whispers.

"Let's just stay in my new favorite place all day," Francesca suggests.

"I am thinking the same thing." Antonio gently, but firmly squeezes his bride.

Francesca frowns. "Wait…we have to get up and feed and water the animals first…then we can meet back here."

Antonio kisses Francesca. "They'll be alright for a little longer.…"

The newlyweds enjoy all the aspects of marital physical intimacy, again, then they tend to their animals and return to the embrace of their arms.

·······ঔৎ·······

"I just can't believe our Francie is all grown up...and now we call her by her given name...Francesca...it just warms my heart." Sophia shares with Leonardo while they eat breakfast. "I just love him. I never thought I would love anyone as much as I do David and Steve...but I do. I love Antonio...and now he is our son." Sophia continues.

"Yep. Like I said...it would all work out." Leo takes a sip of his coffee.

"You did say that. Oh, I wonder how they will all get along if Steve and David are ever stationed here." Sophia wonders.

"That too, will be alright. All things have a way of working themselves out." Leonardo states. "Those three young men all seem pretty mature, plus they know each other. If I was concerned...it would be regarding their wives accepting Francie as a friend of their husbands."

"That is true. You are calmer than I am...I just want to wave a wand and release magic to make all things perfect...now." Sophia slightly laughs.

"I know you would." Leo grins.

"And I miss Sarita so much. She would be ecstatic knowing Francesca and Antonio finally got together." Sophia sighs.

"Yeah. I miss them all as well. They would be so happy," Leo reminisces.

Sophia nods and kisses Leo's cheek while she reaches to remove his empty plate.

Chapter 78

ALRIGHT ALREADY

Blazer and Celestial are walking toward the Chiawauka headquarters.

"I am very proud of you...that you are finally going to communicate your actions to the High Priests. I will come in with you, if you want."

Celestial slightly shakes her head. "I do not have a clue what I am going to say."

"How about just tell them the truth. That is always the best thing to do...and bravest," Blazer encourages his assigned partner.

"Hey you guys!" Razel crosses paths with Blazer and Celestial.

"Hey yourself." Celestial smiles.

Blazer nods. "Hi Razel."

Razel smiles from ear to ear. Razel then reaches out and places one of her hands on each of Celestial's arms. "I am so proud of you. Even if you are scared...it will all be well."

"Huh? What?" Celestial questions.

Razel tilts her head. "Celestial...really? I knew you took those humans the day it happened. I could feeeeel it!" You can see most of Razel's white teeth because her smile is so large, as she removes her hands from Celestial, then raises them into the sky. "I guarantee you; I would have done the same thing."

Celestial shakes her head. "That settles it. I see no reason to tell the High Priests what I did. If you know...well...they most certainly know...why discuss it further?" Celestial pleads her case.

Razel laughs. "Are you for real? You need to...let's use the word, 'confess'...to our High Priests the actions you chose. They are waiting for communication from you. In this instance, your actions will not separate you from them, but lack of communication does separate us." Razel states her case. And certainly, you know if our thoughts or actions are malice or of ill-intent, those actions *do* separate us, until we seek forgiveness.

"I have told Celestial that. I completely agree." Blazer adds.

"Yes, yes. I am aware of everything you both have conveyed to me. Alright already. We are here. I might as well, walk in and talk about something they already know and probably do not want to hear about it...how I failed...." Celestial shrugs.

"Fail? Oh, honey...you did not fail. You and Blazer were assigned to life details...and...you did instinctively what you have been trained as a Chiawauka. There is no failure. Sure, we all mess up...or go on a solo mission and make difficult, but necessary, decisions for the good of all, as we believe at the time. I assure you no one thinks any less of you. Some might even admire you for your bravery and taking care of business." Razel places her hand on the shoulder of Celestial.

"Really?" Celestial perks up.

"Yes. Of course." Razel assures.

"Okay. I will go and reveal to them what I did." Celestial concedes. Then she mumbles, "Even if they already know."

"Yes. Even if...." Razel moves her hands in a manner that pushes Celestial in the direction of the front tall double-glass doors of the magnificent architectural embassy.

Blazer glances at Razel. "Thanks for the additional support."

"No worries. I am glad to be of service." Razel again, lights up with her incredible smile.

⁓

"Celestial is here to see you." The receptionist at the front desk relays to the high priests through a communication device. "I understand. Yes."

The receptionist then exchanges eye contact with Celestial. "They would like you to go to the conference room."

"Thank you." Celestial walks across the large tile floor to the stairs that sport red carpet and are four times the width of normal stairs. Celestial glances and sees Blazer briskly walking to catch up with her. They ascend the stairs together.

"I will wait outside, just in case you need me," Blazer affirms.

"Thank you. I will be alright. I appreciate your encouragement," Celestial conveys as she pats Blazer on his arm.

Blazer opens one of the large double doors to the conference room for Celestial to enter.

⁓

"Welcome Celestial," High Priestess Ammerie addresses from the end of an extremely long conference table. "Come and join us."

Celestial makes her way to the end of the conference table and sees not only the high priests, but also Briele, Reigna of Acheeas. Her heart sinks as she pulls out a chair on the side across from Briele. The high priests then sit.

"Why have you requested to see us today?" High Priest Akshai asks.

Celestial thinks to herself, *if you already know why...and I know why...how about meeting adjourned?* Then she hears Blazer's voice in her head, *humility, repentance, reconciliation, forgiveness, healing, and strength.*

"Celestial?" High Priestess Ammerie attempts to get her attention. "Celestial."

Celestial hears the lovely hypnotic voice of the high priestess and shakes her head slightly. "Yes. I apologize. You have my full attention."

"You appear as though you are deep in thought," Briele notices.

Celestial casts her eyes to Briele. "Yes...I was." Celestial adjusts her position and sits tall in the chair and makes eye contact with the high priests. "I want to tell you...I have been meaning to...actually...I have been putting it off...wondering why do I need to discuss it...but many months ago, while I was on the planet Soleil for a few days, I witnessed an avalanche. At the same time, I heard screams from a frightened little girl and I could hear the prayers of the mothers for their families. I quickly studied the situation and saw they were about to plummet to their deaths into what appeared as a bottomless crevasse. I placed them into a deep sleep and swept them up. I relocated them to your planet...." the eyes of Celestial shift back to Briele. "I placed them in a similar landscape they were accustomed to on Soleil. I failed to tell you Briele, or ask your permission. I also failed to contact headquarters for approval. Honestly, I behaved instinctively and believed I had no time for communications. I had to act fast. I opted to save their lives and relocate them. Honestly, in hindsight, perhaps I should have set them safely away from the crevasse, but the fall over the edge into the crevasse was already in motion, so I chose to relocate them instead of allowing them to perish. I understand by making the choice I did...well...it has fallout as well. I have spoken with the humans and we have discussed the emotional pain they are experiencing along with their sons that are, alive and well, on Soleil. To be honest, if given the choice again...I think I would have handled it the same way," Celestial outlines. "Maybe I could have just set them out of harm's way…maybe that is what I should have done, then they would still be enjoying their lives on Soleil."

The high priests and Briele remain silent after listening to Celestial detail the events of that day, which led her to her choices.

"Celestial, I do wish you would have contacted me. Since there was no time for discussion, I would have appreciated being informed. Regardless, we welcome them to our planet and I am happy to say they have settled in nicely to the nearby community you placed them," Briele discloses.

Celestial cautiously smiles and humbly nods.

"Celestial, we assigned you and Blazer to preserving life…if ever needed. Not just Chiawaukas, but humans as well. We recognize you reacted instinctively from your soul that is, of course, a supreme guardian being. You behaved accordingly…the only issue we have, is that you set yourself apart from us for so long before you told us. Not informing us, even if we already know…well…it will slowly eat at your spirit and isolate you and separate you from us and the Chiawaukas. We are one. We are here to guide our beloved Chiawaukas. Please remember that," High Priest Akshai addresses.

Celestial again, humbly nods. "Yes. I understand. Thank you."

"Blazer and you will remain on the assignment we entrusted you with…that is preserving life…when necessary…if applicable," High Priestess Ammerie communicates.

There is quiet in the large conference room. Celestial is astounded that she is allowed to remain with Blazer on their assignment.

Celestial musters up her confidence with humility and addresses the high priests and Briele, "Thank you so much. I am truly sorry I put off telling you all of what I had done. Communication to you does make my soul feel at rest. Thank you."

High Priest Akshai along with High Priestess Ammerie stand. "You are welcome. Please do not be afraid. Now go, and continue doing your best," High Priest Akshai instructs.

Celestial bows. "I will. Thank you. And Briele, thank you for welcoming the humans from Soleil."

Briele nods. "I am honored you chose my planet to relocate them. They will do very well."

Celestial nods, pushes her chair in, turns, and walks to exit through one side of the large double doors.

Blazer stands tall and walks beside his teammate to the stairs. Neither of them speak a word until they exit the building. They journey the length of a block before they communicate.

"Okay. How did it go? Do you feel better?" Blazer rattles off inquiries.

Celestial slightly grins. "Yes...I do feel better. My heart sank when I saw Briele across from me."

"Wow! Briele was there?" Blazer is in disbelief.

"Well...it is her planet that I placed the families on," Celest maintains.

Blazer nods. "That is accurate. Makes sense she was at the meeting."

"It is bad enough confessing or telling what I did to the high priests who already knew...but to have Briele there as well...ugh," Celestial shares.

Blazer grins. "They all knew, didn't they?"

Celestial stares at Blazer and then slightly shakes her head and replies, "Yes."

"Did they remove you from the mission they selected us for?" Blazer asks.

"No. They said we will remain on the assignment they entrusted us with and to continue to do my best," Celestial outlines.

"Well, that is great news!" Blazer remarks.

Celestial nods. "Thank you, Blazer for encouraging me to go before them. I do feel much better...like a heaviness is lifted from me."

"I'm glad to hear it!" Blazer expresses.

Chapter 79

A YEAR GONE BY

"I cannot believe it has been a year since the accident." Eloise quietly voices, standing by her husband's side at the burial grounds within the Garden of Remembrance.

Theodore takes the hand of his bride and tucks it around the bend at his elbow. "I know. I made a vow along with Antonio that we will make our parents proud and do our best for the kingdom," Theo pauses. "I know...we do not have to do anything...they are already proud of us...but I will keep my word and be the best king ever."

Eloise looks up and gazes into Theodore's eyes. "I too, will do my very best so your parents will be proud."

Theo smiles at his wife and wraps one arm around her. They quietly stand a few more moments contemplating their loss, the future, and their lives together as they lead the kingdom.

"Good morning, Cowboy." Francesca enters the stables where Antonio is taking care of morning chores. "Are we going to the Garden of Remembrance today?"

Antonio stops what he is doing and exchanges eye contact with Francesca. "Yes. Will you come with me?"

"Oh, sweetie…you do not even need to ask. I will be by your side through every step," Francesca reaffirms.

Antonio nods and slightly smiles. "Another reason I love you." Antonio pauses. "I'll finish up in here and I will be ready."

Francesca lovingly smiles and conveys, "Can I help you with anything?"

"No. Not right now. Thank you, though," Antonio answers.

"Alright…I will be ready to go when you are," Francesca assures and returns to their ranch home.

While she is dressing for the day, she glances at herself in the full-length mirror in their bedroom…she notices some changes in her body.

...... ⚬♨⚬ ......

Antonio stands before his parents' burial site holding the hand of his beloved wife. He then drops her hand and kneels. He places his hands together and silently prays. Francesca kneels beside him and bows in prayer. After some time in quiet prayer and meditation, Antonio stands and offers Francesca his hand, and helps her to stand as well.

"My parents would have loved you!" Antonio hugs Francesca. He slides his hands down her curvy waistline and feels a slight change in her figure.

Francesca peers into his eyes. "Yes…we are going to have a baby."

Antonio gently lifts Francesca off the ground in a big hug and spins in a circle. "Did you hear that Mother and Pop? We are going to have a baby!" He exclaims while he sets Francesca down. "What a beautiful gift for us…a year out from when my parents passed…we find out we are bringing new life into our world." Antonio places his hands on each arm of Francesca. Antonio leans in and kisses Francesca.

Francesca smiles.

"Let's go find out from Doctor Gerard when you are due. We have to pick a name…and get a room ready…." Antonio gleams.

Francesca laughs a little watching Antonio's exuberance.

·······⦿⦿·······

Doctor Gerard returns to the exam room that Francesca and Antonio are in. "Well, I can tell you that your baby is due around the third week of Juliah."

"What?" Antonio is ecstatic. He then looks at Francesca and exclaims, "That is the week of your birthdate as well!"

"It is." Francesca smiles and shares in Antonio's enthusiasm.

"You are healthy and fit, I see no reason for you not to continue with your normal activities. You only have around six months to go." Doctor George Gerard outlines.

"Well, she won't need to be active or do anything," Antonio proudly states.

Francesca hops off the table. "I will."

Antonio and Francesca exchange their first stare-off.

"Look…you two will figure it out. Antonio…Francesca is healthy. She is physically fit…her body is used to being active. Her carrying your bundle of joy does not change that. Francesca should remain active. Of course, within reason, but I see no medical reason currently for her to be inactive and sit around during the pregnancy," Doctor Gerard details.

"Within reason…." Antonio repeats.

Francesca remains in her stance. "Yes. Within reason. And I am reasonable and will decide for myself what I believe I can do safely."

Antonio does not break his stare from his wife. Then for some reason, out of nowhere, he hears his pop's voice, "*I hope you meet a woman as tender as your mother and as fierce."* Just then, Antonio softens and smiles at Francesca. "You are truly who my pop wanted me to marry. I trust your judgement. I hope you will forgive me for wanting to put you on bedrest. It is just my way of protecting my family."

Francesca remains on high alert, but her sense of empathy runs deep and realizes Antonio feels he had no control over losing his parents. His protective mode is most likely heightened, which results in him wanting to control things beyond his control. She, too, softens. Her spirit opens. "It is alright. Thank you for caring so much about our baby and me."

"Well, of course. I would do anything for you and our family." Antonio reaches for her hand.

Francesca gives Antonio that smile he loves to see. "I know you would, Cowboy."

"Alright. I will see you back here in one month." Doctor Gerard assigns after he inhales a deep breath, then exhales. It relieves him to see the young Mancini couple work through their differences.

"Thank you, Doctor." Antonio reaches to shake his hand.

"Thank you, Doctor." Francesca smiles and leans into Antonio.

"You two are quite welcome. Antonio, your parents would be so happy." Doctor Gerard mentions.

Antonio nods with a cordial smile. "They would be, indeed." He places one hand on the door handle to open the door for Francesca and places his other hand gently on her lower back.

Chapter 80

MAKING PLANS

"Hey, let's invite our friends over this weekend and have a dinner and game night," Francesca suggests while she lays on her back in their king-size bed with her knees bent, moving them from side to side.

Antonio steps out of the master bathroom with his night pants on, sporting his muscular physique. "I like that idea." He walks over to the bed and rolls his body next to Francesca's. "Can we announce our news then?"

"I like that idea." Francesca quickly adds, "Oh! We must go tell my parents first!"

Antonio reaches up to tousle a few of her curls. "Of course. Let's go see them tomorrow."

Francesca repositions and rolls into the arms of Antonio meshing her body into his. The two relax in the arms of each other and fall asleep.

······◦❦◦······

"Oh, this is the most exciting news!" Sophia sweetly smiles and hugs Francesca and then reaches for Antonio.

Leo glows with joy. He reaches to hug Antonio and then his daughter.

"Thank you for coming over to tell us."

"Well, of course!" Francesca smiles. "You are the first we have told. We thought we would invite Sully, Katherine, Eloise, and Theo over for game night this weekend."

Sophia brings her hands to her chest. "I think that is a lovely idea."

"You both are welcome to come out. We would love to have you," Antonio states.

Sophia and Leonardo both smile. "We appreciate that. How about we pass on game night this time, but we will come out for Sundei family dinner."

Francesca nods. "You *will* come to game night sometimes, won't you?"

"Yes...yes...of course. But not this weekend. We will come out Sundei," Leo reassures.

"This is so exciting. Francesca, honey...your baby is due around your birth date!" Sophia is feeling blissful.

"Yeah. Pretty cool," Francesca agrees.

"Do you have a name chosen yet?" Sophia asks.

Antonio shakes his head. "No...we will let you both know as soon as we do."

"Thank you for coming by today. This is the best news," Leo expresses and wraps one arm around Sophia.

"Thank you for lunch! Delicious as always, Mom," Francesca compliments.

"You are welcome any time," Sophia voices.

Antonio and Francesca hug Sophia and Leonardo. They leave to return to home.

Chapter 81

AT THE CASTLE AND AROUND THE KINGDOM

"Such wonderful news…a new baby to our kingdom!" Eloise says aloud while she makes their bed.

Theodore steps from the bathroom and positions himself behind Eloise. He wraps his arms around her and quietly reassures, "One of these days…we will be adding little ones to the kingdom as well."

Eloise turns and faces him staying within the comfort of his embrace. She stands on her tiptoes and kisses him. "I know. I am so looking forward to our little ones. Until then, we will continue to thrive as a couple…a team…leaders to our kingdom…servants of God…."

Theo rubs his hands up and down his wife's back while they kiss. Then he removes his lips from hers. "I like your plan." He and Eloise exchange another passionate kiss which results in them returning to their bed.

"You are going to have a playmate." Katherine smiles and gives kisses to Ben.

"End of Juliah…then Ben turns three Septembria 14th…so almost three years apart," Sully calculates.

"I am so happy for them! And Ben being older will work out just perfectly. He can help teach their little one." Katherine giggles.

Sully grins as he finishes getting dressed for morning service. "Yep."

......⚭......

Father Romano greets the parishioners as they leave. "Leo…you look like sunshine has settled on your shoulders," Father Romano mentions when he shakes the hand of Leonardo.

Leonardo grins and uses his other hand to pat Father on the arm. "Indeed. I am going to be a Papa. Our Francesca is going to have a baby."

"Wonderful news!" Father Romano expresses.

Sophia also is beaming with joy when Father shakes her hand.

"Congratulations to you all," Father Romano delivers.

"Thank you, Father," Sophia and Leo reply in unison.

Sophia and Leonardo go home, change clothes, rest for a while, then make some sides for dinner, which gives Francesca and Antonio time to get home, rest, and prepare dinner. After they rest and prepare their sides dishes, they head out to the Mancini Ranch for a family dinner.

Chapter 82

MONTHS PASS BY

Francesca lights up when she sees Antonio walking through the door with a bouquet of early blooms.

"I saw these decorating the landscape when I returned from my ride and wanted to pick some for you." Antonio extends the bouquet to his wife.

Francesca smiles. "Thank you, babe...they are lovely!" Francesca takes the bouquet and gently places it on the island while she grabs the perfect vase and fills it with water. She then arranges the flowers into the vase and sets them on the center of the island. "I love it! Thank you!"

"You are welcome. How are you and our little one feeling today? Two months to go...." Antonio grins.

"Doing great! So, are we set on the names we have?" Francesca asks.

"Yes. I like the name Marco...it goes with Mancini," Antonio states.

"Yes...and Alexander is a favorite name of mine," Francesca adds.

"Marco Alexander Mancini…has a nice ring to it." Antonio grins.

"And you are good with our daughter's name…if it is a girl…?" Francesca doubles checks.

"Absolutely! Natalie Alexandria Mancini is perfect!" Antonio reaches for the hand of Francesca and kisses it. "I will be back later."

"Tell Sully and Katherine hi for me. Ben is soon going to have a playmate." Francesca smiles.

Antonio nods. "I will. Enjoy your day." He heads to the door.

"I will just bake and maybe, brush Moondance and Autumn, and play with the fur babies," Francesca voices.

"I like that." Antonio waves. "Be safe. Enjoy your day!"

Chapter 83

JULIAH

Sophia, Leonardo, the Carlisles, along with the king and queen arrive at the Mancini's to celebrate.

"Happy Birthday, honey." Leonardo loudly hollers out when he walks in past Antonio, patting his arm. "Where is that little grandson of mine?"

"Come on in to the family room, everyone." Antonio greets the rest of their guests.

Family and friends enter the Mancini family room and see Francesca in a cute dress already sporting her trim figure while holding the most adorable little two-month-old boy with a full head of brunette hair.

Sophia sets her bags down and exclaims, "Happy birthday, sweetie!" then zooms right over and takes precious Marco from the arms of her daughter. "You are just adorable, pumpkin. Eager to be in the world two months early. And look at you now. How are you feeling, honey?" Sophia shifts her eyes and questions Francesca.

"The incision the surgeon made for the cesarean is still tender and numb. He said it could be that way for a year…maybe two," Francesca informs.

"You are both healthy. That is what matters," Sophia voices.

"My turn.…" Katherine steps next to Sophia. "Happy Birthday, Francesca." The ladies exchange Marco. Katherine sits in a chair so Ben can get a closer look. "Meet Marco, sweetie."

Ben smiles and places his little hand on the top of Marco's chest. Ben attempts to articulate the word 'brother.'

Katherine giggles. "Marco will be like your brother, yes."

Ben pats the baby then searches for toys to hand him. Katherine ends up with a pile of toys on her lap surrounding Marco. The adults find humor in Ben's brotherly behavior.

The guys gather in the kitchen while the women make themselves at home in the great-size family room.

"What an ordeal you two went through. But Marco seems healthy and Francesca is glowing," Theodore notices.

"I don't know how you did it. Katherine delivering Ben on time was an event…let alone a cesarean two months early," Sully comments.

"Yeah. I was filled with so much anxiety. Not being in control. Not being able to protect either of them. It sent me to my knees," Antonio humbly replies.

"I am just glad my daughter and grandson have you," Leo commends.

"I appreciate that," Antonio responds.

The men enjoy beverages and exchange conversation while the women are doting over Marco.

Chapter 84

ON CHIARAS

"I think we should send Celestial and Blazer to Acheeas to show the human families what has been happening on Soleil," High Priestess Ammerie voices.

"I agree. Plus, Celestial will not feel the need to sneak off the planet to show them." High Priest Akshai laughs a little. "It is good for Blazer and Celestial to reveal to the humans how their sons and families have been doing. I believe it will bring them and the humans, peace. Go ahead and notify the team."

High Priestess Ammerie places her index and middle finger to her left temple and communicates. "Blazer and Celestial...please come to the conference room." Ammerie lowers her fingers.

Blazer and Celestial are at a nearby lake when they receive the message. They exchange eye contact.

"I wonder what this is about," Blazer comments.

Celest shrugs her shoulders. "Beats me."

The two Chiawaukas decide to transport themselves directly there instead of walking since they are some distance from the embassy.

Blazer and Celestial materialize just outside of the grand double doors. Blazer opens the door for Celestial to enter.

The receptionist at the front desk addresses, "They are waiting for you."

Celestial and Blazer swiftly move up the staircase to the conference room. They enter and see the High Priests looking out the window that spans the length of the room.

"Ah, thank you for arriving in a timely manner," High Priest Akshai acknowledges.

Blazer and Celestial both nod.

"Be seated," High Priestess Ammerie directs.

Celestial and Blazer each sit down. Both Ammerie and Akshai sit down as well.

"We summoned you here because we want you to travel to Acheeas and show the two families all that has happened since the weddings. We believe it will provide entertainment for them, but also give them additional peace…and hopefully put their worries to rest," High Priest Akshai outlines.

Celestial lights up and Blazer nods.

"Yes. We can do that. Thank you," Celestial responds.

"The humans will appreciate the gesture. Thank you for sending us," Blazer adds.

"Well…we did not want you to feel you needed to sneak off planet." High Priest Akshai raises an eyebrow while peering at Celestial.

"Of course. Not again. No, Sir," Celestial anxiously replies.

"Very good. Leave at once. When you return, give us a report," High Priestess Ammerie requests.

Blazer and Celestial both nod and stand.

"Absolutely," Blazer states.

"Thank you so much." Celestial bows.

"Be safe. Peace to you both," High Priest Akshai expresses.

"Peace to you," Celestial and Blazer communicate in unison.

Chapter 85

ON THE PLANET ACHEEAS

Blazer and Celestial land on Acheeas near the ranch. They get out of their spacecraft and journey up the slope from the lake.

"This view of the ranch is as breathtaking as the ranches on Soleil." Celestial inhales a deep breath.

"Yes. Beautiful scenery," Blazer remarks.

The Chiawaukas approach the cabin and spy Don and Franklin working outside.

"Hey you two. Need some help?" Blazer questions.

"Well, look who the sky brought in." Don grins.

"We thought we would add on to the cabin since this is our new home," Franklin reveals.

"Splendid idea." Celestial smiles. "We have a surprise for you."

"I am pretty sure we can take a break," Franklin states.

Don lays down his hammer. Franklin removes his toolbelt. The men walk around to the front of the house and open the door for their guests.

"Look who the sky brought in...." Don grins at his word selection.

Tabitha runs over to Celestial and Blazer and squeezes them both.

"Hello, sweetie," Celestial greets.

Sarita tosses a towel down after wiping her hands. Marcella comes out from a bedroom. Both women and Tabitha have been busy in the house.

"Our high priests want us to show you what has been going on since your sons got married."

Sarita raises her hands up with her elbows bent. "Just lovely. I can't wait!"

"Let's gather on this sofa and these chairs," Franklin suggests.

"Perfect," Blazer concurs.

The two families and the Chiawaukas sit comfortably on the furniture. Blazer waves his arm in an arc and a screen manifests. Celestial waves her hand, then points at the screen. The first scene that appears is Antonio and Francesca the day after their wedding.

"Oh...Oh, my...." Sarita blushes. "I don't think we need to see this." She says with a nervous laugh.

"I can fast forward...." Blazer informs.

"Aww...our son and Eloise are at the Garden of Remembrance...visiting us...." Marcella is touched.

Franklin places his arm around his wife and daughter.

"There is Antonio and Francesca. She looks like she has put on some...." Sarita notices.

"I bet she is pregnant!" Marcella finishes Sarita's sentence.

Don and Franklin enjoy seeing their wives so happy to watch life on Soleil.

"Shhh...let's listen...." Sarita places her hands as if she is praying.

The eyes of everyone in the room focus on the screen before them.

Antonio gently lifts Francesca off the ground in a big hug and spins in a circle. "Did you hear that Mother and Pop? We are going to have a baby!" He exclaims while he lowers Francesca down.

"Yes! We do hear you, Son!" Sarita reaches her hand toward the screen. The families continue to watch and listen.

"What a beautiful gift for us…a year out from when my parents passed…we find out we are bringing new life into our world." Antonio places his hands on each arm of Francesca. Antonio leans in and kisses Francesca.

Francesca smiles.

"Let's go find out from Doctor Gerard when you are due. We have to pick a name…and get a room ready…." Antonio gleams.

Francesca laughs a little watching Antonio's exuberance.

"I gotta tell you…." Don begins.

The Chiawaukas pause the footage.

"Blazer and Celestial…this is quite a gift for us all. Thank you." Don mists up.

"You are quite welcome." Blazer reacts, then resumes the link.

……⚬♋⚬……

Doctor Gerard returns to the exam room that Francesca and Antonio are in. "Well, I can tell you that your baby is due around the third week of Juliah."

"What?" Antonio is ecstatic. He then looks at Francesca and exclaims, "That is the week of your birthdate as well!"

Marcella takes Sarita's hands in hers and squeezes them. "This is so beautiful."

Sarita rests her head into Marcella's head.

The Chiawaukas continue to play the footage.

"It is." Francesca smiles and shares Antonio's enthusiasm.

"You are healthy and fit. I see no reason for you not to continue with your normal activities. You only have around six months to go." Doctor George Gerard outlines.

"Well, she won't need to be active or do anything," Antonio proudly states.

Francesca hops off the table. "I will."

Antonio and Francesca exchange their first stare-off.

"Uh-oh...oh, boy...." Sarita quietly voices as she and the families wait with anticipation on where this is going.

"Look...you two will figure it out. Antonio...Francesca is healthy. She is physically fit...her body is used to being active. Her carrying your bundle of joy does not change that. Francesca should remain active. Of course, within reason, but I see no medical reason currently for her to be inactive and sit around during the pregnancy," Doctor Gerard details.

"Within reason...." Antonio repeats.

Francesca remains in her stance. "Yes. Within reason. And I am reasonable and will decide for myself what I believe I can do safely."

Antonio does not break his stare from his wife. Then for some reason, out of nowhere, he hears his pop's voice, "I hope you meet a woman as tender as your mother and as fierce." Just then, Antonio softens and smiles at Francesca. "You are truly who my pop wanted me to marry. I trust your judgement. I hope you will forgive me for wanting to put you on bedrest. It is just my way of protecting my family."

Don gently pats Sarita on the knee, "Look there...he listened to me. And he married a girl just like you."

"Well...our son always listens to both of us. He is very obedient," Sarita proudly asserts.

They continue to view the arc.

Francesca softly voices, "It is alright. Thank you for caring so much about our baby and me."

"Well, of course. I would do anything for you and our family." Antonio reaches for her hand.

Francesca gives Antonio that smile he loves to see. "I know you would, Cowboy."

"Alright. I will see you back here in one month," Doctor Gerard assigns after he inhales a deep breath then exhales. It relieves him to see the young Mancini couple work through their differences.

"Thank you, Doctor." Antonio reaches to shake his hand.

"Thank you, Doctor." Francesca smiles and leans into Antonio.

"You two are quite welcome. Antonio, your parents would be so happy," Doctor Gerard mentions.

Antonio nods with a cordial smile. "They would be, indeed." He places one hand on the door handle to open the door for Francesca and places his other hand gently on her lower back.

"That kept my attention. Suspenseful and tender." Franklin glances over to his friends.

"Oh, look! There is Sophia and Leonardo! I miss them!" Sarita places her hand over her heart.

"I do as well. I love them. I am glad they are alive to watch over our sons," Marcella endearingly expresses.

Sarita observes. "And I love that Francesca has the ability to sense where our son is coming from and softened her stance and opened her heart…."

"Ah…Leonardo and Sophia just found out…and look at Leo…Father Romano was right…he is shining like the sun," Sarita adds.

"There is more…." Blazer discloses.

"Yes…please continue," Franklin directs.

"Oh…such a beautiful bouquet of flowers Antonio gives Francesca," Sarita softly narrates.

"What's wrong?" Antonio runs to the door from the stables. He sees Francesca stepping lightly and holding onto her stomach. "Oh, my…what can I do?"

"I don't know…I think I am having our baby," Francesca cries in pain.

"Nope...you hold on...." Antonio rushes back to the stable *and moves at an accelerated speed hooking up the carriage and his fastest team. He opens the doors and comes barreling out...thinking to himself...Times like these are when I wish we voted in vehicles...I could sure use the speed of a truck right now....*

Sarita, Don, Tabitha, Marcella, and Franklin are on the edge of their seats.

Antonio leaps off the carriage and darts to Francesca. He swiftly and carefully places her into his arms and dashes to the carriage lifting her up with the utmost care. "Hold on, babee...I will protect you both...."

Francesca is intently praying.

Antonio drives the carriage as fast as he believes he safely can.

"I love you, Antonio," *Francesca cries.*

"I love you, too." *Antonio glances at his wife. They reach town and take the quickest route to Doctor Gerard's.*

"My parents...our friends...." *Francesca takes deep breaths.*

"Yes...I will let them all know," *Antonio assures.*

Antonio brings the team to a stop, jumps out of the carriage, and rushes to lift Francesca out.

"I can walk...." *Francesca maintains.*

"No. I will not hear of it. Let me take care of my family," *Antonio gently, yet firmly requests.*

"Alright, Cowboy." *Francesca leans her head into Antonio's shoulder while he swiftly carries her to the door. He opens the door while carrying Francesca. He props it with one foot while he maneuvers them through.*

The nurse stands and opens the doors to the exam rooms. "Doctor!" *the nurse yells.*

Doctor Gerard urgently leaves an examination room and sees the Mancinis.

"I think this is it...our baby is ready...." *Francesca quietly mumbles.*

318

Doctor Gerard leads them to the surgery room. "Lay her on this bed...." Doctor Gerard points.

Antonio lays Francesca gently upon the operating bed. "You're gonna be alright...." Antonio is filled with anxiety, but tries to assure Francesca she will be safe. He kisses her forehead.

Doctor Gerard dries his hands after scrubbing them, then positions himself to examine Francesca. "Nurse, get me the twilight mix...."

"On it!" The nurse quickly moves into action.

"Twilight mix?" Antonio quizzes.

"Yes, the mix...it has the sedative and pain block...I have to deliver the baby by cesarean," informs Doctor Gerard. "You may sit with Francesca behind the curtain."

Antonio nods and pulls over a chair as he notices them scrubbing her stomach with a blue liquid. "It's going to be alright, honey." Antonio gazes into the extremely sleepy eyes of Francesca. He caresses her forehead as she calms from the medication the doctor administered.

"Oh, my...I can't take this...will she be alright...will we be grandparents?" Sarita stresses.

"Antonio...I will cut through seven layers to reach the amniotic sac. How is Francesca?" Doctor Gerard asks.

"She is resting," Antonio replies.

"Very good," Doctor Gerard responds while he concentrates on his surgical skills.

Doctor Gerard pulls the baby out and sets the infant in the blanket the nurse is holding. She rushes the baby to the incubator where she cleans the newborn up and stimulates the little one.

"Antonio...you and Francesca have a beautiful baby boy," Doctor Gerard reveals while he is stitching Francesca up.

"A boy?" Antonio lights up still not taking his eyes from Francesca. "Did you hear that? We have a son...." Antonio caresses the face and forehead of Francesca.

"Alright...she has internal stitches that will dissolve. The surface stitches I will need to remove in two weeks," Doctor

319

Gerard instructs. He covers Francesca, then removes the curtain.

"Congratulations," Doctor Gerard offers.

"Will he be alright? I mean...two months early...is he alright?" Antonio expresses his concern.

"He is going to be alright," Doctor Gerard assures.

Just then, the nurse carries the tiny preemie over to meet his parents. Antonio hops to his feet. The nurse places the newborn in his father's hands.

"Hey, little guy...I am your Pop...and your beautiful mother is resting. Welcome to our world," Antonio softly speaks with his deep voice.

If Antonio could emit light, the room would be as bright as the sun.

"Francesca...wake up...we have a son...he has a full head of dark hair...." Antonio quietly speaks to Francesca.

She opens her eyes. She is still experiencing the sedation. Francesca reaches up to Antonio and the baby. "Hello Marco Alexander Mancini...." she whispers.

The nurse takes Marco from the arms of his pop and returns him to the incubator. The doctor will do a thorough exam.

"We have a grandson." Don kisses Sarita on the cheek.

"We do...he is beautiful." Sarita rests her head into Don's shoulder and begins to weep. "We are going to miss out on their lives as if we are dead."

Celestial and Blazer feel deeply for the humans.

"Is there more?" Franklin asks.

"Yes...in Juliah, Sophia, Leonardo, Theodore, Elosie, along with the Carlisles, go to the ranch home to celebrate Francesca's birthday and to see Marco," Celestial answers.

"I do not need to see anymore," Sarita voices. She stands. "I am so happy you shared this with us. It was truly delightful. I am going to lay down awhile." Sarita dismisses herself and goes to her bedroom.

"I would be babysitting!" Tabitha exclaims.

"You sure would, honey." Marcella smiles.

"I am going to go to my wife," Don states. "Blazer...Celestial...thank you."

"Yes...of course." Blazer nods.

"I'm sorry if we upset her...." Celestial apologizes.

"It's alright. Thank you...." Don motions all is well and proceeds to the bedroom.

"Thank you for this," Marcella articulates.

"Yes. Thank you," Franklin communicates.

"Next time you come we will have a huge house! My dad and Don are building bedrooms and bathrooms on each side of the house for each family...and this area we will share," Tabitha details with excitement.

"We saw them working today. It will be wonderful." Celestial smiles at Tabitha.

"We will see you again...." Blazer slightly bows and walks to the door. He opens it and waits for Celestial to make her goodbye hugs to everyone.

"Wait!" Marcella and Franklin both walk over to the door to see them out. "You will show us their lives again...won't you? I mean...I would like to know when our son and Eloise have a baby," Marcella pleads.

Celestial nods. "Yes. We will do that. Of course, honey."

Franklin wraps his arm around Marcella. "Thank you," Marcella and Franklin voice together.

The Chiawaukas leave the ranch home and trek back to their ship.

······⌾⧴⌾······

Don snuggles into Sarita. He whispers, "Are you alright?"

Sarita rolls over. "Don...I do not know that I can do this anymore...see footage of their life and yet, not be a part of it. Is that how heaven will be? That we can see our people...but helpless as to let them know how proud we are of them or how happy we are. We are grandparents…and we will never know our little ones."

"I don't know what lies before us. I do know our lives have been spared. Do not give up hope," Don lovingly reassures Sarita.

"You are right…all will be well…we have a grandson." Sarita lovingly smiles at Don.

"We sure do." Don kisses Sarita.

They fall asleep in comfort of the arms of each other.

Chapter 86

RETURNING TO CHIARAS

"**I** think we should go directly to the high priests...." Blazer recommends.

"I agree. I am not going to wait to consult with them on anything. I want them to be pleased with me," Celestial comments.

Blazer offers a heartfelt smile. "You do know Celest, they are pleased with you because of who you are...not because of your work. You were created as a supreme guardian being. We have been taught all lives...including humans...are precious in the eyes of our Creator."

"I know. I know...I am a work in progress...." Celestial winks at Blazer.

"We all are...." Blazer remarks while he opens one of the large double doors at the embassy.

"I'll let them know you are here...." the receptionist voices while the team head up the stairs.

"After you...." Blazer again opens the conference room door.

Blazer and Celestial see the room is empty. They walk to the large window to view out.

"Just spectacular," Celestial comments.

"It is. The landscape on Chiaras is as beautiful as the other planets," Blazer agrees.

"Except VeNoma...yuck...that was an ugly planet," Celestial remarks.

"It was kind of a dark planet, wasn't it?" Blazer concurs.

"Yes. Just awful," Celestial states.

"So glad you two are here. Please sit." High Priestess Ammerie enters.

The two Chiawaukas step back from the window, walk over to the huge conference table, and pull out a couple of chairs to sit in.

"How were you received?" High Priest Akshai questions.

"Oh...couldn't be better," answers Celestial.

"Very good. And did it give them peace seeing an update?" High Priestess Ammerie asks.

Blazer and Celestial both slightly tilt their heads.

"It did...until they viewed their grandson's birth. It was very emotional," Celestial details.

"In fact, Sarita dismissed herself. She conveyed her deepest thanks and said she does not need to see anymore," Blazer outlines.

"I see." High Priest Akshai nods. "Good work. Let them be for now."

"Okay. Thank you for allowing us to show them what is going on in their absence," Celestial cordially thanks the high priests and stands.

Blazer also stands. "Yes...thank you. By the way, the Chamberlains requested we continue to update them and let them know when their son and his wife have a baby."

High Priest Akshai replies, "I see."

Both high priests stand. "Peace be to you." They express in unison and slightly bow their heads.

Celestial and Blazer exchange the same words and gesture.

......⚬❦⚬......

"What are your thoughts?" High Priestess Ammerie inquires.

"I think we should send Sarita a dream. One that she will witness Sophia, her friends, and family praying for her...Don...and the Chamberlains," High Priest Akshai suggests.

"Oh...that is a lovely idea, Akshai. How about we also let her know that she can communicate through her thoughts...her energy...and they will sense her presence," Ammerie proposes.

"Well...we do not know if she is in the bloodline...but yes...all humans have an energy...they are all connected...yes...let's do it," Akshai agrees.

"Have you given any more thought to how we are going to designate team assignments?" Ammerie inquires.

"I have. Let's discuss it later," Akshai requests.

"Certainly." Ammerie nods.

"Will you send the dream to Sarita?" Akshai asks.

"Yes." Ammerie nods. High Priestess Ammerie stands before the large window and folds her hands in prayer. She then raises her left hand to the sky and her right hand in the direction of the planet Acheeas. Ammerie is deep in prayer and meditation. After some time, Ammerie turns to face Akshai. "It is done."

Akshai nods.

"I do have another idea," Ammerie vocalizes.

"Present it," Akshai invites.

Akshai listens while Ammerie asks, "Remember when we met with the high council about the contingency plans?"

"I do, indeed." Akshai replies.

"All were in agreement that at some point we would anoint more humans than just the leaders of the planets with the golden droplets of our DNA." Ammerie recalls.

Akshai nods. "Go on...."

"I propose we anoint the two families that have been relocated to the planet Acheeas. We do not need to tell them now. We can wait until...." Ammerie pauses, thinks, then continues, "Well, we can even wait until after the Ancient Writings are fulfilled for that matter," Ammerie outlines.

Akshai displays a facial expression of deep thought while he peers out the window of the conference room. He then casts his eyes upon Ammerie and gazes into her eyes. "Ammerie, I believe that is an excellent idea."

"We will visit them when they sleep," Ammerie voices.

"Yes." Akshai nods. He clasps his hands behind his back.

The high priests withdraw from the conference room.

Chapter 87

NEW LIFE

"My love for you grows more each day." Antonio smiles gazing into the blue eyes of his wife who is lying beside him. You are giving me another child in Marleil." Antonio kisses his wife while they caress each other.

"Not much time left…and Katherine and Sully are expecting their second child six months after. How very wonderful." Francesca smiles gazing into the eyes of Antonio. "Marco will be two years old…two months after this little one arrives." She rubs her stomach.

"Funny how things work out." Antonio continues to peer at Francesca with a deep love and admiration. "The Carlisle's second child is due the same month their first child was born. Ben will turn five right when their second child is born, and both of our babies will be spring babies."

"Yeah…it's kind of cool how things happen," Francesca softly voices while Antonio and her continue to tenderly caress each other.

"You know...time has passed...you never did tell me the story of where you learned to ride a horse." Antonio brings up out of the blue.

"Let's save that for another day," Francesca sweetly voices.

"Good plan." Antonio wraps his arms around Francesca and they enjoy the embrace of each other while their bodies melt together.

Francesca whispers, "I sure hope Eloise and Theo have children soon."

"Me too," Antonio quietly conveys.

Peaceful silence fills the room as they bask in the physical intimacy of their love.

Chapter 88

LOVING OUR HOME

Don, Franklin, Tabitha, Marcella, and Sarita all step outside some distance from their ranch home on Acheeas.

"This is just spectacular!" Marcella declares.

"It is…the design is just perfect!" Sarita places her hands over her heart.

Don and Franklin managed to design and build a perfect addition. Each side of the ranch house now sports a master bedroom with a bathroom and two additional bedrooms with a bathroom in the center of the bedrooms. The main cabin will be shared where the kitchen, dining area, family room, and a bathroom are. The bedrooms in the original cabin will most likely be converted to an office and hobby room.

"I love my new bedroom! Thank you, Daddy and Mr. Mancini," Tabitha expresses.

"You are welcome, honey." Franklin places his arm around his daughter.

"You are welcome, Tabitha. And remember…you may call us by our first names."

"Okay…Don." Tabitha grins.

"There ya go." Don winks.

"This will give us all privacy, yet an area where we can come together. I just love it," Marcella articulates.

"We worked as a team. All of us," Franklin acknowledges.

"We did. I love it!" Sarita voices as she and Marcella rest the sides of their heads into each other.

"Well…let's go in and make dinner.…" Franklin motions.

The Chamberlains stroll up the steps of the deck and into their home.

Don motions for Sarita to join him. They mosey a short distance across the yard.

"It is just beautiful. Thank you," Sarita compliments the work of her husband.

"Yes. You are welcome. I want to know.…" Don takes Sarita's hands into his hands. "Are you doing alright?"

Sarita gazes into the eyes of Don. "Yes. I am. Ever since I had that dream that I mentioned to you… the one where our friends and son and Francesca were praying for us…well everyone in the kingdom…and then to see Marco trying to crawl…I felt like I could say, 'Nonna loves you'…he could hear me. It was just such a powerful dream. Well…ever since then…I have felt at peace. I feel like they will be able to hear my thoughts…at least sometimes…does that sound goofy to you?"

"Not at all. God created us in his likeness. He speaks to us through the Holy Spirit…so no…it does not sound goofy…it is like when we can sense something…or someone comes to our mind…we should contact them if possible or pray for them," Don explains.

"Yes. Exactly. I love you, Don Mancini," Sarita states and kisses the check of her husband.

"I love you, too." Don wraps his arms around Sarita and they slowly sway as if a slow dance song is playing.

That night, after both families are deep in sleep, the high priests descend from the sky in their sphere. They get out and position themselves above each human during their visit to the three bedrooms. They visit the bedroom of Marcella and Franklin. Next is Tabitha, and lastly, the bedroom of Sarita and Don. While in each room, the high priests move their hands and arms in a figure eight over their bodies and quietly speak the Ancient Chant. Soon, golden droplets release from their hands and drop onto the humans. The droplets quickly absorb into their bodies. After the Chiawauka High Priests perform this ceremony over each person, colors of gold and golden droplets burst, which momentarily flashes light throughout each room. After they have completed their mission, they touch their emblem and vanish into the sphere. The sphere quickly ascends and disappears.

Chapter 89

A FOAL IS BORN

"Aw...she is just beautiful! I will name her Lady," Francesca reveals.

"Very good," Antonio voices.

"Wow, Autumn sure seems to be a good mother," Marco notices.

Francesca lovingly smiles while she holds Gino. "She sure does."

"I will help train her," Marco asserts.

Francesca and Antonio smile at their son and are proud of his determination at such a young age.

Chapter 90

DURING THE NEXT SEVERAL YEARS

The humans continue to grow as individuals. Their bonds deepen in their relationships. They enjoy what life offers, such as: game nights, dinner gatherings, church, prayer, horseback rides, hikes, rivers, lakes, fishing, work, losses, and sleep.

Francesca and Antonio experience heartache when they have two miscarriages a little over a year apart. Marco is around five, and Gino is around three.

With their wives at their sides, Antonio and King Theodore do their best to honor their parents' legacy. They strive to enhance the prosperity and continued safety of what they have inherited, for the greater good of all, to honor their parents.

Chapter 91

A PICNIC AT MANCINI LAKE ·

"Look at them...time has gone by so quickly...." Katherine mentions while she enjoys watching their sons play at the water's edge.

"Ben will soon be ten...so grown-up...Marco is seven...our Gino is five and your Luke will soon be five. How did you plan Ben and Luke to be born three days apart in the same month...yet five years between them?" Francesca laughs. "Did you ever think we would have all sons?" Francesca leans back while she sits on a blanket, with her legs stretched out in front of her, and her arms angled to the sides behind her, propping herself up.

"No. I figured one of us would have a girl. Sully and I still do not know how we ended up with both boys born in the same month. Well...we know...but we sure did not plan it that way." Katherine giggles. "Maybe Eloise and Theodore will have a daughter...whenever they do have children." Katherine imagines.

"Maybe so." Francesca smiles. Her eyes shift out to their husbands. "I love watching them fish."

"Oh, I do too. They are happy campers," Katherine agrees. "I love that all these years you host family dinners most every single Sundei and game nights once a month on Saturdeis. Your parents must love that," continues Katherine.

"We all do…it is just the right thing to do. We only have one life…." Francesca replies.

"That is true." Katherine nods.

"Let's go get our feet wet!" Francesca stands and sweeps Gino into her arms at the shoreline and walks into the refreshing, chilly water.

Katherine is still rolling up her jeans, but quickly joins her and the boys.

Marco walks out into the water with his mother and brother.

Ben and Luke hold onto Katherine's hand as they walk out a little way into the lake.

"I am not cut out for this chilly water," Katherine states. "I don't know how you do it."

"I don't know…I just love having my feet in a mountain lake or mountain river," Francesca shares.

Katherine and her sons return to the shore. She dries their legs off with a towel and pats their bodies.

Francesca, Marco, and Gino return to shore as well. "Let me dry you a bit," Francesca informs her little boys.

"We are fine, Mother. We will air dry!" Marco asserts. "Come on, Gino." After Francesca pats excess water from her sons, Marco takes the hand of Gino and they run along the shoreline. "See…we will be dry in no time!" Marco declares.

Francesca smiles at her sons and thinks to herself…*that's my boys*. "Marco has the right idea for roughing it…they will air-dry. I have dry clothes and blankets if they need," Francesca maintains.

Katherine nods while she makes sure Luke and Ben are completely dry by changing their clothes.

Chapter 92

INTERVIEWS AND ASSIGNMENTS

Chiawaukas fill the halls and main areas of the embassy. In the large conference room while looking at a stack of applications, High Priest Akshai slightly grins, then shakes his head. He rifles through the pile and briefly scans some. "By glancing at these, we have a wide range of applicants, from seasoned Chiawaukas to barely out of the academy."

"It is a glorious occurrence that so many want to serve to the calling we were chosen for and created to be...Supreme Guardian Beings...." High Priestess Ammerie expresses in her soothing voice.

High Priest Akshai nods. "I suppose it is...let's call in the first applicant on the stack...."

......⚬⚭⚬......

"I am glad we are done with the interviews," High Priest Akshai admits.

"I am as well. We have much to think about," High Priestess Ammerie voices. "But then...you know...it seems we just know who we are going to choose for what teams and which assignments. I could feel their energy and which pairing we should select for teams."

"I agree. We just know…I could sense it, as well, with each applicant we interviewed," Akshai shares.

Ammerie smiles in her whimsical way. "Let's do something fun…let's each write down who we think should be paired and share our insights with each other."

"Like a game?" Akshai raises an eyebrow and frowns.

"No…better…to see what our instincts tells us…to see if we read their energies correctly…to see if we are in alignment with each other as leaders of the Supreme Guardian Beings…." Ammerie details.

"Sounds like…work…." Akshai laughs.

"Now I know you are jesting…coming from one of the most methodical and fiercest workers I have ever encountered," Ammerie compliments.

"Alright…I will agree to your terms…." Akshai concludes.

The high priests sit and write their choice of pairings down. It takes no more than a few minutes.

"Let's swap lists." Ammerie slides her list over to Akshai.

Akshai also slides his list to Ammerie. They each pick up the paper and flip it over to read the suggestions of pairings.

"Oh, my…." Ammerie laughs.

"Well…this is certainly an impressive pairing you have," Akshai comments.

"Yeah…." Ammerie giggles. "It appears to mirror your list."

"Imagine that." Akshai grins.

Ammerie and Akshai delight in their intuitiveness.

"Tell me…why did you choose these for a pairing?" Akshai points at two names.

Ammerie leans and looks. "Ah…I believe he will balance her. He is very grounded…yet witty. I think it will be the pairing she needs when she experiences memories that haunt her."

"I see. I placed them together because she has so much empathy...and it will be good for him," Akshai reveals.

"Alright...so same pairing for different reasons. Very good." Ammerie nods.

"Okay...moving on...definitely these two together." Akshai points at the list. "I agree. What is your reasoning?" Akshai inquires while he points and shows Ammerie.

"Easy. They are both such strong, adamant personalities...no one else could handle them...they are both leaders...." Ammerie informs.

"Yes...one with tremendous empathy and the other with such a serious manner and approach," Akshai concludes.

"They will complement each other nicely. They have a profound respect for the other," Ammerie notes.

"Another perfect pairing." Akshai cracks a grin.

The high priests continue down their list of selections and are astounded they paired the same Chiawaukas.

"What about this pairing?" Why did you choose these?" Ammerie questions.

"Probably the same reason you did." Akshai laughs a little. "He is one of the most seasoned, patient Chiawaukas, among us. Time and time again he has demonstrated his deep patience and the ability to stay on task. I paired him with the newest one out of the academy because, frankly, I think he is the only one who can guide her to maturity while being patient. These two...." Akshai points to names on the list. "...neither of them would put up with her nonsense. They would each be requesting a new partner within no time."

"I completely agree, Akshai. That is why I paired those two as well," Ammerie discloses.

"Though I *am* impressed...I am not surprised. We were gifted our leadership command for a reason...and though we arrived at some pairings for different reasons...it is grand to see we did, indeed, pair them well." Akshai stands tall.

Ammerie also stands. "Yes. I am pleased with our selections."

Chapter 93

PASSING THROUGH

"Mm...love you Mama...I will see you and daddy out at the house this weekend." Francesca releases her mother from a strong embrace.

"Of course. Your dad is certainly looking forward to going fishing with our grandsons and Antonio," Sophia sweetly conveys.

Francesca is sporting a very stylish hat and backing up to the door of her parents' store while talking to her mother. "Very good! See you soon! Love you guys!" Just as she turns to open the door, the door is opened by a tall, well-built man, several years older, and Francesca slams right into his arms.

Horrified and embarrassed, "I am so sorry. I was clearly not looking where I was going. Are you alright?" Francesca backs away from the arms of the man. "I am very sorry."

"That is quite alright, Miss. It is not every day I get slammed into by a handsome woman," The unknown rider admits. "And yes, I am alright."

Sophia steps closer.

Francesca, feeling very embarrassed continues, "Again…my apologies."

"It is quite alright, Miss." The well-built man tips his hat toward Francesca.

"Alright. Goodbye, Mother." Francesca turns and walks out and thinks to herself, *something familiar about him…hmmm…his voice*…then she sifts it out of her mind and refocuses on getting home and seeing her guys.

"You have a captivating daughter," The man remarks.

"We do. Thank you. Is there something I can help you with?" Sophia questions with professionalism.

"I just need to get some supplies." The man pulls out a list from his pocket and hands it to Sophia.

"Oh, sure…we have all of these items in stock," Sophia confirms.

Sophia leads the man to each item and he sets each item into the cart. Sophia tallies his supplies and he pays for the merchandise.

"Thank you for your business. We appreciate it," Sophia continues to be courteous and professional.

"You are quite welcome. By the way, what is your daughter's name? She seems familiar…like I have met her before," the rider asks.

"Her name is Mrs. Antonio Mancini." Sophia makes sure this customer knows her daughter is married.

"So Tony is married now?" the customer asks.

"Yes…very…and with children," Sophia informs.

"I am glad to hear that. I have done business with his dad ever since he was a little one. Don always offered the best Wintuckets," The rider comments. "Well, thank you for the supplies." The rider tips his hat, picks up his merchandise, and leaves the store.

Sophia just watches him…not sure what she is sensing…then is interrupted when Leonardo walks inside.

"Having a good day?" Leo asks.

"Yeah. You missed our daughter," Sophia discloses.

"Oh?" Leo frowns. "Well, we will be out there in a couple of days."

"Were you smoking that pipe, again?" Sophia tilts her head and questions.

"Nothing gets past you...." Leonardo kisses Sophia on the cheek. "I just like it."

"I know...but it is not healthy for the only set of lungs you have," Sophia advocates.

"Well...we will see...just let me enjoy it now and again," Leo requests.

Sophia nods. "I will try. I just do not want to lose you."

"Well, honey...we are all going to pass from this life to the next...." Leo reminds.

Sophia frowns and quietly voices, "I know."

———

Francesca arrives back at the ranch and dismounts Moondance.

"How was your ride to town?" Antonio greets Francesca while he reaches the for reins of Moondance.

"It was good. Dad is looking forward to fishing." Francesca smiles at Antonio.

"You are so beautiful." Antonio stares at his wife.

Francesca giggles. "You're not so bad yourself." Francesca leans into Antonio and kisses him.

"See...I like that." Antonio smiles.

"I know you do, Cowboy," Francesca playfully expresses.

Marco and Gino come running out.

"Hi, Mom!" Gino lights up.

"Hi, Mom!" Marco is happy to see their mother.

"My boys. I love you guys!" Francesca wraps her arm around each son.

"I have some work to do out here. Marco and Gino, I could use your help," Antonio states.

Both boys nod.

Francesca walks up to the house and glances back. "See you guys in a bit."

Gino and Marco help their pop in the stables.

"I love horses," Marco voices.

"I do too. I really love building things," Gino mentions.

Antonio hears a rider coming up their long drive and looks out. He recognizes the man. "Gino, go up to the house and let your mother know we will be having one more for dinner."

"Yes, Sir." Gino replies, then hurries to the house.

Marco stands next to his pop while the rider dismounts his horse.

"Boy, it has been a LONG time, Cash, since I have seen you." Antonio walks toward the visitor and shakes the hand of the well-built man.

"Your name is Cash?" Marco giggles.

"Marco, mind your manners. That is not polite," Antonio scolds.

"It's alright, Tony." Cash smiles with a kind warmth about him.

"You know why we call him Cash?" Antonio questions Marco.

Marco shakes his head. "No, Pop."

Antonio grins. "Because every time Pop, your grandfather...would sell horses to this man...well...he always had such a large wad of cash...so that is how he acquired his nickname."

"I see. So...what is your real name?" Marco asks.

"My name is Miles Cassidy," Cash answers. "But you may call me Cash. Nice to meet you, Marco." Cash reaches and firmly shakes the hand of Marco.

"You arrived just in time for dinner. Let's go up to the house," Antonio invites.

"I appreciate that. I am here to purchase some more horses...and to give you my condolences on the loss of your parents. I guess, to congratulate you also on having a family," Cash conveys.

"Yes. A lot of time has passed since I last saw you," Antonio notes as he opens the side door for Marco and Cash to enter. "How many horses do you need?"

"Three, if you have them," Cash answers as he enters their home.

"There is a bathroom right in there, for you to wash up." Antonio points.

When Cash comes out, Antonio leads him through the kitchen to the dining area.

"This is my wife, Francesca, and our other son, Gino," Antonio introduces.

Cash removes his hat and slightly bows. "I believe I had the honor of meeting you earlier today at your parents' store."

Francesca blushes. "Yes. How did you know it is my parents'?

"I believe you referred to the woman as your mother, when you said goodbye. Also, your mother made it very clear you are married," Cash respectfully answers.

Antonio smiles. "Her parents are very protective."

"Well, I can understand that." Cash nods his head toward Francesca. "Gino, it is very nice to meet you." Cash extends his hand to shake Gino's hand.

"We will pray," Antonio announces.

Francesca, Marco, Gino, and Antonio bow their heads. Cash is a little taken aback, but follows suit and bows his head. Antonio leads them in prayer.

"So, what brings you to Chamberlain?" Francesca inquires while she passes the main course.

"Mancini horses. I have been purchasing horses from Don Mancini for years. I knew your husband here, when he was a little guy," Cash recalls.

"I see. Welcome to our home," Francesca politely voices and smiles.

"I have to say, this is the finest meal I have had the good fortune to enjoy in some time," Cash appreciates.

"Thank you." Francesca slightly nods.

"My mother is the best chef in all the land!" Gino exclaims.

Cash laughs a little. "I don't doubt that."

As the conversation winds down after dessert is served, Gino asks Cash, "Do you know how to shoot a gun, too?" The boys are extremely fascinated meeting someone that knew their pop when he was a boy.

Antonio and Cash exchange eye contact and a grin. "Cash used to be the fastest draw in the entire mountain region. He won many first-place awards in shooting competitions," Antonio informs.

Hearing those words, Francesca instantly feels queasy, like a trigger went off inside. She stands and gathers dishes from the table to carry into the kitchen. The boys and Antonio also stand and carry their plates and their guest's plate and silverware to the kitchen. The table is quickly cleared.

"Tony, this was very kind of you to invite me for dinner. How about you show me what you have available to sell," Cash suggests.

"I can do that," Antonio replies.

Cash turns before he walks out the side door. "Boys, it was very nice to meet you...and Miss...Mrs. Mancini, thank you for dinner. It is truly my pleasure to meet you. You take care...."

At that moment, what Francesca had sensed earlier that she sifted out of her thoughts has returned, barreling to front and center stage...*I know that voice...is it? Could it possibly be...*her thoughts are interrupted when she hears Antonio's voice, "Babe, are you alright? We will be at the stables."

She slightly nods her head and barely smiles. "Yes. Thank you. I will finish up in here."

"Are you sure you are alright?" Antonio notices something odd about his wife.

"Yes. Yes," Francesca assures.

Antonio follows Cash out the door.

"Can I go too?" Marco pleads with his mother.

"No. Let your pop do his business," Francesca answers.

"But if I am going to be like Pop, I need to listen and learn," Marco pleads his case.

Francesca frowns and is not quite on her game. "Stay out of their way and do not interrupt."

"Thanks, Mom! I love you, Mother." Marco hugs his mother then jets out the door. He quietly approaches the stables and for some reason opts to stand in the darkness that shadows cast, to listen to their conversation.

"I have these I can let go of." Antonio shows Cash. "Two geldings and a mare."

"That'll be great," Cash states.

"Hey, whatever happened to those three you had riding with you? Um…I think Devlin, Dylan, and Owen were their names," Antonio questions.

"You don't know?" Cash questions.

"Uh…no," Antonio earnestly answers.

"One was killed by a horse, and I shot the other two," Cash answers.

Marco hears the words his pop and Cash exchange. Shivers run through him.

"You really never heard?" Cash curiously quizzes.

"No. Honestly, not to speak bad of anyone, or question your reasons, but I never understood why you tried to teach them the ways of your life…they seemed worthless," Antonio shares. "I never would have hired them."

"Well…I told their parents I would see what I could do with them," Cash discloses.

"I see," Antoino responds.

"I really cannot believe you do not know…it actually happened in the fall before your parents' sleigh ride accident that winter. Well…it has been so many, many years…I cannot be certain, but your wife looks just like the young girl they attacked," Cash outlines.

"Wait...you are telling me they attacked Francesca?" Antonio attempts to keep his voice lowered while he feels fury flowing through his veins.

"I can't be sure, but her voice sounds the same...and Tony...she *looks* the **exact** same as she did all those years ago, but...I can't be one hundred percent sure." Cash imparts. "Her horse stomped Owen to death...then Dylan shot her horse."

Anger swells inside of Antonio. "What were you doing when this went down?"

"To be honest, I was allowing the guys to blow off some steam, but then I did intervene." Cash pauses and shakes his head. "It haunts me to this day. She was crying and really...they should not have attacked her. She became short of breath...I think she was having an asthma attack," Cash recounts.

"I can't believe you thought it was alright to attack a girl!" Antonio sternly attests.

"I can vouch those were NOT my finest hours, Tony. I am sorry, Tony. She was one tough cookie. She took my gun from me and kept the horses of the dead men. I rode into town to alert the sheriff. I have carried regret with me many years for what I allowed to happen. I was the one who killed Devlin and Dylan," Cash confesses. "Ever since...I have done my best to make it right by helping others...especially women."

Marco comes running from the shadows of the dark and begins to repeatedly punch Cash while he screams, "You hurt my mother!"

Antonio grabs ahold of Marco and firmly clasps him with his arms. "I think you better go, Cash." Antonio releases Marco from his arms. "You get up to the house...NOW!" Antonio, with his deep, resonating voice, instructs Marco.

Marco runs as fast as he can.

"Cash, I cannot even swallow the notion that you allowed a girl to be hurt. We, as men, are created to protect females...not because they are weak...but because they are sacred. I am so angry...it is best you leave...NOW." Antonio glares at a man he has known ever since he was a boy. "Where did this happen?"

"On the Chianne River, up past the C-Fork," Cash answers.

"Tony...for what it's worth...." Cash attempts are abruptly curtailed.

Antonio interrupts. "I need you to leave my property, Cash."

Cash frowns and sighs and reaches to pat Antonio's shoulder, but Antonio adjusts his stance so Cash cannot touch him.

Cash gets on his horse gazing upon Antonio. Scenes of doing business with Don and meeting Antonio when he was a little boy scramble through his thoughts. Cash experiences remorse all over again while he rides away.

······◦✗◦······

Marco runs into the house and straight to his mother and hugs her.

"Hey, what's up?" Francesca embraces Marco.

Marco sobs. "I love you so much!"

Francesca is taken aback and does not know where this is coming from, but she does what she can to comfort her son.

Antonio steps into the house and sees his wife and son swaying in the embrace of a hug. He quietly walks over and wraps his arms around them. After a few moments he reaches for Marco's hand. "How about I take you to bed and tuck you in?"

Marco wipes his eyes and squeezes his mother. Francesca squeezes him back and quietly voices, "Sleep well, my son. I love you."

"I love you, Mom," Marco quietly speaks.

Antonio leads Marco to his room. Marco grabs his pajamas and goes to the bathroom while Antonio sits on his bed. Marco returns from the bathroom and crawls into his bed and lays his head on his pillow. "Is Mom going to be alright?" Marco asks.

"Your mother is just fine. Don't you worry about anything. That incident was long ago. She is safe with us. What were you doing out there anyway?" Antonio assures and asks.

"I wanted to learn how to do business just like you," Marco explains.

Antonio grins. "I see. Well...next time." Antonio runs his hand over Marco's thick head of hair. "If you need to talk about this...please discuss it with me only. Not your mother."

"I understand. So...Cash shot the men that hurt mom?" Marco quizzes.

"I guess he did," Antonio answers while caressing his son's face. "Look, you go to sleep, and if you need to talk about it...please come to me."

Marco nods. "I will, Pop. Goodnight."

"Goodnight, Son." Antonio leans over and kisses the forehead of his son.

Antonio descends the stairs, walks to their large family room, and grabs a blanket on the way to the door of the back deck.

"I knew you would be out here." Antonio wraps a blanket around Francesca and then sits beside her.

He wraps his arm around her and she leans her head onto his shoulder.

"Quite an evening," Antonio comments.

Francesca nods.

"Let's just sit in quiet," Antonio suggests.

Francesca snuggles into Antonio and closes her eyes. She rests in the comfort of his love.

He kisses her head and reaches to hold one hand. After some time, she falls asleep. He lifts her and carries her to their bed, placing her gently on top of the covers.

Chapter 94

A DATE DAY

"**B**oys, come on." Antonio motions. "We will be leaving as soon as your grandparents arrive."

"There are my sweeties," Sophia exclaims as she steps onto the deck and hugs them.

"Thank you for watching the boys," Francesca expresses.

"You two, go enjoy your day. We are happy to spend time with our grandsons," declares Leonardo.

Francesca smiles. "Alright. Love you guys!"

"Love you!" The boys say in unison.

"Be safe," Sophia voices.

"We will," Antonio assures.

Sophia and Leonardo settle in with their grandsons to begin a glorious day.

Antonio and Francesca saddle up their horses. Antonio puts the pack of food and water on his horse.

"Where are we going?" Francesca asks.

"It is a surprise...but a beautiful place," Antonio answers.

They enjoy the scenery of the mountains. They see the crops across the valley and view herds of animals grazing. Francesca is so busy relaxing from hearing the sounds of the Chianne River, she is not even paying attention to where they are, until they stop.

"Further up on this trail is the C-Fork." Antonio points. "I wanted to bring you on this back trail to this beautiful spot." Antonio steps off his horse and reaches for Francesca's hand to assist her off her horse, Autumn.

Francesca scans the area and sees her favorite spot as a teenager. Then she spies the cross her dad made for Aspen. Francesca sighs. "Why did you bring me here?"

Antonio gently reaches for a hand of his wife, "Walk with me."

She walks with him, holding his hand. He leads them to the river's edge. "I wanted to share this beauty with you," Antonio voices.

Francesca feels a bit of anxiety while she scans the area. Then she notices the picnic table and realizes something is different about it. She lets go of Antonio's hand and walks closer to inspect. "Wow. Somebody built a new picnic table. This is beautiful." She turns her head and looks at Antonio. "I remember an old rickety one."

"I know," Antonio quietly voices.

"You know? Have you known all these years?" Francesca quizzes.

Antonio shakes his head. "No. Only since Cash came to our ranch."

"I see. Well, why bring me here?" Francesca interrogates.

"Look, my parents always taught me...if I have a bad experience somewhere which prevents me from returning to that place, I should revisit it and create new memories. Now, there are instances that may not be possible...but in this case...I built that table for new memories. I know you love this part of the river as much as the part that runs through our property...." Antonio grins. "Actually, this is also on our land. Anyway...I want it to be a place we can visit together...an area where you feel safe enough to visit when you ride...to make new memories in a location where something bad happened. I don't know, just hearing my parents teach me this...well, I never thought much about it, until now."

Francesca leaps into Antonio's arms. "You are...without a doubt, the most beautiful soul I have encountered!" She gives Antonio a big smack of a kiss.

Antonio smiles from the depths of his heart. "I am glad you are pleased."

"Your parents' wisdom makes perfect sense...thank you!" Francesca smiles while she gazes into the eyes of Antonio.

Antonio walks to Ranger and removes the pack of food and water. He carries the pack to the picnic table, unzips it, and sets out sandwiches, chips, and water.

Francesca radiates. "This is the best day...I have so many best days with you."

"Glad to hear that." Antonio nods.

After they eat and enjoy small talk, Francesca reaches for Antonio's hand. "I want to show you something...." She leads him to the grave. "This grave is where Aspen, my first horse is buried. I learned to ride her...we even did jumps and a few tricks...but mainly she was my best friend. I was with David and Steve when I picked her out and named her." Francesca pauses. "I never really told them what went down. I regret that now."

Antonio places his arms around Francesca. "I am sure they understand. The three of you were tight and you will always have that. How blessed you are to have forever friends."

Francesca peacefully smiles while she ponders fond memories. "I guess so."

"I know so," Antonio reassures.

"Come on!" Francesca lights up and grabs Antonio's hand.

Antonio slightly shakes his head while he thinks to himself, *I married a woman with endless energy.*

They reach the river's edge. Francesca quickly pulls her boots and socks off, then rolls up her jeans. "Come on, Cowboy."

Antonio follows her lead and leans on the boulder to remove his boots and socks. He begins to mess with rolling up his jeans and then just decides to unbutton his jeans and take them off instead of rolling them up.

"What are you doing?" Francesca giggles.

"I can't roll up my jeans as well nor as high as you...." Antonio declares. He then steps into the river.

Francesca wades out as far as she can. "I LOVE THIS!" she raises her arms toward the sky. "Thank you, Father...Creator of the Universe!"

The two enjoy playing in the river, then end up breaking in the new picnic table with tender intimate, yet heart-pounding passion.

Francesca slightly interrupts their kissing and turns her head.

Antonio raises his head slightly. "Are you alright?"

"Yes...I was wondering...did you plan this?" Francesca quizzes while she studies his eyes.

"No. Not at all," Antonio heartfully answers. He gazes into her eyes. "But I like it." He tenderly smiles at her.

"Yeah...me too." Francesca grins and pulls him back to resume.

They enjoy the afternoon in the arms of each other while listening to the sounds of the river.

······◦⧟◦······

"So, this area is on our property? And, your parents never minded that people would ride out here?" Francesca inquires while she gets dressed.

"Yes, our property. No, my grandfather always said that this is a great place to cross the river. It is wide, and for the most part in this section, shallow enough for people to cross on horses to the other side to trail elsewhere. So, no...he never fenced it. And yes...I imagine my parents knew you buried Aspen here...they never told me though...." Antonio zips up and buttons his jeans.

Before he finishes getting completely dressed, she interrupts his endeavor. Francesca glances at him and positions herself next to him with her body pressing against his. She stands on her tiptoes to kiss him. She wraps her arms around his back and rubs up and down. The two exchange more passionate kisses.

"So…we are not leaving?" Antonio voices between kisses.

"Huh uh…." Francesca and Antonio slip each other's clothes off and enjoy more physical intimacy of their marital bond.

······⚬❦⚬······

"I could stay out here all night." Francesca smiles.

"Me too." Antonio rubs on her back.

"Is Cash a good man?" Francesca searches into Antonio's eyes.

"Honestly…yeah…I believed him to be. I still believe he is. I really do," Antonio speaks from his gut.

"Then I want you to contact him and make peace. Sometimes, even the best of people…well…if they are around bad people an extended length of time…their views and even actions can be momentarily compromised. So yeah…I do…I want you to make peace with him," Francesca thoughtfully advocates.

"You never cease to amaze me." Antonio gazes into Francesca's eyes.

"I sensed his spirit…he seems true and direct…and honest. I can't explain it…but despite the haunting memory, not to mention, what I experienced…I sense he is a grounded man," Francesca shares.

"I have learned to trust what you sense…it is like you have a gift." Antonio grins.

"You think we ought to head back?" Francesca raises her eyebrows and grins.

"Probably ought to." Antonio nods.

"I love you. You never push me...but you are always there...for when I am ready...." Francesca notes.

"I just learned from my parents...." Antonio voices. "I have, however, incorporated a few things on my own...." A large grin decorates Antonio's face.

"I know you have. You are a good man, Antonio Joseph Mancini," Francesca showers him with praise. "...with wise parents too! Do you know where Cash will be?"

"I have an idea...we can ride there together now...or I can go tomorrow," Antonio throws out ideas.

"Let's go now. I would like to ride with you...just means on a date longer. We have time. I will stay back when you approach him, so you guys can visit in private...." Francesca smiles. "And sell him the horses he wants...."

"Well, that would free up some stalls for the new ones that will be arriving." Antonio agrees. Antonio assists Francesca up and they get themselves together. Antonio grabs the pack of remaining food, the rest of their water, and secures it to his horse.

As they ride away, Francesca comments, "Nothing better than hearing the sound of a mountain river...." She glances over at Antonio and winks. "Every day with you is the best day ever...."

"I agree one hundred percent." Antonio holds his head high.

······◦❧◦······

You can hear the hooves of their horses on the trail as they approach. "Look...there he is. Creatures of habit...he always liked to camp in this area when passing through Chamberlain," Antonio recalls.

"I am glad you found him. I will wait here." Francesca confidently nods at Antonio.

Antonio motions Ranger ahead and steadily walks down the trail to the campsite.

Cash abruptly stands and turns. "Tony…I sure did not expect to see you."

"Yeah…about that…we have some unfinished business," Antonio states.

"Hey…if you want to punch me…go ahead…I deserve it…." Cash addresses.

Antonio shakes his head. "No…I have three horses you want to purchase. Are you still interested?"

"I am." Cash looks up at Antonio still sitting tall on his saddle.

Antonio dismounts Ranger and takes a few steps closer to Cash. "I am not happy about hearing what happened to my wife and that you were involved. You did save her though, and…I believe you to be a good and honest man."

Cash is astonished at the compassion Antonio exhibits. "I like to think of myself as a good man, Tony. I would like to ask your wife for forgiveness…whenever you deem it is best."

"She is right over there." Antonio points. "No time like the present…tomorrow is not promised."

"Alright then…." Cash views over in the direction of Francesca. "Tony, I am sorry from the depths of my wretched soul. I want you to know that. There is not a day goes by that I am not haunted by her tears and screams of anguish when she was attacked and then they shot her horse…then to hear her labored breathing…it has remained with me to this day. I hope you will find it in your soul to forgive me…."

"Please…spare me the narrative, Cash. I am still wrapping my head around it. Yes…I do forgive you. I believe you, when you say you have tried to make it right by helping people on your journey," Antonio expresses.

"I have…I have been trying to make right the wrong that was done…." Cash admits.

Antonio motions for Francesca to ride into camp.

Francesca reaches camp and remains on her horse.

"Miss...I ask your forgiveness for allowing you and your horse to be harmed. I...to this day...do not know what I was thinking...it still haunts me. If you do not forgive me...I will understand," Cash sets his case before Francesca.

There is an uncomfortably long silence while Francesca is forming her thoughts. "You cannot be productive if you are haunted daily by your despicable deeds. I believe you are living each day to right the wrong. I forgive you, Cash. My husband knows you to be a good man. I sense you to be a grounded man. I forgive you. I, too...at times, have been haunted by that day...my first horse...Aspen...who was my best friend...she was my baby...but I cannot live in that memory or I will not be productive nor live as I was created to be. Sounds like we both need to live in today."

The words Francesca speaks strikes an emotional chord in Cash and tears form in his eyes.

Antonio decides to let Cash experience the pain alone, but after a few minutes, steps next to him, and places his hand on the shoulder of Cash and then drops his hand to his back and gives him a pat.

Francesca dismounts her horse and steps next to Cash. She extends her hand in an offering to shake his hand.

Cash is deeply moved by how she carries herself. He reaches to shake her hand. No words are exchanged. Antonio places his arm around his wife. They turn, Antonio assists Francesca onto her horse, then mounts his. "Cash, you can swing by tomorrow to purchase those horses."

"I will do that." Cash waves.

······◦❧◦······

Later that night, after the sun broadcasts the last rays of the day across the river, Cash sits in the dark at the river's edge with a gun in his hand, wondering if he should even be alive. His deep thoughts break away when he hears leaves crackle. He rapidly stands and turns, "Father?"

"I saw your campfire as I was riding by and thought I would stop in. What is your name?" The priest inquires.

"My name is Cash...I mean Miles Cassidy. Yes, sit. Would you like some coffee?" Cash nervously asks.

"No, thank you, not this late," Father replies. "Let's just sit here awhile. I enjoy the sounds of nature."

Cash sits back down on the large rock he was sitting on and Father sits on a perfect size rock, the height of a chair.

Father notices the gun leaning against a large rock. "Always good to have protection when camping."

An expression of puzzlement casts across the face of Cash. He then remembers he leaned his gun against the rock. "Oh...yeah...."

The two sit in silence, staring at the beauty of the evening sky.

"I was thinking of using it on myself...that beast," Cash discloses.

"I see. What brings you to such despair?" Father asks.

Cash questions, "Can I confess to you?"

"Of course, my son...." Father quietly voices.

Cash begins with the story of many years ago, then other sins come to his mind. He reveals all that he can remember, to the priest. Cash begins to weep. "Can our Creator of the Universe...God...forgive me? The young lady told me I am forgiven and that I need to live in today, so I can fully live as I was created to be...."

"She sounds like a wise young woman...." Father softly speaks. "Are those all of your sins?"

"Yes. All that I can remember...." Cash admits.

"Continue...." Father instructs.

Cash stumbles through the prayer, and at the precise moment he hears the word *absolve* Father imparts, Cash feels like daggers are being pulled from the top of both of his shoulders. He barely hears the rest of the words the priest speaks.

"Go in peace...." Father unfolds his hands, stands, places his right hand on the shoulder of Cash...and walks away.

Cash stands and turns. "Thank you, Father...." But Cash does not see the priest anywhere. It is as if he vanished. Cash feels a little unnerved and decides to pack up and ride to the Mancini's tonight.

......⚬ℓ⚬......

Antonio happens to be making his last rounds when he hears a rider coming up the drive. Antonio walks out of the stables.

"Tony...may I please bunk here tonight? I will sleep out here in the stables. I would just feel more at ease," Cash pleads.

Antonio, not sure what is causing Cash to be requesting shelter...welcomes him. "Yes. I would have you stay up in the house, in a guest room, but this time...yes...I have a room out here, you can sleep in ." Antonio leads Cash and his horse into the stables and directs Cash where he can sleep. "Are you alright?"

"I think so...I just feel a heavy sense that I should come here for the night," Cash shares.

"I see. There is a frig over there...." Antonio points. "If you need anything, help yourself. We'll do our business in the morning."

"Thank you, Tony. I very much appreciate your kindness," Cash communicates. "Goodnight Tony."

"Sleep well, Cash." Antonio departs from the stables.

Cash lies back on the queen-size bed that is in a spacious guest room up in the loft and peacefully rests.

......⚬ℓ⚬......

Antonio finishes his shower. After he dries off, he wraps the towel around him and walks into the bedroom.

"Is Cash alright?" Francesca asks.

Antonio slightly tilts his head. "How did you know Cash is here? I was just about to let you know."

"I do not know. I just sensed it." Francesca sits on their bed with her legs crossed and her elbows bent.

"For real? You did not hear him riding up the drive?" Antonio is curious.

"Nope. I was most likely in the shower after I told our boys goodnight," Francesca accounts. "I just know things. I sense them…maybe not always…but sometimes…for some reason…clear as day.…"

"I guess so.…" Antonio still expresses a curious look. "He seems a bit off his game. So, I told him this visit he could stay in the stables. We have that nice guest room in the loft. He will be plenty comfortable."

"Yes. Well, before he leaves tomorrow be sure and invite him up to the house. He can have a bite to eat before he sets out. And, you probably need to have a talk with Marco. He was pretty upset the other night. My guess is he overheard you and Cash talking," Francesca shares.

"You do know things, don't you?" Antonio grins, then leans over and kisses Francesca's cheek.

"I don't know…sometimes.…" Francesca smiles while she gazes at her handsome husband.

He lays back on his pillow and places his hand on her back. She lays back and snuggles into his body. They sleep peacefully.

……·⚬⚭⚬·……

"Marco, after you carry your breakfast dishes to the kitchen, I want you to come with me out back before we do chores," Antonio addresses his oldest son.

"Sure thing." Marco carries in his bowl, glass, and silverware, then follows his pop out to the back deck.

"Hey…don't I need to go, too?" Gino asks his mother.

"Your Pop will get you after they visit." Francesca smiles. "What should I make for dessert for this evening?"

"Chocolate pie...yum," Gino chimes.

"I like your thinking...." Francesca winks at Gino.

"Marco, I want to visit with you about the other night," Antonio voices.

"I have been thinking a lot about that...." Marco admits.

"You have? What are your thoughts?" Antonio questions.

"I think you should forgive Cash. You have known him most of your life. Grandfather knew him, and had good standing in business with him...and...I don't know...Cash seems to really respect you...enough to be honest with you about a subject matter that he realizes could have severed his ties to you," Marco explains.

"How did you get to be so smart?" Antonio grins at his son.

"I don't know...I observe you and mother...and I listen to stories you tell of your parents and then, of course, Grandmother Sophia and Grandfather Leonardo...I learn from all of you," Marco outlines.

Antonio releases a breath, and then just smiles. "I have something else to tell you...."

"He is here, isn't he?" Marco breaks in.

"Who?" Antonio asks with curiosity.

"You know...Cash. He stayed in the stable loft last night, didn't he?" Marco excitedly expresses.

"Why do you think that?" Antonio inquisitively questions.

"I don't know...I just felt it," Marco shares.

Antonio slightly tilts and shakes his head in astonishment thinking...*my wife...AND my son*....

"Am I right?" Marco eagerly asks.

Antonio nods his head. "Yes. He is here, and when I do business with him this morning, I would like you to be by my side so you can see how a business transaction is handled."

"Thanks, Pop! And then...I want you to teach me all about our mine...I want to work there as well!" Marco declares.

"You are ambitious," Antonio comments.

"Like my parents...." Marco gazes up into the eyes of his pop.

"Let's go meet up with Cash...." Antonio suggests.

They descend the steps of the back deck and walk over to the stables. They come upon Cash having nearly all the morning chores completed.

"What are you doing?" Antonio questions.

"Hey. It is the least I can do for you putting me up a night. Don't worry...there are still some things for you to do." Cash grins.

Antonio nods.

"Hello, Marco. Are you going to assist in the sale today?" Cash smiles at Marco.

"I am." Marco stands proudly.

The three walk over to the office where the transaction takes place. Antonio teaches Marco about the necessary paperwork. Antonio and Cash also do some role playing as if Cash is a new client.

"Cash, Francesca insists you come to the house before you leave to get some food," Antonio mentions when their business is complete.

"Alright...there is something that happened to me that I am wanting to share with the both of you," Cash informs.

"Alright...look forward to hearing it." Antonio pats Cash on the back, then leads the way.

······◦◦◦······

"I have to agree with your son…best chef in all the land.…" Cash compliments.

"Thank you," Francesca humbly replies.

"Okay…I have something I want to share with you.…" Cash begins.

"Boys, go outside and play," Antonio directs.

"Tony, it is fine if they stay. Trust me," Cash reassures.

Francesca and Antonio exchange eye contact. Antonio communicates, "Alright."

"Last night…I was sitting at the river's edge…to be honest…wondering why I am even alive…when a priest who was passing by saw my campfire. He approached me and sat beside me. We visited. I asked if I could confess my sins to him.…" Cash recalls.

All the Mancinis are filled with wonder of this story.

Cash continues, "I confessed the sins that have been weighing heavy on my heart…and then, more came to mind…so I confessed those as well…and I kid you not…when I heard the words, 'I absolve you'…I didn't hear anything else, because I physically felt daggers being pulled from both of my shoulders. I know it sounds…well.…" Cash pauses.

"It sounds like a profound healing!" Francesca adamantly voices.

"Yes! Yes! It was profound! And I believe I did receive a healing! I wish I would not have waited all these years to seek forgiveness. Anyway…the priest was leaving and I turned to tell him thank you…and he was not anywhere to be seen…it's as if he had vanished!" Cash describes. "So would you please tell your priest, 'thank you', for me?"

Antonio and Francesca exchange eye contact.

"Cash…our priest is out of town for five days. I do not know who you ran into…but it sounds like a life-changing event," Antonio informs.

"It was. It really was. Are you sure he did not come back early? He was wearing his black cassock, like he had some special Mass," Cash continues.

Francesca and Antonio both shake their head.

"What you described Cash, is beautiful. Thank you for sharing with our family," Francesca heartfully communicates.

"Yeah. That is remarkable. What a blessing," Antonio agrees.

"Maybe you were visited by the priestly angel of God because he saw you needed him," Marco proposes.

Gino excitedly exclaims, "Yeah...that's right! How cool! I bet that's it!"

Francesca almost glows from hearing the ideas of her sons.

Antonio calmly adds, "I am sure it was a priest traveling through...."

"Are you sure? How can you be so sure?" Marco exuberantly questions his pop.

"Well...you are right, Marco...I cannot be absolutely sure. Cash...maybe you were visited by a celestial being." Antonio smiles.

"It sure seemed real...as real as you are all sitting here," Cash insists.

"I am very glad. Sounds like a true blessing for you," Antonio maintains.

"It was. That is why I wanted to stay here last night. Just to feel a safety around me," Cash explains.

"Anytime you are through this way, you are always welcome here," Antonio reassures.

"I appreciate that." Cash stands. "I need to hit the road if I want to reach my destination by nightfall."

The Mancini family stands and escorts Cash out.

"It is certainly my pleasure to meet your family, Tony. Marco, Gino, listen to your parents...they are very wise. And Francesca, if I may...your beauty runs as deep as it shines out. Thank you all...for really being here...for experiencing this healing with me," Cash heartfully expresses.

"We are thankful as well," Antonio voices.

"We are, Cash. Thank you." Francesca stands next to Antonio and reaches to shake Cash's hand, but when he reaches for her hand, Francesca steps toward him and hugs him instead. She sends a healing energy through her hug. She does not understand it. She cannot explain it, but she knows she has that ability.

Cash softly voices, "You are a remarkable woman. Thank you. I cannot explain the healing I feel I have received."

Francesca barely smiles. She nods to acknowledge his words while she steps back to Antonio's side.

Cash also nods. "I admire you both. You have a solid family, Tony. I am honored to be here."

"Cash, it is our pleasure. Please, come and stay with us again. Do not wait so many years." Antonio reaches to exchange a hug with Cash.

"Good doing business with you, Mr. Cassidy." Marco extends his hand for a firm handshake with Cash.

"You are quite the business man." Cash grins.

"Keep talking to the priest...I like that story!" Gino smiles.

"I will do just that, Gino!" Cash winks at Gino.

Antonio escorts Cash to the stables and helps Cash get the horses ready for the journey.

Chapter 95

A ROYAL BABY

"Theo...I think it is time...." Eloise calmly speaks to her husband.

"I will have Andrew get the doctor. I do not want to leave your side," Theodore states. Then he leaves their room momentarily to search for Andrew.

Theodore quickly walks down the hall and slightly elevates his voice, "Andrew...."

Andrew hears the king and, without wasting any time, rushes to him. "How can I help you?"

"Get the doctor, please. Eloise is about to deliver our baby," Theo anxiously imparts.

Andrew slightly bows and instantly takes off down the hall. He alerts the guards on his way out. Fortunately, there is a saddled horse that Andrew gets on and rides away.

"Eloise...you are doing excellent! Ah...welcome little one," Doctor Gerard speaks to the baby. He then shifts his focus to the king and queen. "You have a healthy boy."

"We have a son!" Theodore proudly and loudly articulates. Theo leans over to kiss Eloise.

The nurse cleans up the bundle of joy, wraps a blanket around him, and carries him over for his mother to hold.

"Look at you, precious one. I have waited many years for you." Eloise shines while a few tears trickle from her eyes.

Theodore is extremely proud and exceedingly happy. He bends over to kiss his son and his wife. "Thank you, for giving me this beautiful family."

Doctor Gerard cherishes witnessing this long-awaited event. "Do you have a name for him?"

"We do. His name will be Rupert...which means bright fame or shining with glory. And his middle name will be Franklin after my father. Franklin is also my middle name," Theodore declares. "Rupert Franklin Chamberlain. You will one day be king of this magnificent kingdom," Theodore speaks lovingly, in a quiet voice.

Theodore gazes into the eyes of Eloise, "I love you."

"And I you...." the beauty of Eloise radiates the room.

······◌ℓ◌······

Antonio and Francesca, along with their sons, are eating lunch in town with Sophia and Leonardo.

Antonio notices an expression cast across the face of Francesca. He inquisitively questions her. "Are you alright?"

Francesca nods. "Yes...I believe so."

"What is happening?" Antonio inquires.

"What do you mean what is happening?" Leo questions.

"Nothing...I mean...your daughter just seems to know things...." Antonio answers.

"Now you are talking out of my frequency. Senses and feelings...ba...." Leo chews another bite.

Sophia wants to roll her eyes, but chooses to refrain so no disrespect is displayed in front of their family.

"What is it honey?" Sophia quietly questions.

Francesca bursts out a huge smile. "I think Eloise and Theodore just delivered their baby.

"That is wonderful news!" Sophia exclaims.

"I can't be sure...that is just a feeling I have...." Francesca tries to level the energy.

"Trust me...most things you feel or sense...are spot on," Antonio confirms.

"After lunch let's go over and see," Sophia suggests.

"So, I am fourteen and almost three quarters of a year older than their baby," Marco calculates.

Francesca smiles. "I guess you are, if they did have a baby."

Chapter 96

VISITING THE ROYALS

Sophia, Francesca, Antonio, Marco, and Gino are approaching the stairs to the castle, even Leo is accompanying them.

Andrew escorts out Doctor Gerard and his nurse when the group arrives.

"Greetings!" Doctor Gerard voices.

"Hello," Each person of the family speaks.

"She may have visitors. Andrew will show you in," Doctor Gerard communicates.

Andrew leads Sophia, Leonardo, and the Mancini family in.

"We have visitors," Andrew announces.

Theodore and Eloise are pleasantly surprised seeing the faces of their forever friends.

"Come in, come in," Theodore invites.

The ladies, followed by the boys, enter the room. Antonio and Leonardo then step into their large royal bedroom.

"Wow! What a wonderful surprise!" Eloise delights.

Francesca and Sophia take a turn in giving Eloise a hug.

"Gosh, your baby is so tiny," Gino comments.

Eloise laughs. "Honey, he is seven pounds."

Gino smiles and holds the baby's hand.

"We named him Rupert Franklin Chamberlain," Theodore announces.

Marco makes a face of eww while thinking, *worst name ever....*

"I gotta ask...." Leonardo begins, "Where did you come up with that name?"

Marco tries to hide his grin while he thinks to himself, *cool, Grandfather thinks it is an awful name as well.*

"Well...Rupert means bright fame or shining with glory. Franklin is my father's name and my middle name...." Theodore explains, though he feels he owes no one any explanation, however, he is proud of the name they chose.

"I see...it is a name for a prince," Leonardo acknowledges while he nods.

"It sounds like it!" Gino smiles at Rupert still holding his hand. "Hey little guy...I am Gino and this is my older brother, Marco."

The adults experience great joy that Eloise and Theodore, after many years, finally gave birth to a beautiful healthy little boy.

Each person in the room takes turns standing next to Eloise and Prince Rupert.

"So beautiful...." Francesca quietly voices. "I am so happy for you my dear friend." She leans over to give Eloise another hug.

"Thank you. Wait...how did you know we delivered him today?" Eloise questions.

Theodore and Eloise wait for a reply. The other adults glance at each other. After what seems like five minutes, but in reality, is only seconds, out of nowhere, Marco declares, "We just knew it!"

Everyone begins to laugh. "Very good. I am glad you all came to welcome our son into the world. Thank you," Theodore heartfully expresses.

"Yes. Thank you so much. Please let my cousin and Katherine know," Eloise requests.

"Absolutely," Antonio assures.

Francesca and Sophia both give Elosie a hug before they depart.

"Bye, little guy." Marco gently touches the baby.

"Bye, Prince Rupert." Gino smiles.

"Fine looking boy you have there. Congratulations," Leonardo states.

Antonio and Theodore exchange a hug.

Theodore and Eloise rest with joy, holding their newborn.

Chapter 97

NIGHTMARE

Stars decorate the night sky surrounding the waning crescent moon. The residents of the picturesque Chamberlain Kingdom that is nestled in a valley of rich land which hosts farming and ranching, between the fourteen-thousand-feet tall peaks of the Chianne Mountain Range, and the twelve to thirteen-thousand-feet peaks of the Chamberlain Mountain range, sleep deeply, knowing their king and queen now have a prince to carry on their legacy one day.

⬦⬥⬦

Francesca begins tossing about. Sweat forms on her forehead. She turns over again. She feels her body temperature rising, though she is not quite fully awake. After a split second, she sits up and blares out a terrifying scream, which results in Antonio abruptly awakening.

Antonio sits up and places his arm around Francesca. "Are you alright?"

Francesca anxiously searches their master bedroom with her eyes. She then fixes her eyes on Antonio. "Oh, my…I have never experienced such a nightmare."

"What was it?" Antonio asks, while he gently rubs up and down her back in an attempt to calm her.

"I don't know…it was like a cloud formation of the scariest looking evil beings hovering over someone. I sense it is someone I know…I just cannot see the rest of the nightmare," Francesca details.

"Are you alright, Mother?" Marco and Gino bolt into their parents' bedroom.

"We could hear your scream upstairs," Gino informs.

Francesca extends her arms to her sons. Marco and Gino both step close to the bed to exchange a hug with their mother.

"I am well, indeed. I am sorry I awakened you," Francesca quietly voices.

"Okay, we just want to make sure you guys are safe," Marco communicates.

"Try to get some sleep," Gino so maturely offers.

Francesca and Antonio both lovingly smile at their sons.

"I will. Thank you. See you in the morning," Francesca conveys.

The boys leave their parents' bedroom and return to their rooms upstairs. Francesca and Antonio lie back on their pillows.

"Are you feeling better?" Antonio inquires.

"I don't know. It was such a disturbing nightmare," Francesca divulges.

"It must have been…you are sweating," Antonio notices.

"Yes. It was alarming," Francesca voices.

"Try to get some sleep…and know it is only a nightmare," Antonio reassures.

Francesca barely nods, all the while, knowing she is aware she has an inner perception about things. The visions in her nightmare trouble her. Concern for what possibly lies ahead fills her with great anxiety.

Chapter 98

ASSIGNMENTS

The High Priest and High Priestess stand tall at the end of the conference table. They observe each Chiawauka enter the room and take a seat.

They notice one seat is empty. Everyone in the room hears the door, but sees no one enter. High Priest Akshai walks along one side of the table to the door and opens it. Pixel stumbles into the room.

"Oh, gosh. Pardon me. That door...I could not remember if I push it in or pull it out...it just did not work either way. Boy, oh boy...man...I see I am the last one here," Pixel speaks as though she is discombobulated.

"Please take a seat." High Priest Akshai instructs while he returns to the head of the table next to High Priestess Ammerie.

"Welcome. You are the ones we have selected from our list of applicants for upcoming missions. Does anyone have any questions before we begin?" High Priest Akshai addresses.

Every Chiawauka is quiet, that is, except Pixel. She is rolling around in her chair, attempting to position it just right.

"Is there a problem with your chair, dear?" High Priestess Ammerie questions.

All the Chiawaukas turn their heads, staring at Pixel, waiting for an answer. But she is fixated with her chair.

"Pixel, is there a problem with your chair?" High Priestess Ammerie again addresses the Chiawauka.

Pixel raises her head, and realizes the entire assembly is staring at her. "Um…no…I just couldn't get it to roll…you know what…never mind. I am good." Pixel tosses her hand and nods.

The Chiawaukas shift their attention back to the high priest and priestess.

"Alo and Tayen…we are assigning the two of you to the planet Tertammi. The leader Teryk and his wife, Malini (Ma-lee-knee), are looking forward to working with you," High Priest Akshai voices.

"Next up…Stellar and Luna…we have chosen the two of you to serve as a team on the planet Acheeas. You will work with Briele, Reigna of Acheeas," High Priestess Ammerie speaks with her soothing, pleasant voice.

The Chiawaukas are listening intently as the high priests scroll down their list.

Celestial contains her heavy heart. She feels disappointment that she and Blazer are not chosen for Acheeas.

"Ollie and Omar…we are pairing the two of you together. You have been paired together in the past and we believe you complement each other. For now, you will be going to the planet Kareenia. Kehlani (Ka-law-knee) is eager to have you," High Priest Akshai assigns.

"Those remaining, will be sent to what we have titled…Mission on Soleil. This mission is of the utmost importance," High Priestess Ammerie outlines.

"As you know…Chiawaukas imprisoned the evil Cryptolores deep in a cavern on the planet of Soleil. In addition, two unrelated human females were infused with Chiawauka DNA. We will send you to the coordinates the Ancient Writings speak of. You are to locate the two families. There will be a marriage between the two families and then you will ordain them. Also, we want to make sure the Cryptolores remain imprisoned. For this assignment...." High Priest Akshai pauses and glances over to High Priestess Ammerie.

"Razel and Zeek, you will be a team. Piper, we are pairing you with Pixel...."

You can almost hear Pixel begin to comment, but she notices Piper slightly shaking his head and his lips are tight.

High Priestess Ammerie continues, "Celestial and Blazer, we are keeping you as a team assigned specifically to the restoration of life. Lastly, Victor and Viana...we have selected you to be paired as a team. You will be a reconnaissance team. We will keep you posted as to when you will leave for the planet," High Priestess Ammerie concludes.

"For those of you assigned to other planets besides Soleil, you will leave in three days. For those of you assigned to Soleil...it will be some time before we send Victor and Viana, so the rest of you will remain on standby...here on planet Chiaras (Key-R-us). Are there any questions?" High Priest Akshai directs.

None of the Chiawaukas express any indication they have inquiries.

"You are all dismissed, except Celestial and Blazer. Please stay behind. Also, Stellar and Luna...please remain," High Priestess Ammerie instructs.

The Chiawaukas quietly leave the conference room.

Stellar, Luna, Celestial, and Blazer remain at the request of the High Priestess.

"As you may know, the current king and queen on Soleil have delivered their first child. Now...since Marcella and Franklin were very adamant that they want to know when their son has a baby, Celestial and Blazer, we want Stellar and Luna to accompany you to Acheeas. You will introduce them to the humans. Brief them during your voyage. Teach them how you utilize the arc that enable the humans to view their families on Soleil. Luna and Stellar, we paired you to this assignment because you both have great empathy and a sense of purpose…and diligence, which is everything these families are all about. We are not suggesting Blazer and Celestial do not have those gifts, but we have chosen them to be the guardians of life," High Priest Akshai summarizes. "Are there any questions?"

The Chiawaukas understand their mission and ask no questions.

"Alright, leave at once to share the news of their grandbaby," High Priestess Ammerie directs.

The four Chiawaukas each say thank you and depart the conference room.

Chapter 99

RETURN TO ACHEEAS

Celestial and Blazer brief Luna and Stellar on the way to Acheeas.

As they enter the atmosphere and drop into a lower altitude, Stellar and Luna notice the beauty of the planet.

"This is very much like Soleil. I can see why you relocated the humans here," Stellar comments.

"It is just breathtaking," Luna reflects.

"It is the reason…the landscape and atmosphere," Celestial confirms.

They land, exit the sphere, and trek up to the ranch.

Tabitha sees them and runs toward them.

"Oh, my…how you have grown. You must be in your twenties!" Celestial expresses.

"This is Tabitha. Tabitha, this is Luna and Stellar," Blazer introduces.

"It is very nice to meet you, Tabitha." Stellar smiles.

"Hello, it is nice to meet you." Luna extends her hand to shake the hand of Tabitha.

"This is incredible! Getting to meet two more Supreme Guardian Beings!" Tabitha exclaims. "Come on...let's go up to the house." Tabitha motions.

The Chiawaukas follow Tabitha.

"I am surprised you are still living at home...." Blazer comments.

"Yes...I am engaged now...we are building that home over there." Tabitha points. "We will live on this property once our home is completed and we are married."

"Congratulations, honey," Celestial voices.

Tabitha opens the door of the cabin to allow the Chiawaukas to enter. Sarita stands in surprise. Marcella walks out from their side of the home. Franklin along with Don, enter in the front door shortly after.

"What a lovely pleasure it is to have you visit us again," Marcella addresses.

"Thank you. We have some news...this is Stellar and Luna...they are the Chiawaukas now assigned to this planet, and if you need them for anything at all, just call their name. They will hear you," Celestial details.

"Wow...stationed to the planet?" Franklin questions.

"Yes. Every so often our leaders assign us to different planets for a time," Stellar informs.

The adults nod with understanding.

"Welcome to our home," Sarita voices.

"Marcella, you asked us years ago to please return when your son and Eloise gave birth...." Blazer begins.

Franklin places his arm around Marcella. Marcella places her hand over her heart.

"We can show you," Celestial vocalizes.

"Oh, my yes...please...." Marcella beams, then she glances to Sarita." I'm sorry...do you mind?"

"No, not at all. I would love to see your grandbaby," Sarita sweetly conveys.

The humans sit on the large sofa. The Chiawaukas stand behind them. Celestial waves her arm in an arc and within seconds, it is as if they are in the room on the planet Soleil.

"Oh...she is giving birth...." Marcella voices.

"We have a grandson!" Franklin exclaims.

Sarita and Don exchange loving eye contact.

"Aunt Tabitha. That has a nice ring to it," Tabitha declares.

"Wait...." Marcella sees Francesca, Antonio, Leonardo, Sophia, and two boys enter the room. Marcella quickly glances at Sarita. "May we continue to see this?"

"Yes. Certainly," Sarita assures.

Sarita and Don see they have two teenage grandsons.

Marcella reaches to hold the hand of Sarita.

"Will you look at that...Antonio has two sons of his own. Thank you for sharing this with us," Sarita comments.

"You are welcome. We were honoring your wishes by not showing you their lives," Celestial conveys.

"I appreciate that." Sarita nods.

Celestial and Blazer forward to other scenes.

"Look...Rupert is such a doll...the older boys seem to take care of him at gatherings," Sarita voices.

"I just love how our sons, Sully, and their wives are so close. And blessings to Sophia and Leonardo for being steadfast pillars for them," Marcella expresses.

"Thank you, Blazer and Celestial." Franklin nods at the Chiawaukas.

"Our pleasure. Now...because of our new assignments, Blazer and I will not be returning for some time, however, Stellar and Luna are also able to operate the arc whenever you want. If you need *ANTHING*, just call out their name," Celestial outlines.

"We will keep that in mind," Franklin acknowledges as he steps to the front door to open it, as he sees them out. "It was nice to meet you both."

"The pleasure is ours," Stellar communicates.

"Yes, just say one of our names aloud, as though you need us, and are not talking about us…." Luna laughs at her words.

"We will do that." Marcella smiles.

"Be safe out there." Sarita waves.

"I wonder if I talk to Rupert…if he will hear me." Tabitha ponders.

"They say spirits and souls can hear or feel the energy of another," Blazer maintains.

The Chiawaukas trek across the yard and down the slope.

"I guess this is it. You two will be heading to meet with Briele, and we will be returning to Chiaras for now," Celestial imparts, and reaches out to hug her Chiawauka sisters.

"You two be safe," Stellar directs.

"We will. You two as well." Blazer extends his hand to shake the hands of Stellar and Luna.

Celestial and Blazer enter the travel sphere and depart planet Acheeas. Stellar and Luna touch their emblem and vanish. They reappear at the headquarters of Acheeas to meet with Briele for further instructions.

······ঙ৯୦······

The Chamberlains and Mancinis retire to their bedrooms when the sun sets.

"Franklin?" Marcella quietly voices while she is sitting on the bed.

"Yes?" Franklin gives Marcella his complete attention.

"I finally understand why Sarita has not wanted to see any more updates the Chiawaukas offer to us." Marcella pauses peering into the eyes of her husband. "The pain of not being there is just too great. I may request another viewing…but I am leaning toward fewer and further apart," Marcella heartfully conveys.

"I think that is wise," Franklin submits.

"You will be okay with that?" Marcella questions.

"I am alright with whatever brings our lives peace here. Because here is where we are," Franklin asseverates and reaches to squeeze a hand of Marcella.

They lie back onto their pillows with their hands folded across their chests, navigating their life in their thoughts, as they drift to sleep.

Chapter 100

GAME NIGHT

Francesca, Katherine, and Eloise finish clearing the table. Marco, Gino, and Luke are playing with Rupert in the family room. Ben, who will be eighteen in four months, is sitting with the men.

"I think he is almost ready to crawl!" Marco loudly exclaims.

The ladies in the kitchen exchange smiles.

"He is the best baby. He does not fuss. He is so happy. He loves snuggles...I do not know why it took so many years before we had a child, but I can say I am so excited to finally be a mother!" Eloise shares.

"He is adorable," Katherine adds.

"He is just precious. I love holding him," Francesca expresses.

"Gino, you're what...thirteen now? And Marco...just turned fifteen?" King Theodore asks.

Gino nods. "Yep."

"My nephew, Ben will be eighteen and Luke will be thirteen in four months. And our bundle of boy will be one...all in Septembria. I was hoping our children would be closer in age with all of you, but Rupert will have plenty of older brothers to teach him," Theodore remarks.

"Yep." Gino nods.

"Isn't Gwendolyn the most precious little girl you have seen?" Katherine comments.

"She is! Rupert and Gwendolyn are about six months apart. I am glad the Gerards finally had a baby as well. Doc has been wanting one of his own," Eloise shares.

"Yes! What a glorious kingdom we live in," Francesca voices.

Chapter 101

COMMISSION

"I am glad you could join me fishing today," King Theodore conveys to Antonio.

"I am as well. It is nice fishing in the Chamberlain River sometimes." Antonio laughs a little.

"I have something that is important to me, but because I value you, I want to run it by you," Theo indicates.

"Sure. What's up?" Antonio asks.

"I have an aging staff. My chef is retiring. So, I hired a young chef, named Pierre. He will be moving to our kingdom within a month. My four main guards have expressed they are done...so before they retire, I plan to request Tim and Richard to return to our kingdom and serve here. Charles, our equerry (stable manager), is retiring. I found a great man for his replacement. His name is John." Theodore then glances over at Antonio. "And I would like to request Steve and David to also be commissioned here."

"I think that sounds great. Bring everyone back to their home kingdom, plus I think that was their goal...to serve here," Antonio gives his input.

"Will Francesca be alright with Steve and David returning to Chamberlain?" Theodore glances at Antonio.

"Yes. Of course. Why wouldn't she be?" Antonio queries.

"Well, I know they were very close friends when they were kids...like best friends, and observing them, I felt she either had a slight crush on them or maybe they her...I don't know. I just want to make sure you two will be alright with me requesting they be commissioned to this kingdom," Theodore elaborates.

"I see. Sure...they were very close childhood and teenage friends and that will always be a part of who they are. I am sure the notion of one of them marrying Francesca crossed everyone's minds...but the timing was not in sync at that time. They met their women...she met me...and life grows on." Antonio smiles and reaches to pat Theodore on the back. Antonio's deep voice resonates when he adds, "I appreciate your concern. Trust me when I say...all is well. We look forward to meeting their women and welcome them into our lives...games nights...dinner parties...Francesca will be thrilled they will be serving in their home where they have aspired to serve. She will be happy for them and everyone."

Theo smiles. "Alright then. I thought you and Francesca would feel that way."

Antonio grins, "You already submitted their transfer to this kingdom, didn't you?"

Theo slightly bows his head, grins, then looks directly at Antonio. "I did."

"Very good. Well, thank you, still, for running it by me," Antonio expresses.

"I love you like my brother," Theodore admits.

Antonio nods. "Same goes for me."

The two men refocus their attention to fishing.

"Look at all the fish Pop caught!" Gino exclaims.

"Do you want to cook those tonight?" Francesca asks.

"If you don't mind, yes, let's do," Antonio replies.

"Very good. Let's grill," Francesca suggests.

......⚬⟨⟩⚬......

"Did you and Pop always know how to cook? You guys are really good at it," Marco comments on the way to their bedrooms.

"Yeah...I feel so fortunate...and so does my stomach!" Gino giggles while he rubs his belly.

"Alright, my sons...." Francesca steps into Marco's room first and waits for Marco to return from the bathroom.

Then Gino goes to the bathroom while Francesca tells Marco goodnight.

"I want to be just like you and Pop in every way." Marco looks up at his mother while his head is resting on his pillow.

"That is very sweet of you. God bless you. Sleep peaceful." Francesca kisses Marco on his forehead then steps out of his room.

"Goodnight, Mother," Marco voices.

Francesca then walks to Gino's room. Gino is lying in his bed.

"Goodnight, sweetheart. God bless you. Sleep peaceful." Francesca leans over and kisses Gino on the forehead.

"I love you. I love our family." Gino smiles and closes his eyes.

Francesca turns and gazes upon her youngest. "I love you too, sweetie."

As she walks down the hall to return to the stairs she pops her head in Marco's room. "I love you."

"I love you, Mom," Marco whispers.

......⚬⟨⟩⚬......

Francesca swiftly descends the stairs and walks through the family room to the doors of the back deck. She opens the door and slides outside.

"I have a seat with your name on it." Antonio looks over at Francesca.

Francesca smiles from ear to ear. "Your words are music to my soul."

"Well, I have some news for you, that I found out, while I was fishing with Theo," Antonio begins.

"Wait...let me guess...." Francesca requests.

"Alright...." Antonio nods and slightly tilts his head.

"Theo wants the Chamberlain boys back together so he is requesting Tim, Richard, David, and Steve to be assigned to our kingdom...." Francesca grins from ear to hear.

"How did you know that?" Antonio articulates each word distinctly. "I know...because you know things...you sense things."

Francesca smiles. "Well...that too...." She giggles. "I did sense it coming, but Eloise mentioned it while I was visiting her and Rupert. He is just the sweetest baby. Anyway, she conveyed to me that Theo is concerned so he wanted to discuss it with you. She said she assured him all will be well."

Antonio grins. "Yep. He is just protecting those he loves...and he loves them as well."

"Oh, of course. I think it will be wonderful to finally meet their ladies! I hope they will want to participate in game nights and dinners," Francesca discloses.

"That is precisely what I expressed to Theodore." Antonio leans his head into Francesca's head as they view out across their property from their deck. "I like how we think."

"Me too!" Francesca grins.

After sitting next to each other with their heads resting upon the other, enjoying the tranquil surroundings, Francesca abruptly sits upright.

"Wait! I was just thinking, I don't even know how to behave. I know me, and I will be all verbally affectionate...." Francesca slightly rolls her eyes.

"Calm down. All will be well." Antonio places his large, strong hand on her back and rubs it. "If there is one thing I know about you, babe, you try to behave in a manner that makes every person feel special and important," Antonio comforts.

"Well, everyone *IS* important. We are all special in the sight of our Creator," Francesca expresses.

"Yes. Exactly. You be you. If that makes people think you want them, so be it. Our Father knows your heart. If it makes people wonder anything other than you truly want to enjoy them as brothers and sisters, that's on them. Do not change how you behave due to someone else. Be true to what you believe. Be you," Antonio heartfully encourages.

Francesca sits back and rests in the embrace of Antonio's arms and thinks to herself. *I know he is correct. I just so much hope we can all hang out! It has been so, so many years now.*

Chapter 102

NEW STAFF

Queen Eloise and King Theodore host a celebration for the chef and guards that are retiring and to welcome the arrival of the new ones. The castle grounds are full of people from the kingdom to celebrate. After the king and queen make their announcements, they give prestigious recognition for the members of the staff that are retiring, and formal introductions of the new staff. Everyone attending begins to mingle with each other. They each seize an opportunity to welcome the new castle personnel, along with giving their sentiments to those retiring.

Antonio and Francesca stroll around holding hands. Marco and Gino remain by their sides.

Antonio whispers and points, "There they are."

"Boys, I want to introduce you to my very best friends when I was your age," Francesca expresses.

"Wait…they're guys…you had *boy* friends." Marco laughs.

Gino giggles as well. "I get it! Friends that are boys!"

The Mancini boys are certainly being silly.

"Well, yes. We met when we were five and just became the best of friends. Of course, Queen Eloise and Katherine were my best friends as well," Francesca discloses.

When they reach David and Steve, Antonio immediately extends his hand to firmly shake each of their hands. "Welcome home."

"Thank you for that," Steve conveys. "This is Veronica."

"Hi, I am Francesca, this is my husband, Antonio, and our sons, Marco and Gino." Francesca offers her hand to Veronica to exchange a greeting.

Veronica takes the hand of Francesca and conveys, "It is very nice to finally meet you. I have heard a lot about you." Veronica smiles.

Francesca smiles. "It is my pleasure to finally meet you."

The attention then shifts to David and Leah.

"I hope your journey here was pleasant," Antonio offers.

"It was. Great to see you, Antonio," David conveys. "This is my wife, Leah."

Antonio extends his hand to shake the hand of Leah. "It is nice to meet you, Leah. Welcome to Chamberlain Kingdom."

"Thank you," Leah conveys.

"Hi. It is so nice to meet you, Leah. We hope the four of you will join us for a cookout next weekend at our ranch," Francesca welcomes.

"I don't know. I most likely will not be here," Leah mentions.

"Oh. Well, I am sorry to hear that. Maybe when you return," Francesca cordially extends the invitation.

Leah shrugs. "I don't know. I may not come here very often. My home and my family are in Zaltana."

"Oh, yes...." Francesca politely acknowledges while she is thinking, *David is your family...your husband...you should remain here with him....* "Well, know that you are always welcome. Antonio and I enjoy bringing people together for meals and game nights."

"I'll keep that in mind. Thank you." Leah smiles and nods.

"Wow! Steve and David...you two look the same!" Francesca greets her forever friends.

Steve steps forward and gives Francesca a big hug. "Good to see you."

"Oh...it is so good to see you!" expresses Francesca.

They release their hug and take a step back. Steve and Francesca exchange eye contact and smile at each other.

"Look at you, all grown-up," Steve voices and smiles.

Francesca smiles from ear to ear. "And look at you...all muscular and grown-up."

Steve and Francie both grin and giggle a bit.

"Well, the muscles came with my job and age." Steve grins.

"I imagine. You wear it well," Francesca compliments.

Steve remains with a smile on his face and he nods. "Thank you."

David steps forward and reaches to give Francesca a big hug, but switches to a light limp hug, not a David hug at all. "Good to see you, Francie." Then David shifts his eyes to Marco and Gino. "Nice to meet you."

"Nice to meet you," Marco and Gino both vocalize.

"It is great to have you both back!" Antonio voices.

"It's good to be back!" Steve asserts.

"Yeah, it is," David speaks quietly.

Francesca takes the hand of Veronica in hers. "It is just so good to have you all in our kingdom! Steve and David...again...welcome home!"

"It is good to be here." Veronica smiles. "We would love to come out sometime."

"Perfect." Francesca smiles. "Next weekend!"

"We'll be there!" Veronica confirms.

"We'll be on our way. Nice to meet you ladies. Steve and David, again, welcome home." Antonio tips his hat.

Francesca and Antonio, along with their sons, turn and stroll to mingle with others, and welcome Tim and Richard home as well.

Leah and Veronica dismiss themselves from their men and wander across the castle grounds to find a restroom.

David scans the property. He locates Antonio with Sully and Theodore. He also spies Katherine, Eloise, and Francesca.

"Here. Hold my drink." David hands Steve his drink then hurries to where the men are.

Steve raises an eyebrow and wonders what his best friend is up to now.

······ઉૐ······

"Oh, David. I am so glad you and Steve accepted serving our kingdom," King Theodore reiterates.

"Theo, it is our pleasure," David assures.

"A lot has changed since you two have been gone…yet some things remain the same." Sully shakes David's hand firmly as he welcomes him.

"Yes. Thank you for that. Antonio, can I speak to you for a moment?" David questions.

Antonio and David step away from the others.

"Do you mind if I speak to Francesca for a minute…even ask her to dance?" David inquires.

"I don't mind at all, and I think Francesca will like that," Antonio assures. "Thank you for asking."

"Of course." David pats Antonio on his back then quickly makes his way to Eloise, Katherine, and Francesca.

"Oh, hello, David. It is so good to have you home," Katherine imparts.

Eloise smiles. "You have no idea how happy you have made Theo."

"I am glad. Steve and I have waited a long time to return here," David expresses.

"Francesca, would you like to dance?" David gazes into the eyes of Francesca and outstretches his hand to hers.

A curious expression sweeps across the face of Francesca. She glances over to Antonio. She sees him nod and wink at her along with a motion of his hand to go ahead. Francesca then glances back and looks into David's eyes. "I like that idea." Francesca slightly bows.

David takes her hand and leads her away from the others in a dance. Their faces are about six inches apart during this dance. "First of all, you are gorgeous. I thought you were beautiful eighteen years ago when you were fifteen…well, about to turn sixteen…but…WoW!"

Francesca blushes and slightly smiles.

"Second, I want to apologize. I am so sorry I left you behind and was not here to protect you and Aspen. It makes me sick. I can only imagine the pain you experienced. I ask if you will forgive me, Francesca," David bears his heart.

"Well…first…thank you for your compliment. Second…David, you always had your heart set on serving in the Guard of the Kingdoms. The first year…if I remember correctly, the leadership prohibits any of the guards to even have girlfriends. I encouraged you both to go…I knew it was your dream career. I was in no way going to hold you back," Francesca speaks from her heart.

"I just feel so bad you were attacked…and Aspen was shot. I feel…no…I wanted to protect you…always…ever since we met," David reveals.

Francesca sweetly smiles while she peers into the eyes of David. "I know. You are my forever protecter. All is well, we are forever friends. There is nothing to forgive. You are an upright, noble man who has a beautiful wife. I pray God will bless you in all you do."

David's heart is on his sleeve. He gently pulls Francesca close to him and gives her a forever friend embracing hug. "I will always love you, Francie," David whispers into her ear.

Francesca's armor softens and she whispers, "I love you, my forever friend…I always will."

They continue their hug swaying to the music then step back from each other. "And I look forward to attending your dinner groups and game nights," David states.

Francesca smiles. "Antonio and I are very thankful you and Steve and your ladies are back home."

"We are too." David smiles and releases Francesca from his arms. "You know it was never about...."

Before David completes his sentence, Francesca skips to the end of it for him, "I know. It was a timing issue. That is all."

"Yes." David nods.

......⁕......

"You do not mind them dancing together?" Sully asks while the three men observe.

"Nope," Antonio replies and slightly shakes his head. "I know David and Francesca both to be upright and honorable. I imagine this dance is exactly what they both need. Whatever he has to say to her...well...it's long overdue...like unfinished business."

"Tony, you are wise beyond your years," Theodore acknowledges.

Antonio slightly laughs, "I think she is rubbing off on me. She will most likely never admit to me this is what she needed. She may not even recognize it...but I know they had unfinished business and it takes nothing away from her love and devotion to me."

"You, my friend...are a good man." Sully pats Antonio on the back.

Antonio nods. He notices Francesca approaching. He opens his arms. She walks right into his arms and kisses him.

"Thank you for that," Francesca whispers into his ear. "It is like I have received a healing I was unaware I needed. So weird...thank you." She snuggles into the arms of Antonio and he embraces her with a loving hug.

"Mm…wanna go home?" Antonio inhales the faint fragrance in her hair, and asks.

"I do," Francesca answers.

He releases their embrace. "Guys, we are going to get the kids and go. See you tomorrow at church, and then our house for dinner."

"We will be there," Theo confirms.

"You know we wouldn't miss it!" Sully motions with his hand like he is a captain making a command.

Antonio and Francesca find their sons hanging out with Ben and Luke, along with Camille, and other teens around their age.

"Time to go," Antonio directs.

........⁂........

David arrives back at Steve's side. Steve hands David his drink.

"What are you doing?" Steve questions.

"Look…I just needed…I wanted to tell her I am sorry. I asked permission from Antonio if I could speak with her and dance. He gave me his blessing," David details.

"It has been what…eighteen or nineteen years since we have seen her? A lot of time has passed," Steve expresses concern.

"I know. But it is never too late to apologize…and I want her to know I am sorry I was not there to protect her," David communicates.

"Well…I am sorry as well…but she knows that," Steve maintains.

"I know she knows…I guess I had to do it for my spirit as well," David divulges.

Steve nods. "I get it. I understand. Was she receptive?"

"Yeah. She will always love you and I. We are her forever best friends." David smiles and moves his drink in a motion as if he is saying cheers.

Veronica and Leah return.

"Sorry we were gone so long. The bathrooms were quite a journey across the property over by the stables, then we got to admiring their beautiful Wintuckets." Veronica details.

"No worries," Steve answers.

"I may not go back home just yet...." Leah voices.

David smiles. "I am glad. I hope you will give Chamberlain Kingdom a chance."

"I may stay for a week, but I did promise my family I will be back soon. I will see," Leah remarks.

"I know. We will try to make your stay memorable." David raises his drink as if making a toast.

Antonio steps from their master bathroom into the bedroom with only his night shorts on. "The boys sure fell asleep quickly."

"They did. Don't you look inviting...." Francesca playfully admires the physique of her husband.

Antonio crawls up onto their tall bed and climbs over Francesca.

She lays her head back on the pillow. "You are just the best." Francesca smiles.

"I am glad you think so. You look pretty inviting yourself." Antonio leans down and kisses her.

She reaches her arms up around him and he lowers his body onto hers.

Chapter 103

ANOTHER RESIGNATION

"I think I say this every meal…you guys outdo yourselves…each meal is so delicious…." Sully leans back in the chair and rubs his stomach.

Francesca giggles. "I am glad you like our cooking."

"Yeah…Katherine and I joke about moving in with you guys when all our kids are grown." Sully laughs.

Sully's laughter is infectious. Katherine, Antonio, Theodore, Eloise, Leonardo, Sophia, and Francesca are all giggling or laughing.

"Aw…look…those older boys take such good care of Rupert." Eloise notices when she glances into the family room.

"Oh," Theodore speaks solemnly." We have another person who is retiring early."

"Oh? Who is that?" Leo questions.

"Sheriff Wesley Winslow. He informed me after the festivities he plans to retire. He mentioned he may relocate and continue to do the same work. He is just not sure. He wants to live closer to his daughter who lives in the Martinelli Kingdom," King Theo details.

"Aw, that's sweet. I can certainly understand that," Sophia voices.

"Yes." Leo nods.

Everyone gathered expresses the same sentiments.

"Have you thought who will be his replacement?" Antonio questions.

"I have. I hired Sheriff Ryan Patrick. He and his lovely wife, Darlene, will be moving to our kingdom in the next week," King Theo outlines.

"Splendid," Francesca voices. "I know we will love them."

"It'll be great to welcome another couple to our kingdom," Katherine voices.

"I have heard great things about that sheriff," Sully notes.

"Yes. That is why I hired him. I hate to see Wesley go...he has been an outstanding sheriff, but I am thankful we found another great one so quickly," Theo contends.

Chapter 104

RECONNAISSANCE MISSION

High Priest Akshai and High Priestess Ammerie stand next to each other studying The Ancient Writings.

"I believe it is time to send Victor and Viana to the planet Soleil," Akshai contemplates.

Ammerie raises her head and lifts her finger from thoroughly scrolling. "I agree. The time is now, from what I discern from these worn pages."

······⁙⁙⁙······

In the month of Mayella on the planet Soleil, Victor, and Viana land at the coordinates they are given. Sporting their tall bodies, they search the area.

"Maybe we should shrink ourselves to our smaller version. I think we will be less conspicuous," Viana suggests.

"We can, though the humans will not be able to detect us either way. But sure…we can be whatever size we like." Victor nods.

"We need to find a place to dwell while we are on this planet. I think we should fly around the area and scout for a location," Viana puts forth another idea.

"Yes. Let's do that. It will allow us to see the geography of the area." Victor likes Viana's recommendation.

The two Chiawaukas set off in flight to explore the area.

"I see why Celestial visits this planet for getaways," Viana mentions. "This is absolutely gorgeous. The breathtaking mountains, the valley that hosts herds and flocks of animals. Oh, and these rivers!"

"Yes, very impressive. The landscape is designed with the utmost creative artistry," Victor commends.

"Simply spectacular! Over there...I see a ranch." Viana points.

They lower their altitude to get a better look.

"That looks like a tree house," Victor notices.

"Quite an elaborate one at that," Viana observes.

"Aw, look at the banner hanging from the back deck!" Viana points. "It reads, *Happy 16th Birthday, Marco*." Viana notices.

"Let's land and investigate," Victor directs.

The Chiawaukas land on the well-built treehouse.

"I don't think it is being used...." Viana discerns.

"I agree. Look this way." Victor points. "If this was built for those two boys...I doubt they use it much anymore," Victor assumes while he and Viana watch two teenage boys ride horses across the field.

"I bet one of them is the boy that turned sixteen. Isn't that just a lovely sight to behold. I love humans!" Viana speaks from her heart. "Looks like the festivities are over."

Victor nods. "Let's continue to explore the area before nightfall."

"Alright," Viana agrees.

The two take off in flight again and fly over the area they are assigned to.

"Oh, my! That castle!" Viana voices. "Well…it looks like a palace as well…it looks like it is made for protection like a castle, but at the same time, it's beauty is like a palace…just remarkable architectural engineering."

Victor acknowledges the descriptive narrative Viana gives.

"Ah…that must be the royal family." Viana's heart melts. "I am so thankful the high priests chose us for this assignment."

"Yes…well…it just makes sense to me they would choose us," Victor declares.

"Do not be boastful," Viana slightly jests.

"Viana, it just makes sense to me because the other seasoned Chiawaukas, such as Omar and Ollie, were assigned to the planet Kareenia (Ka-ree-knee-a) for now…and we…well…in my eyes…we make an excellent team. In this case, we are a reconnaissance team," Victor explains.

"I see what you were saying. I agree," Viana concurs.

Chapter 105

THE PRINCE TURNS TWO

"Francesca, I cannot thank you enough for helping me with Rupert's second birthday and with the upcoming Annual Fall Around, the first of Octobria. I am so thankful for you," Eloise appreciates.

"You are quite welcome. It is truly my pleasure." Francesca smiles then reaches to pick up Rupert.

Rupert smiles and tightly hugs Francesca.

"Everyone will soon be arriving for the party." Eloise begins to feel anxious.

"Eloise, it is going to be lovely, and this little doll will experience a wonderful second birthday," Francesca assures.

"You are right. You know...I hope we have more children...." Eloise shares in confidence.

"Maybe you will. Antonio and I would have four, but you know...I had two miscarriages...so for us...we guess our two sons is what God intended," Francesca discloses.

"Yes...we were so heartbroken for you both times. Your boys seemed to be saddened by it," Eloise sympathizes.

"They were. It seems like many years ago. The miscarriages were about a year apart from each other. I think Marco was five and Gino was three," Francesca solemnly recalls.

"I am sorry to bring it up," Eloise apologizes. "I am thinking aloud...I would love to have a sibling for Rupert."

"Eloise, nothing to apologize for, and maybe it will work out that you will be blessed with another baby," Francesca maintains.

Eloise smiles. "Honestly, I cannot imagine loving another child as much as I do Rupert, but I am sure I will if we have another baby. How is it having a sixteen-year-old on your hands?"

Francesca laughs. "He will be seventeen in eight months and he has his heart set on working in the mine. He wants to do absolutely everything the Mancini men did before him. We find it sweet, though I do worry since there was that one mining incident where the miner died, not to mention, some who have been injured," Francesca recalls.

Eloise voices, "I remember. It was tragic. I admired you taking the boys to help the family with chores for a while. But you know...overall...the mine is safe. Antonio has made sure of that."

"Yes, he has. Thank you. If Rupert would have been born and old enough, I am sure you and he would have been with us to help," Francesca reassures. "And yes, I feel the mine is very safe. I just wish Marco wanted to do something else."

"Maybe he will. This will give him a taste of work at the mine. He may change his mind," Queen Eloise conveys.

"You are right. Antonio will not let him begin until he turns seventeen. Okay, we should go now, I am sure everyone is waiting to see this little prince," Francesca suggests.

"Yes...I am sure our guests have arrived. Thank you again, my friend." Eloise wraps her arms around Francesca and they exchange Rupert from the arms of Francesca to the arms of his mother.

Chapter 106

ANSWERS IN THE JOURNAL

Francesca rolls over in her sleep. She can feel her heart racing, she tosses. She abruptly sits up. She is out of breath. Antonio feels her body shift. He opens his eyes and sees her sitting up in their bed. He also sits up and turns on the lamp.

"Are you alright?" Antonio asks.

"I guess," Francesca murmurs.

"Another nightmare?" Antonio questions.

Francesca gazes into Antonio's eyes. "Yes. The same nightmare. A cloud-like formation of a hideous being hovering over someone. I cannot make out who it is or where they are going. Ugh. So scary."

Antonio slightly shakes his head. "I am so sorry. Did you have these nightmares before? I mean…when did the first one begin? I believe something is causing them."

Francesca peers into his eyes, then scans their entire room. "I do not recall ever having this nightmare when I was young," Francesca communicates, but she is intensely thinking, trying to recall. "You know what?" Francesca blurts out while she reaches to a drawer in the nightstand by her side of the bed. She pulls out the very soft purple leather covered journal from Eloise and

Theodore so many moons ago for her birthday. The engraving of the moon, stars, mountains, and a river with a few pine trees, including her name, 'Francesca,' inscribed on the leather cover just below the river, is still intact. While sitting next to Antonio in their bed, she flips through a few pages and scans the words. "The first time I had this nightmare was the night Prince Rupert was born. How weird is that," Francesca curiously voices.

"Pretty weird, considering everyone was experiencing so much joy," Antonio agrees. "We were at Rupert's birthday party earlier today."

Francesca is still flipping through pages and is in disbelief. She stares into the eyes of her husband. "Do you realize, every single time I have experienced this same nightmare, it has been after I see Rupert…either the same day or several days later?" Francesca inhales, then exhales with a heavy sigh.

"That is unusual," Antonio comments. He notices some words on a page while she continues to turn the pages in her journal.

"Oh, look…here is the song Fly Fishin' I wrote on our first time fishing together." Francesca smiles and giggles.

Antonio grins and glances down onto the words in her journal. "That was a fun song."

She continues to turn pages. Antonio spies what looks like another song.

"Is that another song?" Antonio asks.

"It is…but it was written before I met you. It was in my old journal but I transferred it to this one," Francesca comments.

"Can I read it?" Antonio asks.

"Sure," Francesca replies while handing Antonio her journal.

Antonio reads the words of the song that she wrote as a teenager. He slightly shakes his head. "You have a real gift…being able to create such a powerful song, full of passion, with words." Antonio pauses. "Maybe sometime you will write a song for me."

Francesca smiles. "Yeah. I just have not thought about that. I love our life each day…but yeah…I like that idea." She kisses Antonio's cheek.

Antonio smiles and hands Francesca back her journal. He places his hand on her cheek. "You know, I feel very fortunate to have you as my wife."

Francesca smiles with her eyes gazing into the eyes of Antonio. She leans in to kiss him.

Chapter 107

MONTH AFTER MONTH

"Viana...it has been nearly eight months now...and we have seen no auras...maybe I am not cut out for surveillance." Victor paces in the treehouse.

"Victor, I have no doubt you are cut out for whatever assignment our high priests give us. It is great that things are so peaceful on this planet. Do you forget the one...." Viana is interrupted.

"I have not forgotten. Please honor my request I made all those years ago to never speak of it...of him...again," Victor adamantly asserts.

Viana nods. "Yes, of course. I just hate to see you edgy for action."

Victor cracks a smile. "Edgy for action. Now that is funny." Victor grins. "You are right. We will continue our reconnaissance mission as directed. I will try not to complain," Victor voices.

Viana smiles.

Chapter 108

THE GARDEN OF REMEMBRANCE

The royal family along with the Mancini family meet at the Garden of Remembrance as they have each year since the avalanche.

"I sure wish I would have known them." Marco takes off his hat.

"You do honey, through all the memories your pop and others have shared," Francesca quietly voices.

"I feel like I know them very well!" Gino contends.

"You would." Marco shoots him a look.

"I just mean…it is as if sometimes I can hear Grandmother Sarita's voice! I have never heard it…but it is as if sometimes I can hear her," Gino describes.

"I feel the same way. I will hear things my pop told me…or my mother." Antonio heartfully shares.

"No…I mean like sometimes I can hear her cheering me on…or encouraging me…as if she is praying for me…and I sense it," Gino astutely describes. "I feel like I *know* Grandmother Sarita and Grandfather Don."

Francesca wraps an arm around Gino. "That is beautiful."

Antonio exchanges an endearing smile with Gino.

"Maybe I hear them too. I think it is just my imagination so I shut it out...but maybe I will listen closely. I want to feel close to them as well," Marco expresses.

Antonio places his hand on the shoulder of Marco.

Eloise and Theodore stand next to their friends. Theodore decides to pick up Rupert.

"I hope one day, Rupert, you will come to know my parents...your grandparents...through memories we share and pictures you'll see," Theodore speaks softly to his son.

Eloise has her arm wrapped through the bend of Theodore's elbow.

They remember their parents and remain in silence before they leave.

$$\cdots\cdots\mathcal{O}\mathcal{L}\circ\cdots\cdots$$

"I take them with me everywhere. Isn't that what we should do?" Gino asks.

"Absolutely. We take our people everywhere we go...dead or alive...." Antonio smiles, while he experiences an impact from the depth his teenage son seems to possess.

"I can't believe you are going to be fifteen in a couple of months. Is there anything special you would like to do to celebrate?" Francesca asks while they walk to their wagon.

"No. I just love our family, so I want to do something with all of us. Luke and Ben and their parents, the royals, my Montanelli grandparents, and you guys." Gino exhales a laugh. "I guess I want to be surrounded with people I love."

"That is the best place to be." Francesca heartfully smiles.

Marco and Antonio both grin.

"Hey...I will be seventeen in Mayella. Remember...you said I can start work at the mine then," Marco adds while Antonio leads the team out of the area at the Garden of Remembrance.

"Yes. I do remember that." Antonio nods.

Marco leans back in his seat next to Gino. He gives his younger brother a proud smile.

Chapter 109

CLOSING THE ARC

Stellar and Luna step onto the porch of the cabin where the Mancinis and Chamberlains reside. Luna knocks.

"Hello, welcome," Marcella invites the Chiawaukas in.

"We were wondering if you wanted to see an update," Stellar communicates.

"Oh. I think I would like to. Let me get everyone." Marcella walks about the large cabin to gather everyone.

Everyone is now in the living area and greets one another.

"I am sorry Tabitha is not here. She is working with Briele today. I think she is applying for an internship," Marcella voices.

"Yes. Briele has mentioned how dedicated and helpful Tabitha is," Luna comments.

"It has been quite a while since we gave you an update. We thought we would ask if you would like to see more," Stellar puts forth.

"Can we? I think I am ready to see…at least one more time," Marcella pleads.

Franklin, Sarita, and Don sit on the sofa.

"Whenever you are ready," Franklin articulates.

Stellar waves her arm in an arc. As before, the scene appears as if they are right there, but observing.

"Oh...Rupert is having his second birthday party." Marcella smiles.

"My Marco and Gino...well...they are teenagers." Sarita places her hands over her heart.

"They still visit the Garden of Remembrance," Franklin observes.

"Did I just hear Gino convey he can hear me?" Sarita brightens up.

Stellar rewinds the viewing. Everyone listens attentively.

"I feel like I know them very well!" Gino contends.

"You would." Marco shoots him a look.

"I just mean...it is as if I can hear Grandmother Sarita's voice. I have never heard it...but it is as if sometimes I can hear her," Gino describes.

"I feel the same way. I will hear things my pop told me...or my mother," Antonio heartfully shares.

"No...I mean like sometimes I can hear her cheering me on...or encouraging me...as if she is praying for me...and I sense it," Gino astutely describes. "I feel like I know Grandmother Sarita and Grandfather Don."

Francesca wraps an arm around Gino. "That is beautiful."

Sarita is astonished. "They **do** hear me. I have always believed if we think of someone...they can feel it or sense it."

Don glances at his wife and smiles.

"Aw...Rupert is so adorable. I will try to speak to him as well in my prayers and perhaps one day he will realize it is Franklin and me. What a cutie he is! Gino and Marco are so good with him." Marcella is touched.

"I am sure proud of our grandsons," Sarita delights.

Don wraps his arm around Sarita. Don inconspicuously wipes at a tear that trickles down his face while he watches his son lead his family.

Franklin notices the pain Don is experiencing and places his hand on Don's shoulder.

"You know…we really appreciate the attention and care you have given us. But from here on forward…when you visit…just visit with us. Please, no more viewings of our sons and their families until we ask," Franklin speaks with authority as a king does.

"I apologize for any grief it causes you," Stellar voices with compassion.

"I can only imagine," Luna expresses.

"We will adhere to your request." Stellar moves to close the arc.

"Will you replay it one more time?" Sarita requests. "That is, if the rest of you do not mind."

Marcella, Don, and Franklin all nod in favor.

"Certainly." Stellar waves her arm in an arc and the replay begins. When it is finished, Stellar raises her arm to close the viewing arc when she hears Marcella.

"Wait!" Marcella anxiously voices. "I just want to see a still shot of all of them."

Stellar nods, and provides a picture of King Theodore, Queen Eloise, Prince Rupert, and the Mancinis: Antonio, Francesca, Marco, and Gino.

Sarita, Marcella, Don, and Franklin sit and gaze upon the love they see in the faces of their sons and families.

Chapter 110

LYRICS FROM THE HEART

The Carlisles and Mancinis finish securing their food for the night. Ben, Luke, Marco, and Gino enjoy the campfire while sitting on their sleeping bags, searching across the lake. Katherine, Sully, Antonio, and Francesca sit around the campfire. They enjoy the sounds of the water that gently splashes against the rocks at the edge of the shore. A peaceful quiet sweeps all of them away to a place of serenity. After what seems like an hour, but is more likely only minutes, Francesca stands with urgency. She casts her eyes on Antonio. "I have it!" Out of her mouth she begins to speak, but quickly shifts to singing these words while she steps around the area. Katherine, Sully, Antonio, and their sons eagerly listen.

With each sentence she sings, she makes hand and arm gestures that represent the words of the song.

> *"Out on the balcony under the moonlit night,"*
> *as the ocean breeze rolls across the summer sky-*
> *I feel your sweet lips...pressed to mine....*
> *As the big snowflakes fall from the mountain sky-*
> *The fireplace crackles, warming inside,*

I feel your sweet lips…pressed to mine….
Oooh Babee, there's a world out there-
Of places to adventure, for us to share-
Take my hand…and we'll go…everywhere….
Dance with me-under the stars-
Hold me close-to your heart-
Take me with you forever-everywhere….
Sit by me at the river's edge-
Listen to the water rushing by-
Smell the scent of the pine trees-in the air-
Oooh, Babee, there's a world out there-
Of places to adventure-for us to share-
Take my hand…and we'll go everywhere….
Dance with me-under the stars-
Hold me close-to your heart-
Take me with you-forever-everywhere…. "

"Oh, Francesca…how beautiful!" Katherine exclaims, shooting smiles at everyone, while she claps.

Antonio stands up and steps next to Francesca, taking her into his arms. He leads her in a slow dance and recites the words, "Dance with me-under the stars-hold me close-to your heart-take me with you-forever-everywhere."

Francesca gazes up into his eyes. "You like it? It just came to me."

"I think it is perfect. Thank you." Antonio places his cheek next to hers while they continue to sway to the music of their hearts.

Chapter 111

VICTOR AND VIANA

"There are some remarkable humans on this planet. I am surprised we have not seen any auras yet," Victor contends.

"I know. With the boys who live on this ranch stopping a fight months ago, along with the dad calming the horses so one of them could pull a child to safety…just very noble humans," Viana recollects. "All are genuinely into sharing and helping, just like this birthday party they are preparing for…so thoughtful and kind."

"I am trying not to be frustrated. We have been here ten months now," Victor calculates.

"I know. It will be alright. All will be well," Viana assures.

Victor raises an eyebrow while he casts his view across the spectacular ranch with one arm bent behind his back.

Chapter 112

SPRING

"Time passes so quickly," Sophia voices while she steps cautiously on the trail.

"I don't know how many more family hikes I can do," Leonardo speaks while catching his breath.

"Stop your smoking...for starters," Sophia quietly voices.

Leo slightly shakes his head.

"I am so glad you all complied to my birthday wish! All of us hiking together." Gino laughs while winking at his best friend, Luke.

Ben and Marco take the lead. Gino and Luke are close behind. Francesca, Katherine, and Sophia keep a good clip. Antonio, Sully, and Leonardo enjoy the hike. They are comfortable at their own pace knowing they are moving slower than the rest.

Gino suggests to Marco, "Maybe we should slow up and walk with our grandparents."

"Yeah. That is a good idea," Marco agrees.

The four boys hold up.

"Are we stopping?" Leonardo asks.

"No, we thought we would walk with you," Marco chimes out.

"Nonsense. We will visit with you when we reach the destination. Now skedaddle," Leo asserts. "Maybe on the way down."

Gino laughs a bit. "Alright, Grandfather."

The boys go on ahead.

Each person enjoys the hike. The boys are not aware the king and queen are at the Mancini ranch preparing a meal and cake to celebrate Gino's fifteenth birthday, a job the royals insisted doing since Rupert is only now two-and-a-half which is too young for the hike.

Steve, Veronica, and David also arrive to surprise Gino and celebrate. Leah has returned to Zaltana.

Doctor George Gerard, his wife Laverne, and daughter Gwendolyn are in attendance, as well, to celebrate when the group returns from the hike.

......⚬⧸⧹⚬......

"What a wonderful birthday for Gino. I am glad my parents agreed to hike at his request," Francesca voices.

"Oh...it just occurred to me...Rupert was here. I hope you do not have another nightmare since Rupert was with us part of today," Antonio shares.

"Yeah...I find it hard to believe that I have the nightmares after I have been in his presence...either the same day or several days out...maybe it is a coincidence," Francesca ponders.

"Maybe so," Antonio quietly replies.

"You know what I do sense though...." Francesca frowns.

"What's that?" Antonio asks.

"I sense, that for some reason...maybe their schedules...but something is going to shift, so that for a while, we will not be seeing much of Steve and David outside of their jobs...nor much of Veronica or Leah. I hope I am wrong, but it is a strong feeling I am experiencing," Francesca outlines.

"I have found that your instincts are better than most people calculating," Antonio assures. He reaches to turn off the lamp and they lie back onto their pillows. "I love you."

Francesca rolls to her left side. "I love you."

417

Chapter 113

THE LAST ASSIGNMENT

"Let's travel to Mount Abdiel. It is time we tell him his assignment," High Priest Akshai suggests.

"I like that idea. You know, I would not be surprised if he becomes a High Priest one day," High Priestess Ammerie vocalizes.

"I agree," Akshai concurs. "He has a natural ability to lead his brother priests and his mannerisms are that of a noble mentor."

"Yes…we are all called to be witnesses…he does have a very unique ability," Ammerie acknowledges.

They land on Mount Abdiel where the architecturally well-built, ancient church remains intact.

The high priests are greeted by those they pass along the pathway to the front.

"He will be back soon. He went for a ride," One of the brothers informs.

Ammerie and Akshai exchange eye contact.

"Thank you," High Priest Akshai voices.

They stroll around the large manicured yard and gardens while they wait.

Finally, who they are waiting for arrives. "The high priests are in the gardens wanting to see you," A brother notifies.

A tall, slender Chiawauka briskly walks to greet the high priests.

"There you are, John Henry. So good to see you," High Priestess Ammerie voices.

"Thank you. It is good to see you both." Father John nods while exchanging a handshake with Akshai.

"We have an assignment for you," Akshai relays.

"I am at your service." Father John Henry slightly bows.

"You are versed in The Ancient Writings...." Ammerie states.

"I am...very well," John Henry replies.

"We will be sending you to the planet Soleil. You will not let the others know you are there until it is time," Akshai instructs.

"I understand," John Henry quietly complies.

"By the way...impressive work you did for the human, Miles Cassidy," Akshai notes.

"Oh, yes...you mean Cash. I have been watching for years...he was ready...I deemed it appropriate," John Henry describes.

"It was beautiful and has made an everlasting, profound effect on his life," Ammerie comments.

"I am just glad I could be there." John Henry folds his hands in a prayer manner and slightly bows.

"You have a natural gift, John Henry," Akshai acknowledges with exuberance.

John Henry slightly bows his head. "Thank you. I do my best."

"Peace be with you, John Henry," Ammerie voices.

"Peace to both of you," John Henry replies.

"We will contact you when it is time," Akshai states.

"I look forward to it," John Henry affirms.

419

"One more thing completed." High Priest Akshai inhales a deep breath.

"Yes…and Father John Henry Lanzreth is such a beautiful soul. He will be an asset for the humans and his fellow Chiawaukas, if needed," High Priestess Ammerie voices.

"He will, indeed. With his skill set along with the fact that since he has been ordained Bishop, the other Chiawaukas will not be able to detect his presence when he shifts into his human form," Akshai reveals.

"Yes…the high priests before us selected well," Ammerie agrees.

Akshai nods.

Chapter 114

AT THE KRYSTYLEEN MINE

Antonio arrives early at the mine. He wants to make sure his crew is aware that Marco will be starting in a few weeks.

"Hey boss, nice to see you," Pearce greets.

Antonio shakes the hand of Pearce. "Good to see you. Is Curtis around?"

"Yes, Sir. He was hoping to see you today," Pearce replies.

The two men walk inside of the mine office building. They proceed down the hall to find Curtis at his desk studying paperwork.

Curtis quickly stands when he sees Antonio. "Hello. Good to see you."

"Good to see you, Curtis." Antonio reaches to firmly shake his hand. "Looks like you have got quite a stack of papers."

"I do. I will tell you about that in a minute. What brings you in so early?" Curtis inquires.

"I want to make sure you guys remember that Marco will begin work here in a few weeks, after he turns seventeen," Antonio informs.

Curtis and Pearce both nod.

"Yes. We look forward to working with the next generation of Mancinis," Curtis discloses.

Antonio stares at the two men. "I want you to treat him like any other worker. No favoritism."

"Of course. We treat all men with equal respect. That is the mine motto." Curtis replies.

"Very good." Antonio nods.

"I will personally teach him, Antonio, the most productive way in which to work, including safety protocol," Curtis states.

"I look forward to working alongside him," Pearce comments.

"Very good. I know he will be in good hands with you both," Antonio confirms. "Now, what did you want to tell me?"

Curtis walks back over to his desk and picks up a couple of sheets of seismic data. "Tony, look at these." Curtis steps next to Antonio so they can both view the graphs. "According to the readings from the seismograph, we have been experiencing some unusual seismic activity the past few days, though we have not felt any." Curtis points to the data on the paper.

"I see, perhaps the seismograph is malfunctioning." Antonio takes ahold of the readings and compares. He then hands them back to Curtis. "Alright. Just let me know if anything changes. I do not want any of you injured."

"Will do," Curtis acknowledges.

Chapter 115

THE ROYALS

"I do so love our kingdom!" Eloise voices.

Theodore smiles. He lifts Rupert into his arms. King Theodore then shifts Rupert to his right side, and holds him securely while he reaches for the hand of Eloise with his left arm. They stroll the castle grounds. "If only my parents were alive to journey through life with us...."

Eloise squeezes Theodore's hand. "I know. I miss your parents and Tabitha so much! Rupert would have loved them all!"

Theodore nods. "Indeed." He slightly laughs while thinking of his younger sister. "Aunt Tabitha...has a nice ring to it...Rupert would have loved her!" Theo gazes into the eyes of Eloise. "I would like to have more children with you."

Eloise lights up. "I would love that so much!"

Theodore, still securely holding their little prince, leans over to kiss Eloise. "Want to try tonight?"

Eloise radiates, "I think that is a grand idea, my King."

King Theodore sets Rupert down. Rupert walks as a toddler does. King Theodore tenderly takes the hand of Queen Eloise. The king and queen along with their son, Prince Rupert, continue to stroll the castle grounds on a magnificent Mayella day.

Thank you for reading the prequel.

I hoped you enjoy the journey...
and follow what unfolds next....
The Chiawaukas
Mission on Soleil
The Ancient Writings Fulfilled
The Quest for Order

Enjoy the Wonders of the Night Sky!!

Alexandria Chiaro spent her childhood and adolescent summers traveling through beautiful mountain states with her parents. During this time, she began writing poems, songs, and lyrics, which later transitioned into writing short stories.

Many years later, an idea for a title came to her while attending church with her mother. However, it was not until an additional three years later that someone asked about the characters in her story, unlocking the treasure chest that is in this trilogy. The particulars of the cast of characters came quickly thereafter, and a few in somewhat prophetic places. The dark of a winter night brought the names of the evil beings, and the name of the supreme guardian beings came to her in her dining room, where she gathers and strengthens her own family. The story itself takes many twists and turns, foreshadowing events which unfold as the reader progresses through the trilogy journey, which has brought to life this prequel.

Sharing her imaginative stories with you brings Alexandria great joy.

Alexandria fills her time with church, family, friends, fur babies, work, writing, and projects. She greatly enjoys the outdoors along with mountains, & rivers, just as she did those summers long ago.

Enjoy!